ZOMBIE BILLIONAIRE

CREATURE QUEST SERIES
BOOK 2

NICK SULLIVAN

This is a work of fiction. All events described are imaginary; all characters are entirely fictitious and are not intended to represent actual living persons. The author does not claim to have seen a Bigfoot and to the best of his knowledge has never been bitten by a zombie.

If you purchased this book without a cover, consider making one from construction paper and gluing it to the front. Draw a menacing businessman in front of a moonlit city skyline and write "Zombie Billionaire" across the top in crayon. You're good to go.

Published by Wild Yonder Press

Cover illustration by Claudio Bergamin of claudiobergamin.com

Cover design by Claudio Bergamin and Chris Sorensen

Copy editing by Eliza Dee of Clio Editing Services

Proofreading by Gretchen Tannert Douglas

ISBN 978-1-966989-00-4

PRAISE FOR ZOMBIE BILLIONAIRE

"Sullivan takes your favorite things—zombies, Bigfoot, a lake monster that puts *Jaws* to shame—and blends them up into a frothy, gory, fun-filled monster adventure!"
    - Chris Sorensen, author of *The Nightmare Room*.

"Gory & Glorious! A monster-mash sequel that's more than worth the wait. The horror elements don't pull punches, but they're matched with smart pacing, comedic relief, and genuine heart.
    - Brian's Book Blog.

"This story has it all, and by that I mean cryptids, carnage, and a cannibalistic corporate CEO. What more do you really need out of a hella fun story?"
    - Rick Gualtieri, author of *Bigfoot Hunters*.

"This book reads like a really great movie exploding off the pages. Sullivan writes with such glee it's infectious. Overall, a fantastic follow up and one I think creature fans will definitely love!"
    - Steve Steed, author of *Mastodon*

"*Zombie Billionaire* is just as entertaining as its predecessor, but this story contained more depth, fun, and adventure than the original; just what a sequel should provide."
    - Quella Reviews.

AUTHOR'S NOTE

You know how some authors say: "This book might be part of a series, but you can read it as a stand-alone?" This isn't one of those books.

If you haven't read *Zombie Bigfoot*, then tuck this book into your impressive and eclectic shelf of literature and go get "*ZBF*". Heck, you could tape the two books together and pretend it's an omnibus. This book picks up directly from the epilogue and the epi-epilogue of *Zombie Bigfoot*.

*To "The Oldsies" (and honorary Oldsies)...
You've all remained such valued and loyal friends over the years.
Our unending text thread has brought a smile to my face most
days... even when I look at it at midnight and realize there are two
hundred new texts since I paused to brush my teeth. I hope you enjoy
your appearances in this book. And here's a little "dedication text
thread" for you:*

*To Brady: "Pudding."
To Mark: "Shut up, Aldrich."
To Kevin: "Eat a pickle."
To Stuart: "Red... hanky!"
To Sharkey: "You build Kristie's sweat lodge yet?"
To Kristie: "Quit dancing with James and finish your novel."*

The boundaries which divide Life from Death are at best shadowy and vague. Who shall say where the one ends, and where the other begins?

—Edgar Allan Poe

CHAPTER ONE

Cameron Carson was dead, to begin with. There was no doubt whatever about that. The young Sasquatch's teeth had torn the side of his throat, severing the carotid artery and lacerating one edge of his vocal cords. Exsanguination led to hypovolemic shock and complete organ failure. In layman's terms, Carson bled out.

Once the billionaire's heart stopped beating, the cells in his body were rapidly starved of the life-giving oxygen required to continue functioning; cellular processes ceased, acidity levels rose, and enzymes started to digest cell membranes from within. Carson's body began eating itself.

Not to be left out, bacteria in the body joined the party and attacked the gastrointestinal tract. It would be some hours before rigor mortis set in, and well before that time, the corpse of Cameron Carson was discovered near the treeline. After efforts to revive him proved fruitless, the former titan of industry was zipped into a body bag and moved to the center of camp. The billionaire's body temperature steadily dropped.

It was at this time that something extraordinary occurred: at the site of the bite, a large number of cells began to *change*. Foreign nucleic acids sought out strands of human DNA and rapidly wove themselves into the helixes of their structure, the mutations multiplying at an exponential rate. Cells that had ceased operation when deprived of oxygen resumed their function, their processes now working in an anaerobic fashion.

Darkness. Then sound. Voices. "You told me he was dead!" That one was familiar... but then another spoke. "He *was*, sir! The side of his throat was torn out. He'd bled out by the time we found him, I swear!"

Fear in that voice. *Good.* There was another sound, too... a low, guttural snarl that seemed to fill the dark place Carson inhabited. *Is that sound coming from... me?* He reached out and his hand met with a surface; it yielded to his touch, but only a little. *Am I in the womb?* The ridiculous notion quickly fled into the remote corners of his mind as another set of thoughts rushed to the fore and blotted out his musings, as if another "self" was standing beside him and shrieking into his ear: *Hungry! Must eat! Those fear-voices, find them kill them tear their flesh eat their faces! This dark thing holding us destroy it find the voices KILL!*

Awareness departed Carson for a time as an all-consuming rage and hunger flooded his thoughts. But in a brief instant, he was able to focus and perceive another voice, one that spoke with calm determination. "Singleton. You must kill it. The dead should stay dead."

Singleton... the name was familiar. "Kill," that calm voice had said. *Yes... kill. Kill kill kill kill KILL!* Carson felt himself being lifted, the strange, dark place around him moving. He tore at the substance in front of him and howled with renewed madness.

Suddenly, a point of light appeared. It grew into a vee of brightness and Carson's eyes strained to adjust to the sudden obliteration of the dark. In moments, he could make out faces. People.

Food! He threw himself at the nearest shape, but unyielding bars halted his progress. He strained, reaching clawed fingers toward this figure. But then it spoke: "Mr. Carson... Cameron... it's me —Bill."

It was as if a switch had been thrown; a rush of memory triggered a return to sanity. *Bill. I know a Bill. Bill Singleton. And that other name: Cameron. That's me.* The hunger/anger began to build again, but Carson forced it back. *No! Damn you, whatever you are, stop! I am Cameron Carson, and I'll be damned if I lose control to mindless urges and gibbering thoughts!* The malevolent voice abruptly stilled and Carson kicked loose from the bag and rose to his feet.

"Mr. Singleton..." His voice sounded ragged to his ear and he could feel his vocal cords scraping in an unnatural fashion. "I seem to be... ill." He felt an odd pressure from within, that monstrous "other" trying to reassert itself. With a surge of will, Carson crammed the beast back into a mental cage, even as he leaned against the bars of the physical one. "Would you... would you be so kind as to get me home?"

"Yes, Mr. Carson," Bill replied softly.

Carson's stomach growled and his thoughts turned to... meat. The "other" stirred again but the billionaire had a notion that might sate these cravings. "And Bill... call ahead... tell my chef I'll be wanting several Wagyu ribeye steaks."

"Of course, sir," said Singleton.

Carson flashed his famous megawatt smile. "Extra rare." He let the smile linger on his face longer than usual, enjoying the sensation of his lips stretching wide, the feel of his teeth clenching powerfully together. His eyes swept over the assembled men and women around him. Relaxing the grotesque grin, he cleared his ruined throat and spoke in a rasp. "I won't pretend to fully understand exactly what has happened to me... but I think perhaps, for the moment, I had best remain in this erstwhile Bigfoot cage. I trust there are no objections?"

A couple of the young National Guardsmen seemed to relax, and some of his surviving expedition members laughed nervously. One man remained absolutely still and unsmiling; Carson shifted his gaze to him.

"Mr. Washakie. Joseph. If eyes were daggers, I suspect I'd have a pair of holes in my face right about now. Correct me if I'm wrong, but I believe I overheard you suggest that someone should kill me." He sifted through additional fragments of memory from his time in the body bag. "And that I was no longer human." He held up his hands and looked at them closely. "I confess I don't feel a hundred percent... but I don't appear to have any fangs or claws. I believe I still fall very much into the 'human' category." The inner voice returned for an instant: *Is that what you think? Well, Cameron, old buddy, just you WAIT.* Then it was gone again. Carson closed his eyes tightly and took a deep breath. *Did I, though? Did I take a breath?* Opening his eyes, he continued. "That young Bigfoot bit me, yes? I imagine I was in severe shock. But surely you aren't still advocating for visiting murder upon me?"

Joseph held Carson's gaze for a moment before turning away and addressing Bill. "I will have no words with that thing. The only wisdom out of its mouth was its offer to stay in the cage."

Singleton puffed up with indignation and opened his mouth to protest.

"I am done speaking to you as well," the Shoshone tracker added before turning and walking away.

Carson felt a powerful flash of anger, but this time he kept it flowing deep within, like a riptide. He forced a wide smile back onto his face. "Mr. Washakie, be reasonable. I would value your input on my current situation."

Joseph stopped for a moment. Without turning, he spoke quietly. "Ask it if its heart is beating." Then he continued to walk away toward the edge of camp.

Carson's grin faltered at the man's words. He brought his fingertips up to the unwounded side of his neck and pressed them against his flesh for several seconds. *Surpri-i-i-ise!* The inner voice seemed to chuckle with dark mirth. Carson forced his smile wider and gave a real-world chuckle of his own. "You almost had me there!" he called after Joseph. "Of course my heart is beating!"

But, of course... it wasn't. He had felt nothing beneath the pads of his fingertips.

Russ Cloud and Dr. Sarah Bishop had watched all of this unfold and quickly followed Joseph as he passed by them.

Sarah leaned toward him, her voice low. "Whatever it was that happened to those Sasquatch to turn them into monsters—or those two geologists who attacked the Spook Stalkers—it's happening to Carson, isn't it?"

Joseph kept walking. "Yes, I think so. But..."

"But, what?" Russ prompted.

Joseph stopped near the edge of the clearing where the monstrous silverback Bigfoot had assaulted the camp. "That alpha we fought... it had completely turned. A remorseless killing machine. A true Wendigo. But the mindless rage, the hunger... Carson seems able to control it. At least partly."

"Well, that's a good thing, right?" Russ asked hopefully.

Joseph looked him in the eye. "I think that could be a very, very *bad* thing."

"Should we warn the authorities?" Sarah asked.

"The question is, *which* authorities?" Joseph gestured toward the masses of CDC employees, National Guard, and other unidentifiable government types that were growing by the minute. "I am concerned our warning might spark the wrong kind of interest. In fact..." Joseph trailed off as he spotted something on the ground near the smoldering remains of an expedition tent. He stooped and retrieved it.

"Your chunk of white buffalo turquoise!" Russ said. "You shattered that failed Molotov cocktail of mine with that thing; saved my life."

"Yes," Joseph bounced the small bluish-white stone in his hand and his eyes went distant for a moment. An instinctual impulse overtook him and he blindly tossed the rock back over his shoulder.

"Joseph!" Sarah blurted. "Why on earth did you do that?"

"Ow! Son of a—who threw that?" A young National Guardsman stormed around a nearby tent. His hair was jet black and he held his helmet in one hand and the piece of white turquoise in the other. An M4 carbine was slung over his shoulder. He came up short, looking intently at Joseph. "Uncle Joe?"

Joseph smiled broadly and went to the guardsman, plucking the stone from his hand and clasping the young man's forearm in greeting. "Luke! Good to see you. Sorry about the rock to the noggin."

"It was so weird. I *just* took off my helmet, and... hey, what are you doing here?"

"Long story. I'll fill you in later, but first..." He turned to Sarah and Russ. "This is my nephew, Luke Redheart. Luke, this is Russ Cloud and Dr. Sarah Bishop. Russ is a survival show host and a moderately skilled tracker—"

"Hey!" Russ protested.

Joseph soldiered on. "—and Dr. Bishop is a primatologist and expert in all things Sasquatch."

Luke took Sarah in. "You study Bigfoot? Mom and Dad said they saw one near Syringa. Mom called it Tso'apittse."

"I've never heard that term before," Sarah said. "What does it mean?"

Joseph shook his head. "My sister always loved that story. The name is from a Shoshone fable. It means 'Cannibal Giant.' Huge creatures made of stone that ate children. I think our ancestors picked that up from Russian traders. The idea of child-eating giants has a distinctly European feel to it."

"And a Bigfoot wouldn't eat a human..." Sarah started before catching herself.

"Well, that's what I always thought," Luke said. "But some of the guys have been talking about what happened here. They said there were at least two Sasquatch that attacked the camp... and a third killed some people out in the forest." He looked at the trio and lowered his voice. "Did you see any of it?"

"We saw plenty," Russ said.

Joseph gathered himself. "We aren't through here. Russ, we need to go back to the geologists' camp."

"Holy... I forgot all about the—" Russ began, but Joseph interjected quickly, placing a firm hand on Russ's forearm.

"Yes, Russ... *that* camp. We've got to get there right away."

"Wait, are you talking about the campsite to the southeast?" Luke asked. "Up on a rise, green tent?" When Joseph nodded, Luke continued. "Well, that's a coincidence. I'm on my way there now. Taking over guard duty for a couple fellas who've been there since we arrived."

Russ gave Joseph a knowing look. The Shoshone spoke quickly. "We'll go with you, if you don't mind."

"I dunno, it's supposed to be a restricted area..."

"I know. We're the ones that told them to restrict it."

"Well... I s'pose that'd be all right, long as the LC doesn't get wind of it. You are family, after all."

"Sarah, care to join us?" Joseph asked.

"Actually, I need to check with Liz and Dhir and make sure our mutual friends have gotten safely out of the area. They said they'd keep an eye out with the little drone, TED Junior."

"Probably just as well," Russ said quietly, throwing another look Joseph's way before clearing his throat. "Luke, those two guys who have been guarding the camp..."

"Sharkey and Farley. Shark and Farl. Good fellas."

"They know not to enter the camp, right?"

"Yessir, the commander was very clear on that point. Take up a position in view of the green tent but don't go into the campsite itself."

"Let's hope they're good at following orders," Russ muttered.

Back in the expedition camp, Carson listened intently as Singleton brought him up to speed, explaining the attack on the camp that had occurred while Carson was bleeding out near the treeline. The infected alpha of the Bigfoot troop had killed numerous expedition members before it had been destroyed in the forest. Carson actually had a vague recollection of battling this beast in the hours before getting his throat torn out; a failed capture attempt had cost the life of his massive bodyguard, Brick—the huge man being piledrivered into the ground by the monstrous alpha.

Several other mercenaries, including Willem Jaeger and Katya Volkov, had been killed by the alpha's mate, although that creature had been eliminated in another part of the forest. And apparently, while Carson was occupying the body bag, the expedition tracker, Joseph Washakie, had burned the zombified Sasquatch remains prior to the arrival of the National Guard and advance elements of the Centers for Disease Control and Prevention.

"Bill, I'm going to need to get out of here as soon as humanly possible." Even with the ruined rasp of his voice, Carson's patrician southern drawl remained intact. "I can't help but notice there are a substantial number of governmental science types in the vicinity and I'm sorry to say that I may not be able to maintain my current level of decorum for much longer."

"I understand, sir," Singleton replied in his clipped British accent. "But the head of the Seattle branch of the CDC has made it quite clear that everyone involved in the, um... 'incident' must undergo a thorough medical check at a temporary quarantine station in Grangeville."

"Oh, no no no, that won't do. That won't do at all." Carson

thought for a moment. Was it getting harder to think? Well, he *had* been clinically dead, after all—perhaps he could cut himself a break. "Is your sat phone functioning?" he asked, reaching a hand through the bars.

"Yes, sir," Bill said, withdrawing the walkie-talkie-esque phone from a jacket pocket and carefully placing it in the outstretched hand.

Carson quickly dialed a number and waited briefly before speaking. "Lawrence, old friend! It's Cameron. I trust Atlanta's treating you well? Sorry about the voice; came down with a touch of the crud. Listen, I'm in a bit of a sticky pickle and could use some of your managerial muscle."

"I ain't going anywhere without my gear!"

"Mr. Sorenson, sir, I was told you needed medical attention," the young National Guardsman protested, "and the first helicopter's leaving for Grangeville right now."

"Well, I'll be sure to wave bye-bye as it flies away, while I'm gathering up my expensive and irreplaceable equipment." The portly audio engineer puffed himself up, balancing on a crutch.

"Bud," Liz Torres said, "I can bring it on the next one. Dhir, you know what Bud brought, right?"

The Pakistani tech smiled. "You mean the audio detection and analysis gadgets that he couldn't stop bragging about between breaths of air? Yes, I am familiar with them."

Liz snickered, then gestured around the tech tent. "I promise I'll bring you all of your toys. Now, go get that broken leg patched up, okay?"

While Bud grumbled and hobbled his way toward the helicopters with the help of the soldier, Liz sat back down in front of the controls for TED Junior, the small drone she'd been operating to search for survivors. She'd placed it on autopilot when the

National Guard had arrived, and after a minute or two of deft maneuvers, she brought it in for a gentle landing behind the tent and turned to Dhir Patel. The young man had taught her how to fly the little quadcopter, as well as its big brother (or "sister"— Dhir had insisted TED the Elder was a "she"). Liz watched him for a moment, admiring his bronze skin and big brown eyes. "So, what's next for you? Aside from getting poked and prodded by the CDC, I mean."

Dhir grimaced. "I'm not overly fond of needles. Puncture wounds and nausea—two worst things, in my book... and for me, the first usually leads to the second."

"Aw, suck it up, ya big baby."

He grinned at her. "Goo goo. But to answer your question, I'll probably return to New York. Mr. Carson will want me to go back to work at Maiden Labs."

"Assuming he doesn't go back to being dead," Liz murmured. She moved closer to Dhir and spoke in a low voice. "I talked to the medic. The guy said Carson wasn't breathing and had no pulse. Throat torn open, a pool of blood under him... skin cold and pale as milk."

Dhir squirmed uncomfortably. "I think, perhaps, with every-thing going on—monsters attacking and all—maybe the medic made a mistake?"

"Maybe." Liz seemed to realize she was very close to the young man; for a moment her concerns faded into the background. "New York, huh? I've always wanted to visit New York."

Carson pulled on a red-and-gold Maiden Media windbreaker, zipping the jacket all the way to the top. He did so not for warmth; he wasn't the slightest bit chilly. At least he didn't *feel* cold. Or hot, for that matter. Actually... he wasn't sure he was aware of any temperature at all. No, the windbreaker was to conceal his blood-soaked shirt, and he finished zipping it up just as the Seattle CDC rep approached the cage with Bill Singleton right on her heels. As the billionaire leaned casually against the bars, the short-haired woman gave Carson a quizzical look.

"Why are you in that cage?"

"I don't know if you heard, but a rabid Bigfoot nearly killed me. I feel more comfortable in here, in the event another furry monstrosity comes traipsing out of the woods."

The CDC rep shrugged. "Mr. Carson, I've been speaking to your secretary—"

"Mr. Singleton is hardly my secretary. 'Aide-de-camp' would be more apropos."

"Yes, well, in any event, he says you'd like to return to New York. I hope you understand why that is out of the question. There is a very real possibility of some form of bacterial or viral outbreak and we must transport everyone to a temporary quarantine next to the airport in Grangeville. Once we've run some tests—"

Suddenly, the rep's sat phone rang. Carson had noticed Bill texting someone from his own sat phone while the woman had been speaking and he threw a subtle nod Carson's way. The CDC rep answered the call and listened intently, an expression of confusion growing on her face.

"But sir, from what I understand, Mr. Carson was bitten. If *anyone* should be going to our quarantine—" The woman abruptly stopped speaking and winced. While Carson couldn't make out the specific words emanating from the phone, he could hear the authority in the voice. The woman threw a suspicious look at the billionaire. "Yes, sir. I understand, sir." Ending the call, she looked at Carson. "That was Dr. Lawrence Whitmore, the new head of the CDC in Atlanta. He said that you and a small group of your associates are free to travel back to New York. He explained you have your own quarantine facility?"

"Indeed I do. I have a Level Four facility on North Brother

Island in the East River. Coincidentally, back in the olden days, they used to quarantine smallpox and typhoid cases on that island. Apart from my labs, North Brother is just ruins and bird nests. No civilian residents whatsoever, and there isn't a doubt in my mind that we have far more stringent protocols in place than anything you've whipped up on the spur of the moment in some podunk Idaho town."

"But... how are you going to get there? There might be a chance of infection at the airports—"

At this point, Singleton stepped in. "We will be taking a Maiden Aviation helicopter to Missoula, where we will immediately board Mr. Carson's private jet. Maiden Industries will have no difficulty clearing the vicinity around our aircraft and I have already made arrangements at LaGuardia. We will have the water-side apron at the northwest corner all to ourselves and a boat will be waiting less than a hundred yards away. Now, I'm sure you have plenty of work to do... as do we. Don't let us keep you."

The CDC rep looked at Singleton suspiciously and started to say something, then thought better of it and abruptly turned away. She called out to a group of National Guardsmen who were waiting in a clump. "Okay, change of plans..."

As the woman stormed off, Carson smiled. "Nicely done, Bill."

"You too, sir. How much will that favor cost us?"

"You can't put a price tag on influence, Bill... although I'm sure Lawrence would beg to differ and will suggest an appropriate sum. Our 'friendship' has already proved mutually beneficial: he fast-tracked the FDA approval for our mosquito eradication program and I got him appointed to run the CDC. Still, I suggest we 'fast-track' our departure in the event our Seattle friend decides to second-guess her boss."

"Yes, sir. The helicopter is fueled and ready and your jet is on standby in Missoula. I've arranged for the expedition medic to be on board and I assume we'll need some 'muscle' to manage the cage. Two of Brick's mercenaries survived and I've added the cook;

he seems sturdy. Between them, they should be able to handle loading and unloading."

"The cook, yes, good thinking. Let me speak to him, if you'd be so kind; I have a few... special requests. And fetch that whiz kid, Dhir Patel. I want him with us."

CHAPTER TWO

"Check this out, Colonel."

The gray-haired man looked up from his laptop as a soldier entered the tent he had commandeered. Although Colonel Ronald Dosset was dressed in Operational Camouflage with National Guard patches, he was not a member of the Guard. The insignia indicating his rank, however, was correct. "What've you got?"

The soldier, also dressed in a new-looking National Guard uniform, held up a digital camcorder. "I had to find a compatible charger; the battery was dead when we found it." He handed it to his superior. "I'm pretty sure this is something you'll want to see."

Dosset flipped open the viewscreen and hit play. After taking in the deliberately shaky footage and atrocious redneck accents, he spoke in a clipped, no-nonsense tone. "Why the hell am I watching this, Jenkins? Looks like a crappy reality TV show."

"It is, sir. *Spook Stalkers*. The men you are watching are deceased. Extremely deceased."

Dosset glanced up from the screen. "The bodies at Location Foxtrot?"

"Yes, sir. Two of the bodies, at least. But that's not where we found the camcorder."

A rasping vocalization drew the colonel's attention back to the screen. A shambling form was entering the viewable distance of the camera's night vision. "That parka... it's from one of the *other* bodies at Foxtrot," Dosset noted. The holder of the camera spoke to the approaching figure and it stopped in its tracks. Suddenly, the figure charged the camera, startling the colonel. Horrific sounds followed and the camera angle went to an upside-down view of trees. He hit the pause button and ran a hand across the top of his high-and-tight haircut. "Jesus..."

"It's pretty horrible, yes, sir."

"Jesus Horatio Christmas, this is what we're looking for!" Dosset rewound the video and paused the playback on the twisted rictus distorting the face of the onrushing attacker. "Beautiful," he said, his voice quiet with awe. "Where did you find the camera?"

"Location Golf. There was a half-eaten bear nearby."

"A what? Wait, don't answer. Not as important as the answer to *this* question: How did that video camera get from Foxtrot to Golf?"

"Well, sir... there is a final video after that one. Not selfie-style; this was filmed properly. You can hear a pair of men recording what they say is a Bigfoot nest. They must have found the camera, carried it to that location, and then dropped it when the bear showed up."

"A bear that wound up dead and eaten."

"Yes, sir."

Colonel Dosset abruptly stood and strode from the tent, signaling to more of his men. "Listen up!" He held up the camera and jabbed a finger at the still image of the twisted face on the screen. "We need to find wherever *that* came from. Those bodies are under quarantine, but we've got their personal effects. I want to know who they were and what happened to them. We figure that out, and I think we'll find what we're looking for." He slapped the camera against Jenkins's chest. "Here, get this to the eggheads. Have them do a voice analysis; I want to know the identity of the two men filming the Bigfoot nest."

"You hear that?"

"I heard. Keep walking."

"They had the camera we took from the *Spook Stalkers* camp!" Russ hissed in a borderline whisper. "When the Zombie Bigfoot was giving that bear a flip-top head, I must have dropped it!"

"No shame there," Joseph replied in a low voice. "I nearly dropped more than that. Keep walking."

Russ, Joseph, and Luke had just left Sarah at the tech tent and were about to head for the geologists' camp when an officer burst from a nearby tent, brandishing the camcorder. Fortunately, unlike the hosts of most paranormal reality shows, Russ had never selfie-pointed the camera at himself or Joseph; they passed by the gathering soldiers without incident.

"Luke," Joseph asked, "I'm not current on Army fashion, but are those men National Guard?"

Luke Redheart risked a glance back without breaking stride. "Well, they look like they are... mostly. But I don't recognize any of them or their patches. Most of the folks here should be from the 126th Engineering Company, out of Moscow, Grangeville, and Orofino... but those guys aren't. Also, the gray-haired fella is a colonel—but my commander is on-site and he's a lieutenant colonel. Seems like rank overkill. Also-*also*... those uniforms are really new. Most of the guys and gals I know don't have the latest Operational ones."

Joseph nodded. "Yes, I noticed the storage creases on the uniforms hadn't been ironed out."

Russ threw Joseph an incredulous look. "Are you even human?"

"Observe and deduce, my Watsonian friend. You really need to read some Conan Doyle."

"Well, here's a deduction. They're going to be looking for the place those zombie geologists came from—the place *we're* going."

"Let's pick up the pace," Joseph said, lengthening his stride. "Those men are likely the last people on earth who should get their hands on that sphere."

"What sphere?" asked Luke.

"Joseph called it the 'Stone that Sings,' a name from Native American lore," Sarah explained to Dhir and Liz. "Greenish, spherical, probably a meteorite of some kind. They found it in the geologists' tent and said it started to affect Russ when he got too close to it. We think the emanations from it caused the geologists to change."

"And the Sasquatch that turned into monsters... you think they came across this sphere?" Dhir asked.

"No. From what Brighteyes told me, the silverback alpha of his troop was bitten while he was fighting the geologists—the... 'zombies.' It changed him, and he went on to bite the matriarch... and she bit the teenage Bigfoot that killed Carson."

"*Almost* killed Carson," Liz interjected from her chair in front of the drone controls.

"Yes... almost." Sarah furrowed her brow. The camp medic had been so certain Carson was dead.

"So, if this sphere can mess with your head if you get too close... how exactly are Russ and Joseph going to get rid of it?" Dhir asked.

"Russ said he had a couple of ideas; grabbed a few things from here before they headed back out."

"Who headed out?" asked a voice from the tent flap. A young man in yellow coveralls with a Centers for Disease Control logo on a lanyard poked his head in. "My boss said everyone is supposed to board the next few helicopters for the CDC temporary quarantine in Grangeville." He held up a clipboard. "I'm guessing you are Elizabeth Torres, Sarah Bishop, and Dhir Patel?"

"You're three for three," Liz said.

The man's mouth twitched in a half-hearted attempt at a smile as he scanned his clipboard. "And Bud Sorenson has already departed, so that leaves Russ Cloud and Joseph... Wa... Wuh-*shock-ee?*"

"*Wah*-shuh-kee," Sarah corrected, stressing the first syllable. "They should be back shortly."

"Where did they go?"

"They just needed to check on a few things. They have permission from the National Guard's commanding officer," Sarah said. "And as for us, we'll be ready to go shortly."

The CDC man remained silent for a moment, lightly tapping the clipboard with the top of his pen. "All right, the next chopper leaves in ten. We'll expect you three to be aboard." He turned abruptly and headed out of the tent. Glancing back down at his clipboard, he examined several words he had scribbled in the margins while he'd stood outside their tent: *Sphere? Meteorite. Geologists. Zombies.* After a moment's thought, he walked quickly towards the field where the helicopters were staging.

Back inside the tent, Liz piped up. "Hey! I think I found them! About four miles north."

Sarah scrambled to peer over Liz's shoulder. "I see some movement. Good eye, Liz, but it could be a deer or elk. The trees are so thick."

Dhir flipped a switch on the control panel for TED Junior, the small quadcopter drone that they'd been using for reconnaissance. "The thermal imaging should help. It's less effective in daylight, but with the overcast sky and the rain from last night... there!"

The image on the viewscreen had gone white for a moment, but as the lenses and software found their sweet spot, two distinct blurs of heat came into view in the forest below. One very tall, one quite small. Sarah breathed out a sigh of relief. She'd been concerned that her newfound friends might have been spotted by the influx of humans and helicopters, but the pair seemed to be well on their way to clearing the area.

"Good luck, Brighteyes," she said.

CHAPTER THREE

Brighteyes heard the buzz above the treetops. It sounded like a continuous cicada song, quite different from the thumping quality of the larger, whirly-winged man-machines. All the same, this was clearly man-made. Littlefoot hooted excitedly and peered up through gaps in the canopy overhead. He smacked the back of his wrist against Brighteyes's leg before thrusting out his arms and making a whirling full-body spin. 'Maple seed machine!' Then he signed further. 'But small.'

The young adult Sasquatch looked down from his eight-foot height at the excitable youngster and communicated with a mixture of hand signs and vocalizations. 'Big or small, it is man-machine. We must stay hidden.'

Brighteyes glanced up at the tops of the trees again before quickening his pace. Daughter of Beardface had said many men with guns were coming; he had to get his little half brother safely away from the growing activity in the south. He plucked the little Sasquatch from the forest floor and lifted him atop his shoulders before picking up the pace. Littlefoot panted with laughter at his new vantage point as they sped northward through the trees.

'Where?' Littlefoot vocalized.

With the diminutive Bigfoot atop his shoulders, Brighteyes couldn't make out the additional signals or facial expressions that had likely accompanied the question. Hand and finger signing when combined with simple vocalizations allowed the Sasquatch to enhance the meaning of the basic concepts behind a grunt or a pant. Still, Brighteyes understood that Littlefoot was likely asking where exactly they were going.

Brighteyes thought about how to answer that question.

When Brighteyes was himself an adventurous young Bigfoot, he had loved to roam far afield. The troop controlled a fairly large territory, stretching from a good-sized creek near a tiny human town to the east, to a salmon-filled river to the south, with old human logging roads providing borders to the north and west. The troop alpha, Silverback, had punished him whenever he went too far or was gone for too long, but his mother, Sky, had been more tolerant of his exploration. She would frequently distract Silverback with grooming, food, or sex when she detected that Brighteyes was about to sneak back into camp from one of his forays.

One bright summer day, Brighteyes had decided to cross the human road to the north. After spending several minutes in the treeline overlooking the old logging road, listening intently while he built up his courage, Brighteyes finally scampered out of the trees and crossed the gray ribbon. Having baked in the summer sun, the surface of the human-made trail was hot on the soles of his feet, and Brighteyes wasted no time dashing across and vaulting up a little overhang. Reaching out with a long arm, he grabbed a sturdy sapling and let his momentum swing him further up the slope, propelling himself forward to another tree... and another. In moments, Brighteyes was out of sight of the road, reaching the top of the small rise.

Cresting the top of the forested hill, the little Bigfoot paused and drew a deep breath. The sun-dappled forest floor shone at his feet and not far ahead he could hear the babble of a brook. The breeze tickled the hairy coat of his back, coming up from the road behind. Young Brighteyes whuffed with pleasure and loped down the gentle slope, heading for the creek he'd heard. Fish would be nice. In moments, he reached the little body of water, but as he neared the water's edge, he discovered that he wasn't the only one with fish on his mind. He froze. Across the creek and a little upstream were two young Sasquatch females! One had an unusually curly red pelt and the other had a bright blond straight-haired pelt. The curly-haired red-body was poised above the brook, eyes intent on the water, a hand poised to strike. The blonde was... well, he wasn't sure *what* she was doing. She seemed to be dancing with a butterfly that was fluttering amongst some nearby flowers.

Brighteyes stared in wonder at the pair. He had known there were other Sasquatch in the world; his mother had told him so. But this was the first time he had ever seen another outside of his own troop. While he watched, fascinated, the curly one suddenly cocked her head and sniffed the air before whipping her head to the side and looking right at him. Brighteyes scolded himself; he had known the breeze was at his back and had failed to wait for it to shift before moving forward! The red-body slowly rose, chuffing to her dancing sister. The blonde appeared to wake from her dance-dream and turned to look where her sister was staring. Brighteyes rose from the foliage he'd been crouched in, glancing down with a subservient posture to put the young females at ease. It was then that the wind shifted.

The fresh scents of the two female Sasquatch tantalized his nostrils but it was immediately swamped by a powerful male scent. Sweat, testosterone, and... age. A shape detached itself from the shade of a nearby tree, just downstream on Brighteyes's side of the brook. A male, an alpha, at least as large as Silverback! The massive gray-pelted Sasquatch moved toward Brighteyes with an unhurried gait, coming to a halt a few feet away. Brighteyes remained still, maintaining his submissive body posture.

The huge alpha looked impassively at Brighteyes for some time before vocalizing and signing. The dialect was quite similar to the one the young Bigfoot's troop used.

'Outsider. Who are you? Where come from?'

Brighteyes swallowed and responded with deferential vocalizations. 'I am named Brighteyes. I come from south.'

Again, a long silence, then: 'You are too young to mate with my daughters. You are too little to challenge me for territory. Why are you here?' The big male's tone was oddly threatening, but not savage or bullying the way Silverback's had been. It simply carried a quiet confidence that—should the need arise—he could kill Brighteyes without breaking a sweat.

'I was exploring. I love to look. I love to search. The world is big and I want to see it.'

At this, the curly-haired red-body Bigfoot let loose a short pant of excited agreement. The alpha turned his head partway in her direction and let loose a sharp grunt. The young female fell silent and the male turned back to Brighteyes. 'The world is big... but this part of it is not for you. This part of the world is *mine*. I am BreakTree.' The giant Sasquatch thumped his chest with one fist in a casual manner, but Brighteyes could feel the impact in the air. The alpha gestured back up the rise. 'You will go back across the man-trail and you will not cross it again. Return to your troop.'

Brighteyes sucked in a breath. He had not mentioned his troop, not wanting to endanger them. Would this male try to take over Silverback's territory?

BreakTree seemed to read the young Bigfoot's thoughts. 'I smell your troop on you, young one. And I see the fear in your eyes. Worry not. My kin have all we require in my lands. I will not fight with others for territory I do not need. Go now. And tell your troop they too must remain south of the man-trail.'

Brighteyes dipped his head further, chuffing softly. He turned and tree-pulled his way back up the slope. At the top, he looked back down. The blond-body female was already dancing with butterflies again, but the young red-body was staring intently at him. Brighteyes found himself staring right back. Movement broke their shared gaze as BreakTree started moving toward the rise, a look of simmering violence percolating beneath the surface.

'Go. You have stayed too long already.'

Brighteyes slid down the reverse slope and dashed across the road, heading back into Silverback's territory.

By late afternoon he reached the troop's current camp. As he came in at a run, Sky had no time to distract Silverback, and the big male was waiting as Brighteyes skidded to a halt. As he opened his mouth to explain, the troop leader smacked him hard across the face.

'You run off again! You miss lunch! You miss grooming!' Suddenly, Silverback stopped speaking. He sniffed the air. Stepping closer, he leaned in and inhaled deeply an inch from the young Bigfoot's hairy pelt before gripping him by the shoulders. 'I smell another male. Where? WHERE?'

Brighteyes winced as the alpha's powerful fingers dug into his muscle. He pointed north. 'Across the man-trail that runs from rising sun to setting sun. But he said we must not ever cross it again!'

Silverback leaned in close. 'Who? Who said?'

'BreakTree, the alpha of the territory across the man-trail.'

Silverback released his grip and thought for a moment, a look of eagerness growing on his face. 'What else did you see?'

Brighteyes hesitated. 'Not much. A stream. But they...' He trailed off.

'*They?* Who else did you see?' Silverback's eyes gleamed.

Brighteyes thought about the pair of young female Sasquatch. He had no doubt Silverback would try to abduct them into his small harem, given the chance. He didn't want that. Besides, he was fairly sure that BreakTree would prove more than a match for his troop leader. 'They... they stopped me. BreakTree... and his brothers.'

Silverback's eager look faltered. 'Brothers? How many? How big?'

Brighteyes launched into a description of a quartet of giants, each larger than the last, ending with: '...and all of BreakTree's brothers had many scars. One had a limp; another was missing his nose. I think they challenged him...'

Silverback's eyes wobbled, but he quickly recovered and puffed up his massive chest. 'Well, if they ever cross the road to *my* territory, they will have new scars to cry about!'

Brighteyes never again crossed that man-made trail to the north.

And now, here it was once more, the old logging road the humans used to drive their vehicles to nearby campsites. Brighteyes stopped in the treeline and lowered Littlefoot to the ground. The young Bigfoot looked down at the road in confusion.

'Brighteyes, this is the man-trail Silverback warned us about. We are not supposed to cross it!'

'We must. Our territory is no longer safe.' He took Littlefoot by the hand and stepped into the road.

CHAPTER FOUR

Cameron Carson watched from his cage at the back of the H225 Super Puma helicopter as his men loaded another body bag aboard, placing it in a row where they had removed the seats. It had taken another call to Lawrence at the Atlanta HQ for the Centers for Disease Control to "convince" the Seattle CDC on-site that Carson's lab would need tissue samples as well. Besides, there were plenty to go around.

"That should do it," Singleton said.

"No, let's take one more," Carson said. "The largest one."

"You mean...?" Singleton began before understanding took hold. "Oh... yes, sir." He hopped down from the side entrance of the helicopter and Carson could hear him call out, "Willis! We need *that* one too. I think you'll need to gather a few more men to lift it."

Another voice, this one unfamiliar. "I need to speak to Mr. Carson."

"Look, we've been through this already with your boss," Singleton said. "We are leaving for an alternate quarantine location—"

"This isn't about that and my boss doesn't even know I'm

talking to you," the man hissed in a rush. "Listen, I think this is something Mr. Carson will want to hear."

"Let him in, Bill," Carson called.

A man bearing a clipboard and wearing yellow CDC coveralls climbed aboard the helicopter. He halted in his tracks when he saw Carson.

"What's the matter? Never seen a rich man in a cage before?"

"No, sir, it's just... your neck..." The man raised a tentative finger and pointed.

Carson reached up and found that the bandage had slipped down from his neck wound. His fingers grazed the ragged flesh and his stomach rumbled. *Mmmmmm... feel that skin and gristle and dried blood? You should be dead, Carson my boy!* Carson squeezed his eyes shut and readjusted the bandage. "Thank you, young man," he said, recovering as the inner voice fell silent. "I'll have a medic spruce that up a bit. Now, what did you want to say to me?"

The man steeled his courage and stepped forward. "Well, sir... I overheard my boss complaining about you going over her head. Seems like you've got a lot of influence and... well, I figured if you've got someone on the inside going *over* her head, maybe you'd like someone going... uh... *under* it."

Carson stared for a moment before bursting into laughter. "I'm guessing oratory is not your strong suit, but I get your drift. Do you have anything else you'd like to say? Perhaps something... specific? Something *useful*, to demonstrate your good faith?"

"Yes, I think so. When I was rounding up expedition members for transport to Grangeville, I overheard three individuals discussing what might have caused the initial... 'infection,' I guess we're calling it." He glanced down at his clipboard. "Elizabeth Torres, Dhir Patel, and Sarah Bishop."

"Actually, I've arranged for Mr. Patel to come with me. But as for your fortuitous bout of eavesdropping"—Carson leaned against the front of the cage, propping his face between two bars— "please, do go on."

"It sounded like some kind of spherical meteorite might be to blame for what happened to the Sasquatches; they seemed to think it was radiating something that causes 'changes' if you're too close. They mentioned some geologists, which I believe are the two infected individuals that attacked a pair of reality show hosts. The three in the tent said two other expeditionary members were going out to look for the sphere, with the blessing of the National Guard commander."

"Do you happen to know who those two sphere-seeking individuals are?"

Another glance at the clipboard. "Russ Cloud and Joseph... Washakie." The man got the name right this time.

"What is your name, son?"

"Alan Robbins, sir."

"Well, Alan, you've been very generous with this information, and it seems only fair that I be 'generous' in return. Are you going to be at the quarantine in Grangeville?"

"Yes, sir."

"Excellent. Then I don't see any reason why our exchange of generosity should not continue." He spied Singleton listening intently at the entrance to the helicopter. "Bill, speak with our new friend here and exchange the necessary details to facilitate our arrangement."

Just then a group of four men arrived, grunting and straining under the load of a massive body bag. Singleton took Alan Robbins aside as the men heaved their load into the helicopter with a collective grunt of exertion. As they stepped back down, the expedition medic hopped aboard and tentatively approached Carson's cage, a pair of med-kits in his hands.

Carson smiled. "Ah, good of you to come. I want you with me for the little hop to Missoula and the flight back to New York."

"Uh, yeah. Mr. Singleton told me to get aboard and that we're leaving in a few minutes." The man stared at Carson, his eyes drifting to his neck.

"I'll need you to apply a new bandage," the billionaire said. "Let's go ahead and err on the side of overkill, shall we? Bleeding no longer appears to be an issue, but I gather it's a trifle... unsightly."

The man swallowed. "Yeah, you could say that." He set his kits down and opened one of the boxes. He quickly selected a roll of gauze and approached the bars but hesitated as he drew close.

Carson made no move to offer his neck. Instead, he simply gripped the bars in his hands and stared at the medic. "Come on. I won't bite." He felt a mental gale of laughter. *Oh, you did* not *just say that, Cameron old boy! After all, you of all people know just how much you'd like to... bite.* The man started forward again. *Yes. Come closer.* The thoughts in Carson's mind were disconcerting and he felt... urges. Some of them quite violent. He recognized these feelings as inappropriate—out of sync with the reality around him—and he felt his grip on control slipping. Although he enjoyed the occasional alcoholic beverage, Cameron Carson never overindulged and he never sullied himself with harder drugs. Loss of control was so *unseemly.* And now, this flurry of unwarranted thoughts and emotions and urges enraged him. The medic must have seen this in his face; the man's own face lost color as he lurched back a step. Carson hurled his indomitable will against these gibbering thoughts and forced them back into the closets of his mind. He conjured a smile on his face.

"You know, I should probably just rebandage my neck myself, hmm? I'm sure you have plenty to do with our imminent departure." He held a hand out through the bars. "Here, hand me the gauze."

The man seemed to sag in relief and reached out to plop the roll into Cameron's hand—a hand that suddenly grasped the man's wrist before he could make the handoff. The medic winced as the powerful grip ground the bones in his wrist.

"One more thing," Carson growled in a low voice, "I understand you've told a number of people that I was clinically dead.

No pulse. No breathing. Obviously, I am very much alive. The fear I'm seeing right now in your eyes? I'd rather not see that in too many other sets of eyes if these *rumors*—based on your hasty initial diagnosis—were to cause unnecessary consternation." Carson continued to speak with his toothy smile firmly in place, but no mirth reached his eyes. "I am hereby requesting you *reassess* what you thought you saw when you examined me. Such a reassessment would be met with substantial gratitude on my part." Carson strengthened his grip and the man winced. "On the other hand, continuing to spread damaging and faulty medical *opinions* would not be in your best interest. Do we have an understanding?"

The medic nodded, terror painting his face. "Y... yes. You... you probably *did* have a pulse when I found you, but it must have been so weak that I failed to detect it. With the monsters attacking the camp and all."

Carson's smile grew wider and this time it did reach his eyes. "Very good." Still gripping the wrist, he plucked the roll of gauze from the medic's fingers with his free hand. "I'm fairly sure you saved my life! I'll make certain the world knows it." He released the man. "Now, while I've got you here, I'd like you to prepare a sedative and keep it handy for when we take off from Missoula. Just between you and me, I'm a *beast* on long-haul flights."

In little more than an hour, the Super Puma had landed on one of the three helipads at Missoula International Airport. A Maiden Air private jet equipped with an extended cargo ramp was waiting nearby and within minutes they were airborne, headed east. Carson's cage was ensconced at the rear of the plane behind heavy privacy curtains. Aboard were a pair of pilots, several mercenaries, the medic, and the camp cook. Most Maiden Air corporate jets boasted a pair of beautiful flight attendants, but they were conspicuously absent on this flight. Bill Singleton and Dhir Patel were locked in conversation in a row of plush seats near the rear.

"So... you want me to spy on the CDC?"

"Certainly not, Mr. Patel. I need you to maintain secure contact with an individual *within* the CDC."

"Right, I got that."

"This individual is an *employee* of the CDC. This is simple information sharing. He'll be letting us know about developments on their end, and we'll do the same, if we learn anything at our North Brother lab. Where you will now be working."

"The lab on the island in the East River near Rikers? The one where they used to keep plague victims?"

"Typhoid and tuberculosis, actually. North Brother Island is mostly a bird sanctuary now, but Mr. Carson offered to maintain the historic buildings and fund research in the local bird sanctuary in return for a small facility underneath the remains of Riverside Hospital."

"What exactly does Maiden do there?"

Singleton opened his mouth to respond but abruptly snapped it closed. "I think we're straying from the purpose of this conversation. Can you maintain a secure pipeline with this CDC individual or not?"

"Why does it need to be secure?"

Bill Singleton pinched the bridge of his nose between his fingers. "Look... Dhir. Mr. Carson has been very generous to you and your projects, wouldn't you agree?"

Dhir thought about the technical ventures that he had applied for funding for within Maiden's Engineering and Software Division. In each and every case, his requests for additional funds had been met with an influx of cash above and beyond the amount he'd asked for, as well as a detailed response from Carson himself, always indicating an intense interest in—and at least a basic understanding of—the proposed research. "Yes, Mr. Carson has always been an enthusiastic supporter."

"Yes. Cameron is, by his nature, an 'enthusiastic supporter.' He supports anything he perceives as a potential advancement for humankind... genomics, space exploration, the quest for limitless energy. He is also quite enthusiastic in his adventurous stunts with skydiving and circumnavigation and underwater speed records. And in his support of archaeology, anthropology, and now... cryptozoology. All of this enthusiasm has made him a number of enemies within the Maiden organization. 'Enthusiasm' doesn't always translate into profits. There have been rumblings of discontent; they aren't loud, but I've heard them. The money lost on the antimalarial project and the disastrous Maiden Galactic moonshot resulted in one attempted board ouster already. And now... *this* debacle."

Singleton leaned closer. "Cameron is a, um... complex man. A bit arrogant, a bit... well... megalomaniacal, if I'm honest. If he can't take credit for something, he's not likely to pursue it. But if everything he dreams up were to come to pass, our planet would be better off. He may do much of what he does to inflate his own ego, granted—but if we end up with fusion? Or a moon base? Or a live Bigfoot?" He raised his eyebrows at Dhir and waited.

Dhir sighed. "Okay. Yes, I can set you up with a form of encrypted communication, outside of the company servers. I can't do much if he calls you directly or uses company email, but if you route messages through my system, I should be able to keep them secure."

"Excellent. Thank you, Dhir. I knew we could count on you." Singleton rose and headed for the rear, pushing past the privacy curtains. He found Cameron Carson with a look of intense concentration on his face, two fingers pressed against the right side of his neck just below the jawline. The rest of his neck was completely swaddled in layers of gauze. He abruptly removed his fingers when he spotted Singleton.

"How are you feeling, Cameron?"

A rueful chuckle. "I feel fine, Bill. Fantastic, even. But just between you and me and the lamppost... all's not well." He lowered his voice. "For one thing, I can't feel my pulse."

Singleton frowned. "Your blood pressure may still be dangerously low from your injuries. I'll fetch the medic—"

"No!" Carson snapped before returning to a quieter tone. "My pulse isn't *low*... it's *nonexistent*." Singleton started forward, raising his hand toward the bars. Carson stepped back. "And I don't think it would be advisable to allow anyone too close to me at the moment. That's another concern I'm having. I'm experiencing... urges. Do you have the sedative?"

"Yes, sir."

"Good. Keep it handy. Now, if you would be so kind, send the cook back."

Singleton nodded, noting a gleam in his employer's eyes after he mentioned the cook. As he exited the rear, Dhir approached him.

"Mr. Singleton, I sent your CDC contact a temporary email and instructions and got an immediate response through the encrypted channel I've created for him." He handed his smartphone to Singleton, who read the message on the display:

Russ Cloud, Joseph Washakie, and an unnamed National Guardsman left camp an hour ago and headed south. I am securing a Guard escort and will attempt to follow.

CHAPTER FIVE

"So... you think this meteor thingie... what did you call it?" Luke asked.

"The Stone that Sings," Joseph responded.

"Man, that sounds familiar..." Luke mused, frowning. "Anyway, you think this singing rock turned those geologists into zombies... then one of them bit a Bigfoot... who bit another Bigfoot... who bit a *third* Bigfoot... and then, that one bit Carson."

"*Killed* Carson," Joseph amended.

"It's all theory, of course," Russ said. "But I can certainly attest to that rock throwing off some powerful vibes. If Joseph hadn't pulled my dumb ass out of the tent when he did..."

"Wait a sec, hold up." Luke stopped and the three of them stood on the trail to the south of camp. "If that thing started messing with your head after just a few seconds, what exactly are you planning to do when we find it?"

Russ shrugged a backpack from his shoulders and unzipped it, extracting a hefty pair of padded headphones. "I borrowed these from Bud Sorenson's audio equipment, as well as one of his digital recorders. It's loaded with some Bigfoot vocalizations, as well as some music he liked to listen to. When Joseph first told me about the legend of a rock from the sky that turned men into monsters, he called it the 'Stone that Sings.' And I have a vague memory of hearing a tone—more of a chord, really—when I got close to it. These thick noise-canceling headphones, combined with something playing through them, might be enough to block that sound. I'll go into the tent with these on, and I've got another headset for one of you in case someone has to pull me out; no player for it, but they block out sound pretty well. Of course, if it's really some sort of radiation, then we'll have to come up with something else."

"And the shovel?" Luke asked Joseph, pointing at the shovel the Shoshone carried over his shoulder.

"This? Oh, this is for bashing Russ's head in if he starts to change into a brain-biter."

"Really?" Luke asked, incredulous.

Russ laughed. "Joseph's your uncle, isn't he? You must know he's full of shit about eighty percent of the time."

Luke grinned sheepishly. "Yeah, Mom told me all about growing up with him; he was always playing pranks and spinning tall tales. Called him the second coming of the trickster god."

"Your mother is Joseph's sister?"

Luke looked down and kicked at a loose rock on the trail. "Was. She passed a couple years ago."

"She was a great woman," Joseph said, pushing through the awkward moment. "And she pulled her share of pranks on me, too. How's your father doing, Luke?"

"Pretty good. He's living in Kamiah in the Nez Perce rez. Opened a little self-run museum and gift shop near the It'se Ye-Ye Casino. Said the tourist traffic is better there, and he likes the local VFW."

"Nez Perce?" Russ looked at the young guardsman. "Aren't you Shoshone, like Joseph?"

"Half. Dad's Nez. Or Nimiipuu, as he prefers to call the tribe."

"Good to hear he's well," Joseph said. "Been meaning to pay him a visit." He lifted the shovel from his shoulder. "To your question, this is so we can bury that meteorite deep, where no one will find it. There were some digging tools in the geologists' camp, but I wanted to be sure we had one with us, in case someone already bagged and tagged the evidence."

"I doubt it," Luke said. "Sharkey and Farley were supposed to guard the site until the shift change and they're probably still there. As far as I know, no one else has been up there yet."

"No one has," Joseph said, examining the trail ahead.

"How do you know?"

"Russ? Care to show my nephew the ways of the tracker?"

Grinning, Russ gestured to Luke. "Over here, grasshopper." Luke followed as Russ walked ahead, looking from left to right. "Heavy rain before you got here, so we've got ideal conditions for... that." He pointed at a boot track in the trail. "Joseph and I have been spotting these all the way from camp. Two males, wearing... hey, press your foot in the trail right beside this track." Luke did so and the structure of the sole was a close match. "Two males wearing the same issue boot you are. You're a size 10?" Russ asked.

"Yeah!" Luke exclaimed, clearly impressed.

"This guy looks like a half size bigger. And that's his friend." Russ pointed near the other side of the trail. "He's about a size 13."

"That'd be Sharkey. Big dude. Hey, how'd Shark and Farl know where the camp was?"

"Russ and I figured out the coordinates from the terrain features on a topo map," Joseph said, an undercurrent of annoyance in his tone. "Told the Guard to lock the site down. That was before Cameron Carson decided to return to the living." He shook his head. "I should've kept my damn mouth shut. Gone back myself."

"Hey, we did have a few things on our minds, if you recall." Russ grasped Joseph's forearm. "At least you made sure the infected Sasquatch were burned before the government types got to them. And we can still get that damn rock out of there before the wrong people get their hands on it."

"Hey, guys?" Luke had gone ahead on the trail, following the tracks. "I think I'm getting the hang of this! Looks like Shark and Farl stood around here for a while... and there, they headed up the rise. Hey, what's that?" He pointed at a red swatch of ribbon tied around a tree limb.

Russ started up the rise and the others followed. "Trail blaze flag. Looks like they marked the route for follow-on groups."

Joseph went to the flag and took hold of it. Unsheathing his large hunting knife, he slipped the tip under the ribbon and cut it free. "Can't hurt to buy ourselves a little extra time." He pocketed the ribbon and pointed ahead. "They cut in toward the camp earlier than we first did. It shouldn't be too far ahead." He turned to Luke. "I know you said the commanding officer gave orders to everyone to stay well clear of the camp..."

"Yeah. Maintain a perimeter, but don't go into the camp."

"Well, just in case"—Joseph pointed to the M4 carbine slung over Luke's shoulder—"flip your safety off."

Fifteen minutes later they came within view of the camp. The neon green tent was easy to spot and they could see a National Guardsman nearby, leaning against a tree, wearing earbuds and bobbing his head to an unheard beat.

"I doubt zombies are music lovers," said Joseph.

"I dunno. Could be listening to 'Monster Mash,'" Russ replied, then immediately groaned at his own lame quip. "Man, I don't even have kids, and I'm burping up dad jokes."

"That's Farley," Luke said. "Where's Sharkey?"

"One way to find out," Russ said. "Flash!"

Farley, deep in his music, didn't budge, but a head popped up beside him.

"Uh... Thunder?"

"Hey, guys, it's Luke! Here to relieve you." He gestured to Russ and Joseph to follow him, looking back over his shoulder at Russ. "Really? Flash-Thunder?"

"Nice one, Grandpa," Joseph chided, pushing past.

"Hey, I binge-watched *Band of Brothers*, so sue me," Russ protested.

"About time you got here, I'm starving!" Sharkey boomed, rising to his full height and stretching. They could now see that he'd been sitting in a camp chair. "I'm gonna eat the heck out of a steak."

Farley, seeing his friend stand up, flipped off his music. "Oh, hey, Luke." He took in Russ and Joseph. "Who are these guys? The commander said not to let anyone in except officials of the US government... and they don't look too official."

"Well, actually, they sort of are. They're... forensic experts. They were part of the Carson expedition and got roped into helping. Joseph here is my uncle too, if you can believe it."

Farley shrugged. "Cool." He pushed off from the tree he was leaning against and stretched. "Let's get back, Shark."

Joseph looked intently at the two men as they gathered up their gear. "Gentlemen, did either of you enter the camp?"

Sharkey showed an intense interest in his bootlaces. "No, course not. Orders were to set up a perimeter, stay out of camp."

Farley became hyperfocused on his smartphone, scrolling through some tunes. "We've been right here the whole time. Hey, we better get back if we wanna catch the helo into town."

The two men exchanged some quick goodbyes with Luke and were soon on their way back, following the red ribbons. Joseph had only removed the two nearest the main trail, not wanting his minor sabotage to be too obvious.

"What's that smell?" Luke asked, wrinkling his nose.

"That's from our geologists, after they turned," Joseph said. "The odor was also in the clearing where we found their remains, only much stronger."

"We better get to it," Russ said. He handed the loose set of earphones to Joseph before donning his own and clipping the recorder to his belt. He stepped into the camp, eyes drawn to a box for rock samples. He emptied it and said loudly, "I'm going to put it in here." He looked at Joseph, who had his cans around his neck. "Keep your eye on me through the tent flap. If you see me getting all blissed out or whatever, yank me out of there quick!"

Joseph gave him a thumbs-up and Russ took a deep breath before turning toward the green tent. Sample box under one arm, he reached down and switched on the recording. Sasquatch howls filled his ears. *Hell no. Too creepy. Besides, I need something continuous.* He looked down at the device and thumbed through several selections until he found a delightful reggae riff. Russ turned up the volume and slowly opened the tent flap, using a loop on the corner to fasten it so that it stayed open.

On a whim, he took off his ever-present do-rag and wrapped it on his hand. He wasn't sure touching the meteorite's surface had anything to do with its strange effects, but it didn't hurt to take precautions. One hand now protected, Russ crouched and entered the tent; the stench was overpowering. *There!* The pouch the stone had been inside of was lying atop the sleeping bag. He edged closer. *I don't hear any zombie choirs, so the earphones must be working.* He gingerly reached for the pouch.

Outside, Joseph turned to Luke and lifted one side of his earphones. "Step back and keep your distance. If one or both of us turns... and attacks you"—he raised the muzzle of Luke's carbine —"headshot."

Luke swallowed and stepped back as the two of them waited. Joseph could see Russ bending down, could see him freeze. Joseph tensed, ready to move.

"Shit!" Russ's expletive was loud enough that Joseph heard it through his cans. He lurched back into the waning sunlight and tossed an empty pouch into the dirt as he tore off his headphones. "It's gone!" Then his eyes widened, "Unless it's somewhere else in the tent!" He started to put his headset back on, but Joseph stopped him, his own ears now uncovered.

"No. It's not in there. That time you went in and it affected you, I could just barely hear a hum, almost like a faulty electrical plug." He held up a hand and listened intently. "It's not in this camp."

"But if no one else has been in the camp... oh." Luke stopped speaking as Joseph pointed to some familiar-looking boot prints in the camp.

Joseph then pointed at several indentations in the moist ground next to a camp chair. "I believe your friend Sharkey may have felt the urge to take a load off and borrowed the companion of this chair."

"There's a size 13 near the tent flap," Russ said. "And here... looks like a scuffle. Both of their prints in a cluster. Then the smaller prints move toward that drop-off and... one very deep print here."

"I know what happened," Joseph said.

"What?" Luke asked, his mouth open in wonder at the rapid-fire display of tracking skill.

"Later. We have company."

Russ heard the sound of approaching voices and signaled the others to take up positions where they'd found Sharkey and Farley. As they scrambled to the spot, Russ gathered up the headsets and stuffed them into his backpack before donning his do-rag. While Luke shouldered his carbine and Joseph leaned against a tree, Russ plopped into the camp chair and feigned a nap.

"Here they come," Joseph said under his breath. "Try not to yell 'flash.'"

"Shut up," Russ muttered back.

A voice called out. "Corporal Redheart?"

"Here!" Luke responded.

"We're coming in." A group of six National Guardsmen and three civilians in white coveralls came into view through the trees and approached the camp.

Joseph watched them carefully as they approached, and Russ waited until they were near before rising from his camp chair, the picture of nonchalance.

"We just took over for the previous guard duty," Luke said. "I didn't expect anyone so soon."

"Yes, we passed the men you relieved on our way here," said one of the civilians. "Good thing, too. Whoever blazed the trail did a terrible job." He tapped his identification in a leather case on a lanyard around his neck. "Matthew Shedd, Department of Defense. We'll take over from here."

Luke started to protest, but Russ was already heading back the way they'd come. "Fine by me! They ain't paying me enough for this weekend warrior shit."

The man glanced at him. "You two are Guard?"

"Yeah, they called us up so fast we went straight from the bar to the motor pool. No time to grab our uniforms."

"Let's go, Luke," Joseph said, "These guys have things under control. It's Miller Time!"

Halfway back to the trail, Joseph asked Luke, "So, young tracker, what did you see?"

The young man thought for a moment. "The guardsmen weren't guardsmen. More of those pristine uniforms, weird state patches. And I looked at their boots! Different make. Betcha they leave different tracks. Oh! And most of the guys I know... well, we're in decent shape and all, but... those men were hardcore. And older than most National Guard guys."

"The kid's good!" Russ said. "And I recognized at least two of them from when we overheard their boss talking in camp. I wonder where he is."

"Probably following up on various leads," Joseph surmised. "I'm guessing they've sent groups to all of the sites. Whoever 'they' are."

As they reached the trail, they spotted another group coming down from the north. Two actual guardsmen and a young-looking man in yellow CDC coveralls, holding a portable GPS and arguing with his escort. One of the soldiers spotted them and called out, "Hey, Redheart, are you coming from the site? Didn't you just get here?"

"Some DoD guy relieved me, Jack. You guys headed up there?"

"Yeah, this CDC guy shanghaied us."

"Mr. Cloud? Mr. Washakie?" The CDC man frowned. "Where have you been? It's almost sundown; you were supposed to take transport to the Grangeville quarantine hours ago."

"We're on our way back to the helicopters now," Russ said.

"The last helicopter will have departed by the time you get back," the man said, flustered. "You'll have to take one first thing in the morning. Return to your tents in the base camp and don't go running off until then." He cocked his head. "What were you doing out here?"

Russ shrugged. "Just had some last-minute things to attend to."

"Did you find what you were looking for?" the CDC man asked.

Joseph appraised him in silence, then: "Who said we were looking for something?"

The man stared back at him before speaking, "Well, where's the camp? There was supposed to be a red ribbon."

Russ pointed up the hill, "Straight up that way. Can't miss it. Just a word of warning: It's getting a bit crowded up there."

On their way back to camp, Russ turned to Joseph. "That was fishy, too, wasn't it?"

"Yes. One CDC man by himself? No gear that I could see."

"Well, maybe they're short-staffed, with the quarantine and all. Speaking of which, I suppose we should hop a chopper first thing tomorrow and get it over with. Besides, I want to check in with Sarah."

"I bet you do," Joseph said, with a ghost of a smile.

CHAPTER SIX

"Mr. Singleton! Wake up!"

Singleton jerked awake. The combination of a vigorous jostling and the note of panic in the cook's voice snuffed out the vivid dream he'd been inhabiting. "What's wrong? Is it Mr. Carson?"

"You better come back, sir. And have that sedative ready. Mr. Carson said so."

Singleton looked around the cabin of the plane. The ambient light was low and everyone appeared to be sleeping. It was pitch black outside the windows; they were probably halfway to New York by now. He pushed past the privacy curtains and came up short. The cage was empty, the door hanging ajar, and there on the floor beside the cage was one of the body bags they'd loaded aboard. It was open.

"What the fuck is going on?" hissed Singleton in an uncharacteristic burst of profanity. "Where the bloody hell is Carson?"

"In there." The cook pointed at the door to the rear stateroom. The cage had been too large to fit through the door, so they had placed it just in front of the suite. "He... he said he needed privacy. He ripped the cage door open! Broke the lock clean off. I thought that thing was designed to be strong enough to hold a Bigfoot!"

"It was."

The man held up a keycard. "Here. He told me to lock him in and give you this."

Singleton took it, a look of confusion on his face. "If he was able to tear that cage open, he's not exactly 'locked in,' is he?"

"I... I'm not sure he's thinking clearly. He..." The cook glanced back at the half-open body bag. "I'm sorry, sir! He was quite insistent, and I owe everything to the man! God forgive me..."

"What... what did you do?"

"Just the arm, sir! I'm so sorry!"

Singleton now noted the bloody galley knife beside the bag. For several long moments, he simply stared at it in silence. "Go to the forward lavatory, wash yourself thoroughly, and have a seat. Say *nothing* to anyone." As the terrified man pushed through the heavy curtains, Singleton went to the aft cabin and raised his knuckles to the door. He took a deep breath and then knocked softly. "Cameron. It's Bill. Are you... are you all right?"

"Bill! Thank God. Come in. Shut the door behind you."

Carson's raspy voice sounded like it was quite some distance away from the door. Bill held the card near the electronic lock, hesitating. *In for a penny, in for a pound*, he thought before swiping the keycard through the lock and opening the door a crack. He didn't see his employer. But he did see a bloodstain on the carpet.

"In the lavatory."

Singleton cautiously entered the stateroom and approached the private bath situated in the corner. Belatedly, he thought about going back for a firearm from one of the mercenary contractors, but by then he was in view of the bathroom interior.

"Hello, Bill."

Whatever he'd thought he was going to see, it wasn't this. Carson sat on the floor beside the sink, one wrist secured to a towel rack by a pair of handcuffs with fluffy pink padding. His beard was caked in dried blood.

"So… bit of an explanation is in order, I suspect. First off, rest assured I am presently in control of my faculties. I remembered I kept some… 'paraphernalia' on hand in the bedside table." He jingled the handcuffs. "You know… to keep things interesting. Once I came to my senses and realized I was out of my cage, I grabbed these and came in here. Towel rack seemed sturdy."

"Where is the arm, Cameron?"

"Oh… that. Yes. In the tub."

Singleton carefully made his way to the bathtub, cognizant of how close he came to Carson. In the tub was the lower part of an arm, cut through at the elbow. There were two healthy bites taken out of it. He felt his gorge rising.

"I suppose I'm lucky it wasn't altogether fresh. I think the foul taste is what snapped me out of whatever was happening to me. Seems my discerning palate is still semi-functional."

Singleton tore his eyes away from the grisly remnant and looked at his old friend. "But you gave that keycard to the cook; asked him to lock you in. A part of you must have possessed a modicum of control."

"I don't know how much control I can give myself credit for, if I'm forcing my cook to carve up corpses for a mid-flight snack. But yes… part of my awareness is still there, when the hunger surges. When… when the rage builds."

"We've got to get you to the lab! Doctors Schneider and Takagawa should already be there. If anyone can figure out how to cure you, they can."

Carson barked a laugh. "I suspect a 'cure' in the truest sense would be for me to crawl back into a body bag… but at this point, I'll settle for control. And on that note, do you have the sedative?"

Singleton dug the syringe from his coat pocket; uncapping it, he flicked it with a finger to jar any air bubbles loose.

Carson snorted at that. "Yes, wouldn't want any bubbles in my bloodstream. If I still have one—"

"*Please*, sir!" Singleton felt a flash of anger as tears stung his eyes. "I don't pretend to know what's happening to you, but I would appreciate knowing *less*, at this point. Could you *not* confide in me any more specifics, at least for the time being?"

Carson was quiet for a moment. "Yes, of course, Bill. Forgive me. I have come to rely on you so much over the years that I may have lost perspective as to how disturbing this would be for you."

"It's all right, sir," Singleton said, taking a breath and setting the hypodermic down near Carson. "If you don't mind, I'll let *you* administer the sedative."

"Sensible as always, Bill." With years of self-administered longevity treatments under his belt, Carson expertly injected himself and set the needle aside. "How quickly will this take effect?"

"The medic said it should work within minutes." Without turning his head, Singleton pointed toward the tub. "I'm going to leave that in there for now. I'll drag the body bag in here and we can put the arm inside. I'll clean the knife the cook used and deal with the stain in the stateroom, then we'll lock this door and hold on to the keycard. After we disembark at LaGuardia, I'll have the pilots relocate the plane to our Westchester facility and arrange a thorough deep-clean."

"I'm lucky to have you, Bill," Carson said.

Singleton went back to the area outside the stateroom and peeked through the curtains. Everyone appeared to be asleep. Even the cook was tucked in a chair, eyes closed. *I doubt he's sleeping, though. I doubt he'll sleep for a long, long time.* Singleton looked at the cage, the door standing ajar, the lock plate hanging askew. Did Carson realize he had done that? Perhaps not... or he never would have thought a pair of novelty handcuffs and an airplane towel rack would hold him. Bill reached up and pushed the cage closed, managing to wedge the mangled locking mechanism shut. If necessary, he would explain to the passengers that Carson had decided it was safe to exit the cage and was resting in the stateroom. He looked down at the body bag. The knife was on the edge of the zippered opening, so he carefully flicked it into the interior before grabbing hold of the foot of the bag and dragging it into the stateroom. As he closed the door and locked it, Carson spoke from the bathroom.

"Bill, we have a problem."

The sedative should have worked by now! Singleton stepped into the bathroom and saw that his employer was wide awake.

"I'm afraid I don't feel a thing." Carson sighed... although the exhalation of breath sounded oddly unnatural. "I realize I just promised you I'd avoid going into specifics as to my condition, but... I'm not sure sedatives will work on the 'new me.' When we land, getting me from the plane to the boat might be a touch dicey."

"I think I've got something," a pudgy man in earphones said, his glasses reflecting the light from his laptop's glow, the only illumination in the cramped studio apartment.

The calico cat, assuming she was being addressed, turned her head to look at her roommate.

"Yes... yesyesyes... I've *really* got something!" the man said, pressing a hand to his headphones and listening intently.

The cat yawned. She didn't know why they were still awake; her roommate stayed up like this every once in a while. At least it was a break in the daily routine.

"Something about an arm... a body... a sedative... cleaning the plane." The man scribbled notes in a pad. The bugs his employer had placed in Carson's executive jet's stateroom were in the main living area, and the conversation fragments he was picking up sounded like they were further away—perhaps in the washroom or maybe just outside in the adjoining cabin. Regardless, he had picked up enough to justify a call. He looked at the clock and grimaced. His employer would likely be asleep, but this intercept was clearly within the prescribed threshold to warrant contact. He grabbed his cell and dialed a number. After just two rings, a voice answered.

"Morgan."

"Ma'am, it's Reggie."

There was a pause. "He's on the plane, heading for New York, yes?"

"Yes, ma'am."

"I know you wouldn't wake me unless it was something good. So, how good is it?"

"The audio isn't the best and I'll have to see how much more I can sort out, but... I think we're talking felony."

There was another pause. "Clean it up, best you can. In my office, nine a.m. sharp." The call disconnected.

Reggie set his phone down and looked at his cat. "We're gonna be rich, Purr-nadette Peters!"

Well, he seems happy, thought the cat. She curled up and went to sleep.

CHAPTER SEVEN

Littlefoot stripped another morsel of flesh from the half-eaten trout in his hands and vocalized, 'Good.'

Brighteyes grunted an affirmation and popped a couple of berries into his mouth. Earlier in the day, they had crossed the logging road at a different point from where Brighteyes had wandered many years ago, but it wasn't long before they came across a brook, babbling away in the trees. On a hunch, Brighteyes had led them along the stream to the west, following it as it curved back toward the man-trail, until they'd reached a spot that seemed familiar; it looked like the very spot where his younger self had encountered the northern troop. The sun was going down and Brighteyes had not been able to spot any Sasquatch sign in the gathering gloom, but this was clearly an ideal fishing spot and would likely be prime real estate for any nearby Bigfoot. He decided they should stay here for the night and move further into BreakTree's territory in the morning, assuming the big male still ruled here. The last thing a wandering adult male should do is blunder into another's territory at night. With the last vestiges of the sun, Brighteyes had managed to snatch a pair of trout from the stream while Littlefoot gathered berries from a nearby bush.

'Berries good?' Littlefoot gave the vocalization an interrogative inflection, an inquiry asking if the berries in his cupped palm were edible. It was now pitch black, the moon hidden by clouds, and the additional hand signals they employed to enhance vocal meaning would be difficult to distinguish.

'Yes. Good,' Brighteyes responded. 'We sleep. Wake morning.'

A screech sounded on the night breeze. A mountain lion, from the sound of it. Nothing to worry the two Sasquatch.

'I afraid,' Littlefoot moaned.

'No fear. Mountain cat.'

Littlefoot snorted in annoyance. 'I know mountain cat, I not baby! I afraid stranger alpha. Mother Silk say Father Silverback afraid stranger alpha. She say stranger have many big brothers and they are scary and mean!'

The little Bigfoot was gesturing as he spoke—fortunately for Brighteyes, the moon peeked from its cloud cloak and he was able to catch Littlefoot's outburst. The youngster had not been born at the time of Brighteyes's short-lived scouting trip. He pulsed a short grunt from his mouth to halt Littlefoot's barrage of voice and hand signing. 'Hey!' When he had the little Bigfoot's attention, he spoke, folding in some of the special hand gestures he had developed.

All Sasquatch communicated with a combination of vocalization and gestures, but Brighteyes had taught Littlefoot a much more complex system of hand signs. Several years ago, he had encountered a hair-faced human, and in the process of nursing that man back to health, he had learned to communicate with him using a variety of gestures that just made sense. The experience had expanded his mind, and Brighteyes and Littlefoot now communicated in a manner far more advanced than any other Sasquatch troop. Brighteyes didn't *know* that, of course; it was just the way he now "spoke."

'The stranger alpha, if he still lives, is named BreakTree. He was very big but he did not hurt me. I did not want Silverback to go north to fight BreakTree, so I lied to Silverback. I told him the alpha had many big brothers to scare him.'

Littlefoot nodded sagely. 'You tricked Silverback.'

'Yes. Silverback would have attacked other troop. I lied to protect them.'

Littlefoot cocked his head in a questioning manner. 'Why?'

Brighteyes thought of the two young females—particularly the curly-haired red-body female who had seemed to look deep inside him. Just then, the moon ducked back into the clouds, immersing them in darkness once more. 'Questions wait morning. Sleep now.'

Brighteyes hadn't had solid rest in many days and his consciousness had to struggle up from the depths of a dreamless sleep. Some part of him had been aware of a knocking sound, but that had not been enough to rouse him fully. The object that lightly struck him, on the other hand, caused his eyes to pop open. He had been sleeping on his side in a temporary nest of boughs and he turned his head slightly. He lay still, looking up at the morning sky, the rosy dawn filtering down through the needled branches overhead. He listened intently: birdsong, a breeze, the burbling of the stream, Littlefoot's gentle snoring. Had he dreamed the sensation of something bouncing against his back? It had felt like...

A pine cone arced down from overhead, crossing his line of sight and lightly bouncing across the needle-strewn ground next to his head. It was immediately followed by a woody knock. A branch striking a tree; a common Sasquatch signal! Brighteyes quickly sat up and looked in the direction the pine cone had come from. Its source stood casually beside a pine tree.

It was a female Bigfoot, about six and a half feet tall, holding a thick stick in one hand and a pine cone in the other. Her hairy coat was very unusual: intensely curly... and red. A bright coppery red that shone in the early-morning light.

Thwack! The red-body playfully smacked the stick against the pine a final time before letting it drop, an amused smile on her primate lips. 'You sleep deep. You miss sunrise,' she vocalized before abruptly tossing the pine cone she was holding. 'Catch!'

Brighteyes twisted his body and managed to catch the hurtling cone. When he did so, the female Sasquatch got a better look at him and her eyes went wide, her mouth shifting from amusement to wonder.

'I... know you,' she vocalized softly.

Brighteyes nodded and gave a short pant of affirmation. 'We met long ago. When we were...' He held up a hand to indicate a short height.

The female moved closer, pointing at the bank of the brook where Brighteyes had been fishing the evening before. 'I was right there.' She looked at the ground at her feet before pointing across the brook. 'And you were watching me from there.'

'Yes.'

'My father told you never to return, but here you are. Why are you here?'

Brighteyes thought about how best to explain everything that happened in the last few days, but before he could begin, Littlefoot sat up and gave a short yelp of surprise. He pointed.

'Pretty red female!'

The red-body panted with laughter, but then some of the mirth went out of her as she asked, 'Is... is this your son?'

'No!' he replied quickly. 'He is of my father by another mother.' Then he added, 'I have no mate.' He wasn't sure why he'd said that, but the female's face changed ever so slightly. She looked... pleased.

Littlefoot stood up. 'I am Littlefoot!'

The curly-haired Sasquatch chuffed and vocalized, 'I am happy to meet you. My name is DawnWaker.' She turned to Brighteyes, who started to give his name, but she stopped him. 'I remember your name. You told it to my father. You are Brighteyes.' She looked closely at him. 'It is a good name.'

Were Brighteyes able to blush, he would have done so, but that was a trait unique to humans. Instead, he looked down at his feet for a moment before raising his blue eyes. 'You were with another when I saw you. Of yellow hair.'

DawnWaker rolled her eyes. 'My sister, DayWaster. She still sleeps.' The red-body puffed up with pride. 'I awake for hours.' She suddenly wrinkled her brows. 'Where is your troop?'

Littlefoot made a mournful sound and Brighteyes gathered the youngster close with one long arm. 'We are all that is left. That is why we came. We want to join your troop.'

DawnWaker looked at them with sympathy. 'My father does not like outsiders, but I will take you to him. I want...' She stopped herself. 'I will speak to him. He must help you.' She looked down at the remains of the two diminutive trout from the night before. She panted a laugh. 'That is all you caught?'

Brighteyes looked at the bones. 'Yes.'

DawnWaker walked past him and positioned herself on the edge of the brook. 'You are terrible at fishing. I will show you how it is done.'

In short order DawnWaker had snagged three trout, all larger than the ones Brighteyes had managed to catch. In addition, she produced several crayfish from a small pocket of still water littered with rocks. Brighteyes suspected she had shifted stones around and created that favorable habitat herself sometime in the past to lure the little crustaceans in.

'Here,' she said, handing over her bounty. 'Someday I will teach you. Now, breakfast. Then I will take you to BreakTree.'

Far to the south, on the bank of a much larger body of water, two young humans were doing their own early-morning fishing.

"Your mom's gonna kill you for stealing shrimp," said one boy, watching as his friend baited a hook with a thawed shrimp.

"Naw, she'll never know. Just took a few from a bag in the freezer. I'm gonna leave you in the dust with these stinky little guys."

"You wish. My dad says to use a green-'n'-silver spoon. Looks like a pike minnow. Salmon think it's gonna follow them and eat their eggs, so they get mad and go after it." The boy with the lure reeled in his previous cast and prepared for a fresh plunk.

"That's stupid. Salmon don't get mad. Besides, we'll be lucky if we get one. Gonna be steelhead again." He cast his freshly hooked shrimp far out into the sparkling waters.

Thanks to four federal dams on the connecting Snake River, there were a lot fewer salmon in the once-aptly-named Salmon River these days. Some locals bitterly suggested that they ought to just rename it Trout River and be done with it, but a few hardy specimens of Chinook salmon managed to make it up here each year.

The instinct to return to their spawning grounds was powerful, and one of these very fish was fighting its way upstream as the two boys cast their lines nearby. The urge to spawn drove the salmon onward until it suddenly felt a different, conflicting compulsion. There was something ahead, near the surface, calling to it. The Chinook turned to investigate, drawn to the strange vibrations traveling through the water.

It wasn't food. It wasn't a mate. But somehow, it was something *more* than those things. A greenish sphere floated gently overhead. Its spawning forgotten, the fish moved alongside the strange object, basking in the pulsing waves emanating from it. Slowly, the salmon began to *change*. Although salmon on the spawn run looked for things to eat along the way, this one found itself overwhelmed by an all-consuming, ravenous hunger.

"Do you hear something?" Lure Boy asked.

"We're next to a river, course I hear something, numbnuts," Shrimp Boy responded.

"No... not the water, it's... I dunno, like a hum. Hey! What's that?" He pointed to a round object floating about thirty feet out.

"I dunno, some trash. But, holy shit! Look right beside it!" Shrimp Boy cried as he finished reeling in his line. "Salmon! Big one! Watch this..."

He executed a perfect cast and plunked the shrimp right beside the fish's head. The salmon lashed the water and struck the bait with such force the boy nearly dropped his rod. He set the hook with a well-practiced jerk and prepared for a lengthy fight.

But no fight was forthcoming. The fish thrashed for only a moment, then stilled, turned in the flow of the river, raised its fishy head partway out of the water, and *looked* right at the two boys.

"What the hell..." Lure Boy said.

With a lash of its tail, the Chinook charged toward the shore, half out of the water, oblivious to the hook in its mouth.

"Uh... can fish be rabid?" asked Shrimp, needlessly reeling in the line as the salmon closed the distance.

Lure quickly dumped his rod at his feet and grabbed a large rock from a scree slide near where they'd come down.

"Jeez!" The salmon reached the shore and launched itself out of the water, narrowly missing Shrimp, who reflexively threw down his pole and jumped back. The Chinook landed on the bank, flopping madly, snapping its jaws in a fit of savagery.

Crunch! Lure brought the rock down hard on the salmon's head, crushing its skull. It went still. "Well... we got a salmon."

Shrimp let out the breath he'd been holding. "Are you nuts? I ain't eating that thing!"

The two boys stared at the fish. It looked wild-eyed, even in death.

"So... you wanna get your hook?"

"Hell no." Shrimp opened a clasp knife and unceremoniously cut the fishing line. "Let's go get a burger."

The two boys hiked up the hill back to a nearby trail. Behind them, a small greenish sphere continued its downstream journey.

CHAPTER EIGHT

"Are you ready, Cameron?"

Carson opened his eyes and looked at the closed door to the rest of the aircraft. He was sitting in the lotus position on the floor of the stateroom. At his request, Bill had given him the key to his handcuffs, and he'd released himself once his assistant had left. The sedative hadn't worked and there was no way they could risk pushing a cage with a man inside across the tarmac, so Carson had convinced Bill to let him do his best to restore his self-control. Seating himself on the carpet near the center of the executive cabin, he'd focused his thoughts inward. Carson had long been a proponent of Eastern meditation techniques; apart from sleep, this was one of the few times that the driven billionaire allowed himself to be still. Cameron Carson was determined to live past a hundred (oh, the irony), and to do so with a sharp mind and healthy body. He had undertaken all manner of treatments to boost his longevity—gene therapy, chemical enhancers, oxygen tents—but he found meditation to be the most effective.

Trying to enter a meditative state was difficult at first; a major component of meditation was attention to the breath. Yes, he could still take air into his lungs and then slowly release it, but the breathing felt... *simulated*. There was a disconcerting sense that the oxygen was not needed and he was simply going through the motions. He forced his thoughts past this sensation and focused on centering himself. When he at last felt a steady, sustained calm, he took inventory. Sure enough, The Other was there... but Cameron Carson exerted all of his will and considerable ego to cow the dark stain hiding in his mind. He summoned a mental representation of the Sasquatch cage and locked this rage-filled part of himself inside of it. After focusing on the image, he then visualized that cage being placed within a second cage and further imagined the cage-within-a-cage being lowered into a deep, dark pit. He had repeated this sequence of images several times when the knock came. And now it came again.

"Cameron? Can you hear me? We've landed and the boat is waiting."

"I hear you, Bill. You can open the door."

The door remained closed.

"Bill, I assure you, I am in absolute control."

A beep and a click, as the keycard opened the lock. The stateroom door opened and Singleton looked inside. "Are you sure, sir?"

Carson rose from the floor, his megawatt smile flashing. "Sure as shiny shit, Bill. Trust me."

After landing at LaGuardia, the Maiden executive jet had taxied to the remote northwest corner of the airport. Various ground support vehicles—luggage carts, catering and lavatory service trucks, mobile boarding ramps—lined the outer aircraft fence. Just beyond, mere yards away, lay the East River and a pair of dilapidated piers. Given the importance of this New York City airport, there was a surprising amount of trash, abandoned boats, and rusting barges along this stretch of shoreline.

Carson strode across the tarmac, his entourage maintaining a respectful distance, but not *too* much distance. To any casual observer, he was just an eccentric billionaire wanting his space or throwing a tantrum, demanding his underlings back off. A single guard manned a gate in the fence near the docks and one of Carson's security detail flashed the clearance he'd gained from his time in the service. There was no need; Carson's government contacts had already cleared the way and the guard quickly waved them through. The group proceeded straight to the pair of docks. Singleton walked beside Dhir, who balanced an open laptop on his arm, monitoring the secure channel with Carson's CDC contact back in Idaho.

At the end of the nearest pier, two Zurn commuter yachts waited, engines thrumming, their red-and-gold hulls sporting the Maiden logo. A gaunt woman in a lab coat waved to them. "Mr. Carson. This boat, if you please," she requested in a pronounced German accent. "Dr. Takagawa is aboard and we'd like to begin our examination immediately."

Carson smiled as he approached. "Dr. Schneider, efficient as always." He instinctively offered a handshake.

Dr. Schneider arched a threadbare eyebrow. "I would prefer to minimize physical contact until we know more about your... condition."

"Of course, Doctor," Carson said, withdrawing the proffered hand and stepping past her to board the sleek Zurn 90 before making his way below. He was met by a stocky Japanese scientist who snapped off a stiff bow and gestured to a corner bench.

"Mr. Carson, if you would be seated, I would like to begin a basic examination immediately."

"Can it wait? I'm famished."

"Your chef is waiting at North Brother," Dr. Takagawa rumbled in his guttural voice. "The ride to the facility only takes a few minutes. In the meantime, I would like to check your vitals."

Carson looked up at Singleton, who entered just as the doctor readied his stethoscope. The billionaire winked at his aide-de-camp and began to unbutton his shirt. "This should be interesting…"

Three hundred yards offshore, a small fishing kayak bobbed in the murky waves of the East River. The occupant held a rod, its fishing line dangling into the water. There was no bait on the hook; she wasn't here for the fish. The young woman lifted her digital SLR camera and adjusted the long-range telephoto lens, making sure not to linger on the two boats at the nearby piers for too long. Anyone in a kayak this close to Rikers Island and LaGuardia Airport was likely to get a visit from the NYPD Harbor Unit if they spent too much time with a camera glued to their face. As the two boats pulled away from the pier and turned toward the north-west, the woman set down her hefty camera in the well in front of her and pulled a cell phone from a pocket on her fishing vest. Raising it to her copiously pierced ear, she placed a call. A voice picked up immediately.

"Morgan."

"He's here. He boarded one of their boats with several others," the woman said with a slight Russian accent. "The German scientist was on board as well."

"Singleton was with him?"

"Yes. And a few expedition members I recognized from the dossiers you sent. I'll send the photos shortly. Although… I didn't see my sister."

"Katya may still be in Idaho. We're still trying to figure out what happened over there."

"Where do you want me?" the woman in the kayak asked.

"He's definitely heading for North Brother?"

"Nearing the Rikers Island Bridge now."

"I'm having a meeting at Maiden HQ at nine a.m. How soon can you join me?"

The woman scoffed. "Not by nine. I'm in a kayak. And west-bound traffic is a nightmare in the morning."

"I'll send a helicopter for you to the executive helipad."

"I can't just paddle up to LaGuardia and hop out, you know."

"Of course not. Be at the Elmjack Little League field in twenty minutes. There'll be a car at the southeast corner to bring you over to the helipad. See you soon, Yana."

Yana Volkov looked at the phone as the call disconnected. Then, for the fifth time in the past twenty-four hours, she dialed her sister's number. After a few rings it went to voicemail. Yana hung up without leaving another message, pocketing the phone and stowing her camera. Hefting the paddle, she brought the kayak around and pointed her bow toward the shore south of the Rikers Island Bridge.

CHAPTER NINE

"Betcha this is the most activity that little town has ever seen," Russ said, his eyes glued to a window aboard the Blackhawk.

Joseph grunted. Off to the side, the Grangeville airport was in view; its small airstrip was clear but the tarmac off to the side teemed with helicopters and vehicles.

Their sunrise flight had taken them out of the heavily wooded center of the Nez Perce–Clearwater Forest and into sparser tree cover and rolling hills. The terrain flattened out as their view was filled with farms and fields, and it wasn't long before the town of Grangeville came into view. With a population of just over three thousand, the small Idaho town sat at the intersection of Routes 95 and 13 and had a decent-sized airstrip capable of operating C-130 airtankers to fight forest fires, an all-too-common phenomenon in Idaho. Situated close to the site of the "incident" but not too close to other towns, it made for an ideal location to stage from.

Luke had remained behind but had given them the lowdown before they boarded. "Grangeville is where my detachment's based.

The armory's in the center of town and the airport's on the northern edge. The CDC set up a quarantine inside the Interagency Dispatch Center. Big building next to the airport; we've used it to stage a few emergency drills." Luke had wished them good luck and watched their departure from the camp clearing, tossing them a wave as the helicopter lifted off.

Now, after a short flight, the chopper banked toward the airport and soon settled onto a vacant patch of apron next to the runway. As a crew member helped them down, they were met by a National Guard sergeant who gestured for them to follow him. Russ and Joseph reflexively ducked, feeling the powerful downwash from the rotor blades. Once they were far enough away from the roar of the helicopter's engines, the sergeant yelled through the cloth mask he was wearing, "Welcome to Grangeville, gentlemen! I'm Sergeant Wilkins. I'm gonna bring you right to quarantine." He led them through a small parking lot and across a road just to the south of the airport. Russ could see police barricades far down the road to either side. Ahead was a long building, surrounded by a hive of activity. Guards were posted at every entrance they could see. Wilkins held the glass lobby doors open and ushered them inside, guiding them to a long folding table with three civilians wearing protective suits and surgical masks. They looked up as Joseph and Russ approached.

"Oh, goody..." Russ muttered. "Let the poking and prodding begin."

"Well, well, well. Russ Cloud. What on earth have ye gotten yourself into, boyo?" The redheaded man lowered his binoculars as Russ, Joseph, and their escort disappeared into the building.

"Who was that other guy with him? Looked Native American."

"Russ sometimes brings along a little local flavor on his shoots." Reality TV star Wolf Wallace turned to the man in the driver's seat beside him. "Thinks it gives his episodes more respectability. Me, I don't need anyone helping me with *my* survival skills."

This was an amusing statement, coming from Wolf, and his driver's lip twitched once. True, the star of *Man vs. Nature* didn't often bring someone with him... *within camera frame, at least.* Wolf's wilderness treks were far from "solo," and he brought a veritable army along for his shoots.

"So, whatcha wanna do?" his driver asked in a mumbled southern twang. Merle Stinnett hailed from the Ozarks and was a former Army Ranger.

"Nothin' to do but wait, laddie," Wolf replied in his atrocious brogue. Few people knew where Wolf actually hailed from, but it certainly wasn't Scotland.

Wolf Wallace was born William Peale and had spent his childhood in South London. Later, he misspent his early adulthood with a traveling pantomime, semi-learning the acting trade and occasionally camping outdoors when lodging was either undesirable or unavailable. One day, after a horrendous matinee for an audience largely composed of crying children, Willy Peale found himself chugging a pint in a local pub. He had just made an internal vow to make his own way in the acting world: come up with his own show, his own hook. As he ordered a second pint to seal the bargain with himself, he happened to glance up at the telly above the bar.

On the screen was an American show, some sort of outdoor survivalist series. Willy's brief camping forays had sparked a basic interest in woodcraft and he had bought a book detailing various tricks for hunting, trapping, fishing, and fire-building. This show, *Survivor Guy,* was fascinating, and the channel appeared to be running a marathon. Willy lost track of how many episodes he watched—or how many pints he consumed. The host of this show, Russ Cloud, clearly knew what he was about, but to Willy's eye, the show lacked flash and style. Its format was simplicity itself: the host trekked into the woods alone and filmed everything himself without outside assistance. Russ was limited by the cameras he could carry and the shots he could compose all by his lonesome... and while this was charming, Willy began to think of ways to jazz it up. If only Russ had a dedicated camera crew. If only he waited for better light for a shoot. If only the man himself were a performer...

Willy Peale sat up straight as the idea rushed into him, fully formed. He ordered an additional pint to celebrate his epiphany.

Over the following weeks, Willy immersed himself in survivalist training and carefully cultivated a new persona as a rugged outdoorsman from the Highland moors, sporting a tartan kilt, dyed-red hair, and an accent that would offend the ears of any true Scotsman unfortunate enough to hear it. Within a few months, Willy Peale legally changed his name, and "Wolf Wallace" strode into the offices of a major cable company to give his pitch. A year later, *Man vs. Nature* was the number one survivalist show on television. His original inspiration, *Survivor Guy*, saw its ratings dip sharply.

Wolf still watched Russ's show and found himself seething with jealousy. Though his ratings dwarfed his competitor's, there was no getting around a simple fact: Russ was leaps and bounds the better survivalist. He had natural instincts and exuded a truthful simplicity that Wolf's flashy show just didn't have.

And it wasn't long before Wolf himself found new competition breathing down his neck. New "survival" shows dripping with reality television conventions swarmed out of pitch meetings and onto the airwaves like termites from a rotting stump. Filled with staged arguments, deliberately incompetent survival choices, fake urgency and phony contests and time limits... even nudity— these newcomers quickly gobbled up market share.

Then, Wolf had gotten a call from his agent. Apparently, Russ

Cloud—the paragon of survival show purity and integrity—was going to hunt for conclusive proof of a Bigfoot! And the expedition would be funded by none other than the eccentric billionaire Cameron Carson. Wolf was furious that he hadn't thought of it first. His showrunner suggested that he should do a Loch Ness hunt, but Wolf quickly shot that idea down. The Loch didn't lend itself to a wilderness survival show format, but more importantly, he was afraid that if he shot an episode full of actual Scots, his invented persona would fall apart like overstuffed haggis.

Wolf had his people reach out to a contact they had in the cryptozoology world and discovered that Carson had an entire division devoted to looking into various legends and beasts. Unfortunately, he also found out that the Bigfoot expedition had already been launched. Wolf gathered a small crew and flew into Boise, quickly learning that some sort of "incident" had occurred. Rumors abounded and there seemed to be a quarantine in effect in a small town named Grangeville, near the western border of the Nez Perce-Clearwater Forest. Questions to a few guardsmen had yielded one important piece of information: Sasquatch had been sighted and some might have been killed... but none had been captured.

Not yet, at any rate, Wolf thought, looking out from his SUV toward the quarantine building. He craned his neck around. "Athena, ya pick up anything new, lass?"

Wolf's tech wiz raised her bespectacled face from the multiband scanner and laptop she had spread out across the back seat. She shifted her headphones off one ear, the earpiece pressing into her vivid purple hair. "Confirmed that Carson has left the area. Confirmed that two or three Sasquatch attacked the expedition and were killed. Scuttlebutt is they were probably rabid."

"Nothin' aboot any live specimens?"

"Not yet," Athena replied, pressing the headphones back into place.

"Here comes Ian, boss," said Merle.

Wolf turned back around and saw his cameraman approaching at a casual trot. Wolf pointed a thumb back over his shoulder and Ian opened the rear door, squeezing into a small patch of back seat that wasn't occupied by Athena's equipment.

"I got something," the man said with excitement. "One of the guardsmen heard from a survivor that Cloud, a blond woman, and an Indian fella were seen in the company of a pair of Bigfoots, one of them a juvenile."

"What?" Wolf spun around in his seat, clamping his hands onto the headrest. "Were these the ones that were killed?"

"No! That's what I assumed, but the survivor says these were different. Near as I can tell, there were five Sasquatch, total... three went rabid and attacked the expedition... and two are unaccounted for."

"That's barry great!" Wolf exclaimed.

"And I also learned that Russ and the Indian were seen going to a site that had been cordoned off. The guardsmen that would've been on duty at the time were..." He consulted a notepad app on his phone. "Sharkey and Farley."

"What are their full names?"

"I asked. No one seems to know; everybody just calls them Sharkey and Farley. Or Shark 'n' Farl."

Athena had lowered one earphone when Ian had entered the vehicle and she was already typing away. "Those are unusual names. I'll have no trouble... bingo. Found them." A few more key taps and she held up her laptop. Two windows were open side by side with photos and biographical information. "And they're stationed right here in Grangeville."

"Russ! Joseph!" Sarah rose from a chair in the large holding room that the CDC was using during screening. Her face lit up and she rushed toward Russ but caught herself. "Good to see you both," she said, a grin still on her face.

"You too, Sarah," Russ said. "Hey, Liz."

Liz looked up, nervously masticating a wad of gum. She thumbed off her smartphone. "Hey, guys."

"Anything wrong?" Joseph asked, noting a touch of concern in the young woman's expression.

"I can't reach Dhir. He should've landed in New York by now."

"I'm sure he's fine, Liz," Sarah said. "Given what's going on, Carson may have instituted a communications blackout. He'll get back to you, don't worry."

"Where's Bud?" Russ asked.

"He's at Syringa Hospital. Same hospital my father was taken to, all those years ago."

"Really? A local hospital? Pretty lax quarantine."

"They tested him first and released him. They know that whatever happened in the forest, it isn't airborne. Everyone has tested clear of any pathogens, so far."

Joseph grunted, then rubbed his arm. "Hate needles." All of them had had blood drawn shortly after they were admitted.

"You two get any test results back?" Russ asked.

"Yes, Liz and I have a clean bill of health. We've been waiting for you two. Did you..." Sarah stopped and looked around, lowering her voice. "Did you find what you were looking for?"

Russ turned to Joseph. "I dunno, did we? You never told me what you think happened to the you-know-what."

Joseph gave a subtle head bob toward a corner of the room. "Let's stick a pin in that for now."

Russ risked a glance and noted a man in a Maiden polo shirt reading a hunting magazine. "I don't remember him in the expedition," Russ mumbled.

"That's because he wasn't," Joseph replied quietly.

Russ blew out a breath. "Great... so we've got CDC guys, Maiden spies, real guardsmen, fake guardsmen—"

"Probably half of whom are DARPA," Joseph interjected in a low voice.

Sarah cocked her head. "DARPA?"

"Defense Advanced Research Projects Agency. Black-ops science."

"Are they after Brighteyes?" Sarah asked in an urgent whisper.

Joseph gave a tiny shake of his head. "No." He started to say something else, then suddenly rose as Sharkey and Farley passed by. "The guardsmen from the site. Come on. I think I know what happened to our mystery rock, but why not get it from the source?"

Sharkey, the big Montanan, was rubbing his arm. "Damn... where do they find these arm-pokers? Took her three tries to find a vein. Ain't like mine are hard to find."

Farley laughed and punched his friend in the arm, eliciting a wince. "Let's hit Three Mile and you can drink the pain away."

"They're not open yet, you lush."

"Then let's get some breakfast burritos at The Trails while we wait."

Russ moved to head them off in a nearby corridor. "Hey, guys. The eggheads clear you?"

"Yeah, looks like it." Sharkey's eyes slid from Russ's face and locked onto Sarah. "Well, hello there."

"This is Dr. Bishop," Russ supplied. "She was in charge of the expedition to track down the Sasquatch."

"Pleased to meetcha, ma'am. I'm Sharkey... this here's Farley."

Joseph moved closer, lowering his voice. "I have an important question to ask..."

"Okay," Sharkey said. "Shoot."

"One moment. I need a visual aid." He grabbed a notice off a nearby corkboard and flipped it over. "Sarah, can I have that pen you have in your right pocket?"

Sarah, accustomed to Joseph's powers of observation, slipped the slim pen from her shorts pocket and handed it to him.

Joseph held the paper against the wall and quickly sketched out a map of the geologists' campsite. He handed it to Farley.

The guardsman glanced at it and his eyes lit up. "Hey, you're good. This is the campsite we were guarding."

"Yes."

"So... what's your question?"

"Two questions... first, do you wear a size ten and a half?"

Farley's eyebrows knitted. "How did...? Uh, yeah."

"Good. Question two." Joseph tapped the pen on the south side of the campsite map. "When you were standing *here*... where did you throw the green rock?"

Farley went pale. "Wh... what rock?"

"The rock that was in the tent. Judging by the boot prints we found, I'm guessing it began to affect Size Thirteen over here, near the tent. When we saw you yesterday, you were listening to music —if you had your headphones on, you wouldn't have been affected at the same level. You grabbed the rock and threw it off the drop-off."

Farley nodded, his eyes wide. "Yeah... but when I was fighting Sharkey for it, my earbuds came out. I think I heard something weird as I threw it."

"Where?" Joseph tapped the map again. "Think hard. Exactly which direction did you throw it? And was it a toss? Or a fastball?"

Farley glanced around, then leaned in to Joseph. "Look, it seemed like it was messing with Shark's head and..." He trailed off.

"It *was*. You did the right thing. But where you threw it and *how* you threw it... we need to know."

"Well... I hucked it pretty hard," Farley said, looking closely at the drawing. "And I came straight from the tent, so... can I borrow that pen?" He took it and drew a couple lines running to the south. "Somewhere between here... and here."

"Do me a favor," Joseph said. "Close your eyes. Throw it in your mind... and listen for when you heard it strike something."

"Uh... okay." Farley closed his eyes and allowed his body to do a half-strength mime show of the throw. He opened his eyes.

"How many seconds?" Joseph asked.

Farley thought for a moment. "About three. Like I said, I threw that sucker pretty damn hard. In a high arc." He opened his eyes, frowned, then closed them again. "Wait... after I turned away and went to check on Shark... I think... I think I heard a splash."

Joseph laid a hand on his shoulder. "Good. Thank you. Enjoy your beers."

Sharkey shifted his big feet. "You won't tell anyone we went into camp..."

"What camp?" Russ interjected. "And who *are* you guys, anyway? I have a feeling I just imagined this whole conversation."

Sharkey chuckled and headed down the hall, tossing a "thanks, man" over his shoulder as he went.

Russ watched them go, then turned to Joseph, who was looking at the lines Farley had drawn. He traced a finger across the paper. "That side of the camp, there was a steep drop-off."

"Yes," Russ agreed. "We need a topography map."

"Well, lucky for us this quarantine site also houses a branch of the US Forest Service," Sarah said. "Liz and I spotted it while we were waiting. This way."

They started toward a glass door at the far end of the main foyer when a man in "hazmat casual" intercepted them. He didn't have the full outfit on, but he appeared to be CDC—at least the badge on a lanyard said so.

"You two! Cloud and Washakie. No commingling with patients who have been cleared. Come with me, please."

"We only got to the fraternization phase," Russ remarked. "Stopped well short of mingling, melding, or merging."

But the man had already turned on his heel, bound for a

curtained area at the back of the main room. Russ turned to Sarah. "Who says 'commingle'?"

Sarah grinned at Russ, then turned to Joseph. "We'll get the maps. What do you need?"

"Topography of the entire area," Joseph said. "As much as you can get."

"I'll try to call Dhir again," Liz said, her face brightening. "I bet he could pull up all sorts of detailed maps for us!"

CHAPTER TEN

Annabelle Graybill stepped out of her green-and-white US Forest Service truck in the parking area behind the Fogglifter Café. Yawning, she closed the door with a thump. Caffeine was sorely needed and this was her favorite place for a strong cup of joe, the popular café being just three blocks from the Ranger Station in downtown McCall. Glancing at a familiar vehicle in the lot, she smiled. A large car magnet decorated the driver's-side door of a white SUV, declaring: *Sharlie Hunters: McCall, Idaho*. Numerous bumper stickers adorned the back, including several touting various lake monster cryptids. Nessie, Ogopogo, and Champ were all in attendance, and McCall's own legendary beastie was there as well: Sharlie, the Twilight Dragon of Payette Lake—although that bumper sticker looked homemade and faded from the sun.

"Morning, Annabelle!" Officer Dwight Flynn was exiting the café with a coffee in one hand and a paper bag in another.

"Morning, Dwight," Annabelle replied. "What're you up to today?"

Dwight groaned and nodded toward his police vehicle.

"Nothing fun. Headed to City Hall—the new mayor called all hands for a meeting."

"This about the festival?"

"Yeah. He's decided last-minute that he wants there to be a boat parade."

"Oh, Lordy... well, good luck with that."

Annabelle entered the Fogglifter Café, got a large coffee, then ordered a breakfast sandwich to go. Sipping her coffee, she followed the sounds of raucous laughter into the corner anteroom.

"Morning, fellas," she said.

Four middle-aged men looked up from one of the few tables in the side room. In unison, their faces lit up, and one cried out, "Graybill! Pull up a seat! The East Indian huevos rancheros are on point!"

"Thanks, Brady, but I need to get up to North Beach. Got a sandwich coming." She looked around at the group and their various orders. Stuart with his thick mop of black hair—a Foggy Burrito. Mark the Ginger, red of hair and freckled of face—eggs Benedict. Kevin, taller than the rest and watching his weight—the McCall Veggie Scramble. And Brady, his remaining hair cropped close to the scalp—the curried huevos rancheros. Sounded so wrong, but tasted so right.

"A breakfast meeting, that's a new one," Annabelle said. "Usually, you boys strategize your lake monster hunts at one of the breweries."

"And that's why we're here," Kevin said with a wink. "We 'strategized' a little too hard at Salmon River Brewing."

"Gotta soak up last night's session," Mark said, waving a forkful of English muffin and ham. "They had just tapped a keg of Big DIPA and we might've overindulged."

"Good to know," Annabelle said. The Salmon River Brewery was right next door, and she'd been known to tip back a pint or two. "So, you boys planning a new search?"

"Kev just got a fish-finder radar we want to try out," Brady said. Then he pretended to have a spontaneous inspiration. "You should come!"

Annabelle smiled. Brady had been trying to get her to go out with him for the past year, and the Sharlie hunts and Sharlie meetings were a popular tactic. "I can't. Litter patrol at North Beach, remember? And someone reported a loose kayak."

"Keep an eye out for any tracks," Stuart said. "Or slide marks."

"Slide marks?" Annabelle raised an eyebrow. "Dare I ask?"

"Sounds naughtier than it is," Brady said. "Drag marks in the sand or mud from when Sharlie pulls herself onto the shore. Stuart here thinks she lays her eggs on the shoreline somewhere. Like a sea turtle. Which is a load of hooey, of course, due to her size. Sharlie gives live birth, like plesiosaurs."

Stuart choked on a bite of burrito. "She's not a plesiosaur! She's a near-extinct offshoot of order Crocodilia."

"In a cold-water alpine lake?" Mark scoffed. "Hardly."

"Nessie is in cold water," Stuart protested.

"And like Nessie," Mark continued, "*and* like Morag, in Loch Morar... Sharlie is a giant eunuch eel. No breeding means nothing but eating and growing."

Brady shook his head. "You're an idiot."

Annabelle turned to Kevin. "What's your theory?"

Kevin held up a finger as he finished a bite of eggs and veggies. "Transdimensional alien." He paused as he swallowed, then: "You know... like Bigfoot."

This sent the rest of the group into a cacophonous symphony of theories and countertheories. Annabelle sipped her coffee and enjoyed the show. Although nowhere near as famous as the Loch Ness Monster—or even British Columbia's Ogopogo or Lake Champlain's Champy—Sharlie was supposedly some sort of thirty-to-forty-foot lake monster, and there had been a flurry of sightings back in the forties. Personally, Annabelle believed Sharlie was likely a combination of half-submerged logs, wind-whipped waves, or—as in the case of one recent sighting—a scuba diver testing his new gear. Payette Lake was too cold, too landlocked, to support any such creature. Bigfoot, on the other hand... maybe. Annabelle had had several "encounters" over her twenty-year career, and while she'd never actually seen anything, the occasional hooting calls and tree knocking had sent a chill up her spine.

"Hey, did you hear anything about the helicopters up north?" Brady asked.

Annabelle nodded. "One of the other rangers said there was some sort of hullabaloo going on in the Nez Perce National Forest. He tried to call the Forest Service office in Grangeville, but some military guy answered. Said they were running an exercise."

"That doesn't sound at all suspicious," Stuart deadpanned.

"Annabelle... sandwich is up," the Fogglifter's owner called from the front room.

"You fellas have a good hunt. And don't run over any scuba divers while chasing giant space-alien dinosaur eels."

"It's the jet skis we gotta watch out for," Mark grumbled. "Those idiots are a menace. Wouldn't know a no-wake rule if it bit 'em in the ass."

Annabelle sighed. "Yeah... that Texan who bought the big house in Wagon Wheel Bay got his twins jet skis for their birthday."

"Twins? There's usually *four* of those douche-rockets zipping around, swamping boats."

"He got each of them two jet skis. Extras for their friends."

"Some folks have too much money," Brady groused.

"Maybe Sharlie'll get 'em," Annabelle suggested, exiting the dining room to fetch her sandwich.

To the north, a pair of frogs croaked and ribbited on a log alongside a southward-flowing creek. A barely perceptible hum approached from upstream, gaining in strength. Slowly, the amphibians turned to face each other. With a sudden pair of leaps, the frogs collided in midair, each attempting to devour the other.

On another body of water, two thousand miles away, Cameron Carson stared down at the surface of the East River. He hated waiting. Their tender lay at anchor, fifty yards from the shore of North Brother Island. Doctors Schneider and Takagawa had gone ashore with several tissue samples to test for pathogens, as well as a small amount of blood... if one could call it that. The efforts to draw that blood had been eye-opening, to say the least. Inside the vial, the viscous liquid almost seemed to move of its own volition. Needless to say, the good doctors had insisted tests be carried out before Carson could be allowed to enter Maiden's research labs.

Carson raised his eyes from the water. The island was over-grown; abandoned, vine-encrusted buildings were tucked into the bushes and trees. A pair of brick smokestacks rose above the canopy, and along the shore lay the ruins of a large dock, many of its pilings rotted away. Off to the side, a pristine new dock seemed out of place.

In the late nineteenth and early twentieth centuries, the island had hosted a hospital for the treatment of infectious diseases. Patients with smallpox, tuberculosis, and polio had been quaran-tined here, including the infamous Typhoid Mary. After the facili-ties closed in 1963, the island was slowly consumed by nature, its buildings falling into disrepair. Off-limits to the public, North Brother had become a bird sanctuary.

And it still was. But now it was a sanctuary of a different sort as well. Offering up nearly four billion dollars, Maiden Industries had acquired the island, maintaining the bird sanctuary, cleaning up various health hazards, and shoring up some of the buildings. In the interests of preserving the island's historical significance, the old hospital and sanatorium buildings were left as they were, apart from structural repairs to keep them from crumbling. If you wanted to look for what Carson had bought for his money, you had to look *beneath* the rotting medical campus.

Situated on the northeast quadrant of the island, the tuberculosis hospital was the largest building by far. From the outside it appeared to be a borderline ruin; shattered windows looked out on the interior of the island and wild grape and Virginia creeper climbed the walls. But looks were deliberately deceiving. The basement had been completely overhauled and now served as the top floor of a multistory research complex.

It was here that Maiden Industries had developed several breakthroughs in cutting-edge technology. Maiden Tech had made strides in robotics and artificial intelligence and was developing a new battery that could theoretically maintain a charge for months —provided they could keep the prototypes from exploding. Maiden Bio was hard at work creating genetically enhanced crops and perfecting new cloning techniques, and the entomology division was doing their best to correct an earlier snafu with a modified species of mosquito. An offshoot of Maiden Galactic operated in one wing, currently studying the possibility of a retrieval mission for the hapless Maiden Moonshot that had missed its orbital window and was presently hurtling toward Venus.

The thought of space brought Carson's mind to the snippets of conversation his inside man at the CDC had overheard about a meteorite. "Bill?" he called out.

His assistant appeared at his side. "I'm sorry for the delay, Mr. Carson. The tests are still ongoing."

Carson waved the apology away. "Any further communication from our mole in Grangeville?"

"Not as yet, sir."

The billionaire gripped the metal rail that ran along the side of the tender. It might have been his imagination, but he had a notion that he could tear the steel loose, if he wanted to. *Go ahead. Do it*, the voice inside coaxed. As if to underscore this urge, his stomach rumbled ominously. *Must... eat.* Carson gave his head a shake and released the rail, then repeatedly tapped a fingernail against it, the impacts ringing it like a bell. He looked up to find Singleton watching him with concern. Carson tucked his hands into his pockets.

"Bill... as I understand it, Russ Cloud and Joseph Washakie urged the first National Guard units on the scene to secure that geologists' camp to the south of our base of operations. Told them to *secure* it... but not to enter it."

"That is my understanding also, sir."

"But he didn't tell them *why*, did he?"

"Not to my knowledge, sir. The operating assumption was that some sort of virus might have infected the campers."

"Whatever it was... I think it's tied to this spherical meteorite they were talking about. And whatever happened to those Sasquatch—whatever is *currently* happening to me—is tied to that hunk of space rock."

"A reasonable assumption, sir."

"Well, then it's pretty clear what we need to do." Carson's gritted teeth pushed through his beard in an unnerving smile. "We need to obtain that sphere."

"Cameron, Cameron, Cameron. What have you been up to?" As the audio clip petered out into static, Hilda Morgan rose from the conference room table and went to the floor-to-ceiling windows overlooking the East River. She clasped her hands behind her back and gazed out at the sun-dappled water.

Hilda looked to her left, taking in the majestic sight of the Brooklyn Bridge with the Manhattan Bridge behind. This view wouldn't have been possible a year ago, thanks to the sixty-story eyesore on the opposite side of Maiden Lane. But Cameron Carson had purchased that building before it could be fully inhabited, bought out all the current tenants, and then shaved the skinny monstrosity down to twenty stories, restoring Maiden HQ's view. Hilda disapproved of Carson's loose hand on Maiden Industry's purse strings and his over-the-top spending on extravagant projects. But in this case, she was pleased with the end result, particularly since Carson had spent his *own* money, rather than dipping into Maiden's coffers.

Back at the conference table, Reggie leaned forward and rotated his laptop back toward himself to silence the audio enhancement program. He stole a glance at the young Russian woman across the table from him. Yana didn't notice, her eyes on Hilda's back.

Hilda Morgan was a striking woman. At an inch over six feet in height, she came from mixed parentage, raised by a single mother in Stockholm, Sweden; her Jamaican father had left them when she was very young. Attending MIT Sloan School of Management in Cambridge, Massachusetts, Hilda found herself working for a number of up-and-coming tech firms, eventually landing at Maiden Industries. It didn't take her long to climb the corporate ladder, and after serving as the company CFO for several years, she settled into her current position: Chair of the Board of Directors. Only Cameron Carson stood above her in the hierarchy. But that was about to change.

Hilda turned to face her two guests, her curtain of tightly braided locks of blond hair swinging across her shoulders. While most women in the corporate world opted for pant or skirt suits, Hilda wore a man's suit, perfectly tailored to her body, a red tie standing out from the expensive gray fabric of the bespoke Savile Row ensemble.

"I apologize again for the quality of the audio," Reggie said quickly. "As I said before, I set the bug up to pick up conversations in the stateroom itself, not the washroom."

"But you did pick up *something* in the stateroom, didn't you?" Hilda said, thinking. "It sounded like an animal…"

"And eating noises," Yana added.

"And that's the only audio you have?" Hilda asked Reggie.

"From the jet, yes ma'am," the technician answered quickly. "But I expect to have some audio from the quarantine site in Idaho shortly."

Hilda frowned. "You don't have any yet? Why the delay?"

"Well, ma'am... our man on the ground planted several listening devices, but there appear to be some federal types on-site —probably FBI or DoD. Maybe DARPA. Anyway, someone's been sweeping for bugs. My guy has to be more careful about where he places them."

"So, they found your little toys?" Hilda leaned on the table with a look of concern. "Can they be traced back to us?"

"Not a chance," Reggie replied with a smug smile. "I've constructed all of my devices with untraceable aftermarket parts, and the signals are automatically encrypted and bounced through half a dozen nodes on three continents."

Hilda nodded. "Well, I hope you brought some with you." She turned to Yana and appraised her; like her sister Katya, the Russian woman had an affinity for tattoos, and her exposed neck and arms displayed a number of them. Combined with her facial piercings and spiky frosted hair, she was memorable. But having worked primarily "in house" for Hilda, Yana was not likely known to anyone at the lab. "The fragments of conversation we picked up from the plane certainly imply some form of wrongdoing," Hilda said, "but it won't be sufficient ammunition for the Board to oust Carson as CEO. We need more. And you're going to get it for me."

CHAPTER ELEVEN

'When you stand before Father, do not look him in the eyes,' DawnWaker warned. 'And do not speak until I say.'

The trio of Sasquatch had been walking north for quite some time; apparently, BreakTree's territory was substantial. Brighteyes opened his mouth slightly and inhaled, tasting the air. He thought he detected the odor of another Bigfoot, but then the wind shifted and he frowned. He sniffed, trying to decipher the confusing scent.

'Raccoon,' he vocalized and signed. 'But also... fox? And elk?'

'BearFriend!' DawnWaker exclaimed. She sniffed the air as well, then pointed. 'This way.'

'Who is BearFriend?' Littlefoot grunted in question.

'He is my uncle. He is very old. And...' She hesitated. 'Do not be alarmed by his appearance. He is sensitive.'

They came over a rise and found a dense stand of huckleberry bushes. Brighteyes could make out a furry form on the far side.

'Uncle! Come meet friends.'

The form froze, then moved around the huckleberries and disappeared behind the broad trunk of a fir tree.

'Don't be shy, Uncle.'

After a moment, the Bigfoot stepped into the open.

Brighteyes stared in wonder at the most bizarre Sasquatch he'd ever seen. The male was probably as tall as Brighteyes, but it was difficult to tell his exact height; old age had bent the primate over, his back humped. But that wasn't what was so jarring: the creature was covered head to toe in a patchwork of animal furs. Deer hides appeared to form the base, hanging from BearFriend's body like the winter clothing some humans wore.

Brighteyes thought back to his encounter with Beardface when he was young. What had the bearded human called what he had been wearing? *Coat.* Yes, that was it. This Sasquatch was wearing a coat! The deerskin had the fur of all manner of creatures affixed to it and it appeared to be lined inside as well. Brighteyes quickly identified possum, elk, bobcat, muskrat, and fox. The thick white fur of a mountain goat was arrayed across the shoulders, and atop BearFriend's head sat a nearly intact raccoon, its tail hanging down the back of his neck. When the Sasquatch moved, the coat parted and Brighteyes was greeted with another surprise. Inside the coat of many hides, the Bigfoot's body was completely hairless! Lack of body hair in humans was something he was familiar with, but they usually had *some* hair. BearFriend was as smooth and pink as a newborn mouse.

Littlefoot started to whine. Remembering DawnWaker's request, Brighteyes quickly laid a steadying hand on the youngster's shoulder. The elderly Sasquatch self-consciously pulled the coat closed and vocalized a query.

'Who are these males?'

DawnWaker explained who they were and recounted meeting Brighteyes as a child. As she vocalized and signed, the old Bigfoot grunted an occasional affirmation. When she finished, he held up a hand.

'I would welcome you... but that welcome is not mine to give. You stand in the territory of my younger brother, BreakTree.'

'They know, Uncle. But they no longer have a troop. I will plead their case. They must join us.'

BearFriend sighed. 'The little one, perhaps. But you, Brighteyes... if BreakTree drove you off when you were younger, he will be even more likely to now. He is older and will consider a mature young male a threat.'

Brighteyes nodded. 'May I speak?'

The mountain goat fur atop BearFriend's shoulders rose and fell as the old male shrugged. 'You may.'

'I do not want territory,' Brighteyes vocalized, adding sign language to enhance his meaning and intent. 'I do not want to threaten your alpha. I only want my sibling to be safe.'

BearFriend watched Brighteyes's hands closely. 'And a mate? You would have no interest in the females that belong to BreakTree?'

Brighteyes started to shake his head but hesitated, his eyes flicking to DawnWaker.

BearFriend cracked a smile. 'Be ready with your answer if BreakTree asks. I would recommend the answer be no... even if it is yes.' He pointed at Brighteyes. 'Your gestures... they are unusual. Some are like our sign speech, but others are nothing I have seen.'

Brighteyes made a conscious effort to simplify his communication, stripping the human sign language from it. 'I learned new gestures from a human when I was younger. I find they allow me to say more.'

BearFriend tilted his head and squinted his eyes. 'Best keep that to yourself, young one. BreakTree is set in his ways. I promise you, he will not like that.'

Brighteyes grunted his understanding. His former alpha, Silverback, had hated the enhanced gestures. Nevertheless, he had taught them to Littlefoot and Scratch. Brighteyes abruptly squeezed his eyes shut and shivered. Scratch—Littlefoot's teenage brother and Brighteyes's own half brother—had been infected by whatever had corrupted their troop's mated pair, Silverback and

Silk. Brighteyes had been forced to kill Scratch, and the memory of that horrible moment flooded his mind. His half brother's wild eyes and snarls... the sensation of the young Bigfoot's skull collapsing as Brighteyes crushed it. A gentle touch on his arm jerked him out of the waking nightmare.

'Brighteyes...?'

He blinked. DawnWaker was looking at him with tenderness and concern. BearFriend moved closer, eyes locked on the pair of them. Suddenly, Littlefoot broke the tension.

'Where is your fur?' he asked BearFriend matter-of-factly.

DawnWaker's uncle smiled, shifting his gaze to the youngster. 'Long gone, little one. Ten winters ago, I wake sick. Not a bad sick. Just a fever. But when the fever broke, my hair began to fall out. By the next moon, my body was bald as a human. And it was winter, so I was very cold.' He looked at DawnWaker. 'Lucky for me, I have a clever niece.'

DawnWaker chuffed in amusement. 'You thought me crazy, at first.'

BearFriend turned from side to side, the fur-encrusted coat billowing as he showed it off. 'Beautiful, yes?'

'There is a human rock-trail north of here, where the trees are thinner on the opposite side,' DawnWaker explained. 'Human wheel machines race by and hit animals from time to time. I found much of the fur there. It took many summers and winters to find enough.'

'How did you attach the skins to each other?' Brighteyes asked.

DawnWaker panted with pride. 'I found a discarded human covering. Took it apart. Saw how put together. I used strips of material from that. Pushed it through deer hide with a thorn.'

Brighteyes looked at DawnWaker with a new appreciation. He too had learned to make use of what humans had left behind, from time to time. 'You are smart,' he said simply.

'Yes. I am.'

'Why are you called BearFriend?' Littlefoot asked. 'I see no bear fur.'

'You have good eyes, little one,' the old Bigfoot said. 'I will wear no bear fur.'

'Why?'

The mountain goat hide shrugged again. 'Because I am Bear-Friend.' He held up a hand to stop the inevitable repetition of the youngster's original question. 'My name was given to me long before I lost my hair. When I was young—not much older than you—I found a lost bear cub that had wandered off from its family. It followed me around until I could find its mother.'

'Who chased you up a tree,' DawnWaker added with a laugh.

'Yes. Until my father came and scared her off. He renamed me BearFriend.'

'What was your name before?' Littlefoot asked.

BearFriend got a faraway look in his eyes. 'I don't remember.' Looking around, he shuffled over to a nearby tree and retrieved a sturdy branch as tall as he was, using it as a third leg. 'Come. We will speak to my brother.'

Within an hour, the sounds and smells of a Bigfoot encampment became apparent. A thick stand of old-growth pines provided obscurement and cover from the elements. The ground, thickly carpeted in needles, was largely devoid of weeds and brush. Brighteyes could make out movement in the waning light, and faint vocalizations could also be heard.

'Wait here,' BearFriend said, his face serious under the raccoon head covering. He hobbled away, leaving the remaining trio to wait on the edge of the pines.

'You look nervous,' Brighteyes said.

DawnWaker raised her eyes. 'So do you.'

'I not nervous!' Littlefoot boldly announced. 'I brave!'

DawnWaker huffed a laugh and shushed him. 'I am sure you are! But not so loud, brave one.'

After a time, the sounds of heavy footfalls approached. Even with a cushion of needles on the ground, the impact of the oncoming Bigfoot's steps was impressive. The gait was not hurried, just... determined. In moments, a massive alpha male appeared. Deliberately shoving a sapling aside with a sharp crack, he came to a halt several strides from them. Brighteyes quickly looked down at the forest floor.

'Father!' DawnWaker called. 'It is good to—'

'I remember you,' BreakTree rumbled.

Even with his eyes averted to the ground, Brighteyes was certain the big male was staring right at him. A shuffling sound announced the arrival of BearFriend, several paces behind his alpha, if Brighteyes judged correctly. He extended an arm toward BreakTree, offering his wrist in a gesture of friendship and submission.

'Long, long ago, I sent you away,' the massive male vocalized calmly. 'Unharmed. And yet, you have returned. BearFriend has explained why... but I wish to hear it from you.'

There was a silence, and Brighteyes raised his eyes, darting them to DawnWaker for assurance. When she nodded, he fixed his gaze on BreakTree's chest; he dared not go higher. 'My alpha... and my matriarch... and my half brother... they are all dead. Littlefoot and I are the last of my troop.'

BreakTree snorted. 'Five? Such a small troop. What happened to them?'

Brighteyes thought for a moment. How to explain? A bite from an infected human had turned Silverback into a ravening monster. Then, after a bite from Silverback, Silk had turned as well. Then Scratch. He decided he'd better simplify. 'They were... afflicted...'

BreakTree split the air with a sudden roar. 'They were *sick*? And you bring that sickness here?'

Startled, Brighteyes tried to explain, gesturing wildly to make himself clear. 'No! We not sick! We escape!'

'Escape? What do you mean? Why did you not stay and care for your troop?'

Brighteyes stammered—or rather, his sign language became hurried and erratic. 'They... *turn*. Like rabies. They attack. We run.'

'What... are... you... doing?' A low growl of menace underscored the question.

Brighteyes raised his gaze further, daring to meet the other's eyes. But BreakTree wasn't looking at his eyes... he was looking at his hands. In his panic, Brighteyes had let loose with a torrent of human-taught sign language.

'All Bigfoot troops communicate differently, but all still understand one another,' BreakTree said. He raised a massive arm and pointed. 'I did not understand half of what you signed.'

Just then, the wind shifted. BreakTree's nostrils flared as he took in their scent. While his manner had been stern and implacable, there had been a calm confidence underlying it. But that abruptly changed. His eyes widened.

'Humans!' he growled. 'You *stink* of humans!'

'Father...' DawnWaker stepped forward, but he turned on her.

'*Silence!* This one is not for you!' Grasping a low-hanging branch as broad as his forearm, the alpha snapped it off with an explosive crack and slammed it into the needle-strewn ground. An unmistakable display. 'You... outsider... you bring sickness! You bring the stench of humans! You bring strange speech that is not our tradition! You have no place here.' He stepped forward, and his bellowing voice dropped to a low rumble, terrifyingly calm. 'Go now... or I will break your limbs as I break the trees.'

Brighteyes dropped his gaze, daring not to challenge the male.

True, he had the strength of youth, but he dared not endanger Littlefoot. Slumping his shoulders, he turned away and headed back south, Littlefoot scampering along beside him. As he crested a hill, he looked back. DawnWaker watched him from a distance, her coppery pelt catching the setting sun.

CHAPTER TWELVE

Cameron Carson ran his tongue across his lips but resisted the urge to lick the plate that lay before him in his executive office. There wouldn't have been much point; the plate was spotless, not a trace of the pooled blood from the extra-rare steak remaining.

His personal chef had transferred over to North Brother, bringing a large assortment of beef and pork, as per Carson's request. The underground facility had a full cafeteria, but he didn't trust himself to eat in front of anyone at this juncture. And that had been a wise choice.

Looking at the fine china plate on the leather blotter atop his desk, he tried to remember eating the insanely expensive zabuton cut of Hitachi-Gyu A5 Wagyu beef. From the flavor that lingered on his tongue, he knew he had. His silverware lay unused on either side of the plate. Small side bowls of garlic mashed potatoes and green beans almondine had been shoved aside, untouched. A cloth napkin lay across his lap, unmarred save for several drops of juice from the steak. Looking down, he could see stains on his shirt. Applying his fingertips to his beard and cheeks, he found more evidence of an animalistic dining experience.

A soft knock sounded at the door. "Mr. Carson?"

Gooooooood. More... meat. Carson shook himself, his mind clamping down on the gibbering thoughts.

The knock repeated. "Cameron? Is everything all right?"

"Yes, Bill!" he called out. "Everything's fine. The steak helped."

"Very good, sir. May I... may I come in?"

"Um... best not, I think. I need a few moments to collect myself."

There was a brief silence on the other side of the door, then: "Shall I send for a sedative?"

"No, no. I'll be fine in a moment. Besides, we both know that wouldn't do anything."

More silence, then: "Doctors Schneider and Takagawa would like to see you in Bio Lab Seven. Contact me when you feel up to it and we'll escort you there."

"We?" Carson smiled. "Escort me?"

"Yes, sir. Until we have a handle on what's happened to you, the doctors think it best."

"As it happens... so do I. Five minutes, Bill." Carson removed himself from behind the desk and went to his executive washroom to clean up, stripping off the meat-soaked shirt and tossing it into a hamper. Once he was clean, he returned to the office and sat upon a floor cushion in the corner, closing his eyes and focusing his thoughts. The *good* thoughts.

Yana Volkov held up her ID to the guard beside the crumbling facade of the old hospital on North Brother Island. Thanks to that nerd Reggie's intrusion into Maiden Industries' human resources files, she now had sufficient clearance to enter the labyrinth of high-tech labs beneath the historical buildings. Reggie had filled her fictional curriculum vitae with a myriad of specialties, giving her sufficient reason to enter a variety of locations. And thanks to a few enhancements to her ID card's permissions, she'd be able to access most of the facility.

The guard looked at Yana, his eyes traveling from her frosted spiky hair to her tattoos and piercings. He scanned the card and his eyebrows rose.

"Multipass," she said with a smirk. He waved her through. An escort rose from a chair in the foyer and led her to a bank of elevators that looked out of place in the old hospital.

The man guided Yana to what he called the "barracks" and directed her to a small room that would be her sleeping quarters, roughly the size of a monastic cell. Once her escort departed, she set down her bag and retrieved a few items from it, then examined a map she had loaded onto her smartwatch. Next, she retrieved a carrying case and extracted a pair of thick-framed glasses. Sliding them onto her face, she tapped a tiny button beside the hinge and made an adjustment on her smartwatch.

Yana glanced around the little room, looking for something to test her special glasses on; her gaze settled on an odd piece of wall art that looked like it had been purchased in the picture frame aisle of a big-box store. She stared at it and tapped an icon on her watch. A brief flash on her smartwatch indicated that a photo of the framed print had been taken. A moment later, the dim heads-up display informed her of the name of the piece and its artist.

Satisfied, she quickly changed into a set of hooded cleanroom coveralls and slipped an N95 mask over her face. Pulling the elastic-rimmed hood of the coveralls over her spiky hair, she exited her room and left the barracks area. With occasional glances at her watch, she navigated the halls, took an elevator up one floor, then stepped out onto the executive level. Doors with name plaques greeted her, and she noted where some of the senior scientists were located. Several of the doors had racks beside them with ingoing and outgoing documents. Glancing at her watch, she noted that Carson's office lay at the end of the next hall. Turning the corner, she spotted William Singleton, Carson's right-hand man, standing beside a dark wooden door at the end of the hall, rapping his knuckles gently against it.

"Cameron… are you ready? Dr. Schneider was quite insistent."

The man looked back over his shoulder just as Yana ducked out of sight and went to the next door beside the executive suite's hall. She quickly grabbed a folder from the inbox and proceeded to examine it, as if she were just now delivering it. Even though she was looking at the materials as part of a ruse, her heart jumped as she read a particular bullet point: *DNA testing indicates significant changes to the genome.*

Footsteps echoed on the hard floors of the executive suite hall around the corner. Yana quickly tapped a button on her watch that would trigger continuous recording. She kept her head down, looking at the folder in front of her as the footsteps neared the main hall.

"How are you feeling, sir?" Singleton's voice asked.

"Considerably more human, after a good meal," Carson's voice replied. Yana had heard the man speak on television numerous times, and his voice seemed oddly scratchy or hoarse. Moments later, he appeared in the main hall, turning left and passing by Yana. She looked up and acknowledged him with a nod, then returned to examining the folder. He barely spared her a glance.

"Where does Dr. Schneider want me?" Carson asked, halfway down the hall.

"The cold room on the bio-level," Singleton replied. "They have parkas in the anteroom."

Carson barked a humorless laugh. "As if I'll need one."

"Please, sir…"

And then they were out of sight and out of earshot. Yana frowned. *Odd thing to say.* Returning to the task at hand, she quickly set the folder back in the basket and went around the corner, unzipping her coveralls as she fast-walked to Carson's door. She tried the handle; it was locked, as expected. She had no doubt that her ID card, souped up though it was, would not only fail to open this door but would likely leave a record of her attempt. Pausing the recording on her eyeglasses, she reached into her coveralls and retrieved a small disk from an inner pocket. Setting it on the floor by the door, she zipped up, then activated a different function on her watch. A tiny screen appeared and she saw a fish-eye-lens view of her own feet.

A few taps on the arrow keys beside this image rotated the view, then sent the little disk rolling through the crack under the door. Much like a commercial robot vacuum, the surveillance device could navigate obstacles on its own, but Reggie had advised she utilize manual operation to ensure the best placement. Yana rotated it from side to side, getting a lay of the land, then sent it to the underside of a bookshelf behind Carson's desk. After ensuring that the microphones were working and the micro-camera was aimed at his chair, she quickly turned on her heel and headed back to the main hall.

She was about to return to the elevator for the barracks level when she paused and looked back at the inbox basket with the folder she'd been examining. She retraced her steps and triggered continuous recording on the glasses. Opening the folder, she quickly flipped page after page, going through the entire report in seconds. She would go over the footage later. Returning the folder, she looked up at the name plate on the door: Dr. Monika Schneider.

"Ah, Mr. Carson. Good. Please, come in."

Dr. Schneider stood at the far end of Bio Lab Seven, one of the larger labs on the bio-level. The gaunt German scientist wore a bulky parka, and other technicians were similarly garbed. Carson stepped inside with Bill following close behind. His two Taserarmed "escorts" entered as well and flanked the exit. The door hissed shut behind them, pneumatically sealing.

Several stainless-steel tables held body bags; most were zipped up but two were partially open: one male, one female. Deceased members of the expedition. From the tattoos on the arms of the female corpse, Carson recognized that one as Katya Volkov.

From the frosty breath emanating from Dr. Schneider and the lab techs, Carson guessed the chamber was set at a very low temperature. He pushed some air out of his mouth but no wispy cloud greeted him. And the room didn't feel cold at all. Not warm, either. Just... nothing. Carson sucked in more air and tried again, to no avail.

He caught Schneider looking at him.

"Fascinating. But not unexpected. Your body is essentially room temperature. And likely, the moisture level in your lungs is negligible. So, the air you draw in remains largely unchanged when you push it back out."

Carson approached the doctor, who casually retreated to the opposite side of a nearby autopsy table, putting the stainless-steel surface between herself and the billionaire.

Carson smiled at her precaution and halted his advance. "Doctor, may we have the room?" When Schneider hesitated, he indicated the two guards by the door. "With the exception of my babysitters, of course. And Bill. I'd simply like to have a frank chat about what you've determined thus far."

"Of course."

Schneider directed the technicians to shift to an adjacent lab until they were called for. As the group exited through an airlock chamber, Carson was able to see into the room beyond.

"Let's have Dr. Takagawa in here as well."

Singleton went to fetch the Japanese geneticist, and once the room was resealed, Carson spoke.

"No more beating around the proverbial bush. Am I dead?"

"Obviously not," Dr. Schneider said without hesitation. Dr.

Takagawa cleared his throat and Schneider continued. "However, by some standards, you aren't alive, either."

"By human standards, at least," Takagawa added. "But if we expand our parameters to include all forms of life, you would certainly qualify as alive."

"But not by *human* standards, is what you're saying. That begs a different question, does it not?"

Takagawa opened a folder he'd brought with him from the adjacent lab. "Your genetic makeup is still composed primarily of human DNA, but there have been substantial... alterations."

"Explain."

"I'm afraid I'm not equipped to provide a comprehensive explanation at this time. We are in uncharted territory, and there are still many tests to be run. The DNA sequencing alone will take some time. Given the nature of the situation, I assume we will do everything in-house?"

"I think that would be prudent," Carson replied. "Don't you?"

"*Hai*," Takagawa grunted with a sharp nod. "Agreed."

"What we can say for sure, based on our preliminary examination and initial bloodwork, is this: whatever has happened to you... it is *miraculous*." Dr. Schneider's eyes shone with excitement. "It will change how we view life and death!"

Carson found his eyes drawn to one of the male corpses on a nearby table. A number of ragged wounds were rimmed in torn flesh. When his stomach rumbled, he tore his eyes away.

"So, what *can* you tell me, Doctors?"

"Well, as I'm sure you've noticed," Schneider began, "your heart no longer functions."

"And I no longer seem to breathe," Carson added. "I can simulate it, but... I don't feel like my breathing is actually doing anything."

"It likely isn't. Your cells appear to no longer require oxygenation. And yet... your circulatory system is still... circulating. In a manner of speaking."

"How do you mean?" Carson asked.

Dr. Schneider went to the counter behind her and retrieved a single test tube of blood, bringing it back to the far side of the table she had been standing behind. In her gloved fingers, she held it gingerly by the top of the tube. Several inches of blood lay at the bottom of the glass cylinder.

"The heart acts as a pump, moving oxygenated blood throughout the body... circulating it."

"And I am... pumpless."

Schneider nodded, removing a glove. "And yet..." She pressed a fingertip to the side of the tube a few inches above the blood. Nothing happened for several seconds, and then...

"Omigod!" Singleton cried out, startled.

A tendril of blood suddenly shot up from the bottom of the test tube, extending a ruby-red pseudopod to where Schneider's fingertip pressed against the glass. The blood expanded to coat the area beneath the pad of her finger, reminding Carson of what happened when you pressed a finger on one of those plasma ball lamps from the eighties.

"Your blood appears to be circulating itself," Schneider said, wonderment in her voice. "It is inert at times, but I have noted it moving of its own accord on several occasions. And heat sources appear to attract it."

"This is why your earlier question about your specific classification as to alive or dead is a difficult one to answer," Takagawa elucidated. "Your blood itself appears to be alive. Its behavior is not unlike that of amoebae or plasmodial slime molds—unicellular organisms that behave as a whole." The geneticist paused for a moment. "Some of my former colleagues at the University of Tokyo just published a study that comes to mind. They took a single type of RNA and suspended it in a solution containing ribosomes and other elements derived from common gut bacteria.

Over hundreds of hours, the single RNA form evolved into five distinct versions, all of them coexisting and cooperating collectively, like a molecular ecosystem."

Schneider grunted. "Not unlike Spiegelman's Monster."

Takagawa shrugged. "Much more complex, but the principle is the same."

"What kind of monster?" Carson asked.

"Dr. Spiegelman was a molecular biologist who created an experiment of self-replicating RNA in the 1960s," Schneider explained. "As they duplicated, they evolved to have shorter genomic chains, which allowed for faster and faster replication. They nicknamed the experiment Spiegelman's Monster. But we're straying from the point. Your blood has developed some... interesting traits. We'll require further study of individual cells, but they seem to be behaving as biological nanobots."

Takagawa's saturnine face conjured a frown. "I'd hesitate to use that analogy..."

"In any event, this explains the lack of livor mortis," Schneider continued excitedly. "Normally, a cessation of cardiac activity would result in blood pooling in the lower extremities. Well... if you were upright, that is. Uncirculated blood is at the mercy of gravity."

Carson thought back to his examination on the tender in the East River. "That's why you asked me to take off my shoes and socks."

"*Ja,*" Schneider replied with a nod. "And there was no sign of discoloration."

Carson looked again at the bodies and unopened body bags in the room. "Several members of my expedition were killed by the three infected Sasquatch. Why am I alive—or whatever I am—and why are they... not?" He gestured to indicate their still forms.

"I believe I may have an answer," Dr. Takagawa said. When Dr. Schneider sighed and started to object, he held up a hand. "A hypothesis only, admittedly. But one that I believe further study will prove true." He went to one of the nearby body bags and zipped it open, revealing a young mercenary whose head was twisted halfway around. "First, many of the deceased died from massive amounts of trauma with little or no sign of a bite. For instance, here we have death by catastrophic cervical fracture."

"But others were bitten," Singleton said with a shudder. "I saw several who had... *bites* taken out of them."

"Correct. And yet, there is no sign of animation in any of them. Here is my theory." Takagawa went to a computer station in the corner and logged in to his account before pulling up two images of DNA sequencing, throwing one up onto an overhead monitor on his left and the other to a monitor on his right. He snapped a quick bow toward Carson and gestured to the two monitors. "Please. Examine these."

Carson came over to the computer station and looked up at the screens. A rainbow of short dashes was stacked in vertical columns, each screen containing many such lines of genetic code. In places, highlighted circles ringed specific sequences. "Are these mine?"

"Yes," Takagawa said but didn't elaborate.

"Well, I'm no geneticist, but... these appear slightly different. I take it that one is from before I was bitten... and the other is from now?"

Takagawa smiled. "Neither is from now. The one on the left is from the first time we sequenced you. The one on the right is from two months ago. There are marked differences."

Carson frowned. "From aging?"

"A reasonable assumption, but no. In fact, quite the opposite. I believe it is from your personal efforts to retard the natural aging process."

Schneider scoffed. "Preposterous. I told you then, and I am telling you now—"

"Go on, Dr. Takagawa," Carson interrupted.

"As I understand it, a decade ago you devoted a sizable amount of the research budget toward longevity treatments."

"I did. Little point in accumulating billions if I'm not around to enjoy them."

"Indeed. And from what I've been able to ascertain, you personally partook of a great many of the experimental methods as they were researched."

"The ones that seemed promising, yes. What of it?"

"Numerous experimental drugs, gene therapy, targeted electrostimulation, sonics... an oxygen tent?"

"Yes to all."

"I believe your DNA has been altered by one or more of these treatments. Some combination of those changes—and the pharmaceuticals you have been taking—have interacted with the saliva from the infected bite."

"A theory we cannot adequately confirm, thanks to the destruction of the three Sasquatch that attacked the expedition," Schneider muttered. "Such a senseless waste. Who ordered their remains to be burned, anyway?"

"A man named Joseph Washakie was responsible," Carson said, returning to the table the German woman stood behind. "It would not have been my choice."

Schneider sighed. "The CDC puts caution ahead of scientific advancement, every time."

"He's not CDC. He was the expedition's tracker." *And he called you a "thing,"* the dark voice teased.

"What?" Schneider blurted in bewilderment. "You let a tertiary subcontractor destroy the find of a century? Why on earth would you allow—"

"It's not important!" Carson shouted, slamming a fist down on the stainless-steel table between himself and Dr. Schneider. The German biologist winced and jumped back. With effort, Carson calmed himself. "I was zipped into a body bag at the time, or I would have prevented the burning."

Schneider's eyes were still wide with alarm. *"Mein Gott…"*

"I apologize for the outburst, Doctor." He noted one of the guards had removed his stun gun and was moving toward them. Carson waved him off. "I assure you, I'm calm now…"

"Cameron… the table…" Singleton was staring at the silver surface in front of the billionaire.

Carson looked down. The edge of the stainless-steel autopsy table was completely deformed where he'd struck it. He looked at his hand, turning it from side to side.

"That impact should have shattered the bones in your hand," Takagawa said with wonder.

"I don't believe it did," Carson said, flexing his fingers. He looked down at the table. "Well… as long as we're running tests…" Several of the autopsy tables were wheeled, but this one was bolted to the floor. He reached down and gripped the table on either side of the impressive dent he'd created. "Dr. Schneider, if you'd be so kind as to step aside."

The scientist needed no urging and scurried to join Dr. Takagawa by the computer monitors.

Carson tightened his grip and heaved. Metal squealed as the table tore loose from its fittings on the side nearest him. Pushing forward, he proceeded to bend the steel legs on the opposite side, until the rest of the base gave way and popped loose. When he relaxed his grip, the twisted mess fell to the floor with a dull, metallic clank. The room was completely silent for several seconds.

Carson looked down at his handiwork. "Well, Doctors… plug *that* into the data."

CHAPTER THIRTEEN

"There they are," Merle said from behind the wheel of the black SUV.

Wolf Wallace leaned forward in the passenger seat. Up ahead on East Main Street, two National Guardsmen exited The Trails Restaurant and Lounge and approached a dark green Dodge Dakota pickup. "Is it ready yet?" he asked.

"Almost," Athena answered from the back.

Merle started the SUV, preparing to follow Privates Sharkey and Farley. It hadn't been hard for Athena to find each man's vehicle registry, and Grangeville's Main Street was pretty much the go-to place for eats, so they'd driven down it and spotted Sharkey's Dakota in short order. Wallace would have liked to have approached the men in the diner, but Athena hadn't been ready for him yet.

But rather than get in and drive away, Sharkey leaned in and grabbed something from the back seat. The two men then continued up the sidewalk.

"What is that he's got?" Wallace asked.

"Looks like a sixty-four-ounce growler for craft beer," Merle said. He checked the GPS map on the dash. "There's a brewery on the next block." He tapped the icon and laughed. "And they just opened." He killed the engine.

"Perfect timing," Athena said. "I'm finished."

"Great. Hand it here." Wolf reached back to take the proffered item. He looked toward the cameraman, who sat beside Athena. "You... um..."

The man sighed. He'd been working with Wolf for nearly six months. "Ian."

"Ian! I knew that. Proper Scottish name! Bring your gear, boyo." He clapped his hands together. "Well? What say ye, lads and lass? Fancy a pint?"

"You sure you're going to be all right?" Sarah asked.

Bud Sorenson chuckled from his hospital bed. "Now that I know my equipment is safe... yeah. Thanks for taking care of that, Liz."

"No problem, Bud."

After Russ, Sarah, Joseph, and Liz had cleared quarantine, they'd come straight to Syringa Hospital in downtown Grangeville to check on Bud. The portly audio engineer was in good spirits.

"The doctors say I can get out of here shortly. Then I'll hobble on back to Colorado and let my wife pamper me."

"I'm going to stay with him," Liz told the others. "Help him gather his gear and get to the airport."

"What about you three?" Bud asked Sarah. He looked into the corner of the room where Russ and Joseph were examining a map they had partially unfolded. "Don't tell me you're going back out there."

"There's still some... unfinished business," Russ said.

Joseph's cell rang and he glanced at it. The contact was unknown, but the area code and prefix pegged it as a local call. "I better take this. Back in a moment." He stepped out into the hall.

"Where's Dhir?" Bud asked.

"New York," Liz said. "He flew back with Cameron Carson. I've been trying to reach him, but it just rings and rings and goes to voicemail."

"I'm sure he's fine," Bud reassured her. "Hey, Sarah... what's with the thousand-yard stare? You okay?"

Sarah nodded. "Sorry. It's just... this is the hospital my father was brought to after his encounter with Brighteyes. It's bringing back memories, is all. He was in a room down the hall."

The door opened abruptly. "It's Luke," Joseph said. "He remembered something. Luke, you're on speaker. Say it again."

"Oh, okay. Um... like I was telling my uncle, when you guys called that rock 'the Stone that Sings,' it sounded familiar. It just now hit me. My dad had a weird rock that he found at this big mound in Kamiah, called Heart of the Monster."

"And he calls it the Stone that Sings?" Russ asked.

"No," Luke said. "The Stone that Sleeps."

Russ, Sarah, and Joseph left their backpacks of belongings with Bud and Liz and exited the hospital. After turning left on Main Street, they walked east. Nearly all the buildings were single-story structures, even the hospital.

"So, where's this place Luke mentioned?" Russ asked. "Where Sharkey and Farley drink."

"Three Mile Brewpub," Joseph said. "Bud's nurse said it's just four blocks away."

"And why are we looking for them?" Sarah asked.

"Because last time I checked, none of us has a car," Joseph explained. "And we need a ride to Kamiah. I want to see my brother-in-law and this rock of his. Since our two National Guardsman friends already know about the stone that started all of this, they're a good option for us."

"Good call," Russ said. "Also, they may know more about what's going on with all the 'men in black' types who seemed to be swarming in like mosquitos to a bug zapper."

They continued into town. Numerous mom-and-pop stores dotted Main Street, many of them serving double or triple duty: a pharmacy/gift shop/portrait studio, a jewelry store that sold musical instruments, a coffee shop that sold mobile phones, and a department store that looked like it had been around since the sixties.

"It's like stepping back in time," Russ commented. He gestured across the street. "When was the last time you saw an actual video store?"

"Hold up one moment," Joseph said, opening the door to the pharmacy-and-more shop. "Back in a sec." In a few minutes he returned, tearing open some packaging and stuffing it in a sidewalk trash can.

"What'd you get?" Sarah asked.

"Some ibuprofen for my ribs. I think I cracked two of them when that Sasquatch swatted me across the clearing." He popped two tablets out of a blister pack and dry-swallowed them, then proceeded down the sidewalk.

"You were just at a hospital and didn't have them look at you?" Russ shook his head.

"They would have told me I have two cracked ribs... I already know that. They would have told me to rest... which we can't do." He shook the blister pack. "And they would've given me these for fifty bucks a pill. This whole pack was five bucks." He shoved the remainder into a pocket.

"There's Three Mile." Sarah pointed at a wood-and-glass storefront with a wagon wheel above the door.

Stepping into the cozy interior, they found Sharkey and Farley planted at the bar on swiveling stools. Sharkey spotted them and raised a half-full glass. "Hey! They let you out, huh? Come have a beer! We were just about to have another."

"Sure thing," Russ said, bellying up to the bar. "Ooh! A hazy IPA."

"Why don't we grab a table," Sarah suggested with a beckoning nod of her head.

"Oh, right… I'll bring the beers."

After giving Russ their preferences, Sarah and Joseph pulled a pair of tables together and Sharkey and Farley joined them. Russ brought over a trio of pint glasses and began to hand out the beers.

"Hey, Shark, what are the odds?" Farley said. "Two TV stars in one day?"

"Oh, yeah! That's right!" Sharkey grinned at Russ. "You have a survival show too!"

Russ looked puzzled as he sat. "So my agent tells me." He took a sip of Three Mile's hazy and sighed. "That's tasty."

"Who's the other celebrity you mean?" Sarah asked.

"That Scottish guy," Farley said. "Wolf Wallace! He was just in here shooting a scene."

"Wolf is here?" Russ added with surprise and an undercurrent of loathing. "Of course he is, copycat vulture. Oh, this keeps getting better and better…"

Sharkey plopped a blue-and-white canvas bag on the table and lifted several items out of it. "Check out the swag! We each got T-shirts, coasters, water bottles… a compass. And a multitool! How cool is that?"

Sarah lifted a coaster emblazoned with the words *Man vs. Nature*. The logo in the center was of a bearded, burly, shirtless man in a kilt wrestling a bear. "Wow. Just… wow." She waggled it in front of Russ's nose. "*This* is your competition?"

"Don't get me started," Russ muttered into his beer.

"Yeah, he was asking about you," Sharkey said. "Wondering if you found Bigfoot."

"What did you tell him?" Sarah asked with sudden urgency.

"Our commanders said we weren't supposed to say anything about that, so… I didn't say nuthin' 'bout that."

"Yeah, you were real smooth," Farley scoffed. "'I can neither confirm nor deny blah-blah-blah.' Staring down that purple-haired goth chick's cleavage the whole time."

"Hey, she was hot."

"No argument from me." Farley clinked Sharkey's glass in solidarity.

"So... you told them the expedition didn't find a Bigfoot."

"Well... I just told them I couldn't say." Sharkey shrugged and took another sip.

"Crap," Sarah muttered.

Russ sighed. "He must've heard I was doing a Bigfoot episode. Wolf's always chasing my ideas. With his million-dollar budget."

"You said they were shooting some video in here," Sarah prodded. "Did he say anything about *what* they were shooting?"

"Idaho survival episode," Farley replied.

"Yeah, right," Russ mumbled. "Look, Sarah... Brighteyes is long gone."

Sarah gave Russ her best shut-up-you-colossal-idiot glare, but fortunately Joseph intervened.

"Say, fellas... any chance either of you could do us a favor tomorrow?"

"Probably," Farley said. "What can we do ya for?"

"I have a brother up in Kamiah I need to see. I'd rent a car, but..."

Sharkey laughed. "Here? You'd have to rent a car to *find* a rent-a-car. No sweat, I can run you up. What time you need to be there?"

Joseph's phone rang and he fished it from a pocket. "I believe I can give you an exact time in a moment," he said to Sharkey before answering. "Jonah, you old dog, thanks for getting back to me." He listened a moment. "Yes, Luke was looking good. He suggested I call you. Listen... what are you up to tomorrow?" He nodded. "Nine o'clock?" He raised an eyebrow in Sharkey's direction. When the big man gave a noncommittal shrug, Joseph returned to the call with "How about ten? We're bumming a ride from some overworked guardsmen. Okay, great, see you then."

Sharkey grinned as the Shoshone hung up. "Thanks, man. I'm off tomorrow, and I'm not a morning person unless I gotta be."

"After what we've been through," Sarah said, "a little extra sleep won't hurt."

"Speaking of which, where y'all bunking?" Sharkey asked. "I'd offer up my couch, but my dog's pretty protective of it. And Farley's place is a pigsty."

"That's cuz your mom doesn't know how to clean," his buddy replied, sipping his beer. "Hey, there's a motel down the road just off 95. Got a nice little coffee shop in its parking lot. My sister's family stays there sometimes. It's just past the hospital, you can't miss it."

"We just came from the hospital, actually," Sarah said. "And left our bags with friends. We can grab those and go get a room."

"Sounds great," Russ said. "I feel like I could sleep for days."

'I tired,' Littlefoot signed. 'When rest?'

'When sun sets,' Brighteyes replied. 'But now, we must go far.'

At Brighteyes's suggestion, the two Sasquatch were minimizing their use of vocalizations. Ever since they had reversed course away from BreakTree's territory and headed south, Brighteyes had been on a heightened state of alert. Many humans and their machines were likely still around the camp that Silverback had attacked, so Brighteyes angled to the southwest, staying as quiet as possible as he looped around the area of activity.

'I liked BearFriend,' Littlefoot said wistfully.

Brighteyes grunted in agreement.

'And you liked DawnWaker.'

Brighteyes stumbled and stubbed his big toe on a tree root. He panted in pain, then shook it off. 'Come. We must find a place to sleep for night, then forage for food.'

"Now that is one fine-looking burger," Russ said appreciatively.

"Yeah, they got some great eats," Sharkey said, popping a chunky french fry in his mouth.

Joseph, Russ, and Sarah hadn't eaten since breakfast, and at Shark and Farl's urging, the group had decided to stay here and grab an early dinner. After they devoured their meals, Joseph rose, unfolded one of the topographical maps Sarah and Liz had found, and spread it on a nearby table.

"This is the area where Carson's base camp was," Sarah said, pointing out a relatively flat area. "Meadow... plenty of room for the helicopters."

"Yes... and down here," Russ said, tracing his finger along a dotted line. "This trail went south, and this hill here would be where the geologists' camp was."

"And here, there is a steep drop, just to the south-southeast." Joseph tapped the spot. "This is where you threw that rock from."

"Yeah, that seems about right," Farley said.

"There's a creek at the bottom," Sarah noted, leaning in.

Joseph nodded. "And with heavy rain the night the creature attacked the camp, it would be flowing well." He looked to Farley. "I call on your memory again... that stone... was it heavy? Like a typical rock?"

"No!" Farley answered almost immediately. "When I grabbed it away from Shark, I was surprised how light it was. I mean... heavy enough that I could huck it pretty good, but not as heavy as it seemed it shoulda been. Oh! And y'know what else? It was warm. And kinda green."

"And back at the quarantine, you said you think you heard a splash after you threw it?"

"Yeah. Pretty sure."

Joseph grunted, then opened up the map further, exposing more to the south. "Do you think it would float?"

"Definitely."

"There are a lot of creeks and streams down there," Russ said. "And they seem to feed into this river here... Salmon River." He traced a creek that split to the south. "French Creek... that seems to be running along a drop in elevation."

Joseph opened the map a bit further. "Upper Payette Lake... then a bigger lake below that..."

"Payette Lake, that's where McCall is," Sharkey said. "Big recreation area. My dad used to take us down there for water skiing in summer and ice fishing in winter. I still go there to fish. Some great breweries there too!"

"Beer me, fellas," Annabelle said, bellying up to the bar at McCall Brewing Company. The four members of the Sharlie Hunters turned on their stools.

"How'd you know where to find us?" Stuart asked.

"Well... you said you were at Salmon River Brewery *last* night, so I figured you'd change it up." The Sharlie Hunters often alternated their choice of venue, limited only by the days one establishment or the other might be closed.

"Couldn't stand being away from me, huh, Graybill?" Brady said affably, pitching his voice down an octave but trying his best not to leer.

"Oh, crap... *you're* here?" Annabelle did an overblown about-face and took two steps toward the exit but spun back around when her beer arrived. She grabbed the pint and took a deep sip, then grinned at Brady. "You need better material."

"That... and a full head of hair. And the return of my youth."

Annabelle clinked glasses with him. "How'd the dinosaur hunt go?"

Brady rolled his eyes. "Plesiosaurs are *not* dinosaurs. They're marine reptiles."

"I stand corrected. So, you fellas find anything?"

Kevin sighed. "We were going to check out the waters around Cougar Island, but the motor conked out before we hit the narrows. Had to call for a tow. Took 'em a while to get to us."

"That explains the sunburn."

"Good thing Mark was suited up in long sleeves and a Panama," Stuart remarked. "With that Irish skin of his, he's lucky he didn't baconize."

"Mmm... bacon." Mark raised a finger to the bartender. "Hey, Pete, can we get some menus?"

"How about you?" Kevin asked. "You find anything interesting on the north end?"

"No, pretty dull day. Looked everywhere for that empty kayak. No joy. Oh! But we got a weird call at the Ranger Station. Apparently, two boys were fishing early this morning, and they were attacked."

The Sharlie Hunters all set down their beers. "By what?" Mark asked.

"It came from the water..." Annabelle whispered, looking furtively around.

"Omigod, was it Sharlie?" Stuart rasped.

"That depends... is Sharlie a rabid salmon?" At the confused looks, she laughed. "These two kids caught a salmon and claimed it attacked them. Said it leaped out of the water and tried to bite them. The dad called us. Thought it might be rabid."

Kevin rolled his eyes. "Fish don't get rabies."

"We told him that." She shook her head. "The kids probably got bit trying to take out the hook."

"What're you up to tomorrow?" Brady asked.

"Back to the north end. Might head into The Meanders up that way. See what there is to see."

As the sun kissed the tops of the hills to the west, the fisherman hauled in his line and prepared to follow the river back south to Payette Lake. Curving sharply with frequent bends, the shallow river on the north side meandered to and fro and was quite popular among kayakers and fishermen alike. The earlier rains had given the water level a significant boost, and the normally calm river flowed into the lake with gusto. Opening the cooler by his feet, Chris "Critch" Critchley looked upon a good day's work with pride: two smallmouth bass, a walleye, and a variety of trout. He reached in and selected a rainbow trout, giving it a peck on its fishy lips.

"You're dinner tonight, beautiful."

Critch was about to put it back and start the engine when a thump sounded from the side of the jon boat. He leaned over, expecting to see a tree branch bumping along his hull, but instead...

"What the heck is that?" Setting the trout back in the cooler, he got down on all fours and reached for the odd greenish sphere as it floated past. It eluded his fingers, but all of a sudden, his thoughts became fuzzy and his ears filled with a hum akin to a musical chord. He rose to his knees, intending to start the motor and go after the object, when his eyes lit upon the open cooler full of fish.

Five minutes later, Critch blinked and stared down at the mass of fish guts and bones in his hands, the raw rainbow trout nearly bitten in half. He spat, ejecting fish scales from the surface of his tongue.

Ten minutes later, the sphere entered Payette Lake. Five

minutes after that, four hundred feet down at the bottom of the lake, something ancient stirred, awakening from a fifteen-year slumber.

CHAPTER FOURTEEN

"Fascinating," Dr. Schneider said quietly, her voice coming through a speaker beside Carson's head.

Cameron Carson waited semipatiently for her to elaborate. He had been lying in the full-body MRI machine for several hours now, and it was beginning to remind him of his awakening in the interior of that body bag. His stomach growled violently, echoing in the enclosed space. They had been running tests on him throughout the entire day, but he had eaten again right before entering the MRI—*two* steaks this time.

Schneider's voice came again. "Your brain activity is surprisingly energetic. And areas are lit up that are reminiscent of the mental processes of an individual under the influence of psychedelic drugs."

"Somehow, that doesn't surprise me," Carson replied. "My mind has felt a bit 'crowded' since the... incident." As if to agree with his assessment, The Other rattled its cage, and Carson felt a few of the links in the metaphorical chains around its prison begin to bend under the strain. "Doctor, how much longer will this take?"

"Why? Are you finally feeling tired?" she asked, excited interest in her voice.

"No, not in the slightest. What I *am* feeling is hungry and irritable... and I can assure you, that is not a healthy combination."

"And yet, you just ate."

"I am well aware of that, Doctor!" Carson snapped. "We're done for now. Let me out!"

Yesyesyes... letmeoutletmeoutletmeout! Carson squeezed his eyes shut, focusing on maintaining control as a wave of urges swept through him, the inner voice babbling away inside its cage.

Fortunately, the examination table hummed and began to slide out of the MRI machine; Carson squinted at the bright overhead lights.

"When you are ready, come out to the diagnostics room," Dr. Schneider said over the intercom.

"Give me a moment or two, Doctor. And... have the security men stand by."

"They are already right outside the door, waiting to escort you."

"Prudent," Carson muttered before sitting in a chair and focusing on a restoration of control.

Five minutes later, Carson entered the diagnostics room. Dr. Schneider was waiting with Singleton beside her. Multiple monitors displayed different portions of the imaging scans, some a collage of stills, others playing out like videos.

"We'll need to make this quick," Carson said. "Given how ravenously hungry I feel at the moment, it feels like my stomach is dissolving itself."

"Funny you should say that..."

Singleton looked askance at the doctor. "Is Mr. Carson's body breaking down?"

"Oh, no... far from it. In fact, I'm seeing signs of rapid regener-ation. But no, I was referring to his use of the word *dissolve*. As near as I can tell, his stomach acids aren't functioning as they should, and yet..." She brought up the results of a recent scan, showing his stomach cavity. "You see here, the blood flow through the arteries?"

"Yes. What's happening there?" Carson pointed toward what he imagined was his stomach.

"That is a pooling of the blood. Ordinarily, this would indicate some form of internal bleeding, and yet... well, here, let me cue up a time lapse."

After a few keystrokes and mouse clicks, the image showed several dark objects in the stomach.

"This is right when we began. Those are bits of steak. Now... watch."

As the video advanced, blood flow seemed to redirect itself, swarming into the stomach and smothering the foreign objects. Near the end of the playback, the blood retreated, leaving no sign of the meal.

"Your blood seems to be behaving like white blood cells on steroids, adapting a version of phagocytosis as a means of diges-tion. You'll remember how the blood reacted to a fingertip on the test tube? It's almost as if your blood is a predatory organism, dissolving the meat and distributing nutrients throughout the body, leaving nothing behind."

"Well... that will certainly save money on toilet paper."

Schneider looked at Carson with interest. "On that subject, have you...?"

"No. Not since my brush with death. Neither one nor two. Haven't slept either."

Singleton frowned. "Am I imagining things, sir, or does your voice seem much less ragged and hoarse than it was this morning?"

"I don't believe you're imagining things at all," Dr. Schneider said. "I mentioned signs of regeneration? Mr. Carson, would you kindly remove the bandage on your neck?"

Carson obliged and Singleton gasped.

"Still unsightly, is it?"

"No, sir... I mean, the scarring isn't pretty, but the wound... it's completely gone!"

"That could explain your extreme hunger," Schneider suggested. "Regeneration is energy intensive."

"In that case, I'd better see to a late-night snack."

"Would you like for me to arrange for your chef to—"

"No, Bill, you go get some sleep. I can scare up something." He turned to the two security men. "Keep ten paces back." With that, he departed the room.

He was on his way to the elevators when he paused near one of the bio labs. This was where Maiden Bio ran longevity treatments on rats. He took out his master keycard and swiped the door open. "You two, stay here."

"But, sir..."

"It's three in the morning, no one is inside. Well... except for the lab rats."

"I still think one of us should—"

"Stay... here," Carson growled, locking eyes with the man. The guard staggered two involuntary steps back.

"Yes, sir," he rasped.

Carson ducked inside.

After a few minutes, he returned to the hall, carrying an aluminum sample case by its handle. Without a word, he headed for the elevators. Neither guard dared ask why there were squeaks and squeals coming from the case.

Yana sat in front of her laptop, examining the video of the lab results folder, pausing the footage after each page flip. The bulk of the bloodwork and DNA tests were for a "Subject One," but there were additional sections for several other individuals, albeit only a page or two for each. But one thing definitely caught her eye: Subject Three was described as a deceased female, approximately five foot nine, brown hair, brown eyes... with extensive tattoos. *Could this be Katya?*

Her watch abruptly pinged and a notification popped up, indicating that the bug in Cameron Carson's office was picking up motion and sound. She tapped an icon and threw the feed to her laptop. Not surprisingly, the Maiden Labs facility was extensively shielded, with Wi-Fi operating on a heavily encrypted, closed system. While Yana couldn't contact the outside world, she had no trouble connecting her watch, glasses, and laptop to each other via Bluetooth. The bug was piggybacking its operation on the lab's secure servers, so while she could receive the information it gathered on her devices here, she couldn't pass it along to Hilda. Not yet, at any rate; she'd need to go outside for that.

Activating the feed, she was greeted with the dim interior of Carson's office. She heard footsteps, and then a thump, as if something heavy had been set down on a hard surface. A faint noise followed. *Squeaking?* She paired a set of earbuds to the laptop and ensured the volume was all the way up. Definitely muffled squeaks... like a rodent. After a moment, a desk lamp was switched on and she could see what she assumed were Carson's expensive shoes between desk and chair. From the underside of the bookshelves, Yana didn't have much of an upward angle, but given how quiet the room seemed, she didn't want to risk rolling the little device forward.

An odd, guttural sigh came from Carson and she heard the unmistakable sounds of latches on a hardcase being flipped open. The squeaks became louder and were joined by a new sound: a throaty growl. The squeaks shifted to terrified shrieks, the growl crescendoed to an animalistic roar, then both of those noises abruptly ceased with a loud, wet crunch... followed by ravenous tearing, chewing, and slurping.

Forget stealth, I need to see this! Yana brought up the controls and commanded the drone-bug to roll forward, then panned the micro-camera up. The device's fish-eye lens treated her to a nightmare. Carson had a white lab rat gripped firmly in his hands, its belly and rib cage bitten clean through. The billionaire's face was covered in gore, his expensive white shirt spattered with blood. He buried his beard into the rodent's belly for another bite.

What the f—? Yana quickly confirmed that recording was occurring, then she adjusted the angle and zoomed in even further.

In profile, Carson chewed... swallowed... then paused. After a moment, he tossed the disemboweled rat into what looked like a boxy briefcase and spoke. "Forgive my manners. If I had known I had company, I would've brought one for you." Then he turned his head and looked down, right into the camera, his mouth stretching into a blood-soaked grin.

Yana gasped, tensing with fear as if she were right there in the room with this nightmare visage. She quickly tapped the "reverse" button and retreated under the bookcase. The image went dark... but then immediately went light again with a loud crash. The view once more showed Carson's bloody grin, leering down at the camera.

Did he just toss aside a fully loaded bookcase? Yana had seen the floor-to-ceiling display of books when she'd set the bug. She was about to send the device forward and make a run for the door when Carson's hand suddenly lashed out. In an instant, the view was replaced with an extreme close-up, the tiny robo-bug now sitting on the billionaire's palm.

"Ingenious little toy... no doubt created with *my* tech." One eye, madness bubbling behind its pupil, filled the image. "I have a digital firewall around this facility, so whoever is controlling this device... *you're in here with me.*" That last phrase was a gravelly snarl, and Carson's fingers curled over the lens, blotting out the view. The microphone registered a nanosecond of crunching noises, then the feed flickered with static and went dark.

Carson opened his hand, looking at the tiny mangled device. Crushing it had been an impulsive act, and in retrospect he might have made it harder for the techs to trace the signal. *But it felt good, didn't it?* the inner voice asked.

"Yes... yes, it did," Carson admitted before dropping the listening device on his desk, careful to avoid the blood spatters from his impromptu snack. He looked over at the toppled bookcase. Doing that had felt good, too. But what a mess—biographies, fiction, science, business books, once perfectly organized, now splayed across the floor like fallen soldiers after a pitched battle. The Other enjoyed the warlike imagery and rattled its cage again.

"Perhaps... if we find our little spy... I'll let you out to play," Carson said aloud. "But for now, I need to think." He picked up the remains of the rat from inside the open case and took another bite as casually as one might munch on an apple. Yes, the need to think was paramount. "I need that sphere," he said to the room, dropping the masticated rat back into the case. He snapped it closed, removing the distraction. "If I have that... perhaps I can undo what was done to me."

The Other laughed. *You do that, and you'll be dead, won't you?*

"You heard the doctor... my body has already repaired the damage that killed me."

But would you really want to give up all that you have become?

"If it means shutting *you* up, then yes... perhaps." He took out his smartphone and thumbed the fingerprint reader. No good... the phone remained locked. Had his fingerprints changed like his DNA? Then he laughed as he realized there was simply too much blood on his thumb.

He found a patch of shirt that wasn't bloody, wiped both

phone and thumb clean, and tried again. Once the phone unlocked, he went into his contacts and found who he was looking for. He called the number; it rang once and went to voicemail. He hung up. "Why, Mr. Washakie, I do believe you're shunning me. No matter. If at first you don't succeed…"

Sarah sat up in the motel bed and picked up her ringing phone, squinting at the unfamiliar number. *Who would be calling after one in the morning?*

"Tell them your car warranty is fine," Russ mumbled into his pillow beside her.

"It's a New York number," Sarah said. "Maybe it's Dhir." She answered the call. "Hello?"

"Sarah, please forgive the lateness of my call, but it is rather urgent."

The upper-crust southern drawl was unmistakable. "Mr. Carson!" she said, instantly wide awake. Beside her, Russ rolled over, alert.

"Please, call me Cameron. Listen, my medical staff think they can… 'correct' some of the less-than-desirable traits I've recently acquired, but to do that we need access to the source of the whole mess."

"Mr. Carson, the Bigfoots that were infected have all been destroyed. The others are long gone and need to be left alone."

"I'm not talking about the Bigfoots; I mean the sphere."

After a pause, Sarah answered, "Sphere?"

Russ sat up fully, violently shaking his head and dragging a finger across his throat. Sarah held up a hand as Carson continued talking.

"A spherical meteorite, I assume. Your friends Russ and Joseph know all about it. We need to get hold of it before the government does."

"I'm... sorry, Mr. Carson, I don't know anything about that. Listen, it's late and I've had very little sleep in the past few days. Good night."

You lying bitch! the inner voice shrieked as the call went dead. "Now, now..." Carson admonished, tamping down the urge to crush the phone in his grip. "We *know* she knows about the sphere... she was discussing it when our CDC mole overheard her. Her little lie confirms that Joseph is likely still looking for it."

Carson's eyes strayed to the crumpled listening device. Raising his uncrushed phone, he called Singleton. His assistant answered on the second ring.

"Sir! Are you all right, sir?"

"Hey diddle diddle, fit as a fiddle, Bill. Listen, I need you to ring up security and lock this place down."

"Oh... sir... what did you do?"

"Not *me*, Bill... I'm right as rain. But I'm afraid we have a spy in our midst. I found a sophisticated surveillance device in my office, and it reacted to my movements as if it were being controlled. Given our electronic umbrella, I assume the operator is in the facility."

"Who do you think it is, sir?"

"Who knows? The government, perhaps. But more likely one of Hilda's little lackeys. She's been gunning for me for a while now. In any event, the North Brother Labs are already no-entry/no-exit from midnight until six. I want to seal this place completely so they can't get outside and send their footage."

"Why, sir?" Singleton's voice was dripping with trepidation. "What were you doing when..."

Carson sighed—or simulated a sigh—before speaking. "I was hungry, Bill. And steaks weren't cutting it."

"Oh, no, sir—"

"No humans were involved, Bill. But... I owe Dr. Schneider a rat."

Hunger. Hunger like she had never known. Sharlie—the Twilight Dragon of Payette Lake—glided through the depths, on the hunt for fish. It wasn't uncommon to experience ravenous hunger after a prolonged sleep, but *this*... this was something else.

An hour ago, Sharlie had been awakened from hibernation by strange emanations in the water. Swimming toward the source of the sound, she had encountered a small spherical object bobbing on the surface. It had called to her, and its song was so entrancing that she had made the decision to devour it... so that its song might be with her always.

There had been a series of odd twinges from her gut—not exactly painful, but not altogether pleasant. The sensations felt as if the thing she had swallowed had rooted itself to the walls of her digestive tract. And now, the bewitching tone was deep inside her, resonating in her body, the object lodged firmly in her stomach. The lake monster felt an odd discomfort in her gut, amplified by growing hunger pangs.

As she neared a shoreline on the northern side of the lake, a bass broke from cover, spooked by her passage. Quick as lightning, Sharlie's long neck whipped to the side and her jaws, lined with razor-sharp teeth, snapped shut on the fish, closing with such force that the bass was scythed in half, sending one chunk falling away. Swallowing her mouthful, she retrieved the rest of the fish and gobbled it down before continuing toward shore. Another fish bolted and Sharlie followed, moving into the shallower waters of the North Fork Payette River.

Three fish, two turtles, and a sleeping duck later, the hunger remained. Sharlie needed more. Something... substantial. She rose to the surface beside a small beach on the riverbank, her heightened sense of smell detecting a large mammal drinking at the water's edge. Arcing her neck high above the surface of the water, Sharlie opened her mouth wide, her eyes locked on what she knew to be a deer.

Lodged inside the beast, the sphere she'd swallowed continued to pulse with its strange emanations; the long throat of the lake monster acted like a funnel, amplifying and directing the song of the sphere.

The deer detected the motion and was about to bolt but paused as a distant sound reached its ears. Entranced, it took two steps into the shallows, front hooves sinking into the silt as it stared up at a swaying shape, silhouetted by the moon.

Striking like a cobra, Sharlie's head plunged downward, her gaping jaws clamping down on her victim's neck. The deer didn't even cry out as Sharlie tore it apart.

CHAPTER FIFTEEN

Brighteyes knew the sun had risen, but he and Littlefoot had been traveling for the better part of three days, and the Bigfoot figured they could both sleep a little longer before they'd need to rise and forage for some breakfast. After all, the bed of pine needles they'd found made for a very comfortable nest.

He was just slipping back into a pleasant dream when an object bounced off his head, eliciting a flash of déjà vu. He abruptly sat up, coming wide awake.

There, leaning against a stout pine, stood DawnWaker. The red-body Bigfoot chuffed a laugh, then tossed another pine cone, this one thumping against Littlefoot's sleeping form, waking him as well.

She panted a laugh. 'You missed the dawn.'

'You!' Brighteyes scrambled to his feet and looked around, scanning for any other Sasquatch.

'DawnWaker! Is BearFriend here?' Littlefoot asked hopefully.

'There are no others. I am alone.'

'You... followed us?' Brighteyes asked.

'I did.'

'Why?'

DawnWaker made a basic gesture that simply meant *I want*. She stepped away from the tree and elaborated. 'I want to see more. I want to know more. You have seen much. You know much. The way you speak with your hands—so different—I want to learn.'

She approached the pair. 'I wish to be with you,' she said softly, then caught herself and opened her arms wide. 'Both of you. If you will let me join your troop.'

'But... we have no troop,' Brighteyes replied.

'You *are* a troop! *We* can be a troop. If you will have me.'

'But... BreakTree—'

'My father will not follow. His territory is more important than any member of the troop.'

'We go south!' Littlefoot said. 'We look for other Bigfoot!'

'You must not journey with empty stomachs,' DawnWaker declared. She went around the tree she had been leaning against, then returned, carrying a wide strip of bark containing fish, huckleberries, and hickory nuts. She set it down in the bed of pine needles in front of Brighteyes and Littlefoot. She gave a shrug. 'I come?'

Brighteyes laid a hand on her shoulder and gave a gentle squeeze. 'Even with no food... I say yes.'

"You should not have answered the phone," Joseph said, staring straight ahead at the RV park across the road from the motel. Beside him, Sarah and Russ sipped their coffees from the parking lot coffee shop, the trio waiting for Sharkey to show up with his truck.

"I told you, I thought it might be Dhir," Sarah protested.

"C'mon, Joseph, give her a break... it was the middle of the night, New York number..." Russ trailed off. "What a minute... he called you first, didn't he?"

Joseph looked over at him. "I sent it to voicemail. No message was left."

"Well, like I said, he asked about that weird rock you two found," Sarah said. "I told him I didn't know anything about it."

Joseph grunted, then tilted his head, thinking. "How did he sound?"

"Charming and polite with an undercurrent of arrogance," she replied. "Pretty much the same."

"No, I meant his voice. When we spoke to him in the cage, his voice was ragged. Hoarse."

Sarah frowned. "I remember. But... no, his voice sounded completely normal."

Joseph shook his head, then took out his cell, thumbing the power button. "Turn off your phones."

"Isn't that a little paranoid?" Sarah asked, taking hers out and powering it down.

"Only if I'm wrong. But if Carson wants the sphere and knows we're looking for it—and I'm not sure how he knows that—he may try to follow us digitally."

"Hey, I was wondering..." Russ said, turning off his phone, "this sphere... let's say we find it. What exactly are we going to do with it?"

"Destroy it," Joseph answered without hesitation.

"Yeah, great, okay. But how? Bury it in a hole? Drop it in a volcano? And how do we keep it from zombifying our brains while we do that?"

"That is something I wish to ask my brother-in-law. He knows more of the old stories than I do."

"And there's that 'Stone that Sleeps' Luke said he has."

"Yes. I hope it is somehow related."

"Okay, fine, but... hear me out," Russ said. "What if we turn that rock over to the CDC?"

Sarah looked at him. "You want to give a rock that turns humans into cannibals to the Centers for Disease Control?"

"Well... aren't they tasked with defending us from diseases? And isn't this sphere's 'effect' kind of like a disease?"

"No!" Joseph said. "The CDC itself would likely have the best of intentions, but if they have the sphere, the *government* has it. And that means DARPA will have it." He crossed his arms. "No. We must destroy it ourselves."

A rumbling engine heralded the arrival of Sharkey's pickup. No longer in uniform, the burly Montanan had an elbow out the open window, flannel sleeves rolled up to his biceps. "Hop in, gang," he called as he pulled into the parking lot.

"Why don't you take shotgun, Joseph," Sarah suggested, "since you know where we're going."

Russ and Sarah hopped into the back seat of the crew cab. "Roomy," Russ declared.

"Yeah, some of my buddies are large fellas," Sharkey said.

"Bigger than you?" Joseph asked with a smile and lifted eyebrow.

"Well... large side to side," Sharkey replied, pulling out of the parking lot. "Sorry about the mess on the floor back there."

"What is...?" Sarah asked, lifting up a red plastic object she'd just kicked. It was hollow with a handle and a funnel at its mouth.

Sharkey glanced in the rearview. "Oh, uh... that's for super-long drives. Don't worry, I washed it."

"Ew." Sarah grimaced and tossed the item down at Russ's feet.

"Hey, now... everything's far from everywhere else out here, and there ain't a lotta rest stops."

"How far is Kamiah?" Russ asked.

"About forty-five minutes. I'm gonna take us up US-12. Few minutes longer that way, but a heckuva nice drive along the Clearwater River."

The drive was indeed pleasant, winding along the river as they made their way north. Out the right windows, the terrain sloped upwards, the hillsides covered in a variety of pine trees.

"Good Sasquatch country to the east," Joseph remarked. "A commanding view and plenty of cover."

"Too bad the freshwater source is across the road," Russ remarked. "Although, I'm guessing they've got a better understanding of roads and cars than deer do."

"I hope they got away okay," Sarah said, her eyes searching the pines.

The road angled away from the river and Sharkey yawned. "Almost there. The bridge to Kamiah's just ahead," he said.

"Slow down!" Normally stoic, Joseph appeared quite animated, looking across the big Montanan to the left side of the road.

Sharkey obliged, and with no traffic behind them, he slowed to a crawl. A low post-and-rail fence ran along the left side of the road with a meadow beyond. In moments, an odd mound came into view, looking a lot like a child's idea of a volcano. About seventy feet in height, the mound was covered in patches of grass and low shrubs and ringed by a second post-and-rail fence.

"There it is," Joseph said.

"What are we looking at?" Russ asked.

"That mound is a part of the Nez Perce creation story and a sacred site for the tribe."

"What's the story?" Russ asked.

"I am Shoshone. Our creation myth involves Wolf. The origin story of the Nez Perce involves Coyote. I'll leave that for Jonah to tell. More importantly for us, according to Luke, this is the location where Jonah found the 'Stone that Sleeps.'"

"Is it a burial mound of some kind?" Sarah asked.

"No. This place is called Heart of the Monster."

"What the...?" Annabelle Graybill brought the Custom Weld Storm toward the shore; the Forest Service's shallow-draft boat came in handy in the winding river north of Payette Lake, known to locals as The Meanders—so named for the plethora of S-curves that wandered from side to side as the river spilled into the lake. She had just rounded a bend when she'd spotted something shiny on a low bank to the north. As she drew closer, she could see what had caught the light. Bone. And blood. Wet and glistening in the late-morning sunlight.

Nudging the boat into the shallows, she killed the engine and pulled on a pair of wader boots. Stepping down into the gravel-and-mud bottom, she slowly approached the grisly remains at the edge of the water.

"What on earth happened to you?" Annabelle asked the deer carcass. She was only able to tell what it had been from a few scraps of hide. Whatever had killed and eaten this animal had *obliterated* it. Almost no flesh or organs remained and sections of ribs appeared to have been snapped off. Only one leg was visible—well, *half* of a leg. Even the head was stripped clean. Flies buzzed about, but there was a faint odor in the air. Annabelle had been around plenty of dead animals in her time and this smell was unusual. Not the typical smell of death; something was off about it.

She'd been up here yesterday, and this kill was fresh; it would be odd to have a strong decomposition smell so soon. She scanned the trees beyond the little beach. Black bears were extremely common in Idaho, but she doubted one of them had done this. Mountain lion? Unlikely. A cougar would have dragged the carcass into cover, away from the creek. Coyotes... doubtful. She didn't often see them around here, and Idaho coyotes were too small to have done this so quickly. That left wolves. There were roughly 1,500 in Idaho, and Annabelle knew there was a documented pack in the area: the Jungle Creek pack. But given how many kayakers and fishermen plied these waters, she had a hard time imagining a group of them gorging themselves right beside the water. Still...

Annabelle stepped back from the carcass and cast her eyes around the sand and dirt beside the kill, looking for wolf tracks.

She found the cloven hoof tracks of the deer just beside the water. And they weren't alone. There, on the edge of the water, was a track from another animal.

"Holy..."

Annabelle clawed her smartphone out of her pocket. She had no cell service this far from McCall—the sat phone in the boat was used for emergency calls—but she found she used her personal phone's camera often. She made use of it now, snapping several photos of the strange track. It had splayed toes that webbed outward in a fan, almost like the track from the front foot of a raccoon if it had been crossed with a duck. But last time she checked, raccoons and ducks didn't have feet over a yard in length.

She took several photos of the carcass, then moved closer, eyes scanning for anything else out of the ordinary.

Well, I'd say that qualifies. Annabelle crouched beside the deer's head. The skull was plainly visible in spots and cracked in a number of places. She reached out for what had caught her eye. Gripping it tightly, she worked the object out of a crack in the skull and held it up for inspection.

In her grasp was a large conical tooth, over six inches long.

Cameron Carson worked the floss through his flawless teeth as he stared into the mirror in his office's executive washroom. The impromptu late-night snack had left something stuck between his teeth and he sought out the offending rat hair.

Success. He rinsed and spat and returned his gaze to the mirror. He probably ought to shave them next time.

Where's the fun in that? The Other chuckled.

Carson narrowed his eyes. The reflection did the same... but had he seen it actually grin and laugh when the inner voice had spoken?

Back in the office, the phone on the desk rang. Carson tore his eyes away from the mirror and exited the washroom, grabbing the phone on the third ring. Singleton always called Carson on his cell phone, so this was someone else. "Yes?"

"Mr. Carson, sir. This is Bob Cummins with security. We've gone through the footage since you arrived and we may have found something, sir."

"I'll be right there, Bob." He hung up, and his eyes strayed to the metal case sitting on the edge of the desk. He picked up the phone again and punched a button for the kitchen. "Yes, this is Cameron. I need two steaks brought to my office." When the chef on duty asked him how he wanted them prepared, Carson grinned. "You know what I haven't had in a long time? Steak tartare. But leave out the minced vegetables... I'm trying out a paleo carnivore diet."

Hanging up, he left the office and made his way to the security station, greeting the woman at a desk just inside. "Where's Mr. Cummins?"

"CCTV room."

"Thank you." Having designed the entire facility himself, Carson knew it like the back of his hand; he went straight to the appropriate door. Inside, three of the walls were covered in monitors. On the right and left, the camera feeds were for the laboratories, grouped by the various disciplines. Along the larger center wall were the feeds from all of the common areas, cafeteria, lounges, hallways, and the entrance. In one corner were monitors for various outdoor cameras hidden along the coast of North Brother Island.

"What have you got for me, Bob?"

"Well, sir, Mr. Singleton explained you found a bug in your office, so I've been searching through the footage outside your door since you arrived."

"Sensible. And?"

Bob tapped a key on his keyboard and the frozen video on the center monitor went into motion. William Singleton stood outside

Carson's office door and after a few seconds, it opened. The billionaire joined his assistant, and the two of them walked up the hall, disappearing from the frame. Moments later, a figure in baggy cleanroom coveralls and a mask approached the door and tried the handle, then appeared to retrieve something from inside the cleanroom suit. The figure's back was to the camera, so it was difficult to tell what they were doing, but a few seconds later, they stooped and set something down.

"We think that's where they put the bug on the floor," Bob said.

The figure straightened and lifted a wrist, doing something on the face of what appeared to be a smartwatch, then turned around and started back down the hallway. When the individual was just about to pass out of sight in the lower frame, Bob froze the image.

"Hard to say with the mask, glasses, and hood... but I'd say this is a female."

"I'd say you're right," Carson said, squinting at the image. "The eyes... there's something familiar. Bob, has anyone attempted to leave the labs, despite the lockdown?"

"No sir, not as yet."

Carson gripped Bob's shoulder. "Good work." When the security man winced and stiffened, Carson quickly let go. "Oh, I'm sorry about that."

"Quite the grip," Bob gasped.

Carson went to the door. "Check the other feeds in the vicinity of those time codes. I want to know where that person came from and where they went. And figure out who they are."

Exiting the security offices, Carson made his way back to his suite, feeling the pangs of hunger surging. When he arrived, he was pleased to discover a double portion of steak tartare on a plate at his desk. He resisted the urge to simply plunge his face into the raw ground meat and forced himself to pick up the fork. Seating himself, he ate as slowly as he could manage. Temporarily sated, he picked up his cell phone and called Singleton.

"Bill... where are they?"

"Sir, I was just about to call you. We were able to trace Dr. Bishop's phone to a hotel in McCall, Idaho, one mile southwest of the quarantine site. But the phone went dark just after nine a.m. their time."

"The morning after I called them," Carson muttered. "That was a mistake. I fear I'm a bit more impulsive of late."

"Understandable, sir."

"Well, have our techs keep an eye on it. And Washakie and Cloud's phones, too. Now, if you'll excuse me, I believe I'm late for an appointment with Dr. Schneider."

"Get a move on, boyo!" Wolf Wallace shouted. "Pass that blasted numpty!"

"Hold your horses," Merle drawled. "After that blind curve up ahead, I'll get around 'em."

They had gotten a late start. After gathering supplies and renting a ten-foot U-Haul truck, the group had finally gotten on the road at a quarter past ten in the morning. Merle drove Wolf and Athena in the SUV while Ian trailed in the U-Haul. They had followed their quarry's route north along US-12, but were now stuck on this two-lane highway behind a farmer on a tractor.

Most of Wolf's production crew had just landed in Boise and would be arriving in Grangeville this evening at the earliest. If Wolf was able to locate the Bigfoot before then, he'd have to attempt the capture himself. He swallowed. The star of *Man vs. Nature* might portray himself as a warrior Scotsman, but at his core, "Wolf" was still a British actor playing a part. Hopefully the ketamine-xylazine tranq darts they'd procured would do the trick.

"If it's good enough for grizzlies..." he said under his breath.

"What was that, sir?"

"Nothing." He pointed as US-12 wound around a curve and

revealed a straight shot with no oncoming traffic. "Now's your chance! Go, go, go!"

Merle crossed the centerline and passed the tractor, with Ian and the U-Haul in his wake. Suddenly, Athena spoke up from the back seat.

"They've stopped."

Wolf turned in his seat and looked back at her. "Where?"

"Three miles ahead. In a town called Kamiah."

CHAPTER SIXTEEN

"Right on time," a leathery man called out as the occupants of Sharkey's pickup piled out into the parking lot near a small building beside the It'se Ye-Ye Casino.

Jonah rose from a red plastic Adirondack chair beside the glass door to his shop. He had a bit of a paunch, but his weathered skin held a healthy tan. Like Joseph, he wore his long black hair in a ponytail, although his was streaked with gray. A sign beside the door declared the store to be the Nez Perce Emporium.

Joseph strolled across to the man and clasped arms, then pointed at the sign. "Surprised it isn't the Nimiipuu Emporium."

"It would be, if I was catering to the tribe and not the tourists." Jonah turned to the others. "The Nez Perce name came from the French trappers. The phrase *nez percé* means pierced nose." He snorted. "Which has never been a cultural affectation in our tribe, so I'm not sure what those Frenchies were smoking. We call ourselves the Nimiipuu. 'The People.' Well... not *this* one." He waved a dismissive hand at Joseph. "Shoshone interloper that he is."

After Joseph introduced the group, Sharkey jerked a thumb

over his shoulder at the casino. "Hey, I'll leave y'all to catch up for a bit. Maybe hit the slots at the... uh..."

"It'se Ye-Ye," Jonah said, rattling off the pronunciation with ease.

"Right. That."

"We'll come find you," Russ said.

While the big man headed across the parking lot, Jonah held the door open for the others. "Please, come in. *Ta'c 'éetx papáayn.* Welcome."

Glass cases topped by a cash register lined the back wall of the Emporium while the rest of the little shop was dominated by shelves, clothing racks, and rotating display stands. Joseph lifted a toy tomahawk festooned with dyed feathers and raised an eyebrow at Jonah. He wobbled the rubber head. "Really?"

"One of my best sellers. You want historical accuracy, go to a museum. I make good money for the town."

Russ was drawn to a sculpted papier-mâché mound in one corner. "Very cool! Kind of reminds me of that Devil's Tower model Richard Dreyfuss was building in *Close Encounters*. This is Heart of the Monster, right?"

Jonah appeared surprised. "You know of it?"

"Joseph showed it to us on the way here. Said you'd tell us the creation story behind it."

"It's a simple tale. A great monster was eating all the animals in the land, and so It'se Ye-Ye decided to—"

"Hey, that's the name of the casino!" Russ blurted. When everyone stared at him, he collapsed in on himself. "Sorry."

"Couldn't even let him finish his first sentence," Sarah whispered with a smile.

"It'se Ye-Ye is Coyote, the trickster god," Jonah explained. "I'll use Coyote, so you won't feel the urge to interrupt again. So... *Coyote* decided he had to destroy the monster. He tricked the creature into eating him, then killed the great beast from within, cutting out its heart.

"With the monster dead, Coyote cut up the body and distributed the pieces across the lands, creating all the tribes, but when it came time for the Nimiipuu, he realized he had nothing left. So, Coyote washed his bloody paws in the Clearwater River and sprinkled the water on the lands nearby, and thus created The People. The mound is the remains of the heart of the monster."

Russ raised his hand. Jonah gave him a look, then gestured for him to speak. "Okay, so... you said Coyote used up everything before he made your tribe, but... that's a pretty big chunk of heart still left over..."

When Sarah smacked Russ on the back of the head, Jonah burst into laughter and explained, "It's a creation myth! Don't get me started on Adam and Eve."

Joseph cleared his throat. "Jonah... Luke said you found a special stone at the mound. That is why we are here."

"That old thing?" He shrugged. "Okay. Come in the back."

The group followed him through a door behind the cash register, where they discovered a dimly lit room that seemed to be part man cave, part museum. A comfortable-looking recliner flanked a leather couch, a big-screen television topped an Xbox and controllers, and a small fridge sat in one corner. Several tables along the walls held a number of artifacts along with colorful minerals and gemstones.

"Won't find any rubber tomahawks in here," Jonah said. "This is my sanctuary, and it's where I keep some of the real artifacts."

"Whoa! Joseph, look at this big hunk of white buffalo turquoise," Russ said, pointing at a sizable whitish rock threaded with streaks of black.

"Yes. Although this isn't really turquoise." Jonah picked it up. "It's actually a form of dolomite."

"Is that the 'Stone that Sleeps' that Luke mentioned?" Sarah asked.

"No." Jonah set the white buffalo down and pointed at the wall. "It is there."

Joseph stepped forward and examined what Jonah indicated: feathers dangled from a leather-wrapped hoop, crisscrossed with strands of sinew like the web of the spider. A small, irregular stone was threaded into the center.

"A dreamcatcher?" Joseph frowned. "Not part of our culture."

"Not originally, no. The practice comes from the Algonquian peoples—the Ojibwe, specifically. But many tribes across America have adopted it in the last century. And... they're popular with tourists. Although I wouldn't sell *this* one. This one is to protect my business."

"I thought they were for preventing nightmares," Sarah said.

Jonah grunted. "Not all nightmares come in your dreams." He took the dreamcatcher down from its nail and held it up. "Think of it as a form of protective charm. The web catches anything that might do the owner harm and absorbs it in the stone." He laughed. "Although, I plan on letting my security cameras and alarm do most of the heavy lifting."

Joseph held out a hand and lightly touched the stone in the center of the web with his fingertips. There was a faint iridescence to the yellowish-green coloring, and its surface was pitted with tiny indentations. It had been threaded into the sinew webbing through several naturally occurring holes in the rock. "You found this at Heart of the Monster... and you stuck it on a dreamcatcher. Why?"

Jonah shrugged. "Seemed like the thing to do. I recognized it from stories my grandmother told. This stone was known to contain powerful medicine, to protect against a Great Evil. Why not enhance one protective charm with another?"

Sarah leaned in and peered at the dreamcatcher's center. "And is she the one that named it the Stone that Sleeps?"

"In the story, two rocks dropped from the heavens: one brought peace, the other... war. And the kind of war that the other brought... involved cannibalism. Humans becoming monsters."

"This other stone... the, uh... cannibalism one... did she call that one the Stone that Sings?" Russ asked.

Jonah straightened. "She did." He looked at Joseph. "You told him this, yes?"

"I did. And explained that our tribes didn't have a monopoly on the concept."

"True. Some say the first mention of that stone comes from the lore of the Ojibwe"—he lifted the dreamcatcher higher—"the very people that are credited with this charm. The Ojibwe tales of the creature known as the Wendigo may refer to one who has been altered by the stone's song."

Joseph placed his ear close to the dreamcatcher.

"What are you doing?" Jonah asked.

"Listening." After a moment, Joseph straightened.

"Hear anything?" Russ asked.

"No." Joseph looked at Jonah. "We believe we have encountered the *other* stone in your grandmother's stories. And it emitted a..." He trailed off and turned to Russ.

"It gave off a hum... or a chord. Very faint, but it was..."

"It *sang* to you?" Jonah hissed the question and stepped back, raising the dreamcatcher.

Russ waved his hands. "Don't worry. Your brother-in-law dragged me away from it before it Wendigo'd my brain. But it... well... it did cause some 'evil' as your mee-maw might've said."

Jonah was about to ask something but Joseph spoke first. "Why did they call the rock you hold the Stone that Sleeps? How did it bring peace to the 'war' that the other stone brought?"

"Well... the two stones are sometimes called brothers. I hate to mix up too many cultures, but it's like a yin-yang thing. This one here is the older, wiser brother... and it can seek out the other. Supposedly, it 'pulls' toward its sibling." Jonah moved the dreamcatcher like it was being drawn to something unseen.

"What, like a dowsing rod?" Russ asked.

Jonah looked like he was about to scoff at the suggestion, but after a moment he shrugged. "I guess so, yeah."

"And what happens when the stones find each other?" Sarah asked.

"Story goes that when this stone finds the other, it can make the bad one...well... sleep. The singing stops."

Joseph reached out a hand. "May I?" He took the dream-catcher and held it aloft. "Jonah... have you tested this little rock in any way?"

"Well, yeah. There's been a lot of mining in the history of this part of the country, and I've collected quite a few artifacts. They used to mine uranium in the nineteenth century—mostly to give glass a yellow or green color... or yellow-green like that stone. Took them a while to figure out the stuff was radioactive." He went over to a rickety desk in the corner and tapped a box with a corded wand attached to it. "I have this old Geiger counter from the early thirties and used it on our little friend there. Very faint radiation, but nothing crazy."

Joseph's eyes remained on the assortment of items on the corner desk. "What is that box there? The wooden one with the shoulder strap?"

"Oh, that's a lead-lined sample box. It was part of some old uranium mining equipment I won at an auction."

"Can we borrow that?" Joseph asked before raising the dream-catcher. "And this?"

"Well?" Wolf asked as Merle got into the SUV.

"The only one in the casino is the big guardsman, Sharkey."

"The motel clerk back in Grangeville said he saw Russ and the other two get into his truck," Wolf said. "And it's right there!"

The trio were in the It'se Ye-Ye parking lot. Ian and his U-Haul were parked at a supermarket across US-12; the moving truck would have been conspicuous in the lot of a casino.

"I'm registering two of the tracking devices here," Athena said as she zoomed in on a map on her laptop. "One in the truck... the other in the casino."

"When I walked past Sharkey's truck, I spotted the *Man vs. Nature* swag bag in the back of the cab," Merle said. "Sharkey must have a bugged item on 'im as well."

Wolf had given the guardsmen two bags of show souvenirs back at the brewery; some of the items had a little bonus hidden inside, courtesy of Athena.

"What about the other trackers?"

"At Farley's mother's house, back in Grangeville," Athena replied immediately.

"Dammit." Wolf ran a hand across his dyed beard. "Sharkey must've dropped off Russ and his mates somewhere along the way."

"I don't think so," Athena said. "I've examined the history of their route and they never left the highway. Apart from pauses at intersections, they didn't come to a complete stop until right here."

Wolf pondered this. "Maybe they're using the casino loo?"

Athena scoffed from the back seat. "All three of them?"

"Athena, do you have a bug? For sound?"

"Somewhere back here," she said, retrieving a fishing tackle box at her feet. She popped it open and scanned a variety of electronic gizmos and assorted parts.

"Get one ready. Merle, I want you to put it in their truck. Maybe we can—"

"Wait... there they are," Merle said, looking across Wolf through the passenger side window. "Coming across the side street. They just left that little shop over there."

From behind the tinted glass of the SUV, Wolf stared at his

survival-rival as the trio crossed the street, headed for Sharkey's truck. "Russ has a metal box with him…"

"Forget the box," Merle said. "Check out what the Indian guy's holding. Some kinda hoodoo voodoo thing."

"It's a dreamcatcher, you redneck," Athena said from behind them, and you could practically hear her roll her eyes. "I have one over my bed."

Merle snorted. "Really? I woulda figgered your walls were full of posters for death metal bands."

"Oh, I've got those, too."

"Shut yer gobs and text Ian to get ready to roll out," Wolf said, looking out the front windshield. "Sharkey's left the casino and is headed for his truck."

"Did you win anything?" Sarah asked the back of Sharkey's head as they buckled their seat belts.

"Naw. But I'm only down five bucks. Hey, I'm gonna take us back the other way. More turns, but it'll shave off a few minutes." He turned left onto US-12 and almost immediately slowed and barked a laugh. "Well, *that* place is new! Y'all want some ice cream?"

On the south side of the highway was a business with the sign "Sassy-Squatch Ice Cream."

"Amusing and appropriate as that is, I think we should get back to Grangeville," Joseph said.

"Fair enough," Sharkey said, turning left at the next street. "I'm lactose intolerant anyway."

CHAPTER SEVENTEEN

Dhir frowned as he examined his laptop screen. He had been monitoring the secure communications link with Alan Robbins, their mole in the CDC, but as the radio silence went on and on, he'd gotten bored. Sitting in his quarters inside a facility with insane levels of digital security, Dhir finally gave in to temptation; he had decided to play around to find out just *how* secure.

After half an hour he'd managed to slip through a few cracks. He had just begun to snoop around when he saw it: a signal. Several paired Bluetooth devices working in tandem... but unlike everything else in here, they didn't bear the Maiden Industries coding, a form of IFF—Identification Friend or Foe—that told the Maiden security systems whether a signal belonged in the network or not. It was well masked, and Dhir would likely never have spotted it if he hadn't dug so deeply.

The signal seemed to be on the move at the moment. In all likelihood, whatever was generating it was gaining in strength as it neared one Wi-Fi node and dimming as it passed. Dhir took a sip of his energy drink and began to track the signal.

Clad in her hooded cleanroom suit and mask, Yana made her way to the cold room. The entire facility was locked down. She had gone to the lobby to try to get outside for some "fresh air"—and to upload her videos to Hilda—but the solitary lobby guard from before was now a quartet. No one was to be allowed in or out; some form of quarantine, they said. But Yana knew better. She shuddered as she recalled the madness in the face that had filled the mini-drone's camera. Carson had locked the facility down to trap her inside.

Just as well, Yana thought. *I'm not through in here anyway.* She had thoroughly examined the files she had filmed outside Dr. Schneider's office door, and the description for Subject Three was an exact match for her sister Katya. Yana had to know for herself before attempting her escape.

Looking through the glass window to the cold room, she spotted two technicians inside. One wore a parka and was examining a massive body on an autopsy table. The other technician was gathering samples; after a moment, that one left through a door into another part of the lab.

Yana triggered continuous recording and adjusted the folder of files in her hand. Lifting her ID and keycard lanyard, she swiped the electronic lock and entered the cold room. When she was young, she had worked in a restaurant in Brighton Beach; walking into this climate-controlled room reminded her of the abrupt chill from her visits to the walk-in freezer to retrieve meat for the cooks.

There was a row of parkas on hooks. Yana put one on, then walked around the room, keeping one eye on her folder with occasional glances at every table in the room. Some were bolted to the floor and some were on wheels. Only the corpse of the giant was currently unbagged, and the rest of the tables either held body bags or were empty. However, there was one other table that would likely never again hold a corpse. Yana halted in her tracks.

Near one side of the room, a stainless-steel examination table had been ripped free of its mountings. The legs and part of the table's surface had been deformed. She noticed the remaining technician watching her. She was about to ask him what had happened to the table, but her mind quickly sifted through all of the information she had gathered. She remembered Carson tossing aside the massive bookcase. She recalled the page count of the file on Subject One, easily dwarfing the amount of information they had on the other subjects.

Yana gestured toward the crumpled table with her folder. "Subject One do this?"

The man nodded. "Apparently so. I wasn't here when it happened, but Dr. Schneider was all excited about it."

"I bet," Yana responded, trying to keep her Russian accent at a low simmer while minimizing her verbiage. She approached the man and nodded at the huge figure on the table. "Which one is this one?"

"Subject Two. Carson's bodyguard. Or... former bodyguard, I guess. Used to be a pro wrestler. Brick Broadway."

Yana gave a grunt of mild interest, but inside she was shaking. Her sister had told her of this man. Apparently, his old wrestling persona would sing Broadway tunes while beating the snot out of his opponents... until the producers decided to bust him down from "heel" and make him a "jobber"—a wrestler who was basically paid to lose all the time. Katya had said that a neck injury forced the man into retirement... and from the looks of it, another neck injury had forced him into a second, more permanent retirement.

Brick's skull was partially caved in and his deformed head lay on the table at an odd tilt; Yana had no doubt his neck had been broken in multiple places.

"Poor bugger," the tech said. "Apparently, that rabid Bigfoot flipped him upside down and slammed him straight into the earth, like driving a nail into a board. The top of his skull was fractured in three places and several of his cervical vertebrae were pretty much reduced to powder."

When Yana heard "rabid Bigfoot," she spared a glance at the HUD in the lenses of her glasses to be sure she was still recording.

"You new?" the man asked.

Yana gave an ambiguous grunt and looked down at her files before closing the folder. "Where is Subject Three?"

The man pointed to a table in a corner of the room. "We haven't processed her yet."

"I know. That's why I'm here."

"Great. I'll let you get to it, then." The man gathered up a small rack of vials full of fluids and scrapings. "Need to get these to Dr. Takagawa."

Yana thanked the technician as he departed. She pretended to be engrossed in her files until he left through a door in the back wall, then moved quickly to the corner of the room. She reached the autopsy table, set her folder down on a wheeled instrument stand, then turned to face the body bag. She took a deep breath... took hold of the zipper...

Dhir stopped in front of the cold room and looked inside. Two figures in parkas and coveralls were speaking at a steel table with a body on it. He glanced down at the laptop he held across his left forearm. The signal was definitely coming from one of the occupants. Singleton had given Dhir a pass that would allow him into several parts of the facility, but he wasn't certain it would work on this door. *Only one way to find out.* He swiped his keycard and the panel blinked green as the door clicked. He pushed his way in just as one of the figures exited the room through a door at the back. The other went to a table in the corner.

Probably supposed to wear a cleanroom suit in here, he thought, then decided to set down his laptop and throw a parka on. The room was freezing and the coat would help him blend in. He lifted his laptop and checked the signal; there was no doubt where it was coming from. As he started across the room, he froze, staring at a massive figure on a steel examination table.

That body... it's Brick! Dhir knew that Carson's huge body-guard had died in the conflict with the infected alpha male Sasquatch; he'd watched the surviving mercenaries zip his battered corpse into a body bag. But why on earth was he here? Shouldn't his body be back at the government quarantine facility in Idaho? Dhir had felt uneasy about a number of things he'd seen during his time in North Brother and he added this one to the list.

Before he could ponder any further on the subject, a gasp and moan came from the technician in the corner. He looked up to see the figure stagger back from the body bag they stood in front of. It had been partially unzipped, and Dhir could see a woman's face staring up at the fluorescents with unseeing eyes.

Dhir stepped forward to assist the female technician as she continued to moan with emotion.

"Oh... *moya sestra*," the woman whimpered.

"Miss... are you all right?"

The woman whirled around, startled. Her face was obscured by a surgical mask and coverall hood; large glasses magnified her tear-filled eyes.

Dhir looked at the lenses... there was something unusual about them. He glanced down at the laptop, then back at the distraught woman. "Who are you?"

She straightened and held up her ID on its lanyard.

Dhir ignored it, looking again at his readouts. "Your glasses... some form of recording device?" When she didn't reply, he continued in a low voice, "Are you CIA? Defense Department? Do you work for a rival company?"

"I work for Maiden Industries," she spat.

Dhir noticed a distinct accent in her speech—Eastern European or Russian. The woman must have realized it too; when she spoke again, the accent was muted.

"I am recording faces and identifying marks on the victims," she said, turning back to the female corpse on the table. "HR wants a record for the families."

There was a hitch in her voice as she spoke. Dhir looked at the body on the table and put two and two together.

"This is the Russian mercenary I saw at the base camp," he said. He came closer and spoke softly. "Are you... are you related to her?"

The woman nodded. "She is my sister." She looked up from her sister's face, then noticed Dhir's laptop held across his forearm. She frowned at the readout on the screen. "What is this?"

"I've been tracking your signal."

"Impossible."

"Well... obviously not." He lowered his voice again. "I had to hack into their system a little."

The woman fiddled with her watch, then looked up at him; although her eyes were pointed in his direction, Dhir could tell she was reading something from the inside of her glasses. Then her eyes focused directly on his. "Dhir Patel... I need to show you something."

"Let me get this straight..." Cameron Carson ran a hand across the side of his neck where the teenage Bigfoot had bitten him. There was still evidence of a wound there, but even the scar tissue seemed to have diminished from the previous day. "My cells are repairing themselves at an accelerated rate... more so than before the bite?"

"We're not seeing the cell death and rapid decay we might expect in a person who has... well... expired," Schneider explained. "Your body seems to be healing itself at a level I've never seen. In a human, anyway. Perhaps the axolotl salamander. I'd be curious to know if you can regenerate a limb."

"I'm afraid you'll have to remain in unfulfilled suspense as far as that hypothetical goes," Carson replied.

"I can't explain it," Dr. Schneider said. "Not yet, anyway."

"I may have a theory," Dr. Takagawa ventured. He lifted a digital tablet and scrolled down a list. "Among the various longevity treatments you have subjected yourself to... I see the peptide BPC-157."

"Yes."

"Supposedly, this peptide promotes injury recovery in muscle and cartilage. Not approved by the FDA, and the only proper trials on that particular amino acid chain were conducted on rats."

At the mention of rats, Carson's stomach gurgled. "What of it?"

"BPC-157 is whimsically referred to as the 'Wolverine' peptide."

"Ah, I see," Carson said, nodding.

Dr. Schneider frowned. "I, however, do not. What is the significance of this name?"

"Not much of a comic book or movie fan, I take it." Carson waved a hand. "It's a character in the *X-Men* who heals rapidly. But I confess, I thought that moniker was just a marketing strategy."

"It may well be," Dr. Takagawa said. "Or it may be that the saliva in the creature's bite interacted with those amino acids. Enhanced them. But I'll have to run more tests."

The door to the lab beeped and clicked and Singleton rushed in. "Sir! We have a problem!"

CHAPTER EIGHTEEN

"He... he ate a rat," Dhir whispered when the video from Yana's camera drone ended in a burst of static.

"I'm more concerned that he's throwing floor-to-ceiling bookcases around and deforming steel tables like Twizzlers. Listen... I wasn't lying when I said I work for Maiden. Hilda Morgan sent me."

"Morgan... she's the president of the company, isn't she?"

"Close enough. Chairperson of the Board of Directors. She needs to see this video. And everything else I've recorded."

Dhir looked up from the laptop on the desk in Yana's quarters. The Russian woman had removed her surgical mask and dropped her hood, revealing short spiky hair, dyed blond. She had a tattoo of some kind on her neck and several facial piercings. But while her overall aesthetic implied a toughness, the look in her eyes betrayed fear.

"Dhir... I need to get out of this facility."

Dhir blinked. "They've locked it down." He looked at her. "*You're* the reason they did that, aren't you?"

Yana nodded. "And if he catches me... Carson will kill me like he killed my sister."

Dhir shook his head. "Carson didn't kill your sister. One of the Sasquatch did."

"Carson sent my sister into the woods to hunt monsters with a *yebanyy* net gun!" Yana spat. "I know. She told me. His orders were nonlethal weapons only. Carson might as well have killed her himself."

Dhir sighed, then slid her laptop aside and replaced it with his own. "If I'm honest... I've been pondering an exit strategy myself." Typing and scrolling, he brought up a schematic of the facility. "When I was poking around in their system, I found *this*." He turned the screen toward Yana and pointed at a spot on the map.

Yana peered at the screen, then nodded. "Good. Let's go." She shoved her laptop into her go-bag.

Suddenly, a klaxon sounded and there was a buzz and click from the door to the hallway. A red light on the lock pad glared angrily at them.

"*Nyet!*" Yana ran to the door and swiped her card; the lock pad taunted her with a disapproving buzz. "We're sealed in."

"I'm on it," Dhir said as his fingers flew across the keyboard. "The ID code above the magnetic stripe on the back of your card, read it to me!"

Yana did so and Dhir entered it into the system. "Try it now."

She did, and the panel treated her to a happy green light and a cheery beep. The door opened.

"How did you...?"

"I'll explain on the way. Turn right... then right again... staircase at the end."

"Fifteen minutes ago, Dhir Patel and an unknown person entered living quarters that were assigned yesterday morning to an envoy from Maiden Corporate," Singleton said as he hurried alongside Carson. A member of Maiden's security detail followed behind, talking to Bob Cummins, who was monitoring CCTV cameras in the security control room. An alarm blared, forcing everyone to raise their voices.

"What are they doing in there?" Carson demanded.

"No idea, sir... that room's camera feed appears to be on a loop," the guard answered. "But we've initiated a Level Three internal lockdown. They're sealed inside."

"Good," Carson growled. *Yessssss, very good*, the inner voice concurred. Carson glanced at Singleton. "When we get there, you two stay outside. I'll handle this." *You certainly will*, The Other cooed. *Clean-up on aisle four!* The thoughts dissolved into mad mental laughter, and Carson gave his head a violent shake.

"Hold up, sir," the Maiden security guard said, coming to a halt in the corridor and pressing two fingers to his earpiece. "Say again, Bob?" The man frowned.

"What is it?" Carson barked with impatience.

"The cameras on the living quarters level just went down and their door is now unlocked."

"What?" Carson roared. "Who unlocked it?"

"Um... *you* did, sir."

Dhir and Yana dashed down the steps, their footfalls echoing in the dimly lit stairwell.

"How deep does this place go?" Yana asked.

"Four stories under the ground floor level, in most places," Dhir panted. "This subbasement is even deeper."

Abruptly, the stairs ended at a steel door that proclaimed itself to be the Auxiliary Generator Room.

"Through here?" Yana asked. "You sure?"

"Yes."

"Pretty clever, swapping Carson's credentials for mine," Yana said as she swiped her ID card through the reader beside the door.

"I came across the employee security clearance database when I was sniffing around," Dhir replied as Yana opened the door. "Figured if anyone had access to every part of the island, he would."

"Just a pair of generators in here. I don't see any other doors. It's a dead end!"

"Not according to these blueprints. The exit is hidden." He stepped past her and lifted the lid on his laptop, scanning the schematics he'd left open. "The generator on the left isn't functional. Should be hollow. Hit that emergency override button on the corner."

Yana did so and the side of the dummy generator popped open. She stuck her head inside. "There's a concrete tunnel," she called out, her voice echoing off the tunnel walls. She looked back at Dhir. "Are the cameras still out?"

Dhir checked his laptop. "No... they rerouted the feed. No idea how long ago. Here, hold my laptop."

Yana took it from him and Dhir closed the door to the stairwell. After a momentary delay, there was a dull clunk as the locking mechanism triggered the bolt. Dhir grabbed a wall-mounted fire extinguisher and smashed it against the keycard mechanism until it broke loose.

"This door is the only way in from the main complex," Dhir explained.

"Well, then, we better hope the builders finished that tunnel," Yana said.

As he hurtled down the stairs two at a time, Carson heard the pounding sounds echoing up from the bottom of the stairwell. Snarling, he grabbed hold of the railing and vaulted it, leaping down to the next flight. As he repeated the process several more times, Singleton's voice sounded from above.

"Sir! Wait! They might be armed."

Cummins had restored the camera feed just in time to spot Dhir and the unknown woman entering this stairwell. Carson knew exactly where they were headed. Finally, he reached the bottom of the stairs and dug his keycard out of his pocket. He swiped it through the pad beside the steel door. Nothing. Not even a red light or "access denied" buzz. Remembering the pounding noises he'd heard, he realized what had happened. Grabbing the handle, he pulled with all of his might. The bolt held. The handle did not.

Carson roared with rage and hurled the metal handle aside with a clatter as the security guard arrived. Singleton limped down the steps behind him.

"What the hell happened to you?" Carson asked.

"Sorry, sir. I turned my ankle trying to keep up with you."

"They're going for the old exit tunnel I had installed. Useful in case of a fire on an upper floor... or in the event of an unsolicited visit from any federal law enforcement agencies."

"I remember," Singleton said. He winced as he hopped down the last steps. "It lets out in the bird sanctuary."

Carson glared at the door. "They disabled the card reader. Smashed it on the other side, I suspect," he muttered, trying to control the urges that were bubbling up inside.

"I could try to break it down, sir," the guard offered, stepping forward.

Carson stopped him with a hand to his chest. "Please. Allow *us*..." he growled.

"Us?" Singleton asked nervously.

Carson stepped back and locked his eyes on a spot on the door beside the locking mechanism. With an animalistic roar, he kicked with all of his might. The door shuddered and the concrete around the access panel cracked in three places. Gray dust puffed outward from the impact.

"Jesus..." the guard whispered, involuntarily taking a step back.

"Oh, I'm afraid *He* has very little to do with it," Carson

quipped, mirth in his voice. He kicked again and roared with triumph when the bolt broke free, sending a small chunk of concrete spinning into the room beyond. The door swung open and rebounded when it reached the limits of its hinges.

The security guard drew his gun and entered. Carson started to follow but turned back to Singleton.

"Bill... you go back upstairs."

"Sir, my ankle's not that bad. I'll try to keep up."

"No... it's not that. I'd rather you not be around when I... catch them."

Carson's voice ratcheted into a gravelly purr as he spoke, and Singleton must have seen something behind the billionaire's eyes; the assistant staggered back a step, almost stumbling when his heel hit the bottom stair.

Carson's toothy grin split his beard as he turned and rushed out of the stairwell.

For a high-tech facility, this exit was decidedly low-tech; the tunnel had narrowed as they went, culminating in a puddle-strewn cul-de-sac with a short flight of six rough-hewn steps, topped with something like a pair of slanted cellar doors.

After unlatching the rudimentary locking bar, Dhir and Yana got onto the top steps and pushed together with their shoulders against the exit doors above them. After a prolonged creak, the doors opened and dropped to either side with a pair of clangs. Rain fell from a gray sky, pelting their faces.

"Now what?" Dhir asked.

Yana was already digging through her go-bag for her phone. "We call for extraction."

"They're probably jamming cell phone signals during the lockdown," Dhir said, looking nervously back at the cellar doors. Did he hear something in the distance? Hard to know with the rain hitting the trees around them.

"They *are* blocking cell signals," Yana confirmed. "But Ms. Morgan gave me a phone with limited satellite functionality, in case of emergency. And I'd say this qualifies." She punched in a code, listened, then spoke. "Yes, this is she. I need an exfil, ASAP. Do you have my location?" She listened again and seemed to relax. "Copy that. See you at the shoreline east of my position." She hung up. "They had a boat on standby. ETA five minutes."

A spine-tingling gale of laughter sounded from the tunnel below them and Dhir swallowed. "We may not have five minutes."

Yana grabbed him by the arm and pointed into the vines and trees. "That way! Run!"

Four and a half minutes later, Carson burst from the treeline beside the East River, skidding to a stop on the rock-strewn shore just in time to watch a small boat speeding away. A figure sat at the stern, manning the outboard, with Dhir and the unknown blonde sitting near the bow. In moments, the boat faded from view, obscured by the rain. As the rain pattered down on his tailored dress shirt, Carson's chest heaved, his simulated breathing sparked by rage, rather than an actual need for oxygen. Eyes wide, lips pulled back from his teeth, Carson snarled with frustration, then whirled and headed back toward the exit at a loping run. His thoughts became chaotic and his vision filled with a haze of red.

The voice within echoed in his mind, and this time... it opened the door of its mental cage and slipped through. *You owe me.*

Armand Gualtieri was in great shape for a man of thirty-two, but his security detail at the facility didn't involve many foot pursuits.

Cameron Carson had left him in the dust during the chase, outpacing him in moments. Gasping for air, he leaned against a tree to catch his breath and get his bearings. He saw movement in the trees ahead and squinted against the rain. It was Carson... coming toward him at a run.

"Sir! Did you find them?"

Carson did not answer, did not slow. He began to laugh as his pace increased, bespoke Italian loafers throwing up splashes of rainwater.

The last thing Armand saw was the billionaire/innovator's face —a face that had once graced the covers of some of the most prestigious magazines in the world—hurtling toward him, perfect teeth bared in a grimace that was half-snarl, half-smile. Carson launched himself through the air. As the billionaire's eager face dipped below his field-of-view, Armand felt a flash of pain and a surge of moisture when Carson's teeth tore his throat apart.

CHAPTER NINETEEN

'I like the color of your hair,' Littlefoot announced, giving DawnWaker's arm a gentle brush with his fingertips.

DawnWaker smiled down at the youngster as the trio walked through the forest. Brighteyes led the way, but he looked back when his half brother spoke.

Littlefoot added gestures to his grunts and pants to articulate a more complex thought. 'Red... like a maple leaf in before-winter.'

'That is beautiful, Littlefoot. Thank you.'

'*You* like her hair too,' Littlefoot signed to Brighteyes. 'I know this because you look at her all the time.'

Brighteyes started to protest with a basic sign of negation but then simply shrugged.

DawnWaker panted with amusement, then halted as she spotted a patch of edible morel mushrooms under a leafy tree. She left the game trail and gathered some to share with the others.

'My favorite!' Littlefoot declared as he took one of the honey-combed mushrooms and bit into it.

'How much further do we go?' DawnWaker asked.

Brighteyes thought for a moment. He had swung wide around the place where the men with guns had been, and that was making it difficult to gauge the distance they would have to travel.

'I do not know. A few more days? My mother... Sky... she said that to the south of Silverback's territory there was a river with many salmon. And beyond that... a big lake. Humans are at the south side of the lake, but not many at the north side. I think there will be much food there. And maybe we can find a safe place to call home.'

After clocking out from the Ranger District HQ, Annabelle Graybill drove her Forest Service truck through downtown McCall, heading toward the Salmon River Brewing Company. Traveling along East Lake Street, she noted some vendors setting up canopies and tables amidst the food trucks that gathered next to the yacht club in The Spot, McCall's new food truck park.

The recently elected mayor, a California transplant named Gary Vance, had gotten together with some of his rich friends and declared this weekend to be "Vancefest," as a thank-you to the residents for electing him. In addition to live music and various raffles, the festival would culminate in a boat parade.

Annabelle slowed and rolled down her window as she neared the site of the old McCall Mall, now rebranded as The Waterfront. Strolling across the crosswalk ahead was one of the Sharlie Hunters that she was on her way to meet.

"Kevin!"

Startled, Kevin looked up from the enormous ice cream cone he held, a smear of fudge at the corner of his mouth.

"Hop in!"

Kevin scurried the rest of the way across and got into the truck. He guiltily raised the cone, the towering triple-scoop of ice cream bursting with chunks of candy and cookies. "I missed lunch. Didn't want to drink on an empty stomach."

"Whatever helps you sleep at night. What the holy heck is that?"

"One of the best sellers from Squatch Sweets. The Notorious B.I.G.foot. Reese's Peanut Butter Cups, Oreos, cookie dough, fudge, caramel... and edible glitter."

"Lucky for you I know CPR." Annabelle gave the tantalizing treat a second glance. "Though I gotta admit, that looks amazing."

"Wanna bite?"

"Mayyyyybe. But let's wait till we get to the brewery," she said, turning the corner past the McCall Hotel.

"So... you said you found something you wanted to show us?" Kevin prompted.

"Yep. But, again... let's wait till we get to the brewery. You're gonna want a beer."

"You guys wanna beer?"

Sharkey held open the door to his fridge and swept his hand across an eclectic selection of local craft beers alongside Bud Lights.

"Thanks, but we better get rolling," Russ said.

"Yeah, I figured. Sorry I can't go with ya, but I'm back on duty shortly. Oh, here are the keys to the Jeep." He took them off a hook near the door and tossed them across to Russ. "I've been fixing her up. Should do all right by ya. But you'll need to gas her up."

"Thanks, man."

"No prob. Hey, lemme go grab the camping gear." Sharkey left the three of them standing in his kitchen as he made his way to the basement.

"Look at this crap," Russ muttered as he sifted through the Wolf Wallace swag bag that Sharkey had emptied onto the counter. He lifted a compass that was set into a rubberized blue housing;

the *Man vs. Nature* logo was embossed in raised white lettering, curving along the top. He held it level. "Well, that's a surprise. It works."

"Good. We need one," Joseph said. "I'm sure Sharkey won't mind parting with it."

"No need, I've got mine..." Russ trailed off as he fished his own compass out of his pocket; it was smashed. "Spoke too soon. Probably busted it when that zombified Silverback was tossing us around."

"Don't remind me." Joseph rubbed his rib cage and retrieved the ibuprofen from his pocket.

Sarah waved a dismissive hand. "I'm the one who's technically still under a concussion protocol. The camp medic thought I was okay, but I'm supposed to take it easy." She laughed. "Not sure if what we're about to do qualifies."

Russ pocketed the gaudy compass. "I'll take this, then... but we still have a portable GPS."

"I'll be shocked if they're not jamming GPS signals in the area around the incident." Joseph spread out the topographical map on the kitchen island and Russ and Sarah joined him as he tapped a point on the map. "Here's where Farley threw the Stone that Sings. The West Fork Crooked River."

"The woods around the expedition base camp are likely swarming with feds and who knows who else," Russ cautioned.

"Correct. I suggest we drive around to Orogrande..." He traced a line along a road east from Grangeville, then cut southward.

"My father drove through there before he went into the woods... and later met Brighteyes."

"Yes, I remember that from the journal. And we'll follow his original route along here, Crooked River Road... also called Buffalo Hump. It runs alongside the West Fork for a while, and we'll ditch the Jeep here, where the road is closest to the river. From there, we'll hoof it to the West Fork and follow it to a spot below the geologists' camp."

"At which point we whip out the dreamcatcher," Russ prompted.

"Yes. With luck, the Stone that Sings will be snagged in the river somewhere nearby, and the Stone that Sleeps will guide us to it."

"What happens if we come upon it suddenly?" Sarah asked. "You said the tone from that sphere started affecting Russ pretty quickly."

"Only when I was up close," Russ clarified. "We'll just have to keep our ears peeled," he warned. "Stop and listen every so often."

Joseph nodded. "Yes. But I am hoping my brother-in-law's artifact will give us some advance warning."

"And I've got two sets of headphones from Bud's equipment," Russ added.

"Still, it wouldn't hurt to have a little extra insurance," Sarah suggested, just as Sharkey clomped up the stairs with several sleeping bags, two backpacks, and a bagged collapsible tent dangling from his hands. "Hey, Shark... you go hunting? Or shooting at a range?"

He chuckled as he dumped the camping gear on the floor of the kitchen. "You're asking a Montanan living in Idaho—who's with the National Guard—if he goes shooting?"

"Thought so. What do you use for ear protection?"

"I've got a set of earmuffs. But most times I just carry some of those little squishy earplugs."

"Can we borrow those?"

"Sure thing. You want some guns to go with 'em?"

Sarah smiled and waved the suggestion away. "No, that's not—"

"Actually," Russ interrupted, "might not be a bad idea."

"I'll open the gun safe and you can take your pick."

Fifteen minutes later, Russ, Joseph, and Sarah loaded up the Jeep with food and water and camping supplies, as well as a 20-gauge shotgun and a hunting rifle from Sharkey's stash. A few minutes later, they were heading east toward the forests of Idaho.

"One of the tracking devices is on the move," Athena announced.

"And the other?" Wolf Wallace asked.

"Still at Sharkey's house."

Wolf pointed at the dot that was leaving town on Highway 13. "That's Russ. I'm sure of it. Where ye goin', boyo? Zoom out!"

Athena did so.

"That's the way you'd go if'n ya wanted to go to the Nez Perce-Clearwater Forest," Merle observed.

"That's where the Bigfoot attacks happened!" Wolf grinned. "Call... the cameraman. Um..."

"Ian," Merle supplied.

"Tell Ian to bring the U-Haul with the gear around to the parking lot. And I'll need him on camera, so tell 'im to bring that intern we just hired. Well... *hired* is probably the wrong word. But I want someone with the U-Haul in case we have to leave it."

"Not sure the kid has a driver's license," Merle advised.

Wolf rose and planted his fists on his hips, above the waistband of his camouflage tactical kilt. "We're moving out! Next stop... Bigfoot country!"

"Holy moly!" Brady choked out the exclamation on the tail end of a spit take of beer.

Annabelle had just set the enormous tooth down on the outdoor patio table. And if she was honest with herself, she *might* have deliberately timed the reveal for when Brady had taken a big sip of his IPA. The four Sharlie Hunters were seated under the shade of an outdoor umbrella, beers in front of each of them.

"Where did you—*cough*—find that?" he managed to splutter.

"Up north. On a shore of The Meanders," she said. "Just up the right fork at the third bend in the river."

"Is it a fossil?" Stuart asked, slipping a pair of reading glasses out of a pocket.

"No." Mark picked the tooth up and turned it this way and that. "This looks fresh—like it just came out of something's mouth. Although... no blood on the roots."

"Conical... slight curve... the shape is consistent with a plesiosaur," Brady observed.

"Or a saltwater crocodile," Stuart countered.

"I found it embedded in the carcass of a deer, right beside the water." Annabelle was already pulling up her photos and set the phone down on the table. "Whatever left that tooth did *this* to the deer."

"Whoa." Mark set the tooth down and grabbed his beer for a fortifying sip.

Kevin gestured with the remnant of his ice cream cone, his hand glistening with melted vanilla. "A croc or a plesiosaur would've dragged their kill into the water."

"Let me guess... your extradimensional, space-alien Sharlie did this, then teleported back to her lair in the fifth dimension," Mark scoffed.

"Well, it sure as hell wasn't a neutered eel!" Kevin popped the tip of the ice cream cone in his mouth with an air of finality.

"Actually, I thought this might be the work of a pack of wolves," Annabelle suggested, "until I saw... this." She swiped back from the carcass shots and revealed a photo of the odd track in the mud.

Their beers forgotten, the Sharlie Hunters practically vibrated with excitement as they leaned over the table.

"Ha! Not flippers!" Stuart crowed. "Looks like a croc foot."

"No... check out the webbing," Brady argued. "More like a

flipper with vestigial claws." He turned to Mark. "But there goes your eel theory."

Mark ignored him. "How big was this?"

"*Big*. Here..." She flipped to a picture where she had put her foot next to the track; her wading boot was dwarfed by it. "Over three feet long... maybe two feet across at the widest point."

"And whatever head this belongs to," Brady said, raising the tooth, "it's a whopper."

"So, fellas?" Annabelle raised her pint of stout and took her first sip. "You up for a monster hunt?"

"This is even better than I hoped," Hilda Morgan said when the video came to an end. The lights had been dimmed in the conference room and Reggie sat beside her, with Dhir and Yana sitting across the table from them. "*Far* better," Hilda added, a note of glee in her voice.

"Don't you mean worse?" Dhir asked.

Hilda rose from the conference table and straightened her suit coat. "In this particular instance... 'bad' is good." She tapped a file folder full of papers. "And thanks to the transcripts of the cleaned-up audio from Carson's jet... as well as the information we've gleaned from our people on the ground at the quarantine site... plus, some interviews from a few survivors of that fool's errand in the forest... we've got a good bit of 'bad' to work with."

Reggie appeared shaken. Although the video had been projected on the screen of the conference room wall display, he was staring at the laptop he had played it from. The final frame was a wash of static. "He... he was eating a rat. Like... a raw rat. It was still alive..."

"Yes, we all saw that, Reggie. In fact..." Hilda leaned over him and rewound the video to a point where the little drone camera was looking up at Carson, his face and hands covered in blood, a bitten-through rat carcass in his grip. She paused the image. "There's the money shot. I want a screencap of that to use in a PowerPoint presentation."

"He needs to pay for what he did to my sister!" Yana hissed. "We need to take all of this to the authorities."

"Oh, we will," Hilda said in a distant voice. "Eventually. But first things first." She turned toward the back of the darkened conference room. "Leo?"

"Yes, ma'am," came a quiet voice from a shadow in the corner.

"Gather the Board of Directors. Tomorrow morning, nine a.m. sharp. Penthouse conference room." She looked up at the grisly image frozen on the screen. "We're going to oust that lunatic. It's time for new leadership."

CHAPTER TWENTY

"This is the spot," Joseph announced. He crouched over a topographic map that was spread out on the ground, its four corners held down by a pair of rocks, the lead-lined mineral case, and the toe of one of Joseph's cowboy boots. The Wolf Wallace-branded compass lay on the edge of the map. "The camp where the geologists dug up the sphere should be at the top of that rise across the river."

Russ looked across the babbling waters of the West Fork Crooked River—really more of a creek—and up at the hillside above the opposite bank. He reached down and tapped the compass with a fingertip, then looked up at the position of the sun. The swag compass seemed to be working. "I think you're right."

"The GPS is down." Sarah held the portable device in one hand, thumbing some of the controls. "It was already a bit spotty when we left the Jeep back on the roadside a half mile back."

"Another indication we're in the right spot," Joseph said. "The DARPA perimeter likely extends past the geologists' camp... and we're inside their jamming radius." He swept a hand across a segment of the river. "If Farley's memory of where he threw the sphere was accurate, it would have come down somewhere over there."

"Well... let's get down to business." Russ unzipped the fanny pack he'd taken from Sharkey's camp supplies. He found the pair of Bud's headphones and put them on, then carefully extracted Jonah's dreamcatcher and put the hanging loop on his finger. Holding his arm level, he walked slowly toward the river.

Sarah found Sharkey's bag of earplugs and offered it to Joseph, who was folding up the topo map.

"No, thank you. I prefer to listen. But you can be our 'designated driver,' if you will. As long as one of us is protected, they can intervene if the other two come under the influence of the sphere."

Sarah plugged her ears and the two of them left their camping gear where it lay and joined Russ at the shoreline. He stood stock-still, arm extended, the dreamcatcher dangling from his index finger.

"I feel pretty darn silly, truth to tell."

Sarah removed one earplug. "Anything?"

"Don't think so. Wait..." The object moved ever so slightly. "Maybe..."

"No. The breeze picked up." Joseph reached out and bent Russ's arm at the elbow, bringing his hand close to his chest. Then he turned him ever so slightly. "The breeze is coming out of the east-southeast. Shield the dreamcatcher with your back."

With Russ in this new position, he waited for nearly five minutes while Joseph and Sarah searched the shoreline.

"Nothing," Joseph announced. He retrieved the mineral sample case. "Let's cross over to the north shore."

They waded across the knee-high water, then repeated their search on the opposite side. After several minutes, Sarah waved at everyone to gather.

"Look, Farley said he thought he heard a splash after he threw it, right? And the night everything went down, it was pouring rain.

This creek was probably twice this depth, and flowing hard. I suggest we head downstream."

Joseph nodded. "Agreed. We'll follow the river until the sun starts to set, then make camp."

Russ held up his finger with the dreamcatcher. "Joseph... you and your brother-in-law aren't punking me with this, are you? Your nephew said you were quite the prankster. And I'll feel pretty silly if this turns out to be gift shop gewgaw."

Joseph grinned but did not answer as he led the way back across the creek. The trio returned to the south shore and gathered up their supplies, then started down a trail that ran along the West Fork.

Sarah paused to look up at sloping, forested hills on the north side.

"You're thinking of our furry friends, aren't you?" Russ asked.

"Yes. When we parted, Brighteyes signed to me that they were heading north. I hope they're okay."

"I'm sure they're fine," Russ reassured her. "They had a good head start; they were long gone by the time all of the army guys and government types showed up."

"Sir! Over here!"

Colonel Dosset strode across the campsite to where a pair of men were examining something at the base of a tree. Their National Guard uniforms were crisp and clean and only one of them wore combat boots. His companion was wearing some basic hiking sneakers and held a Geiger counter, which was ticking away at a pace that indicated mild radiation.

As he approached, Dosset examined the tree; it didn't look like any tree he'd ever seen. Gnarled and twisted, it almost appeared to be in pain and exuded an oddly malevolent quality.

"What have you got?"

"Look here, sir." The boot-wearer pointed at an excavated area at the base of the tree; there was a cluster of roots that curved around an empty spherical space. Some of the roots had been cut.

"Something was in there. Something round." Dosset knelt down for a better look, but the sneaker-wearer put a hand on his arm—and just as quickly removed it, at the colonel's glare.

"Sorry, sir, it's just... I wouldn't get too close. I'm getting residual radiation readings."

"Dangerous levels?"

"I don't think so, sir... but it's not background radiation."

"The geologists that were affected... they dug something out of here," Dosset declared. He rose and looked down at a pickax and shovel that lay nearby. "I want samples taken of that tree, particularly the roots. Have those tools tested... they may have scraped against our mystery rock and picked up some material."

"Yes, sir."

"Tell him about the tent," Boots urged Sneakers.

"What about the tent?" Dosset asked.

"We found traces of radiation in there too. In the back of the tent... between the two sleeping bags."

Dosset was about to reply when his radio crackled to life. "Hobbit Hole to Gandalf. Priority call. I say again—"

Dosset cut the man off. "Go for Gandalf." God, he hated these call signs.

"Sir, voice recognition has ID'd the two men on the *Spook Stalkers'* camera video. The ones that picked it up after the attack... then later dropped it?"

"I remember. Tell me."

"Uh, sir... on an open line?"

"Jumping Jehosophat, Hobbit Hole, these radios are encrypted six ways to Sunday. Tell me now."

"Yes, sir. Russ Cloud and Joseph Washakie. They were survivalists and trackers with the expedition, sir."

"Washakie... wasn't that the Injun that burned the Bigfoot bodies before we got there?"

"Yes, sir."

"Where are they now?"

"They cleared quarantine in Grangeville yesterday morning."

"I want them taken into custody! Find them!"

"Found them!" Wolf shouted. "Back up! Back up!"

Merle braked, bringing the SUV skidding to a halt. Behind them, Ian managed not to rear-end them with his U-Haul truck. Normally, *Man vs. Nature* had its own cargo truck for hauling the ATVs and gear, but it hadn't been brought into Idaho yet.

Merle rolled down the window and signaled Ian to pull off to the side of the road, then he backed the SUV up until Wolf swatted him on the arm.

"There! In the trees on the north side."

"That's not Sharkey's truck," Merle said.

"Nae, but it *is* the Jeep that was parked at Sharkey's house beside the drive," Wolf said. "Athena... where did you lose their signal?"

"A quarter mile after they turned right at the fork in the road. About a half mile back from this point."

Wolf's posse had been roughly forty minutes behind Russ's crew when all of a sudden, the tracking signal became intermittent, then winked out. Athena thought jamming could be involved and was indignant when Merle suggested the tracking bug might have simply crapped out. The signal had been traveling at about forty miles per hour when they'd lost it. Fortunately, it hadn't died until *after* Russ had turned off the road through Orogrande; they knew they had come down the road they were currently on.

"Pull over next to the Jeep."

Merle did as he was told. Ian was standing beside the U-Haul just up the road.

"Bring the camera!" Wolf called out, then pointed at the pimply-faced intern, an eager fanboy they'd come across in Grangeville. "You! Um..."

"Keith."

"Keith, stay with the gear. Ian... let's roll some video."

When Ian was ready, Wolf walked over to the Jeep and placed a hand on the hood. He turned to face the camera. "Engine's cold."

Athena tried a door; it was unlocked. She ducked inside and did a quick search. "Nothing in here... so they probably have the tracker with them."

"Well, boss? Which way do ya think they went?" Merle asked.

While Wolf had begun his career as a bit of a charlatan, he was not without sign-spotting skills. It took him only moments to locate a few tracks. "Toward the river. This way."

At the edge of the creek-sized river, Merle and Athena joined Wolf by the shore. "They spent a fair bit of time here," he said, pointing out multiple prints in the soft ground beside the water. He squinted at the creek; it was shallow, and the late-afternoon sun was low enough in the sky that he could make out the bottom. He beckoned Ian over and pointed out what he'd spotted. "See here? And here? They crossed over."

The quartet sloshed across and after several minutes of searching, they returned to the south side of the creek. "Looks like they went west along the river." He took out a portable GPS device. "Let's see where they might... huh. Ian, cut." He slashed a hand across his throat, then handed the GPS to Athena. "What am I doin' wrong, lass?"

Athena frowned. "Nothing. But... it makes sense. My bugs that we put in the souvenir items use GPS signals, and the bug they had with them conked out in this area. I think I was right about the jamming. Probably from the military after that 'incident' with the Bigfoot."

"Well… nothin' to do but follow the river."

"What about the rest of the film crew?" Merle asked. "They should be in Idaho by now."

Wolf shook his head. Normally, they would film with three cameras. But if Russ could make do with one, so could he. "There's nae time! Let's get back to the road and have a talk with Ian and… um…"

Athena sighed. "Keith."

Fifteen minutes later, they had a plan: Wolf, Merle, Athena, and Ian would leave the SUV and follow the river on foot. Athena would keep an eye on the GPS; the jamming radius likely wasn't limitless. Once the signal was clear, she would check her tracker and try to get a bead on Russ and friends. Keith would take the U-Haul and travel along the road. It roughly paralleled the river, although it strayed quite far from it in parts.

"It'll be dark soon, so let's grab the camping gear and film equipment and get crackin'! Anything we'll need from the SUV, move it to the U-Haul." Wolf pointed at the intern. "*Keith* will shadow us with the ATVs and capture equipment."

"If we took the ATVs, we could catch up with them a lot quicker," Merle suggested.

Wolf shook his head. "They'd hear us coming a mile away. And any Bigfoot they may be tracking would hear us even sooner."

Brighteyes raised a hand, signaling the group to halt. He sniffed the air and listened intently. Turning back to DawnWaker and Littlefoot, he signaled without vocalization, 'Humans. And man-machines. East.'

'Yes. I hear,' DawnWaker agreed.

'Close?' Littlefoot asked.

'No. Far.' Brighteyes beckoned them closer and added soft vocalizations to enhance the meaning. 'We are passing by the edge of my troop's territory. Where the bad things happened. We will continue south. It will be dark soon.'

'Hungry,' Littlefoot signed.

'There is a small creek on the other side of the next ridge. We will fish.'

DawnWaker thumped her chest. '*I* will fish. I fish better.'

As the sun set on Payette Lake, Chris "Critch" Critchley finished affixing a Bucktail lure to his hook and eyed a chunk of pine tree that was floating nearby. Reaching back, he triggered the little tiller motor and repositioned himself closer to it. His quarry might use such a floating tree for cover, and he was going to need every advantage he could get.

Critch could catch trout in the lake till the cows came home, but tonight he was after more elusive prey: tiger muskie. He'd never caught one before. A sterile crossbreed of pike and muskellunge used to stock certain fisheries, the tiger was a voracious and aggressive predator. One of his buddies had managed to land one last night—an impressive three-footer—and had done so in the middle of the lake.

The fishing might be better over on nearby Little Payette Lake, but Critch's dock was on the peninsula of the main lake and he hated messing with the trailer. Payette Lake was nearly four hundred feet deep where his friend had caught it, but it was likely the muskie had been closer to the surface, chasing baitfish coming up from the depths. Open-water fishing could be an exercise in frustration, but Critch liked his chances tonight. With a clear sky a few days shy of a full moon, it would be a beautiful evening for fishing.

He strapped a headlamp to his head; there was enough waning light from the sunset that he wouldn't need it right away, but he didn't want to go hunting for it in the dark if a stray cloud decided to pay the moon a visit. Opening his cooler, he dug in the ice and grabbed a can of Keystone Light. Normally, he'd do his best to gradually replace the consumed beers with trout he caught, although a good-sized tiger muskie would likely leave little room for anything else.

Critch was about to close the lid but found himself staring into the cooler; he shuddered, remembering the previous night when he'd found himself taking a bite out of a raw fish. He'd tried sushi a few times in Boise, so the fresh trout wasn't all that bad... but he had no recollection of having made the decision to do it. *Probably one too many beers*, he thought as he closed the lid with a thump.

Popping the brewski, he took a long swig before placing it in a cupholder set into the corner of his seat. He grabbed his rod and reel and lined up his first cast of the evening.

Two hours and four beers later, with the moon casting a river of ghostly light across the surface of the water, Critch was thinking of packing it in. Not a single bite, not even a nibble. He was just about to drag out his phone to look at the picture of his buddy's catch—see if maybe the jokester had Photoshopped the fish or something—when all of a sudden, his line jerked taut and the rod bowed with a severe bend. He held on tight as the entire jon boat was spun around 180 degrees, then dragged for a good twenty yards.

"Hoo-ee!" Critch shouted. "Got a doozy!" It *had* to be a tiger; he'd never felt a strike like that before. He was about to start reeling his catch in when the line abruptly went slack. "Dagnabbit!" *Did I lose him?*

He risked removing a hand from the rod to flick on his headlamp, then started reeling in the slack. After a moment, the line went taut again and Critch grinned. "Still gotcha." He sat back and braced his feet against the forward bench, getting ready for the fight of his life... but there was no fight. The fish started to come up of its own accord. In moments, the moonlit waters were disturbed as something *enormous* breached the surface just feet from the boat.

Critch stared in disbelief as a massive head rose out of the water... and kept rising. The fishing line dangled from a mouth jam-packed with countless sharp teeth. The creature's head was balanced on a long neck that arced gracefully as it rose high in the air, the moon forming a halo behind it. A powerful stench emanated from the shape.

Good golly, Mike 'n' Molly... it's Sharlie! She's real!

The top of the beast's back, dark in the moonlight, floated at the surface, extending well beyond the reach of the headlamp, but Critch only noticed that in passing as his attention was drawn to the thing's mouth.

Sharlie's jaws opened and there was a *sound*. Not a monstrous roar or serpentine hiss... it was a hum. Or... several hums, blended together in a soothing chord. A beautiful sound. Critch's mouth dropped open as well, unwittingly mimicking the gaping maw above him.

The head reached its apex, high above the boat, and the line went taut again. Still gripping the rod, Critch let the pull of the line bring him to his feet as he stared up at the creature, basking in the tones emanating from above.

Sharlie's mouth yawned wider. This time the hum was joined by a menacing, throaty hiss, then the massive head shot forward and down in a split second, its gaping jaws completely engulfing Critch's head and shoulders. Massive conical teeth met... then passed each other... as the jaws snapped shut below the man's collarbone. Wrenching back into the air, Sharlie tore off the fisherman's head and a respectable chunk of his upper body. Swallowing her prize whole, Sharlie lined up for another strike. Critch's hook was still embedded in the creature's mouth, and the line and fishing pole swung gently in the night air. For her second bite, the Twilight Dragon of Payette Lake chose a leg.

CHAPTER TWENTY-ONE

The call came at three in the morning. Cameron Carson sat at his desk in his North Brother office, going through a slew of reports on an electronic tablet. One of the side benefits of no longer needing to sleep: He had a lot of extra time in the day. Ironically, one of the reports he'd been reading a few hours ago dealt with the effects of sleep deprivation on a person's sanity. That being said, as far as madness was concerned, he suspected a lack of sleep was small potatoes compared to the ongoing rants of The Other inside.

The phone rang again. Very few people had Carson's private cell number and even fewer would dare call him this late at night. He slid the phone closer and looked at the screen: Alan Dusk. Carson sighed—or simulated a sigh—as he debated answering. Alan was no doubt calling to rub his nose in his latest breakthrough or acquisition.

Billionaire Alan Dusk was nearly as rich as Carson and owned multiple high-tech companies. Referring to himself—loudly and often—as a "venture technologist," Dusk had his fingers in numerous technological pies. Carson tapped the screen and answered the call on speaker. "Alan, what an unexpected surprise. What time zone are you in, if I may ask?"

"Oh, sorry, Cameron, old pal, did I wake you?" Alan didn't sound the least bit sorry.

"No, not in the slightest... I'm burning the midnight oil. What's up?"

"Me!" Dusk snorted a laugh. "*Up*, that is. And as for time zones, let's see... I'd say I'm in... well, whatever it's called in Korea. No... make that Japan... now Guam..."

Carson rolled his eyes and reached over to the Tupperware container on the side of his desk, slipping a raw steak from inside and dropping it on a still-bloody plate. "I'll bite... where are you?"

"In the exosphere, Cameron, old buddy! My reusable space plane is a success. I've already tested the reentry and subsequent return to orbit. I just had to share this achievement with you!"

"How kind."

"And with this success, I can move forward with another project of interest to you... Project Daedalus."

"And that is?"

"Well, you remember your failed moonshot? The one that sent those poor astronauts hurtling toward the sun?"

"Venus, actually."

"Really? Well, I'll have my eggheads check with your eggheads for the exact trajectory... but I'll be sending a rescue mission to bring your astronauts home!"

Carson sank his teeth into the steak and tore off a chunk, chewing violently.

"Cameron? You there, old chum?"

Carson swallowed the meat morsel. "The astronauts have been dead for weeks, Alan."

"Yes, but I'm sure their families would appreciate getting their bodies back."

And I'm sure you'd enjoy the publicity... and the thrill of one-upping me, Carson thought. But he said, "That's very noble of you, Alan. Let me know what Maiden Industries can do to help."

"Actually, that reminds me... on the subject of Maiden Industries... I had another, more pressing reason to call you. A little birdie told me something that I felt you should know."

"Go on."

"Well... it may not surprise you that I have a few people keeping tabs on what you're up to... as I'm sure *you* do with my companies. After all, what's a little industrial espionage between friends?"

"Get to the point, Alan."

"Of course. After all, time appears to be of the essence. Were you aware that Hilda Morgan has called an emergency meeting of the board for nine o'clock tomorrow morning?"

Carson's hand clenched, squeezing the steak he held in a white-knuckled grip. He said nothing, beef juice dribbling on the plate.

"Listen, Cameron, old friend... I think she's gunning for you. And from one CEO to another... a Board of Directors should never be allowed to get above themselves. They are there to serve *us*! Shareholders be damned."

"On that... we agree," Carson growled.

"I better go... I'm nearing the next reentry window. Listen, Carson, once I'm back on terra firma, we should get together. Chew the fat."

Carson's grin spread across his face. "Capital idea, Alan. My chef has been doing some amazing things for me. I'd love to have you for dinner sometime."

Carson hung up and tore another hunk from the steak, chewing contemplatively. "Hilda, Hilda, Hilda... just what do you think you're doing?" he muttered through the meaty mouthful.

Oh, you know very well what that ladder-climbing bitch is doing... and what's more, you know what YOU have to do.

"The Board is in my pocket," Carson assured The Other.

All of them?

Carson thought through the roster; the board totaled seven, including Hilda. "Four are firm."

How "firm" do you think they'll be once Hilda shows them whatever her little spy dug up?

"I can charm my way through a vote—"

Maybe the "old you" could... but now? Who knows? Especially when they see THIS.

Suddenly, Carson's vision was replaced by a memory so real, it was as if the event were happening at that very moment. A half-eaten rat lay in his palms. Then he buried his face in it for another vicious bite before the real world returned with a flash. Carson found himself standing behind his desk.

That bitch got all of that on camera, Cameron. Oh, that's fun to say... camera Cameron camera Cameron. And who knows what else she filmed during her stay?

Carson lifted a paperweight globe of Earth from his desk. Clenching it in a vise grip, he squeezed, actually deforming its surface before the transparent acrylic gave up the ghost and cracked down the middle. He tossed the ruined tchotchke aside. "Hilda is going to call for a vote of no confidence and boot me from my own company," Carson growled.

No. She's not. Because we—

"—are not going to let her." Carson and The Other spoke of one accord.

Carson wiped the steak juice from his fingers on the napkin beside his plate, then retrieved his smartphone. He accessed an app entitled "Tunes," then tapped on a password-protected folder labeled "Golden Oldies." The phone's screen was replaced with a list of Maiden properties.

Carson had always been a hands-on CEO and liked to be able to check in on his minions from time to time. He was probably violating a few privacy laws, but the intelligence he gained was worth the risk of a slap on the financial wrist.

He selected Maiden HQ in Downtown Manhattan, then navigated to a backdoor interface that emulated the security control hub, segregated by floor. He selected "Penthouse." The top floor of Maiden HQ was split down the middle by an executive conference room; this was usually where the board held its meetings. Apart from a few smaller rooms, the remainder of the floor was devoted to two massive offices: Cameron Carson's... and Hilda Morgan's. Both offices had a small living area attached as well as a full bath. Hilda was a night owl and often continued to work long after Carson had gone home.

"And with such an important vote tomorrow..." Carson grinned and selected the feed for Hilda's office. Sure enough, she was there at her desk, typing away furiously. Her suit coat and tie were draped over a nearby chair and her tightly woven blond braids cascaded down the shoulders of a pressed dress shirt. As Cameron watched, the woman snickered and said something with a sneer on her face. Then she punched her forefinger into a key with finality, watching something on her screen. After a time, Hilda smiled and tented her fingers, then pressed the intercom button on her office landline phone and spoke. In short order, a tall man appeared at the periphery of the camera image: Leo. Just as Carson had his Bill, Hilda had her Leo. An idea began to form, one far more elegant than The Other could ever dream up.

Carson closed the app and crammed the remainder of the steak in his mouth, gnashing his teeth against the uncooked chunk as he called Singleton. He chewed and swallowed the raw meat as the phone rang twice before his assistant answered.

"Sir? Is everything all right?"

"No, Bill... we have a problem. Have my helicopter prepped. I want it on Field 41 on Randall's Island as soon as possible. Arrange for transport off North Brother and meet me at the docks in ten minutes."

Carson thumbed the call dead, then made his way down to the morgue to look in on an old friend.

The tender left the dock on North Brother Island, bound for nearby Randall's Island and its many ballfields. Even though he'd been dragged from the depths of sleep, Singleton managed to look dapper in a sport coat and slacks, although he hadn't yet tied his tie. Carson was dressed in his usual corporate attire: a thin-lapeled suit coat, no tie, and an untucked dress shirt that cost more than most people made in a month.

"The last time we used Randall's for an impromptu helipad, I was dealing with the blowback for weeks," Singleton groused.

"Closest option, Bill. Not my fault the city wouldn't let us have our own helipad on North Brother Island."

"Well, sir..."

"I know, I know... Rikers Island and LaGuardia are too close." At that moment, the silhouette of Carson's executive helicopter came into view, running lights blinking as it settled into the nearby ballfields.

"Cameron... what's going on?"

"A coup."

"What? Who?"

"Who do you think?"

Singleton was quiet for a while as the tender ate up the distance to the rocky shore of Randall's Island. Then he spoke, his voice strong despite a slight tremor. "What are you going to do?"

Rip her dreadlocked blond head from her shoulders and drink from the neck-fountain of blood, then gorge myself on her organs, one by one—

"I'm going to have a little chat with her," Carson said. "Change her mind."

Change her mind into nutrition, the inner voice cackled.

As the tender reached the bouldery shore, the skipper brought it as close as the shallows would allow. "Sorry, Mr. Carson... this is as close as I can get."

"Close enough." Carson rose, grabbed a duffel bag, and jumped over to the rocky shore with ease. He turned back to Singleton, who was trying to figure out how he could get across. Carson hadn't told Bill what had happened to Armand Gualtieri when Dhir and that interloper had gotten away. When he had returned, covered in blood, he'd explained to Bill that the security guard had swum after the departing boat, but then Carson had been overcome with hunger and devoured a possum—hence the blood-drenched clothes. Singleton had seemed disturbed by that explanation, so Carson wasn't about to involve him in what he had to do tonight.

"Bill, I need you to head back to North Brother. Man the fort, as they say. I'll call you with further instructions."

"Sir, please—"

But Carson was already running toward the helicopter. When he reached it, the pilot—Mason, Carson thought his name was—triggered the rear door. He was about to come aft and deploy the stairs, but Carson leaped up into the passenger cabin.

"Whoa! Guess we're in a hurry!" Mason said. "Where to?"

"Get out," Carson said. "I'm flying solo."

Carson's route was simple: cross over the ballfields to the Harlem River, then fly down the East River, passing over the Queensboro, Williamsburg, Manhattan, and Brooklyn Bridges. The Pier Six heliport was only four blocks away from Maiden HQ, and the company leased two of the fourteen pads on the double pier. But that wasn't where Carson was going.

On the final approach to the heliport, he turned off his transponder and diverted back upriver, then climbed sharply and set down on top of Maiden's skyscraper. While there was no large painted H atop the building, Carson had made sure that the roof had been sufficiently reinforced so that a helicopter could land there in case of emergencies. And in his mind, this situation qualified.

The rotors were still spinning down as he dropped to the roof and made his way to the access door to the stairway. Before stepping through, he brought up his personal security app and confirmed that the roof cameras were still offline; he'd disabled them on approach. One of the security guards on duty might come and check, but he doubted it. The outdoor cameras occasionally had weather-related issues, and at this late hour of the night, they'd likely wait for daylight to assess the outage.

Passing the main roof access, he made his way around it and slid between two massive ventilation units. There, at his feet, was a metal maintenance hatch; at least, that's what it was supposed to look like. He set down the duffel bag and brought up the security app again, triggering the lock remotely. There was a dull clunk and the hatch swung open ninety degrees, revealing metal rungs set into a shaft. Dim emergency lighting came on below.

Carson had always had a healthy amount of paranoia and had designed a means to access the roof directly from his office, much like the secret exit he'd had installed on North Brother—although that one had come back to bite him, allowing Hilda's spy to escape.

In fact, one of the tricks Dhir and his Hilda-spy friend had used on him, he now used himself. "Oh, the irony," he whispered as he put all cameras on the penthouse floor onto a loop, setting it to repeat the last hour of footage. His bit of digital sabotage had another level of trickery to it, employing artificial intelligence video generation to "smooth" the transition between real time and the loop.

Satisfied, he climbed down the rungs into a small chamber.

In the alcove next to the ladder shaft, he pressed a button on the side of a panel, eliciting a soft click. Pressing gently, Carson swung the panel open into his office. The access panel was set into the back of a full-length mirror, hinged on one side. He pushed it back against the wall, then made his way through the darkened room.

Carson's office was spacious and furnished with the usual CEO adornments: shelves filled with books and awards and mementos were flanked by priceless works of art. A massive desk—its polished surface spotless and uncluttered—dominated one side of the room, with seating for lesser mortals arranged opposite. Behind the desk, a floor-to-ceiling window of reinforced glass offered a view of the downtown Manhattan skyline.

Carson set the duffel bag down on the seventeenth-century Persian carpet and extracted a pair of leather gloves. As he pulled them on, he looked out the window; a few lights were on in some of the nearby skyscrapers. Banks, corporate law firms, hedge funds, tech companies... most of the offices in view pulsed with money. He wondered if anyone behind those lit windows was currently plotting the downfall of their CEO? Or whether anyone was plotting what he was about to do?

Doubtful.

Carson lifted the bag and exited his office. Crossing the small lobby, he paused by the open door to the penthouse conference room. He heard the rhythmic whir of a laser printer coming from inside. Hilda must be printing something remotely...

Perhaps... but smell the air, The Other suggested.

Carson inhaled, tasting the odors emanating from the room. Cleaning solutions and coffee were at the forefront, but there it was. Cologne... and underneath that, a hint of male musk. Carson entered the room and turned to his right, where the corner console tables held several printers and copiers.

"Hello, Leo."

The big man jerked in surprise, turning away from the printer that was currently spitting out page after page. Dressed in a navy suit, Leo had loosened his tie from around his thick neck. "Mr. Carson!"

Carson set down his bag. "Working late?"

Leo appeared to be working up an explanation, but then realization—and fear—arose in his eyes. He'd probably read all of the reports that the spy had brought them. "What... what are you doing here?"

"I heard tell there was going to be a meeting this morning. Figured I'd get a jump on things. You know me, Leo... I've always been 'hands-on.'"

"Look, Mr. Carson—"

"I'm sorry, but I'm afraid I'm on the clock and don't have time to chat. Your boss didn't leave me a lot of wiggle room. But you being here, close at hand... that'll make things a teensy bit easier."

"What do y—"

With blinding speed, Carson's hands shot forward, one hand gripping Leo's chin, the other grabbing the back of his head. Jerking savagely, Carson twisted the man's head around nearly 180 degrees with a sickening crack. Like a puppet with his strings cut, Leo collapsed to the floor in a limp-limbed heap.

"Consider that your severance package."

Yes... yessss... now, we feast!

"Not *this* one, my friend. We need him relatively intact."

Just a finger...?

"No! I need to avoid any evidence in the conference room." Carson saw that blood was bubbling out of the man's mouth. Swiftly, he turned Leo's face upright, then grabbed several stacks of collated copies from whatever Hilda had been printing and spread them out under the man's head. "I'll be back before that soaks through," he told the corpse. "Don't go anywhere."

Once more lifting the duffel bag, he exited the conference room and went to Hilda's office. The door was unlocked. Without hesitation, he entered, then closed the door behind him.

Hilda Morgan sat at her desk, eyes on her laptop. "Leo, did you print all twelve copies? I want extras available for some of the department heads."

"I believe he's only printed four or five thus far."

Hilda's wide-eyed face shot up from her laptop, a cascade of blond braids jumping off her shoulders.

"Although I applaud your ambition, Hilda... if there's one thing I value most in an employee... it's loyalty."

The look of surprise on her face was quickly masked. She replied calmy, "I *am* loyal, Cameron. To the shareholders. In the end, *they* are my boss. Yours too."

"Perhaps in spirit... but not in practice."

"So... someone told you about the vote. Who squawked?"

"No idea. I heard it secondhand. And they only told me that you'd called for an emergency meeting of the Board. They didn't actually say anything about a vote."

Carson came closer and held his arm out, releasing the duffel bag above a glass coffee table, where it landed with a thump. Hilda's eyes followed it.

"So, this... *vote*. What vote would that be, Hilda? A stock split? A pay raise for yourself? New board members?"

Hilda glared at him. "You'll find out at nine o'clock."

Carson affected a petulant whine. "But I want to know *now*. Mama Carson always said I was never any good at waiting for something I wanted. Christmas morning, I'd sneak down to the tree while it was still pitch dark out... and *rip* those presents open."

As he finished that sentence, he leaned on the edge of her desk and grinned at her.

"You know very well that it's a vote of no confidence," she said, her voice betraying the slightest tremor.

"I dunno, Hildy... I'm feeling pretty damn confident."

"You have squandered our company's resources on your childish escapades. Half of your expedition into the woods of Idaho *died* because of your incompetence. And... and I have footage of you eating a live rat."

"Don't knock it till you try it... after all, they eat guinea pigs in the Andes. And from one New York resident to another... I think the city might benefit, adding rat to the menu." Carson put a hand to his chest, miming clutching his pearls. "Or are you offended because you're a vegetarian?"

"You are unfit to continue in your capacity as CEO. *I* know it. *You* know it. And after the meeting, *everyone* will know it."

Carson flashed his pearly whites. "You say that, but..." He pushed off from her desk, went to the coffee table, and opened the duffel bag with a long, slow *z-z-z-z-i-p.*

"What's in the bag?"

"I'm tempted to say 'a bribe,' but we both know that even a bag this large wouldn't hold enough money to dissuade you. But *this* might."

He extracted a fire axe from the duffel. Hilda stiffened and her right hand crept to the side.

"Hands on the desk, Hildy dear." Carson hefted the axe, looking at it quizzically. "Spotted this in a stairwell at the North Brother complex. Didn't realize these were actually a thing; always seemed like a Hollywood invention."

"What are you going to do?" Hilda whispered.

Carson took two casual steps closer. "If you're worried I'm about to launch into that whole 'Here's Johnny' shtick, don't you worry your pretty little head. I'm all about the shortest route to the desired outcome." He grinned ear to ear and spoke through clenched teeth. "I'm just going to split your skull down the middle like a ripe pumpkin."

Carson raised the axe, but suddenly a voice came from the adjoining living area.

"Ms. Morgan? Is that Leo? If the Wi-Fi printer is on the fritz again, I can fix it."

A rumpled, doughy man shuffled into view in the doorway to the back room, rubbing sleep from his eyes. Carson didn't recognize him, but the disheveled individual exuded "tech geek" vibes. When he saw Carson, he froze, confusion and alarm on his face.

"Mr. Carson!?"

Carson flashed a lopsided grin. "In the flesh."

"Reggie, call security!"

The techie's eyes shot to the door to the hall, then he took off around the far side of Hilda's desk. As Carson moved to intercept him, he spotted movement out of the corner of his eye as Hilda went for a desk drawer. Carson reached Reggie in two strides and grabbed him by the back of his belt, halting his escape. He dropped the axe and seized the man by the collar with his other hand. Lifting Reggie off the ground, he hurled him into a wall of bookshelves. The impact sent books and knickknacks flying and the man slumped to the ground, appearing incapacitated.

"Now... where were we?"

Hilda answered the rhetorical question by raising a snub-nosed revolver, a look of determination on her face. "Hands where I can see them."

Carson advanced slowly, hands open and held out to his sides. "A week ago, I'd have been quite concerned, looking down the barrel of a gun."

Hilda reached for the intercom and Carson's hand shot forward and ripped it free of the desk. Hilda responded to the sudden movement by squeezing the trigger twice. The revolver roared and Carson felt something push against his chest. He dipped his chin and looked down at a pair of holes in his shirt; two small red stains spread between the buttons.

"Nice grouping."

"You left me no choice!" Hilda said with finality. It sounded like she thought this was over.

"That's *my* line," Carson purred, looking up at her from under his brow.

Hilda's eyes widened. She brought the gun up again, but Carson snatched it from her hand before she could fire a third shot.

"That's quite enough of that." He tossed it aside.

Hilda snatched a letter opener from the desk and took a stab at Carson, but he grabbed her wrist with uncanny speed, then gripped her throat with his other hand. Lifting the tall woman off the ground, he slammed her down on her desk, hard enough that he heard ribs crack. She gasped, the air driven from her lungs.

Carson looked at his dress shirt. "What a mess." He unbuttoned several buttons and opened the shirt to reveal the wounds. "I'd rather not leave any of my blood in your office, so...let's try an experiment, shall we?"

He cleared his mind and concentrated. What Doctors Schneider and Takagawa had told him—had *showed* him—about his blood had stuck with him. It seemed to behave like a living thing. So perhaps... he could control it. He focused on the blood in the wounds, and in moments the blood seemed to congeal and retreat into the holes.

"Nifty."

Hilda rasped in a shaky breath and managed to find her phone. Carson plucked it from her fingers and pocketed it.

"What *are* you?" she managed to wheeze.

"That's the billion-dollar question," Carson said, retrieving the fire axe from the floor and strolling back to Hilda. "I suppose 'zombie billionaire' might come close. Although, I confess I haven't taken up the practice of eating brains. But you know what they say." He raised the axe high above his head. "There's a first time for everything."

CHAPTER TWENTY-TWO

At five in the morning, Carson landed the helicopter at Maiden's Westchester helipad. In the waning darkness, he spotted the black Range Rover in the adjoining lot, Singleton standing beside it. He texted his assistant: *Stay by the car. Be there in five.*

Carson shut down the engines and gave the interior a last look. There was nothing overt that he could see; nevertheless, a proper cleanup would be advisable, likely requiring a call to an "outside expert" along with a substantial payment. Overall, though, Carson was pleased. The Other, however...

You should have consumed them, Cameron! Eaten the evidence!

"I've already explained this to you a thousand times, now shut the hell up. I'll make it up to you later." Carson slammed shut the door to the mental cage. He would need to be sharp.

He stripped himself naked. He'd managed to reabsorb all of his own blood from the bullet wounds. In addition to being somewhat animated, as an added benefit, his blood appeared to be denser now; there had been no discernible spatter from the impact of the rounds back in Hilda's office. Unfortunately, he'd had quite a bit of the traitor's blood on him. He crammed the bloodied clothes into the overstuffed duffel, then stripped off his gloves and added them as well.

Carefully removing the change of clothes he'd brought from his office, he dressed in slacks, a dark blue dress shirt, and a pair of brushed-leather oxfords. Grabbing the duffel bag, he jumped down before turning back and sealing the helicopter. Striding across the pad, he waved to Singleton.

"Good morning, Bill! Thanks for the pickup."

Singleton looked at him closely as he approached. He would see nothing out of the ordinary. He reached for the duffel, but Carson held it away from his grasp.

"I'll hang on to this. No one touches that helicopter without my authorization."

"Sir... Ms. Morgan... were you able to reason with her?"

Carson worked his jaw for a moment, then smiled. "Alas, I was unable to locate her. So, we have to assume she'll be making her move to oust me. I'll explain later. Right now, we need to get back to North Brother." Carson climbed into the back of the SUV, setting the duffel on the seat beside him. As Singleton left the Maiden Aviation complex, bound for Maiden's pier in Hunts Point, Carson replayed his busy night.

After he'd buried the fire axe into the crown of Hilda's head, Carson had acted quickly. First, he'd revived the hapless techie he'd hurled into the bookcase. Okay, that wasn't true. *First*, he succumbed to Hollywood tropes and helped himself to a handful of brains from Hilda's newly renovated, easy-access skull. The flavor was... interesting. Honestly, he didn't see what all the fuss was about; muscle and fat were far more delectable. Once he'd satisfied his morbid curiosity, *then* he sat the nerd down for a little chinwag.

Reggie had been a busy boy... bugging Carson's executive jet and arranging for additional listening devices to be placed in Grangeville. He had also provided Hilda's spy with the gadgets necessary to breach security and gather data at the North Brother facility. He identified the woman as Yana Volkov, a Russian expat and sister to Katya Volkov, who was currently occupying a slab in that facility.

Fortunately, Reggie was a centralized-hub control freak and had access to all of the recordings and accumulated data in all of their uploaded locations. Even more fortuitous, he was amenable to a simple carrot-and-stick offer: the carrot was working for Carson with a seven-figure salary; the stick was to be eaten alive, limbs first.

Carson watched as Reggie wiped every single megabyte of incriminating evidence from every location it had been uploaded to. He even had Yana Volkov's laptop in his possession, which was an unexpected bonus. And, as it turned out—hackers gonna hack—Reggie had hacked into Hilda's own laptop. After providing Carson with unfettered access to the traitor's laptop as well as Reggie's and Yana's, Carson had asked the techie if there was anything else he should know. Reggie replied that every scrap of evidence had been deleted. Carson thanked the man and killed him. Once more, he used the fire axe. To his credit, he did it quickly and cleanly, and despite the protestations of The Other, he didn't take a single nibble of the plump young man.

At this stage, he removed four body bags from the duffel; he'd brought more than that, as he had no idea if he would encounter security—or Yana or Dhir, two loose ends he would later need to account for. He quickly bagged Hilda and Reggie, then crossed the lobby to the conference room with the two remaining bags.

The blood that had been seeping from Leo's mouth had burbled to a conclusion and had only reached about page forty-seven in the "placemat" of reports that Carson had stuck under the man's head. Carson opened the two body bags on the floor and carefully placed Leo into one. Next, he gathered every single printout—bloody or otherwise—and dumped them into the other bag; for good measure, he unplugged the printer and put it in as well.

He zipped the two bags closed, then dragged them into the penthouse lobby. Leaving the one with reports behind, he brought Leo into Hilda's office, zipping his bag back open. Gingerly, he retrieved the axe in his gloved hands and pressed Leo's cold, dead fingertips into the handle in a number of places, then placed the axe into Hilda's body bag. On a whim, he tracked down the letter opener Hilda had tried to stab him with. He gripped it firmly in his gloved hands and stabbed Leo in his right pectoral, careful not to bury the blade too deeply; wouldn't want a gout of blood at this point. He dropped the letter opener on the floor behind Hilda's desk.

Inspired, he now took Leo's phone from his pocket, accessed it with the dead man's thumb print, opened his contacts, found Hilda, and texted her. He kept it simple. *You bitch! You'll pay.* In his pocket, he felt Hilda's phone buzz. He checked it and stifled a giggle. He was about to use Hilda's thumb or face to unlock hers but realized he was overcomplicating things. Instead, he powered both of their phones down and pocketed them.

Next, he zipped the bags closed and brought all three corpses and the bag of reports to his office, leaving them in the hall outside the door.

Finally, he returned to Hilda's office. He located her revolver and put it into the duffel along with her powered-down laptop. In the living quarters, he gathered up every bit of Reggie's electronics he could find as well as Yana's laptop and powered them all down as well. Returning to Hilda's main office, he looked at the destruction around the bookshelves and the blood dripping off the side of her desk. There were definitely signs of a struggle. *Poor Leo... the stress of working for Hilda must have gotten to him.* Satisfied, he locked the door to Hilda's office, took off his shoes and put them in the duffel, then returned to his own office.

Carson brought the body bags up to the helicopter, one at a time, then returned for the duffel. Catching sight of himself in the full-length mirror that concealed the access shaft, he halted at the grisly sight. He knew better than to clean up here and grabbed an unbloodied pair of shoes and a change of clothes from the living quarters to bring with him.

Up on the roof, he revisited his clandestine security app and returned all of the penthouse-level cameras to a live feed, with the exception of the one in Hilda's office. There she was, hard at work at her desk. He left that feed on the loop and climbed into the helicopter. Once he had taken off and dropped down to the river, he reactivated the rooftop cameras. Satisfied, he increased speed and headed south.

Twenty minutes later, Carson flew over the Verrazano Bridge. As he passed beyond the massive span, he tossed all three smartphones out the window. The devices might have all sorts of interesting information on them, but the first thing the authorities were likely to do was track them. They were all powered down, but it didn't hurt to be careful. That step complete, he continued past The Narrows to the edge of the bay that led to the Atlantic Ocean. Descending toward the water, he consulted his GPS and steered toward Swinburne Island, a tiny uninhabited spot of land that was once used to quarantine infected immigrants from Ellis Island. Like North Brother, it was also a bird sanctuary dotted with the remains of ruined buildings. Carson had once debated purchasing this man-made island and had even toured it; he remembered a large, flat concrete slab foundation, just the right size for an impromptu helipad. He triggered the helo's searchlight when he was over the island and located the spot.

Setting down, he got to work. With Leo still in the helicopter, Reggie and Hilda were dumped unceremoniously into the collapsed ruins of one of the old hospitals, then Carson set the axe down beside Hilda. This island was off-limits to the public and so choked with bird feces and unsafe structures that even the most adventurous would be unlikely to stumble upon them until they were nothing but skeletons. And if they *were* discovered, so too would an axe with Leo's fingerprints on it.

The hardest part of this whole endeavor had occurred here, with The Other insisting that the best way to clean up after this crime would be to consume the evidence right here and now. But Carson had crammed it back into its mental cage, knowing that if his helicopter had been spotted, he dared not linger here too long.

Before departing, Carson hefted the bulky printer and hurled it into the water on the south side of the island, where either it would sink or the tides would carry it out to sea. The body bag filled with reports went into the duffel alongside the revolver and laptops, and the two empty body bags were folded up and stuffed in on top.

Back at the helicopter, Carson freed Leo, stuffed his body bag into the duffel with the others, then belted the bag into one of the seats. Dragging Leo toward the cabin door, he positioned the body so that its knees were just at the frame, the lower legs and feet dangling out. Leaving the door open, Carson took off, careful not to bank the helicopter. Not yet. When the Verrazano Bridge came into sight he banked to the left and felt a slight lifting sensation as the helicopter lost 220 pounds of Leo.

Carson triggered the cabin door to close, then flew north. He would take the helicopter to Maiden Aviation's Westchester complex, where it could remain idle and untouched for as long as was required.

"Sir? We're here."

Carson blinked, disoriented as he came back to the present. "Where is here?"

"North Brother."

Carson frowned. "We already drove to Hunts Point?"

"And boarded the tender and drove across to the island. You were... not yourself."

"I... I didn't do anything to hurt you, did I?"

"No, sir."

"Did I... say anything?"

"Very few actual words, sir. Though I distinctly heard 'You should have let me,' several times."

Carson knew what that was about... his inner friend was upset he hadn't eaten his fill. "Listen, Bill... I need to get my hands on that meteorite or whatever it is. Are we still in contact with our CDC mole in Grangeville? Or did we lose that communication when Dhir betrayed us?"

"I terminated the encrypted connection Mr. Patel set up, sir. But we have Maiden personnel on-site there; I'm sure we can contact him."

"Good. Get it done. And we may need to return to Idaho on short notice. Has my jet been...?"

"I brought in an outside expert. The jet has been thoroughly cleaned and we believe we've found all the listening devices."

"How many did they find?"

"Three."

That's all of them, Carson thought. With the threat of imminent death hovering over him, Reggie had been very forthcoming. "Have the jet prepped and standing by. And scare up another tech for me. Someone who's good with computers."

"And what about this Manhattan meeting, sir?"

"We'll take the high-speed tender. I just need to grab a bite to eat and spruce up a little bit. I'll call you when I'm ready to go. In the meantime, why don't you get a half hour of sleep."

'Tired,' Littlefoot complained from atop Brighteyes's shoulders. 'It full dark. Sleep now?'

DawnWaker grunted her agreement with the little one's suggestion.

When they had reached the creek some hours ago, Brighteyes had intended to stop for the night after they'd eaten their fill of fish and berries, but the sounds of man and man-machine had continued. The noises were far away, but he had decided they should push on until the sounds of the night forest were all he could hear. He had picked up the pace from their afternoon travels; the trio loped through the darkness, relying on the moonlight filtering down through the trees.

'Soon,' he grunted back. He pointed ahead. 'One more ridge, then rest.'

"Rise and shine."

Russ started from a deep sleep, Sarah awakening too with a sharp intake of breath. The entry panel was zipped shut, but a flashlight lens was pressed up against the tent, shining down on them. Russ sat up in his sleeping bag. "What time is it?"

"Just after four," Joseph's voice replied. "I want to be on the move before the sun rises."

"Early bird gets the worm?"

"Coffee in five." The flashlight clicked off and it was pitch black again, except for the diffuse glow through the tent wall of last night's campfire that Joseph must have restarted.

As the Shoshone's boots crunched away from the tent, Russ leaned over to Sarah and spoke with a husky voice. "Should I ask him for fifteen?"

Sarah shoved his face away from hers. "Not with that breath."

Five minutes later, Russ and Sarah joined Joseph by the campfire. The Shoshone was sitting cross-legged with the dreamcatcher dangling from thumb and forefinger.

"Anything?" Sarah asked as she sat beside him and retrieved the percolator pot of coffee.

"No. But I want to rely more on this 'Stone that Sleeps.' Increase our pace. We will take turns—one of us wearing ear protection at all times—just in case we stumble across the meteorite. I feel certain it moved along the waterways during the period of heavy runoff. Every five minutes we will stop and use the dreamcatcher."

Russ cleared his throat and scuffed his boot along the ground. "Um... I hate to be the doubting Thomas here, but... how do we know that thing even works? I know your brother-in-law found that Stone that Sleeps at that special place, but... sometimes a rock is just a rock."

Joseph poked at the fire. "I confess we are putting a lot of faith in a legend, but I believe it is as Jonah claimed. To me... it *feels* like more than just another rock. I ask that you have faith that it will work when our quarry is close."

"Fair enough," Russ said. "Not like we have a choice at this point." He held out an enamel camping mug when Sarah offered the coffeepot. He took a sip. "So, what's for breakfast?"

"Whatever you decide to cook," Joseph replied. "I made the coffee."

"Who has the coffee?" Annabelle asked as she slammed the door of her truck. It was just after five in the morning, although it felt much earlier. Not surprising. McCall was inside the part of Idaho that had declared itself Mountain Standard Time and jutted out to the west like an interloper on Pacific Standard. Just to their north, it was still four a.m. But the sun didn't know that.

"Step right up, Graybill. Barista Brady has you covered. Got the beans from North Fork Roasters." Brady lifted one thermos from a cluster of three in the flatbed of his pickup. "And Stuart brought bacon-and-egg sandwiches. Got some OJ in the cooler too."

Annabelle joined Brady and Stuart at the back of the truck. "Where are Mark and Kevin?"

"They're bringing up the boat from Mile High," Stuart answered. "The marina mechanic just got around to fixing Kevin's motor after our last outing. I guess the guy is swamped, trying to get some of the older boats in shape for Mayor Vance's boat parade."

Brady gave a derisive snort. "Vancefest. What a douchebag. I tried to get him to call it 'Sharliefest.' Seemed like a no-brainer, right? But nooooo... it's all about him."

Annabelle grabbed a coffee cup from a sleeve of them and poured herself some joe. She took a sip of the paint-peelingly strong brew and sighed as she looked out at the dark water. Stuart lived in a small cabin nearby, so they'd chosen this pair of public docks north of town. At the moment, they had the parking lot all to themselves; not surprising, as this area was fairly quiet, accessible only from Easy Does It, a road that doubled as a ski trail once the snows came. The whole of Payette Lake would freeze over in winter, and this summer playground would become a winter wonderland.

"So, what kind of gear have the world-famous Sharlie Hunters brought for our hunt?" Annabelle asked.

Brady gestured to several bags and storage boxes that were in the truck bed beyond the impromptu breakfast bar. "We've got the usual: binoculars, camera with a telephoto lens, a decent video recorder. We have a camera drone, but the battery's a bit iffy. Don't want to risk it over water, but maybe along the shore. Brought a night vision scope, too, but that won't be much use if the boat doesn't get here soon."

"Kev finally got that stronger fish-finder he'd been looking at," Stuart said. "The mechanic hooked up the new transducer while he was working on the engine. It's got better low-frequency ultra-sound, so we can scan a lot deeper."

"Sounds great. And I brought a couple things too."

Annabelle walked to her Forest Service truck and retrieved a long bag, which she set on the tailgate. She unzipped it and took out a rifle that looked like a cross between a sci-fi blaster and an Airsoft gun.

"Tranquilizers?" Stuart surmised.

"Yep. And I borrowed a few of the darts we use on bears. But if that's not enough… I've got Gertrude." She lifted the other occupant from the gun bag, a bolt-action hunting rifle she'd inherited from her dad.

The rumble of an approaching boat brought their attention to the water. Annabelle put her weapons back in the bag and pounded the rest of her coffee. From the south, a spotlight came around the bend.

"There they are." Brady grabbed some of the equipment and headed down to the dock.

Given that the Sharlie Hunters had always been more of a social club than a crack team of hardened adventurers, the boat they preferred to use on their outings was the one currently trundling their way: a spacious pontoon boat with plenty of room for the gang, a few coolers of beers and snacks, and maybe a dog or two. In fact, it appeared that Mark had brought his dog along this morning. Cilantro—"Silly" for short—panted excitedly from a bench seat at the bow, a doggie life vest snugged onto her body with a little handle on top. If she fell in, Mark could pluck her from the water like a briefcase. A Chihuahua-beagle, Cilantro had fairly short legs and wasn't the best of swimmers. The half-breed was known as a "Cheagle," but most of the gang insisted on "Be-huahua."

Annabelle brought her gun bag down to the dock and helped tie the boat up. She chuckled at the name Kevin had stenciled on the side: *Slimy Slim*. That sobriquet was one of the lesser-known nicknames for Sharlie. And from a small flagpole above the canopy frame, a flag fluttered, its faded surface bearing a stylized sea serpent with three humps and "Sharlie Hunters" in big letters above. "Payette Lake, McCall, Idaho" lay below the artwork, in a smaller font.

"All aboard who's coming aboard!" Kevin called out.

Once everyone had transferred their gear and food to the boat and climbed aboard, the *Slimy Slim* slipped away from the dock and motored north.

"Come on, let's get cracking," Wolf Wallace urged. "Who knows how far ahead Russ and his mates are by now."

"We gotta eat something first; I'm starving." Merle stretched... then immediately winced and froze. "Damn, I shoulda brought better padding. My back is killin' me."

Wolf thumped his chest. "A night on the ground is good for your soul, boyo." He, of course, had slept on an air mattress—one that he was careful to deflate, roll up, and stash before exiting his tent.

"What's the rush?" Athena asked. "Sunrise isn't for a while, and you need light to track them, don't you? We're still inside that GPS dead zone, so I can't pick up their signal yet."

"How much longer till we're free 'n' clear of the interference, lass?"

"Oh, I dunno... should we call up the military and ask them what their jamming radius is?"

"Point taken. All right, let's have a decent breakfast. Soon as we have the light, we'll get back on their trail."

CHAPTER TWENTY-THREE

As the Maiden high-speed tender skimmed down the East River, Carson beckoned to Singleton to join him in a corner of the cabin. The two guards that Carson had insisted on bringing along started to follow, but he held up a hand.

"Sensitive information, boys. Stay where you are for now." He started aft and took a seat on a corner bench. Singleton sat nearby, but not *too* close. "Don't worry, Bill… if I get riled up, my babysitters can rush over here and zap me with Tasers in no time. And you have that special concoction that Dr. Schneider worked up, yes?"

"I do, sir." He patted his suit's left breast. "I made sure each of our escorts has one as well."

"Ever prudent, Bill."

When every sedative she tried had had no effect, Schneider had suggested that they approach the problem another way. Carson no longer appeared to sleep, and loss of consciousness also seemed to be off the table. Instead, she'd worked up a powerful paralytic. This muscle relaxant was at a strong enough dosage that it could never be used on a human; it would shut down the lungs and heart. But neither of those issues applied in Carson's case at the moment, so this paralytic might at least lock up the muscles in his arms and legs. And jaws. And in a similar vein, the stun guns the men carried might cause his muscles to lock up long enough for one of them to administer the shot.

"Our man in Grangeville... any news?"

"He hasn't heard anything about Russ, Joseph, or Sarah since they left quarantine. Two other members of the expedition, Liz Torres and Bud Sorenson, are in the hospital in downtown Grangeville."

Carson frowned. "What for?"

"Mr. Sorenson broke his leg quite badly when he was attacked by the female Sasquatch. I'm not sure why Ms. Torres is there."

"And the sphere?"

"It sounds like DARPA is looking for something that may have radiated an emission that turned the geologists into the, um... the 'patient zero zombies' that bit the Sasquatch. But he hasn't heard any talk of a 'sphere' other than what he overheard from Sarah and the others."

Carson nodded. "So, only 'Joseph and friends' know of it. Is the jet ready?"

"Yes, sir."

"Good. Well, first things first. Hilda called an emergency meeting of the Board. That's why we're hustling down to Maiden HQ. A vote of no confidence is in the offing, if I'm not mistaken."

Singleton sighed. "I... suspected that might be the case."

"Not to worry, Bill. I'm fairly sure I can get them to see it my way." *And if not...* Carson silenced the inner voice and grinned. "Time to put my game face on. But first... I have one last thing to take care of."

He rose and went outside to the stern to place a call. "Dr. Schneider? It's Cameron. I've got something to attend to in Manhattan, but I'll be back by around noonish. No, no, everything is fine... and yes, my 'handlers' are coming with me. Listen... all those blood samples you've taken from me, how much have you got? A pint? Two?" He listened for a moment. "Good. More than enough. Here's what I want you to do."

"What do we do?" Kevin asked.

"Let's stay in the boat," Annabelle replied, her eyes straying to the gun bag that lay on the deck by the portside bench. She raised a pair of binoculars and tried to steady them against the rocking of the boat.

It was just past sunrise and the *Slimy Slim* was idling off the shoreline a mile south of North Beach. The eastern shore of Payette Lake was less developed than the west, and the Sharlie Hunters had decided to search along it as they made their way north to The Meanders, where Annabelle had found the deer carcass. And now... they'd found a different carcass. Far larger than a deer.

"Moose," Mark said with authority.

"What gave it away? The Bullwinkle antlers?" Brady snarked.

"No... it was the resemblance to your mom."

"Boys, boys, you're both pretty," Annabelle mumbled, examining the shore near the kill. *Kill* certainly seemed the appropriate word. While a full-grown moose might have expired of old age and been descended upon by a pack of wolves, this looked too fresh, and there was far too much carnage. The distinctive antlers were one of the few recognizable parts of the animal left. Annabelle braced her elbows on the grab rail to steady the binos, then scanned the shore to the left and right of the hapless moose.

"What are you looking for?" Mark asked.

"Tracks. Either wolf, cougar, or... 'other.' Kev, can you bring us in a little closer?"

"Not much. It's pretty shallow. Stu, gimme an eyeball on the bottom?"

Stuart took up station at the bow as Kevin nudged the throttle forward. As they drifted closer, Cilantro began to growl. Closer still and the growl became a whimper, then the dog retreated between Mark's legs.

"You smell that?" Brady asked.

Stuart wrinkled his nose. "Whew! Not a good smell."

"The dead deer smell like that, Graybill?" Brady asked.

"Yeah, but not nearly this strong. And I was right next to it that day, but we're still ten yards out."

"Hold up." Stuart held up a hand and Kevin reversed the engines. "Too shallow up ahead." Then he rose, squinting down at the water. "Hang on. Hold right here if you can, Kev." He went through the pontoon's bow gate and knelt on the platform. "There's a deep gouge in the sediment leading to shore! Like something big was dragging along the bottom!"

"Let's get some pictures," Brady said, going to one of the gear boxes.

Just then, Annabelle's smartphone rang. She set down the binoculars on the bench and looked at the screen. She answered when she saw it was her boss at the Rangers HQ in McCall. "Hey, Chief, I was about to call you. Just found a moose carcass on the eastern shore." She listened a moment. "Okay. We'll head there right away."

"Head where?" Kevin asked when she hung up.

"Back through the narrows to the middle of the main part of the lake. I'll explain on the way."

Payette Lake was just over six miles long from its northeast shore at North Beach to its southwest shore in downtown McCall. The lake was split into two parts by the Ponderosa State Park peninsula, with the largest—and deepest—part of the lake on the western side of that spit of land. That part of Payette Lake was a mile and a half across at its widest point.

As Kevin brought the *Slimy Slim* back around the peninsula, Annabelle explained what her boss wanted her to check out.

"There's a boat adrift in the middle of the lake. A fisherman called it in. Said it looked like Critch's jon boat."

"That's weird," Mark said. "He usually fishes up north."

"Might've broken loose from shore," Stuart suggested. "Current runs north to south. He lives alone, not far from me. I'll give him a call." After a while, Stuart said, "Voicemail," then continued to speak. "Hey, Critch, it's Stuart. You lose a boat? Call me when you get this."

"There it is," Annabelle said, pointing ahead. The small boat was clearly unoccupied, bobbing in the light chop.

Kevin maneuvered slightly to bring them downwind of it, then waved Stuart over. "Stu, grab a line from the cubby under the starboard bench. We can lash her to the side and bring her to the dock Critch uses."

Cilantro abruptly stiffened, hackles raised, then dashed to the bow gate and sniffed the air. A growl rose in her throat and she began barking.

"Easy, Silly." Mark took hold of the handle on the cheagle's life jacket. "It's just a bo—"

He halted mid-speech as they came up on Critch's boat. Cilantro's barks segued into whines; she pulled free of her master's grip and retreated aft.

Annabelle stepped up beside Mark. "Oh my God..."

The interior of the jon boat was awash with blood.

"Hope I'm not too late." Carson, dressed in business casual, strolled into the penthouse conference room at a minute past nine. "I stopped for some bagels. Emergency board meetings always leave me famished."

Four men and two women lined the sides of the conference

table, shock and surprise on their faces. Carson reached back toward Singleton and took a large paper bag from him, then set it in the center of the table. "I got a mixed dozen with a few spreads. Rumor has it, the scallion schmear is to die for."

Mr. Reese, one of the oldest men in the room, cleared his throat nervously. "Mr. Carson... we, er... we were unaware..."

"That I would be attending?" Carson supplied as he went to the head of the table and pulled out the chair. "Why? Was this gathering supposed to be hush-hush?" He sat, then swung his feet up on a corner of the table. "One of you, who shall remain name-less, was good enough to inform me of this meeting."

This was, of course, a lie... but there was no harm in sewing distrust amongst the Board. He flashed a Cheshire cat grin. "I am in your debt... whoever you are." He suppressed the urge to pick one of them at random and toss them a wink.

Carson's two "handlers" came around the table and flanked him. They were actually there to protect the Board from Carson... but the Board had no way of knowing that; to all appearances, Carson had brought along a pair of goons to intimidate them.

"This is a privileged meeting!" up-and-comer Lucinda Croft spluttered through coral-red lipstick, waving a finger in the direc-tion of the two guards.

Carson swiveled his chair from right to left with casual glances over his shoulders at each of the men. "Oh, don't mind them. They've signed so many nondisclosure agreements, they're more NDA than man. Their presence is purely a security precaution. As I understand it... I might be under threat." He paused to look around the room. When no one spoke, he continued, "And on that note... where is our gracious host? I thought this was Hilda's ballgame."

"Still in her office, I expect," Mortimer Winslow drawled in his old-money mid-Atlantic accent; the man had a way of speaking that sounded like his jaw had been partially wired shut. "But I must say, it's somewhat irregular that there wasn't anyone here to greet us. Ms. Morgan's assistant, at the very least." He slid his well-manicured fingers in opposing arcs across the empty conference table in front of him. "And no board deck or other materials? She shouldn't have called us in if she wasn't prepared. It's quite a commute for some of us."

"Leo isn't here?" Singleton frowned. "He's always quite punctual."

Carson sighed and took out his phone. "Bill, give him a ring-a-ding while I call Hildy." He glanced around at the Board. "We all have important work to do... we didn't build Maiden into the megacompany it is today by sitting around staring at an empty table."

Singleton and Carson both placed calls and waited. Singleton frowned and hung up. "Voicemail," he stated.

"Same." Carson held up a finger, then left a message. "Good morning, Ms. Morgan. This is your CEO. I'm sitting here in the conference room with six captains of industry, all of whom are waiting on you. We'll give you five more minutes, then I'm going to take over the proceedings." He hung up and frowned. "Odd. Bill, call security and see if Hilda checked into the building this morning."

While Singleton placed the call, Carson looked over at Maximillian Hedrum, the head of the newly formed Artificial Intelligence division. The rotund board member had taken it upon himself to lay out the bagels and had helped himself to a poppy-seed, slathering it in scallion cream cheese before taking an ambitious bite. Midchew, the man spotted Carson looking at him; he slid the cardboard bagel tray toward the head of the table.

Carson smiled and held up a hand. "Oh, thank you, no. I'm off gluten this month."

"More for me!" Max chuckled through a mouthful of bagel.

Carson's stomach growled. He used to love these bagels, but the most delectable thing in view was pudgy Max, stuffing his face. *Wonder how he'd taste with a schmear of cream cheese?* Carson wasn't sure if that thought had been his own or if it had come from his brain's unwanted roommate. He clenched a fist beneath the table, reasserting control.

Singleton ended his call. "Sir, I just spoke to the morning shift. Hilda logged in yesterday at eight in the morning and hasn't left the building. They checked her office's security feed and she's in there right now."

"Probably dotting the last of the i's and crossing the last of the t's," Carson said. "Lucinda, you're her current favorite, why don't you go fetch her?"

While Lucinda exited the conference room, Carson toyed with his phone. "Let's see how Maiden's stock is doing, shall we?" Holding his phone below the table so his minders couldn't see the screen, he quickly entered his security program and turned off Hilda's office camera entirely, then closed out and opened his favorite stock ticker app. "Looks like we picked up a little lost ground."

Lucinda returned, flustered. "Her door is locked."

"Did you knock?" Carson asked.

"Of course. And called her name. No reply. Her shades are drawn."

Carson sighed and clapped his palms down on the table. "Right. Well, I, for one, am not willing to wait here all day. Bill, have security come up and open Hilda's door."

Singleton looked up from his phone. "Actually, sir... they're already on their way up."

The next hour moved surprisingly swiftly, as Hilda's door was unlocked, copious blood was found, and the previous night's looping camera feed was discovered. Police arrived to take statements; these were brief, as the only people on the floor at the time of the manipulation of the camera feed had been Hilda, her assistant, Leo, and a technical consultant by the name of Reginald Brice. APBs were issued for all three individuals. Under the circumstances, the morning board meeting was canceled.

"Well, Bill... I believe the vote has been postponed... perhaps indefinitely," Carson opined as they rode the elevator down, his two escorts standing at the back of the compartment.

"Yes. Convenient."

Carson looked askance at his aide-de-camp. Singleton was unreadable, his eyes locked on the descending numbers on the elevator control panel: 16, 15, 14... 12, 11, 10...

"Something is not right," Yana Volkov murmured. "It shouldn't be taking this long."

"I'm sure Ms. Morgan will let us know when the vote is over," Dhir assured her, eyes on the screen of his laptop.

They had arrived at eight thirty and gone to the twentieth floor to a waiting room; the penthouse level was restricted until the board meeting concluded.

"Where the hell is Reggie?" Yana asked no one in particular. "He was supposed to wait with us. And he has my laptop."

"My guess is Ms. Morgan shanghaied him into running the PowerPoint presentation," Dhir offered.

"Fuck this." Yana placed a call to Hilda, then cursed when it went to voicemail. "I'm going up."

Two minutes later, the elevator doors opened onto the penthouse floor and Yana and Dhir were greeted with a barrier of crime scene tape. Police—uniformed and plainclothes—swarmed the foyer.

"Dammit, Vince, you were s'posed to shut that down once Carson and the Board left!" One of New York's finest held up a hand. "Sorry, folks. This floor's closed."

"What happened?" Yana asked, trying to keep the alarm out of her voice. "Where's Hilda Morgan?"

"We're trying to ascertain her whereabouts," a plainclothes detective replied. "Why? You work for her?" He stopped the elevator door from closing with a blue-gloved hand on the edge.

Yana opened her mouth to answer in the affirmative but stopped herself when something she'd overheard registered. "No, I just know that's her office behind the police tape." She pointed at the open door to Hilda's office, which appeared to be a beehive of activity. Yana had a strong feeling something terrible had happened inside. "Actually, I was supposed to speak with Mr. Carson. His office is at the end, there." She looked past the detective to the uniformed cop who'd stopped them. "Did you say he left?"

"Yeah, you just missed him. Headed for the ground floor. Hey, sorry, but we gotta shut down this elevator. What floor you going to?"

"Ground floor," Yana supplied.

"Okay... last ride before we pull the plug."

Several minutes later, they reached the massive lobby of the Maiden Headquarters building. Yana dashed for the glass revolving doors, as if expecting Carson to be loitering around on the sidewalk outside.

Dhir touched her shoulder before she could reach the exit. "Yana, wait. He's probably long gone, but even if he isn't... I don't think you want him to spot you here. Besides... I have an idea where he's going."

"Where?"

Dhir motioned for her to join him in a seating area in a corner of the lobby. He opened up his laptop. "When we fled North Brother, they locked me out of their systems... but I've still got my hooks in a few less secure Maiden servers. While we were waiting for the vote, I sniffed around. Look what I found in Maiden Aviation."

Yana looked at the particulars on the screen. "I recognize this.

That's Carson's private jet... the one Reggie bugged. And this is a flight plan?"

"It is. From Westchester to Missoula, Montana. That's where we flew to New York from, after taking a helicopter from the site of the Sasquatch attack. I think he's going back there. He seemed very interested in a sphere—probably a meteorite—that Joseph and Russ found. I've since been cut off from the conversation, but he was asking about it with a mole he's got in the CDC at the Grangeville quarantine site."

Yana worked her jaw, thinking. "Why does Carson want this space rock?"

"Maybe to counteract what's happening to him? Not sure. But I know someone who can help." He took out his phone and dialed. "Liz! Wait, wait, slow down... I'm all right. I'm sorry, the North Brother facility was blocking incoming calls. Yes, I'm fine. Are you still in Grangeville? Okay, good. Listen..."

CHAPTER TWENTY-FOUR

"Look!"

Sarah's shout brought Joseph to her side. Up ahead, Russ didn't respond; with his noise-canceling headphones, he continued west along the rocky shoreline of the Salmon River. On either side, the land sloped upward toward distant mountain ranges. They had just crossed over French Creek, a smaller waterway that forked off to the south.

"What did you find?" Joseph asked.

Sarah crouched in a patch of silt between the scree and boulders that lined the river. She pointed at what she had found, looking pleased with herself. "And here I thought you two were the trackers."

"A Bigfoot track," Joseph declared without hesitation. "Pointing south. And it is fresh." Frowning, he unslung the hunting rifle from his shoulder. "But Brighteyes went *north* from the expedition's camp, did he not? And we are far to the south of there."

"I know. Perhaps it's a Sasquatch from another troop."

"Perhaps..." Joseph ran his gaze across the slopes to their south. Suddenly, Russ called out as he approached. "Hey, guys...

what's up?" He removed the headphones from one ear, leaving them atop his head at an angle.

Before he reached them, he suddenly halted and looked down at the ground. "A print. Looks like a barefoot human, but..."

Sarah rose and examined the additional print he'd found. "No... look at the elongated arch... this is a juvenile Bigfoot! And look what I found." She pointed out the original.

"Brighteyes... and his younger brother?" Russ asked. "All the way down here?"

"I'm not sure about that. There was a *third* Bigfoot here." Joseph was crouching nearby. "Adult... but not as large as the first print."

"All three prints heading south," Russ mused. He lifted his arm and pointed along French Creek. "Looks like they left the river and headed that way. Should we... whoa!"

The finger he pointed with had the dreamcatcher dangling from it, and the webbed circle with the stone in it suddenly lifted, the dangling feathers extending toward the south along the creek.

Russ held his arm rock-steady for nearly ten seconds. "That isn't wind."

"No... it isn't." Joseph hefted the rifle again, scanning the trees that lined French Creek. "Whatever it's drawn to... if it's related to the Bigfoot tracks..."

Russ took the hint and unshouldered his shotgun, then slipped the dreamcatcher loop from his finger and transferred it to the barrel of the weapon, holding it level so that it dangled once more. Almost immediately, it rose again, hovering a few degrees shy of horizontal.

Joseph nodded. "Good thinking. Sarah, if you could take the lead-lined box, I'd like to keep the rifle at the ready. And let's have you put in some earplugs."

"Don't be trigger-happy, fellas... for all we know, Brighteyes and his little brother might have doubled back south and met up with another troop."

"Understood." Joseph reached up and reseated Russ's head-phones in place, then signaled for him to lead the way. Scanning the ground ahead, he searched for more tracks.

"You lost them, didn't you?" Merle's tone hovered on the border between fatigue and annoyance.

Wolf kicked at the scree at the side of Sheep Creek. "Ach! There's nae a track to be seen."

"So... keep going... or go back?" Merle asked from astride one of the two-seater ATVs with Ian crowding him from the rear seat. "I vote back."

The going had gotten rough, and as roads had given way to trails, Wolf had sent Keith and the U-Haul all the way back around to Highway 95—on the western side of the mountains—to await instructions while Wolf, Merle, and Athena continued their pursuit with the all-terrain vehicles. The ATVs had allowed them to make speedier progress, but spotting sign had become nigh impossible and they had lost Russ's trail quite some time ago.

Wolf went back to the other ATV; Athena sat on the back seat, her eyes glued to one of her gadgets. Wolf was just throwing a leg over the forward seat—something he did with care, considering the tactical kilt he wore—when Athena suddenly squealed in surprise.

Wolf nearly jumped out of his skin at the shrill exclamation behind him. "*Jings crivvens*, lass!"

"I've got a signal!" Athena shouted.

Wolf abandoned his attempt at mounting the ATV and leaned in eagerly. "Is it Russ?"

"It's the same ID as the one we were following, so yes... proba-bly. Looks like they've finally left the military's jamming radius... or *we* have. Either way, I've got a blip on the tracker."

"How far from us?"

"Eight miles."

"That far? Where? Show me!"

Athena made an adjustment to her tracking signal detector, which was more of an oversized GPS device with three antennae atop it. She turned the screen to face Wolf. "Here... the blip is on French Creek... about a quarter mile south of the Salmon River."

Wolf brought up his own GPS and quickly located the spot. "And there's a road there..." Setting the GPS down on the front rack next to the steering column, he dug his sat phone out of a kilt pocket. "Kevin! I mean... Keith! I need you to get to the Salmon River Road... take it east to French Creek Road and pull over and wait for instructions." He turned back to Ian. "What's the range on your drone?"

Ian had handed his camera to Merle and was already unlimbering a case from the back of his ATV. "Twelve max... ten comfortably. But with all this topography, might be a bit touch and go." He pointed at a ridge above them, too steep for their vehicles. "I'll launch from up there."

"Do it!" As Ian started up the slope, Wolf grabbed Merle, turned on the camera and shoved it into his hands, then maneuvered him toward the ATV Athena sat atop. "Roll film." He moved behind Athena and looked over her shoulder at the GPS screen.

"Ach, Russ... it's been a merry chase... but I'm coming, boyo. And if ye have a Sasquatch with ya... so much the better."

DawnWaker sniffed the air, then wrinkled her jutting brow. 'Bad smell.'

Brighteyes froze, grunting, 'Stop!' He recognized the odor. The "not-humans" that had started it all—one of which had bitten Silverback on the hand—had stunk like that. Not a true death smell, but something *other*. Alive-Dead. Silverback, too, had taken on that stench before he turned into a mindless killing machine.

Littlefoot was whimpering, but all of a sudden, he stopped and pointed. 'Look! I think that what smell.'

Brighteyes spotted movement beside the creek that ran southward from the larger river they had crossed the night before. Whatever it was, it wasn't large. Cautiously, he moved forward, picking up a bleached branch from the rocks that lined the water.

'Stay.' He gestured for Littlefoot and DawnWaker to remain where they were as he slowly approached the object and lifted the branch above a shoulder. It was a frog. But something was clearly wrong with it.

Its body bulged to near-bursting and Brighteyes could clearly see the leg of another frog extending from one side of its mouth and the tailfin of a fish sticking out of the other. As the Bigfoot drew closer, the frog's bulging eye on the near side swiveled in its socket and looked up at him. It managed to burble a throaty croak past its mouthful of fish 'n' frog, then turned and leaped toward Brighteyes. Its distended belly didn't allow for much of a jump and it landed two feet shy of its target. Brighteyes planted his enormous feet and swung the branch in a downward arc, pancaking the amphibian and splattering the contents of its stomach in a gory puddle around it. A familiar odor permeated the air.

Littlefoot barked a sound of disgust; the youngster had ignored his half brother's admonition to stay put and was standing right behind him. 'Frog bad. Frog sick?'

Sick like Silverback... and Silk... and Scratch, Brighteyes thought, but he didn't share those specifics with Littlefoot. 'Yes. Sick. We should—'

Suddenly, DawnWaker uttered a low grunt of alarm. She had remained twenty yards to the north and was now scenting the air. Brighteyes gave her a silent gesture that indicated a simple interrogative. She came his way, hackles raised, signing all the way.

'Humans! Close!'

"Bigfoot hair!" Sarah exclaimed as she plucked the patch of hair from Joseph's fingers. She took one of her earplugs out. "It's copper-colored! I've never seen a ginger Sasquatch before."

"It was in that blackberry bush there." Joseph pointed at a brambly patch just upslope from French Creek. "And in the area around where I found it... no blackberries."

Downstream, Russ had halted. His shotgun remained level ahead of him, and the dreamcatcher continued to float upward, but his eyes were cast downward. He glanced back at the others, pointed two fingers at his eyes, then indicated the ground beside him.

Joseph held up a finger to his lips and Russ nodded. Sarah put the red hair in a pocket and followed the Shoshone as he joined Russ.

"Two sets of barefoot prints," Russ whispered, lifting one headphone off an ear. "The big one and little one again... wait... what's wrong?"

Joseph was scanning the creek ahead, his body tense and rifle held at the ready. He'd only given the tracks a cursory glance when he'd suddenly smelled it: a familiar deathlike stench.

"What is it?" Sarah asked.

"The odor from the geologists' camp... and the infected Sasquatch. Faint, but..."

"I smell it too," Russ looked at the barrel of his shotgun. "I hope our dreamcatcher isn't picking up a zombified Bigfoot."

Joseph shook his head. "The Bigfoot hair I found has none of that otherworldly stink. The scent is faint... and look. The dreamcatcher is angling more to the side now. Toward the edge of the water."

The trio cautiously moved forward, and it didn't take them long to find the source of the smell.

"Holy...!" Sarah exclaimed. "What the heck is that?"

"An ex-frog from the looks of it," Russ replied. "And some fish... and is that a chunk of turtle shell? I can't tell if something puked that up or smashed it flat."

"Smashed it." Joseph took a step closer, looking down at a spot between the small rocks that lined the creek. "The largest of the three Bigfoot was here... and this print in the dirt is quite a bit deeper. Probably grounding itself before attacking this thing."

Russ had the shotgun pointed at the pool of goo and he swung the barrel slowly from side to side. With each adjustment, the dreamcatcher continued to point toward the dead frog. And it did something else now.

"Look at the stone!" Russ squinted at the little hunk of rock in the center of the dreamcatcher's web. "Is it glowing? Hard to tell in the sunlight."

Joseph came over and reached for the dreamcatcher below Russ's shotgun barrel. "Finger off the trigger, Cloud," he said with a crooked smile. He leaned in and peered at the stone, then cupped his hands around it and peeked inside. "Yes, it is definitely glowing. A faint amber light. Let's get closer. Hover it over the smashed frog."

Russ did as instructed and the glow strengthened so that it was clearly visible, even in the sunlight.

"Well... at least we know it works," Sarah said. "So... I'm guessing the sphere floated by here and messed with this frog... and then a Sasquatch smushed it."

"I don't like the sound of a smash-happy Sasquatch." Russ looked at the slopes on either side of the creek. "And those prints look fresh."

'Humans there!' DawnWaker frantically signed. 'With boom-sticks! We must run!'

The forest here was much sparser than to the north, and there weren't many trees lining the creek, but the three Sasquatch were well hidden in a thick copse of blackberry bushes and could barely see the trio of humans near the remains of the Bad Frog. Brighteyes was about to lead them away when he spotted blond hair on one of the humans—a female who looked familiar. *Daughter of Beardface!* He carefully moved his head from side to side, peeking through various gaps in the bushes. Yes, it was her! And he knew the other two humans as well. One of them wore a cloth tied over his head: this was the one who had built a snare that had hobbled Silverback during their final battle. The other, with raven hair braided at the back, was descended from the native peoples of this area. Suddenly the man looked his way, locking eyes with him.

'They see us!' DawnWaker grunted in panic.

'Wait. I know them. They are friends.' The red-body looked incredulous, but Brighteyes laid his knuckles on her forearm. 'Trust me. You two, stay here.'

He picked his way through the brambles and stepped into the open. When the blonde saw him, her face lit up and she called out the human word he knew well: "Brighteyes!"

Striding down the hill, he employed the sign language this female's father had taught him. He had been "dumbing it down" for DawnWaker, but now he could express himself in more detail.

'Daughter of Beardface. Friends.'

Both of the males returned the "friend" gesture and Sarah stepped forward. "I thought you were going north," she signed while speaking her human tongue. "Are you well? Where is Littlefoot?"

'We are well. The alpha of the north troop turned us away. I come south with Littlefoot. And another.' He beckoned up the hill and chuffed out a call: 'Safe! Come!'

Sarah watched as two additional Sasquatch appeared. Littlefoot led the way with an adult female following close behind. Half a head shorter than Brighteyes with a shiny and curly copper-colored pelt, this newcomer appeared wary. Littlefoot, on the other hand, toddled right up to Russ and signed. Sarah translated.

'I remember you.' The diminutive Bigfoot pointed at Russ's weapon. 'I remember boom-stick!'

Russ laughed. "Not the same one, but yeah... close enough." Several days ago, the monstrous thing that Silverback had become had nearly killed them all, only being stopped by a groundbreaking instance of primate tool use: Littlefoot had used a mercenary's tactical shotgun to blow the alpha's brains out.

Brighteyes gestured to DawnWaker and introduced her to Sarah in their shared sign language as 'She who wakes at dawn.'

Sarah signed and spoke. "I greet you. We are friends. Brighteyes... we search for a round rock. Your troop... this rock is what made them sick." In truth, the "Stone that Sings" had first made the geologists sick, and they had passed their infection on to the alpha, but given the basic nature of their shared sign language, it was simpler to truncate the chain of events. "We wish to destroy this rock."

"Tell him we think it made that frog into a monster," Joseph suggested. "Ask him if it attacked him before he smashed it."

Sarah did her best, and Brighteyes confirmed that, yes, the frog had been "Alive-Dead" and had tried to attack him before he'd pulped it with a branch. She was about to ask another question when a high-pitched buzzing sound interrupted the gathering. Everyone looked around and Littlefoot pointed at the sky.

'Maple seed machine!'

"I've got you now, boyo!" Wolf howled, looking over Ian's shoulder at the drone feed. Athena, sitting beside them, had vectored Ian's drone straight to the site of the tracker's signal. Wolf squinted at the grainy image. "Holy shite! Is… is Russ talking to a Bigfoot? Get closer! And why is there so much static?"

"We're at the limits of my range, boss. And they're in a creek gully. If I bring her down for a closer look, we may lose the feed entirely."

"Ach, it's worth the risk! Get closer!"

Russ squinted at the sky until he finally spotted the drone. *That little Bigfoot's eyesight must be a heck of a lot better than mine.* "What do you think, Joseph? Government?"

"Perhaps."

"We should head for cover!" Sarah cried.

"What cover?" Joseph gestured at the thin vegetation around them.

Littlefoot was spinning in a circle, arms outstretched. His own experience with drones had been positive; Dhir and Liz had rescued him with one.

The drone swooped down and came to a hover ten yards from the group. It pivoted from side to side and wobbled a bit. Brighteyes took DawnWaker by the arm and turned toward the hillside they'd come from. 'Littlefoot! Machine no friend!' he grunted, then began to lope away from the creek.

"Damn static!" Wolf snarled. The video feed was spotty at best, but he was fairly sure there were two—maybe three—Sasquatch alongside Russ and his pals. Suddenly, the blurry, furry figures turned and started to run.

"They're making a break for it," Ian commented needlessly. "Controls are sticky, but I'll follow them."

"Wait! Before you do, give me one good close shot of Russ Cloud. I want viewers to see the look on his face."

Ian made an adjustment and the static managed to clear for one blessed moment. Unfortunately, the look on Russ's face wasn't despair or helplessness. It was calm determination. Wolf's nemesis racked the pump on a shotgun he held and leveled the barrel at the drone. There was a flash and the video feed went dead.

"Nae!!" Wolf howled.

"He shot it," Ian declared matter-of-factly.

"No shite, ye numpty!" Wolf clawed his sat phone out of a pouch pocket on his tactical kilt. He dialed the last number he'd called. Fortunately, the name of the callee had finally found a home in his memory. "Keith! How close are ye?" He listened a moment, then yelled, "I don't care if ye've never driven a big truck before, hurry it up!" He hung up. "C'mon, you two!" Wolf rose and scramble-slid down the slope to their ATVs. "Merle! We're rolling out!"

Ian came huffing and puffing down the hill, Athena on his heels. "I've plotted the fastest route down to the spot where they were," she said.

"Good! Ian, what about the footage of the Bigfoots?"

"Well, what we got on the receiver isn't usable, but if we can get the drone's SD card... that'll have crystal-clear video."

"Nice shot," Joseph said as he toed the drone with a boot.

"Thanks," Russ replied. "Did some skeet shooting as a kid."

When Russ had filled the drone's camera lens with 20-gauge buckshot, he'd followed up with a blast that took out one of its rotors, sending the drone plummeting into the shallow creek, where it had started to float downstream. Since Sarah was wearing shorts, she'd volunteered to wade in and retrieve it. Ditching her hiking boots and socks, she quickly caught up with the drone and brought it to shore.

Joseph picked up the drone and turned it over in his hands. "Well... at least it isn't military."

"How do you know?" Sarah asked.

He held it out so that she and Russ could see it. On the bottom was a sticker depicting a bearded kilt-clad man wrestling a bear, with "Property of *Man vs. Nature*" on it and a phone number to call.

"Wolf Wallace," Russ growled.

Sarah seemed distraught. "He's got footage of Brighteyes!"

"Not really. High-def drone footage is stored inside the drone itself." Russ popped open a compartment and located the SD card. "I used a drone in a few of my episodes. But since I was shooting everything solo, I decided it was just extra weight that I didn't need." He slid the SD card out, then placed it on a river rock and smashed it repeatedly with another stone before tossing the mangled chip into the creek. "Done." Then he smiled and dug out his smartphone to take a picture of the sticker on the drone. "Might have some fun with Wolf's production office phone number later."

"How on earth did he find us?" Sarah asked.

"Heck if I know," Russ said. "We're in the middle of the wilderness. Last time he was anywhere close to us, he was talking with Sharkey and Farley... giving them all that stupid swag..."

Russ realized it even as he said it, but Joseph was way ahead of him. He held out a hand. "The compass. Give it to me." He took it from Russ and pried the compass face from the blue rubber housing. There, embedded in the rubber, was a small microchip.

"Sneaky prick," Russ muttered. "Let's smash it."

"No... I have a better idea." Joseph looked at the ridges on either side of the creek, then pointed to the western slope. "That way is more heavily wooded. And a difficult climb... for a human."

"I see where you're going," Russ said with a grin. He picked up the drone and reopened the compartment on the bottom. "This likely has some sort of tracking element too... for retrieval. Gimme that doohickey from the compass." He took the little tracking chip and jammed it into the SD card port, chuckling as he did so. "Just a little 'eff you' to that reality show prick."

Sarah turned to Brighteyes and started signing.

Brighteyes nodded, understanding what they wanted him to do. He wasn't sure of the why, but apparently, this would make it hard for the "bad humans" to find them.

Daughter of Beardface unshouldered a bag from her back, took some things out of it, then stuffed the strange flying machine inside of it. Then she hung it around Brighteyes's neck and signed, "You can use both hands to climb. More fast."

Brighteyes grunted in understanding, then turned to Dawn-Waker. 'I go... put this'—he pointed up the steep slope—'up there.'

'I go with you!'

'No. You stay with Littlefoot and human friends. I meet you downstream soon.'

Before she could protest, Brighteyes took off at a loping run. Once the land grew steep, he used his long arms to propel himself from branch to tree to sapling, giving his speedy ascent an extra boost of momentum. The bag with the "maple seed machine" thumped against his chest. When he finally reached the summit, he extracted the flying machine and tossed it down the opposite slope.

CHAPTER TWENTY-FIVE

Annabelle and the Sharlie Hunters were towing Critch's jon boat south to the Mile High Marina when flashing blue lights caught her eye; Payette Lake's lone police boat was skimming across the waves toward them. Annabelle had only seen the marine patrol's lights flashing maybe four or five times in all the years she'd worked the lake. Drunk boaters were the usual reason... and the marine patrol had to chase down the rich-boy jet skiers from time to time. In general, the boaters here were reasonably well-behaved, although there had been a fatal crash all the way back in 2009.

When she'd discovered the blood in the abandoned boat, Annabelle had called it in to the police and they were the ones that requested they tow the boat into the marina; the *Slimy Slim* was only minutes away from reaching it.

"Guess we're getting a police escort," Kevin surmised.

"Is that the mayor?" Mark asked from the bench by the bow.

In moments, the police boat pulled up alongside. Officer Dwight Flynn was at the helm and, sure enough, Mayor Vance was right beside him.

"Annabelle," Dwight called out with a head-nod greeting as he coasted toward them at an idle.

"Morning, Dwight... sorry about the fuss. You want us to follow you in?"

"Actually, Ms. Graybill," the mayor interjected, "I'm going to need you to turn around and tow the boat to Mr. Critchley's dock. Forensics will look at it there."

"But that's all the way back up the peninsula! The marina's right there!"

"Exactly! And so are the boats that are gathering for the Vance-fest Boat Parade! Along with press and tourists and some of my influential friends. We can't bring a blood-soaked boat into that environment! I mean... just *look* at this mess!" The mayor waved a hand toward the boat where a human being had likely met his demise.

"I think murder takes precedence over a little self-aggrandizing party," Brady spat.

"It isn't *little*! Or self... whatever you said. Besides, we don't know that this is a murder! Maybe... maybe he was boning a fish and the knife slipped."

"You're an idiot," Brady muttered.

"He wasn't carving up his catch in the middle of the lake, Mr. Mayor," Stuart insisted. "Critch always did that at his dock or in his kitchen. And he certainly wouldn't do it while night fishing."

"Well, it doesn't matter! The forensics team from Boise is going to meet us at Critchley's dock, and that's that! Now hurry it up and turn around... I need to get back to the marina to preside over the festivities."

Cilantro "read the room" and started barking at the mayor.

Vance scowled. "What's his problem?"

"Her." Mark gave the dog an encouraging ear scratch. "Not a thing. Silly's just a good judge of character."

Sharlie had never tasted people before. That had changed last night, when she had feasted on the man in the boat... a man that had been trying to catch the very fish she had been hunting, a large predatory fish the humans had begun introducing to the lake half a century ago. Those sterile hybrids were tasty, but not nearly as delicious as the fisherman had been.

Lashing her tail, she ascended and raised her head above the surface of the water, scenting the air. At present, she was near the less populated shore of the lake. Her keen olfactory senses didn't detect much of interest... but then the wind shifted. From across the lake where human dwellings lined the shore, tantalizing aromas reached her nostrils. Descending once more, she undulated through the water, heading west. For over a century, Sharlie had done her best to avoid humans... but that was the old Sharlie.

"Best... purchase... ever!" the drunk in the floatie declared.

Buoyed by an inner tube on the western shore of Payette Lake, the young man kicked leisurely in the chilly morning water. Around him were three of his friends, each with their own floatie. The long-awaited package had arrived last night and he couldn't wait to try it out, even if it meant starting their day drinking a bit on the early side.

The Water Donut Bar was a collection of five inflatable rings, each one patterned after a different donut: three with frosting—chocolate, vanilla, and strawberry—and one with sprinkles. The fifth floatie was the Donut Bar mothership, a larger inner tube designed to look like a Boston Cream with a padded circular cooler built into the center. Each satellite donut had a carabiner on a line that you could hook up to the cooler floatie and "belly up to the bar" with your donut.

The proud new owner of the Donut Bar had selected "sprinkles" for his floatie. He pounded the rest of his beer, then crushed the can and tossed it aside with a watery plunk.

"Hey!" a young woman protested from another inflatable. She was seated in hers, long tan legs dangled over the strawberry-glazed surface of the water donut. "Don't litter!"

"This thing doesn't come with a recycling bin," Sprinkles said as he reeled his donut in and hooked up to the Boston Cream. Strawberry was a bit of a tree hugger, but she was smokin' hot and he'd been trying to get into her pants for weeks. He would probably be more successful if he *didn't* throw his trash in the lake, but Sprinkles's games of mental chess didn't extend too many moves ahead. And if he ever tried to play an *actual* chess game, his brain would likely implode when he tried to figure out how the horsey moved.

"Beer me, bro!" his buddy in the chocolate donut called out.

Sprinkles dug into the ice and grabbed a can, tossing it across to his old high school chum… who whiffed the catch, forcing him to swim after his beverage before it bobbed out of reach. Sprinkles helped himself to another cheap beer that had more in common with water than lager.

His friend in the vanilla donut hooked up on the opposite side of the cooler. "Love your new toy, dude." He reached to the rear of his ball cap and retrieved the vape pen he'd clipped to the snapback strap.

"What flavor you got?"

"Trainwreck, dude. Grew it myself." He took a hit and offered the pen across the Boston Cream.

"No, thanks. I wanna keep my head clear," Sprinkles demurred before downing half of his freshly popped beer.

"Hey, you gonna be in the boat parade this evening?" Vanilla asked. "For that Vancefest thing?"

"Nah. I asked my dad if we could bring the SunCatcher down and join the parade, but he hates the new mayor. Said he'd probably start ramming boats."

"Yo, that sounds rad! I wanna do that!" Chocolate had floated close enough to hear tidbits of the conversation.

"Hey, let's float down to Cindy's," Vanilla suggested. "See if she wants to join the party."

"More the merrier. But she'll have to bring her own floatie."

"We can grab one from her neighbor's pool," Vanilla suggested. "I saw an inflatable alligator in there yesterday. No one's around, man... everyone's down in town for the festival."

As the four adventurers made their way downstream, they were being watched. Hunted. When the group passed a cove in the shoreline... the watcher struck.

"What the f—!" Sprinkles started to shout as an object rushed straight at him with a roar. Specifically, the roar of an engine, as a jet ski hurtled from behind concealment, turning at the last second and slapping his face with a cascade of lake water as the bow wave skirted past his donut, the fiberglass hull missing him by inches. The jet ski was followed by another...and another... then a fourth and final one zipped up toward Strawberry before cutting a hard one-eighty and drenching her with the output of its jets. Startled, she capsized, sending her bikini-clad body into the drink. Cackling, the four jet skiers floored it and headed south.

"It's the Osgood twins!" Vanilla spluttered, holding his vape pen aloft, high and dry.

Sure enough, the Osgood brothers—along with two of their "rich kid" pals—were out for a joyride with the new toys their daddy had bought them. This was a no-wake zone, but rules didn't seem to apply to the twins; their father had a lot of influence in town, and the odds of a citation were next to nil. The wealthy Texan was probably glad-handing it with the new mayor at this very moment, as he presided over the festival in town.

Sprinkles felt a surge of jealousy as Chocolate helped Strawberry back into her donut—especially when his buddy got a little handsy with her and she didn't seem to mind. Sprinkles thought about popping Chocolate's floatie, but his mind went the extra mile and reminded him that he would be destroying his own property.

An hour and three beers later, the quartet had become a quintet, with Cindy joining them on a pilfered alligator pool float. She looked *good*, so Sprinkles decided to switch targets; if Chocolate was gunning for Strawberry, then he'd just have to settle for some alligator tail. But first... a little fortifying nectar.

"All right, everybody! Hook up! Time for Jäger shots!"

Sprinkles had initially debated turning the entire interior of the cooler into a punch bowl and filling it with "Green Goddamn" —a concoction of Mountain Dew, four-dollar champagne, green food coloring, crushed ice, and Everclear—but he was all out of the latter, and that was the keystone ingredient. As everyone kicked toward home base, Sprinkles dug a bottle of Jägermeister out of the ice, then grabbed a sleeve of plastic shot glasses and started handing them out.

Cindy seemed reluctant. "Oh, I shouldn't."

"You should," Sprinkles countered.

"Okay, then."

Once shots were in hand, Sprinkles held the bottle aloft. "Prost! Here's to... um..."

"To Sharlie!" Cindy suggested, hanging off the side of her gator float, snugged up against the Boston Cream between Chocolate and Sprinkles. Not a surprising suggestion, since she lived on Sharlie Lane on the west shore.

"To Sharlie!" the group cheered and downed their shots. For good measure, Sprinkles helped himself to an additional chug from the bottle.

An onlooker might have assumed that the unfortunate choice of toast had summoned the beast, but Sharlie didn't hear the words— nor would she have understood them, even if she had. No... what had enticed her were five sets of legs, kicking beneath the waves. Ten delectable morsels, conveniently clustered around a central object. One thing gave her a momentary pause: a greenish creature, about five feet long, floated at the surface beside the humans. Living in an alpine lake, Sharlie had never seen an alligator before, but from its shape, the creature appeared to be some form of predatory reptile.

Sharlie decided to take out this competitor first and was about to strike when her keen olfactory senses informed her the "reptile" was inanimate and no different from the round objects that held the humans. Satisfied, Sharlie reared back her head, bent her long neck, took aim... and struck. Lashing her tooth-packed jaws from leg to leg to leg, Sharlie feasted. When the slaughter was complete and every morsel consumed, she swam toward deeper water. Yes, humans were indeed delicious... although the last one had possessed a strong licorice taste.

She prowled along the shore for a few minutes when the approach of a boat drew her attention. Normally, Sharlie avoided boats—her back bore the scars of numerous propeller strikes—but boats meant humans. And humans, Sharlie now knew, were delicious. Whipping her powerful tail and pressing her webbed claws against her side, Sharlie shot after the boat. As she neared, she straightened her neck and lifted her head just above the surface of the water, like a submarine's periscope.

The boat had a single occupant and was towing something long and yellow with three humans riding on its back. The boat and its companion were going quite fast, but Sharlie was up to the challenge. The mindless hunger was tempered by cunning, and she oriented herself with a spot ahead of the boat, then ducked under and shot forward toward deeper water.

At the public dock on the peninsula, Annabelle watched as the forensic unit went aboard Critch's boat, which was tied up on one side of the missing man's dock. The police boat and the *Slimy Slim* were moored opposite. Officer Dwight and the Sharlie Hunters clustered nearby while the mayor stood on shore, shouting into his phone.

"I told you to pick me up! No excuses, get up here now! What? The Osgoods? Well, a jet ski's a boat as far as I'm concerned, so if they want to be in the parade, I don't care." The mayor paced away from the group, yelling at Dwight over his shoulder, "Officer, I'm going to walk to the main road. My ride's on its way. Take care of all this."

Cilantro the Be-huahua puffed a disgusted sniff at the man's departure.

"You said it, girl," Mark agreed.

"Sorry about this, folks," Dwight apologized. "Annabelle, I think you guys can go, if you want. Do you need me to—"

Suddenly, the radio on the police boat crackled to life. *"All units, we have a 10-54 on the west shore. Multiple victims. And, uh... I guess a 10-91V?"* the dispatcher ventured.

"What's a 10-54?" Mark asked.

Dwight was already stepping across to his boat. "Possible dead body. And 10-91V is a vicious animal." He grabbed the radio mic. "Dispatch, this is Dwight. I'm on the peninsula and can be across the lake in five. Text me the location. And you said multiple victims... how many?"

"Uh... not sure."

"How about the animal... is it a dog? Bear?"

"Uh... no... the witness who called it in said it was a... a sea monster."

As one, the Sharlie Hunters rushed for the pontoon boat. Annabelle grabbed her rifle-carrying case. "Guys, I'm going with Dwight! See you over there!"

The police boat was quite a bit faster and pulled far ahead of the Sharlie Hunters; halfway across the lake, the radio squawked to life.

"Marine Patrol? Dispatch. Officer Dwight, you there?"

"Still en route, Dispatch."

"Well, hold up. We have ground units heading to the incident, but we may need you for something else."

"Go ahead, Dispatch."

"A kayaker called this in... an out-of-control boat, towing an inflatable banana float, driving in circles. She gave the location—about a half mile west of the Deep Water Launch—but then I lost the call. She screamed, 'What the hell is that?' then the call went dead."

"Where was the kayaker?" Annabelle asked the radio.

"She didn't say, but in view of the banana, I'm guessing."

"Okay, we're on it." Dwight swung the wheel to port and raced south.

The pontoon boat was catching up to them, and Annabelle got out her phone and called Brady.

"Whassup, Graybill? Why you turning around?"

"We're heading south. Might be another incident. You guys keep going. And listen, I know you're Sharlie Hunters and all, but once you get to the... well... scene of the crime... wait until the police arrive on the shore."

"Got it."

Dwight brought them over deep water and in moments they spotted the speedboat and its trailing banana, carving a perfect circle in the middle of the lake. "I'm going to step over and take control. I know you're good with that forestry boat... can you drive? Bring me in close?"

"Sure thing."

As they neared, Annabelle watched the unoccupied banana

bouncing across the waves. At first, she thought the neon-yellow inflatable had a red saddle for riders, but as they came within fifty yards, it was clear it wasn't a saddle.

"There's blood all over the top of the banana!" Dwight shouted as he tightened the straps on his life vest and gathered up a coil of line. "I can't see a pilot at the controls. Bring me in close."

Annabelle matched the circling boat's turn and speed and came alongside on its starboard. Dwight flipped two fenders over the side, then jumped across near the stern and dropped the coil of line on the deck. Annabelle watched as he took two steps toward the helm, then froze, his face going pale. He raced forward to pull the throttle down to neutral, then turned away, dropped to the gunwale, and vomited over the side.

Annabelle dropped her speed and bumped up against the speedboat. "Dwight! What's wrong? What—"

But her eyes provided the answer before Dwight could speak. The area around the speedboat helm was a pool of blood and the interior of the windscreen had been sprayed with it. Seated at the captain's chair was the bottom third of a torso, a few inches of spinal column jutting up like a fence post. The rest of the skipper —ribs, chest, arms, head—was gone.

CHAPTER TWENTY-SIX

Sarah cracked a smile as she watched Joseph and Brighteyes continue their game of hide-and-seek. The playful contest had begun about two hours ago; one would rush ahead of the group and hide, then try to scare the other. With both man and beast possessing such finely tuned senses, the seeking was always more successful than the hiding.

Littlefoot was endlessly amused by the back-and-forth and even DawnWaker had come out of her shell and panted with mirth when the seeker discovered the hider, usually by throwing a pine cone at their hidden foe.

In addition, the dashing ahead served another purpose; it kept the group moving at a faster pace. Now that they knew the Stone that Sleeps could detect its darker counterpart—and detect the *effects* of the meteorite—they could rely more on the dream-catcher. They had come across a salmon on the shore, wild-eyed and dead. The talisman was drawn to it, which supported Joseph's hypothesis that the lightweight meteorite had floated downstream when the waterways had become swollen with the downpour the night of the attack.

The other reason they had picked up their pace was because of

Wolf Wallace. An hour after Brighteyes had tossed the drone and the tracking chip from the summit of the western ridge, they had heard ATVs to their north in the general vicinity of their misdirection.

"They may give up and go back to the Salmon River, but they might continue to follow us south," Joseph said. "We should be out of the jamming; is the sat phone working?"

Sarah was the keeper of the phone; she took it out of her backpack and powered it up. "Yes!"

"Good. Call Sharkey."

She punched in the number they had programmed and handed the phone to Joseph as they walked.

"Hey, guys!" Sharkey answered. "I was wondering when you would call."

"Shark, this is Joseph... we're in a bit of a pickle. You remember that Wolf Wallace character? The one who gave you all that TV show swag of his?"

"Yep."

"Any of his stuff that you've got on you, or in your truck... get it and bring it into your house. Tell Farley to do the same. Some of the items have tracking chips in them."

"That sneaky sumbitch," Sharkey muttered. "Why don't I just burn it all?"

"If they suddenly go dead, Wolf will know you're on to him. This way, it'll just look like you two are in your homes."

"Roger. Consider it done."

"Two other things... one: we had to leave your Jeep on the side of the road near Orogrande." Joseph gave him the location, then moved on to item two. "I know it's a lot to ask, but... can you and Farley bring your trucks down and meet us north of Upper Payette Lake? There's a dirt road that splits off to the northwest of Warren Wagon Road and heads up toward Jackson and French Creeks. I'll text you the coordinates."

"I think I know it... we'll have to go all the way south down to

McCall and then back north from there. That'll take two or three hours. And it'll probably take an hour to track down Farley and get the thumbs-up from our CO."

"You'll get there before we do... we still have a ways to go."

"All right, then, I'll get rolling. You want me to bring anything?"

"Yes. Two big tarps. One for each truck."

"Damnation!" Wolf shouted as he watched Keith pull up in the U-Haul... then promptly drive off the edge of Big Salmon Road and partway down the embankment. The left rear tire spun impotently in the silt and scree as Keith frantically tried to back up. Ian ran toward the truck, waving his arms at the intern to stop what he was doing.

Merle sighed. "Well, this ain't going well."

Wolf had to agree. They had found the drone, but the SD card with all of the high-def footage of the Bigfoots was missing. Instead, they found Athena's tracking chip shoved into the card slot. Russ and friends had tricked them! Without the tracker, they couldn't be sure which way their quarry had gone, so they needed one of the other drones Ian had in the U-Haul to make a visual search. Remounting their ATVs, they raced back to the intersection of Big Salmon and French Creek Roads to meet Keith... who had immediately served up another delay with his piss-poor driving.

"Anything on any of the other tracking devices?" Wolf asked.

Athena seemed distracted by something on her tablet. "Hmm? Oh... no, nothing new... Sharkey and Farley are still in Grangeville."

"What are you looking at?"

"I'm logged in to a forum that monitors police scanners. There's something weird going on in McCall."

"Weird? How d'ye mean?"

"Something about a monster..."

Could it be? Wolf thought for a moment, then took out his GPS navigator. There was no way Russ and his furry friend could have gotten down there so quickly. *Could they?* Finally, he made a decision. "All right, me clan... huddle up!"

"What's the plan, boss?" Merle asked.

"First, we get that idiot back on the road before he rolls into the creek. Then... Ian... get one of your other drones out and search around the area where we spotted Russ and the Bigfoots. Athena... see if you can scare up any more information on what's going on in McCall. Merle... gas up the ATVs in case Ian spots anything."

"What if we've lost 'em?" Merle asked.

"Then we'll get back on the road and head for the main highway south. And *you'll* drive!"

"Brighteyes... what happens if there is no troop to the south?" Sarah signed the question as she walked alongside the gentle giant.

Brighteyes gave a very human shrug. 'Do not know. There are lakes there. We will fish.' He panted a laugh and pointed at Dawn-Waker. '*She* will fish. She is better at fishing.'

DawnWaker watched this exchange and followed the gist of it. 'You say to human I better at fishing. Yes?'

'Yes.'

'Good. Truth. Show me more of this sign language.'

Sarah's sat phone abruptly rang. Sarah saw who it was and quickly answered. "Liz!"

"Sarah! I've been trying to call you! Your regular phone went to voicemail and your sat phone went to voicemail..."

"Sorry, Liz, no cell service out here, and we think the sat phone was jammed for a while."

"Where are you?"

Thanks to a recent huddle over the topo maps, Sarah knew the answer. "About twenty-six miles north of the resort town of McCall." Sarah wanted to tell Liz of their furry traveling companions, but she didn't know who might be listening in. "How's Bud doing?"

"He's good. They're going to release him later today. And guess who called me? Dhir! He told me Carson is coming back to Idaho!"

That's not good, Sarah thought, then asked, "What else did he say?"

"Some pretty dark stuff. Said Carson looked all better, but he was acting really strange... and apparently, he's like... super-strong now. Dhir suspects he may have killed some people."

"Listen, I need to conserve my battery," Sarah said. "Stay away from Carson... he may come looking for you."

"Way ahead of you. Bud and I are going to get out of town as soon as the hospital lets him out. But I'll call you if Dhir tells me anything else."

She hung up to find Russ looking at her. "What was that about Carson?"

"He's coming back."

Carson had just shoved a second helping of seared pork belly into his mouth when the knock came at his North Brother office door. He swallowed the fatty morsel, licked the plate, then grabbed a napkin and wiped his beard. He went over to the door and opened it a crack, remaining out of view.

"Bill? Is that you?"

"Yes, sir. The jet is fueled and ready."

"Good. I want to be wheels-up by one o'clock."

"Then... shouldn't we depart, sir?"

"I'm... waiting on something. Not sure if it worked. Give me a moment, and we'll go visit Dr. Schneider together."

Carson closed the door and returned to his desk, looking at the empty plate. Not a trace of meat remained. Not for the first time, he wondered if he was actually feeding himself... or whatever it was that his blood had become. He went to the washroom and looked in the mirror to see if he'd need to change his shirt after his lunch. The shirt was in pristine condition... but the mirror wasn't. A spiderweb of cracks radiated out from a central spot, the impact point roughly the size of a fist. *I don't remember doing that.* He looked down at his knuckles. Dried blood... and all-but-faded remnants of cuts and scratches. The inner voice chuckled and he gave his head a violent shake. Once the voice was silent, he washed his hands and face.

Outside, Singleton waited with Carson's two security guards. As Carson approached, he heard one say to the other, "They found one of Gualtieri's shoes not far from the shore. No sign of him. It was raining so hard, no prints or anything."

"Weird. He go for a swim or something?"

"Come along!" Carson interrupted as he breezed by them.

As the group came within sight of the main bio lab, it was clear something was very wrong inside. The illumination in the interior of the lab was strobing, with a strip of LED track lighting swinging crazily from the ceiling, flashing on and off and hanging by one end. In one corner, orange flames flickered from something burning. Suddenly, a man in a lab coat collided with the window that lined the wall beside the entrance. His horizontally oriented body bounced off the thick glass before falling from sight.

The door slid open and Dr. Schneider rushed out, blood spatters on her lab coat. "*Gott im Himmel!*" Breathing hard, she spotted Carson and pointed toward the lab. "Well... it worked. Too well, I fear."

"What worked?" Singleton asked with trepidation. "Doctor... you're injured!"

Schneider looked down. "Oh, this isn't mine. But I'd rather not let him kill my entire staff."

"Who?"

Singleton's question was partly answered when a large cylinder of oxygen was hurled through the viewing window beside them, the metallic tank clanking to the hallway floor as shards of reinforced glass tinkled to the ground beside it. From inside the lab, a deep, gravelly voice shouted, "Everything's Coming Up Roses!"

"What on earth?" Singleton rasped.

In the flickering light of the lab, a massive shape approached the shattered glass. A seven-foot-tall nude man stepped up to the broken window and looked out at them. His bluish skin was striped with scars and bulged with muscle. The figure held his head at an extreme angle, a look of aggression and confusion struggling for dominance on his pale features. He stuck his face through the broken glass and looked at the group. "Who Am I?" he rumbled, the semblance of a tune in his bass voice.

"It's Brick!" Singleton blurted.

The massive former bodyguard looked at him. "I Am Sixteen, Going on Seventeen."

"He's magnificent!" Carson grinned.

"You... you reanimated Brick?" Singleton shouted, aghast. He shook his head in disbelief. "After everything that has been going on with *you*, why on earth would you do such a thing?"

"Where we are going... I wanted some extra muscle. And this man is *all* muscle. Plus, he's an excellent fighter."

"I Got Rhythm," Brick spoke-sang.

"As you instructed, we transfused him with your blood," Schneider explained to Carson. "Given his size, we used two pints. Unfortunately, I'm afraid his mind was far too gone. He has been spouting nonsense ever since he snapped his restraints and rose from the table."

"Well... having the top of his skull partly caved in by that infected Bigfoot might have rattled his brains somewhat," Carson suggested.

As he heard the description of the attack that had killed him, Brick's face darkened. "Memory..." he growled. "Pore Jud Is Daid."

"See what I mean? Brain death was too extensive." Schneider sighed. "Word salad."

"No! Song titles!" Singleton blurted.

"What?" Dr. Schneider looked at him.

"I don't think what he's saying is complete nonsense," Singleton asserted, his earlier dismay giving way to excitement. "Brick's wrestling persona—Brick Broadway—was known for singing Broadway show tunes in the ring!"

Carson nodded. "He didn't sing them *well*, of course... the man's voice is like rocks in a garbage disposal... but I think you're right."

"Why just the titles?" Schneider asked. "Why not communicate with longer stretches of lyrics?"

"He explained to me the reason he only sang the titles when I was interviewing him for the job," Singleton said. "You see, song *titles* can't be copyrighted. But early on, he sang whole sections of songs... *that* was copyright infringement, and his wrestling federation was on the hook for licensing fees. They took it out of his salary for years."

"If I Were a Rich Man," Brick lamented.

"It's almost as if he understands us," one of the guards said.

"Whether he does or does not, he must be restrained," Schneider declared. She looked at Carson's guards. "You two... you should have the muscle immobilizer shots, *ja*?"

When the two men pulled hypodermics from their coat pockets, Brick's demeanor changed again, his brows lowering. He beckoned toward the guards through the shattered glass. "Send In the Clowns." With that, he stepped away from the shattered glass.

The two guards entered, syringes at the ready. Brick stood in the center of the room, his head canted to the side, one massive arm leaning on a chair. His scalp had been shaved and the top of his head appeared lumpy.

"He looks like shit," one of the guards whispered.

Apparently, Brick didn't agree. "I Feel Pretty," he muttered.

Cautiously, the two men moved closer.

"Shall We Dance?" Brick rumbled, then suddenly whipped the chair he'd been leaning on at the men. It slammed into the nearest and sent the guard staggering backward, his hypodermic clattering to the floor. The second man stabbed his needle at Brick's chest, but the ex-wrestler grabbed him by the wrist and took the syringe from him, tossing it aside. He clamped his massive fingers on the man's throat and lifted him from the ground. At that moment, the small fire in the corner finally generated enough smoke that the sprinkler system activated, showering the room with conical jets of water.

"Singing in the Rain!" Brick bellowed, lifting the guard high above his head.

"That will be quite enough of that, Brick," Carson snapped as he stepped into the room and walked right up to the naked mountain of muscle.

Brick turned his head, gristly pops sounding as the broken cervical vertebrae in his neck ground against each other.

"Cameron! What are you doing?" Singleton cried out.

"Testing a theory."

Brick tossed the guard aside like a rag doll and turned to face Carson. "Hello, Dolly."

"Cameron, actually... but I suspect you're telling me you recognize me."

"Memory," Brick concurred with a crooked nod.

"Good... you should know that I'm the reason you are now alive. Although, I suppose, in some small part... I was also the reason you became dead in the first place."

Brick growled and cracked his knuckles. "Ya Got Trouble."

"I don't think so, but give it your best shot."

Brick roared and swung a meaty fist that seemed on track to take Carson's head off, but the billionaire raised a hand and the punch halted in midair. Grunting and straining, Brick couldn't seem to move the arm.

Carson smiled. "It appears my hypothesis was correct."

Brick swung his other fist, but that one too seemed to become stuck before it could reach Carson. "Shipoopi!" Brick swore.

"Ah... *The Music Man*. Obscure reference." Carson closed his eyes and focused, then opened them again.

Brick's enraged face softened and he lowered his arms. Moving jerkily, he picked up the chair he'd thrown, set it down, and took a seat.

"There we are. Bill, have security cut the damn sprinklers, would you?"

"How on earth...?" Dr. Schneider stared at Brick, her mouth agape.

"It was something Dr. Takagawa said... that my blood was behaving like it was alive. Like an organism. And you, Doctor... you made the comparison that my blood was acting almost like nanobots. I recently discovered I could control it, to an extent."

Carson couldn't share the circumstances of when he had discovered this trick—when he had pulled the blood back into his own body, after the soon-to-be-dead Hilda had shot him, and shortly before introducing his CFO to the business end of an axe.

Carson gestured and Brick raised an arm, then dropped it to his lap. "The transfusion of my blood into Brick did more than reanimate his corpse... it has also given me partial control of his body."

"Astonishing," Schneider declared. "We must run an entire battery of tests!"

"And we will... *after* I get back from Idaho." As the sprinklers finally shut off, Carson turned to Brick and let his consciousness reach out to touch the man. He was instantly aware of a bloodstream, but with additional focus he was able to brush against Brick's thoughts. "You will come willingly, won't you, Brick?"

The enormous naked man rose from the chair. "I Cain't Say No."

"Good. Now let's find some clothes for you before you put someone's eye out."

CHAPTER TWENTY-SEVEN

At the helm of the police boat, Annabelle followed in the banana's wake as Officer Dwight Flynn brought the speedboat toward Payette Lake's western shore. The forensics team from Boise had already left Critch's boat on the peninsula and driven all the way around the lake to the site of the other attack, so it made sense for Dwight to bring their nautical crime scene to that location. But first, they had circled the area, looking for any sign of whoever had been riding the banana. Spotting no one, they decided to bring the boat in and return later to continue the search.

Dwight drove slowly, piloting the speedboat awkwardly as he was forced to stand to the side of the "demi-skipper," whose partial corpse still occupied the captain's chair. Ahead, Annabelle could see flashing blue lights at the shoreline in an area between two lake houses.

Annabelle spied a cluster of inflatable inner tubes snugged up against an area of low vegetation along the shore. As she drew closer, she could see they were decorated like donuts, designed to look like an assortment of strawberry, vanilla, chocolate, and sprinkles... but all of them appeared to have acquired an additional raspberry glaze on their surfaces. Two were partly deflated, and up against one of the nearby docks, she could see the sad remains of an alligator pool float, only the head still holding its shape.

Dwight aimed for one property's dock and Annabelle went toward the other, which currently hosted the Sharlie Hunters' pontoon boat on one side. The gang was spread out along the dock, staying clear of the yellow-tape cordon that had been hastily set up around the part of the shore nearest to the floatie massacre. Brady was filming, Kevin was glassing the shore to the north with binoculars, and Stuart was stretched out flat on the dock, looking down into the water with a hand shielding his eyes. *Probably scanning for prints or drag marks on the bottom*, Annabelle thought. Cilantro was nowhere to be seen, but her master, Mark, was aboard the boat, struggling with an odd contraption that appeared to be a collection of galvanized plumbing pipes.

As Annabelle motored slowly up to the dock, the Sharlie Hunters stopped what they were doing; as they helped her tie up, they all began speaking at once.

Brady: "Graybill! Glad you're back! You brought your rifles, I hope."

Stuart: "It's definitely Sharlie! The witness got a good look as she swam away!"

Mark: "Cilantro's been hiding under the helm seat since we got here. That smell from the moose... it's very strong here."

Kevin: "Dear God, what happened to that banana?"

Annabelle grabbed her long rifle bag and stepped across. "Did they find any bodies?" She gestured toward the bloody donuts.

"*Entire* bodies?" Mark cleared his throat. "No... a lot of blood... and a few, um... chunks."

"Was there somebody on that speedboat?" Kevin asked.

"Half of somebody," Annabelle replied. "And it seems pretty clear at least one person was riding the banana. We didn't see anyone in the water, but Dwight's going back out to search. I suggested we could come along and help."

"The more eyes, the better," Brady agreed.

Annabelle set the padded carry bag on the dock and sat down beside it. She unzipped the case and took out the hunting rifle and a box of .30-06 cartridges. "Whatever did this... it's big." She started loading the rifle. "If we come across it, we need to kill it right away."

"But..." Stuart started to protest but then shook his head. "You're probably right. Capturing it alive doesn't seem like an option, does it?"

Mark sighed. "So much for my homemade harpoon gun. I nearly had it ready to go! Just had to screw in the compressed air cylinder."

"Finish it up. We may need everything we have. Brady, take the tranquilizer rifle out of the bag. It has one dart loaded and two backups snapped to the stock."

Brady took out the weapon and examined it, then held it at his side. "I don't get it. Plesiosaurs are fish eaters! They wouldn't go after a human."

"Not a lot of plesiosaurs in the wild to help you confirm that," Kevin said dryly. "And we still don't know what it is... that flipper print had claws, remember?"

Ashore, Dwight skirted the crime scene tape and joined them at their dock. "So... as far as this 'donut massacre' goes... forensics is debating whether one or two people were killed by a propeller strike out on the lake and the inflatables ended up here. But the eyewitness swears he heard screams and then..." Dwight cleared his throat. "And then saw Sharlie swimming away. The lead detective thinks the eyewitness is a crank."

"What do *you* think?" Annabelle asked.

"I think they're gonna have to reevaluate once they look in the speedboat." Dwight took out his cell phone. "I also think the boat parade needs to be canceled." He placed a call, then waited. *Ring. Ring. Ring.* "Dammit, Vance... quick sucking off the corporate sponsors and—oh, hey, Mr. Mayor! It's Officer Flynn. Listen, we've got a situation here!" He listened for a moment, then swore under his breath. Tapping his screen, he put the call on speaker. "I understand you're very busy, sir, but I'm currently on the site of what appears to be multiple deaths."

"What? How many?"

"Not sure, sir... only one partial body has been found so far."

"What? Then why do you say 'multiple' deaths?"

"It's just... well... the evidence suggests there were more victims."

"Murder?"

"No, sir. At least, not... not by another human."

"What on earth are you talking about?"

"We think Sharlie attacked a bunch of swimmers and boaters," Brady blurted.

"What the hell...? Who's speaking?"

"That was Brady Johnson, sir," Dwight explained. "He and some of his friends are assisting with a search for—"

"Brady?! The bald guy who wanted to change Vancefest to Sharliefest? What the hell is going on?"

"Sir, *something* attacked a boat... and possibly some swimmers. Combine that with what happened to Critch..."

"And the moose," Stuart added.

"Moose? Look, Officer... I've got a festival to run!"

"Sir, people are dead! Is the chief of police with you?"

"The chief is out on the water with his personal boat, wrangling the other boaters... we'll be leading the parade, and—"

"Mr. Mayor! You have to cancel the parade!" Annabelle shouted.

"Who is *this*, now?"

"Annabelle Graybill. I'm a Ranger with the Forest Service. We believe there is a large marine animal attacking boats, and—"

"Oh, for the love of... not you too! Listen, you idiots, there's no such thing as a Sharlie! It's just a local-yokel fish story for the tourists! And speaking of tourists, there are a *lot* of them here for the festival! *And* press, *and* donors! We are not going to cancel *anything* for a bargain-basement Loch Ness Monster hoax! Whatever happened to that boater, Officer Dwight... *you* handle it. The Vancefest Boat Parade will go forward as scheduled!"

"He hung up," Dwight muttered. "I'll try the chief... he said he'd be off duty today, but I'd say this takes precedence." He called, but the chief's voicemail came on after only one ring. Dwight left a detailed message, then looked out over the water. "The parade isn't for several more hours. We should go back out and search for whoever else was with the speedboat."

"When people ride those waterskiing floaties, they almost always have life vests on," Annabelle suggested. "They may have fallen off in another part of the lake, before the boat went out of control. Can you find out where the boat owner lives? We could backtrack from where we found the boat to its dock."

"Good plan. Maybe the bottom half of the victim has a wallet. You wanna go with me?"

"No, I'll stick with these fellas." Annabelle nodded toward the Sharlie Hunters. "They may need my firepower. And you might want to borrow one of the officers at the crime scene. Some extra backup couldn't hurt, in case we run into Sharlie... or *whatever* it is."

The beast known to locals as "Sharlie" didn't really know what she was either. Her long neck and head certainly looked "plesiosaurical," but she was far larger than even the titanic Elasmosaurus, and her snout was longer and her teeth more robust. Her "fins" were scaled and structured more like webbed, clawed feet. Her overall body shape was somewhat crocodilian, but elongated... her tail almost eellike. In some ways, each of the Sharlie Hunters—with their varying guesses as to her nature—was right. Well, all except

Kevin; extradimensional creatures were an absolute fantasy. At least in *this* lake.

Regardless of what she was, Sharlie knew this: she was still hungry. Very, *very* hungry. A tiny part of her mind that still possessed shards of memory knew that this all-consuming hunger was odd... because she was used to eating a bunch of fish and then hibernating. For *years*, if need be. But in a short span of time, she had eaten countless fish, two deer, a moose, and *eleven* humans. And yet... she was still ravenous.

One thing was for certain... humans were absolutely *delicious*. And Sharlie knew where she could find more. A *lot* more. At the south side of the lake, many humans lived and congregated around a shore that was lined with low structures and docks. She normally avoided this area; there were so many boats and so much noise and light. But now... she thought of that place as a veritable smorgasbord.

Unfortunately, before she could go there and enjoy another eating spree, she had an issue to take care of... one that she'd been working at for the past hour. Something was wrong with her digestion; her instincts told her she had devoured some inorganic material when she'd wolfed down her prey. Something about what she had eaten was interfering with her buoyancy, making her lighter than usual. Bracing herself on the bottom with her clawed paddle-like feet dug into the silt, she tried once again to bring up the blockage from her stomach. She felt the strange singing object shift slightly at her efforts, but whatever had fused itself to her innards held fast. But that wasn't what she was trying to get rid of; heaving and retching, she finally regurgitated a bright orange object. It immediately shot to the surface.

After she had eaten the five humans near the shore, she had gone after swifter prey. Three of the humans that she had plucked from the back of the yellow bouncy-boat had been wearing these orange vests; in her feeding frenzy she had swallowed them whole. She had taken more care with the human on the boat, snapping off the top of it, before the boat suddenly roared ahead, out of reach. By then, she was struggling with what she had eaten and had dived for the bottom.

With one of the orange floating things vomited up, she braced herself anew and began to work on the other two. Soon... she would swim south... and feast.

"New York, New York," Brick purred. He was seated in a window seat, and the angle of his broken neck was such that he had a good view of the distant skyline of Manhattan.

"Yes. Very good, Brick," Carson encouraged. Even though he could take outright control of him, that required a lot of concentration. It would be easier if the man became a willing ally, as he had once been... before the infected silverback had piledrivered him into the forest floor. Carson had posited that an infusion of his blood might grant Brick healing abilities similar to those he himself possessed. It had restored the wrestler's nervous system, but he supposed the regeneration didn't go as far as chiropractic readjustments. Without surgery, it was likely the odd tilt of Brick's head would be permanent. The top of his skull could use some work too.

Focusing on the ex-wrestler, Carson sent him to sleep, then rose and joined Bill and the two security guards. "Brick will need some form of hat, I think."

"I thought of that, sir. When I gathered clothes for him from his quarters, I packed his ballistic helmet. I also brought his body armor."

Carson smiled, thinking of the minimal effect from Hilda's bullets when she'd shot him in the chest. "Not sure he'll need that, but... couldn't hurt."

He glanced around the cabin at the other occupants. In addition to Singleton and Brick, his two guards were along to keep him from misbehaving; they'd also be useful in the event they came across Joseph and needed to "persuade" him to reveal the location of the sphere. Finally, there were four technicians with varying specialties.

"What time will we land?" Carson asked.

"Per your request, the pilot will maintain maximum speed once he is at altitude. Flight time is just three hours. But we will burn a lot of fuel."

"Time is money, and it's more valuable to me than fuel. When do we actually land?"

"The time zones work in our favor, sir. Missoula is Mountain time, so we'll actually land only an hour after we left. And Grangeville is in Pacific time, so... if we transfer to the helicopter and get airborne quickly enough, we'll essentially land at the same time on the clock."

"Good." Carson winced as a hunger pang gripped his stomach. His gaze flicked to one of the guards sitting nearby. *Such a thick, meaty neck.* "If you'll excuse me, Bill... I need to retire to my stateroom for a while. I'm not to be disturbed."

He rose to go aft, then paused, looking at his reanimated bodyguard. *I'm not sure whether he needs to eat or not... but if his blood is like mine...* "Brick. Come with me."

Carson led the way back to the galley and grabbed the cooler he'd ordered loaded aboard. Bringing it to his stateroom's washroom, he set it in the tub and opened the lid. Various cuts of raw meat glistened; the ice they lay atop was stained pink from blood and juices.

Brick leaned over and looked at the contents. "Food, Glorious Food."

But not as glorious as the meatbags in the airplane cabin, The Other sang.

Carson shook his head violently, then directed Brick to eat a pork chop. He hoped the contents of this cooler would be enough to sustain them until they found the sphere. Carson selected a T-bone, sank his teeth into one side of it, and tore half of the steak from the bone.

"Now what?" Sarah asked.

The group of humans and Bigfoots stood at the edge of French Creek. Ahead, the waterway split in two, one stream heading southwest, one southeast.

Russ held the dreamcatcher aloft, hoping for a sign. "C'mon... right or left?"

Joseph set down the lead-lined sample box he'd been carrying and shrugged the rifle and backpack from his shoulders. He took the topographical map from an outer pocket and spread it on the ground.

Sarah retrieved the GPS navigator and sat on a rock beside him. "We're here." She showed him the coordinates. While Joseph found the spot on the paper map, Sarah watched Brighteyes as he signaled to DawnWaker. Sarah couldn't understand most of their "Sasquatchese," but she picked up a word here or there. Years ago, when her late father had taught Brighteyes a small lexicon of sign language, the young Bigfoot had shared some of his own, creating a combined mini-dictionary that Professor Bishop had recorded in his journal.

She rose and called for their attention with a decent facsimile of a Bigfoot grunt, then signed as she spoke. "The bad rock we seek... we don't know which way it went." She pointed at their two waterway options.

Brighteyes gave a pant of understanding, then shared this information with DawnWaker. Littlefoot, who had learned Dr. Bishop's signs, needed no help.

"French Creek continues to our right... and that is Jackson Creek on the left," Joseph explained. "Jackson continues to the south, toward Upper Payette Lake and other waterways... French terminates in a gully to the southeast. We might be able to get to the end of French Creek and eliminate that option... but it would take a lot of time."

"And if Wolf is still looking for us," Russ said over his shoulder, "that would give him a chance to catch up."

Brighteyes clapped his massive hands together to draw everyone's attention. He signed and vocalized a suggestion, then he turned to DawnWaker and explained what he wanted to do.

Sarah nodded and signed back. "Good. Yes. Try." She turned to the others and translated. "Brighteyes points out that the dead frog and salmon we came across—the ones that the stone 'turned'—gave off a distinctive odor. What he calls 'Alive-Dead.'" She demonstrated the double gesture as she said it. "He's offering to scout ahead. He'll take one creek, DawnWaker the other. She'll bring Littlefoot, since he'll recognize the scent they're looking for."

Joseph seemed pleased. "A good suggestion. And we can rest and prepare a meal while they search."

Brighteyes indicated by the sun how long they would go before returning, then he headed down the Jackson while DawnWaker and Littlefoot took the French Creek fork to the right.

As Russ and Joseph sat down to prepare lunch, Sarah traced a finger along the map. "It looks like our meeting place with Sharkey is closer to the Jackson Creek branch. He should be arriving there shortly."

Joseph thought for a moment. "Call him... tell him we may be another four hours... or more, depending on where we think the stone went."

Sarah placed a call on the sat phone; Sharkey picked up on the first ring.

"Hey, gang. I was about to call you. Ran into a bit of a snag. Buncha cops closed the road that runs along the west side of Payette Lake, so Farley 'n' me have to go through downtown McCall to get to the eastern shore road. But there's some kind of festival happening and it's slow going."

"That's all right… we're still four hours out from the road we're meeting you on. Maybe longer." Sarah explained their dilemma, then asked, "Why was the road closed?"

"Not sure. There was a roadblock and they were checking cars, then turning folks around. I saw some McCall police… and there was a pair of Idaho state troopers, too. Told 'em we were Guard and asked what was up, but they were cagey about it."

"Okay, thanks for the update. We'll call you again once we're on the move." Sarah hung up and was putting the phone away when a call came in from Liz.

"Hey, Liz, what's up?" Sarah said. She listened for a moment, then interrupted, "Hang on, Liz! Lemme put you on speaker so Russ and Joseph can hear. Say again."

"Something's happening! Dhir has been talking to a guy in the Grangeville quarantine site, and there's some kind of activity going on in McCall! Rumors about a 'monster' attacking people in the lake there. Most of the hardcore army guys are still out in the forest where the Bigfoot attacks happened, but it sounds like they're sending down a single helicopter to check it out."

"A monster… another Sasquatch?" Russ asked.

"No… it had something to do with a local lake monster story, so it might be a hoax… but some people definitely died from *something*. I know you're just north of McCall, so I thought you ought to know. If Dhir finds out anything more, I'll have him call you directly."

Joseph was already poring over the map again as Sarah stashed the sat phone and traded it for the GPS device. "Payette Lake is only about sixteen miles from here," she said. "And if we follow the Jackson Creek branch, eventually the flow of water leads there."

"You think this monster talk is related?" Russ asked.

"Don't you?"

Suddenly, there was a series of sharp raps, coming from the southeast. *Thump thump…* pause… *thump.* A moment passed, then: *Thump thump…* pause… *thump.*

"Tree knocking!" Sarah exclaimed. "Sasquatch use that to communicate over distance. Brighteyes is telling us to come." A single knock sounded from the southwest, followed by two more, spaced out with several seconds between. The sequence was not repeated. "And that's the female, acknowledging."

"I guess we know which way we're going!" Russ declared.

Joseph hurriedly folded up the map and gathered up his back-pack and rifle. Russ wolfed down the rest of his lunch with one hand while packing items away with the other. Sarah found two large river rocks and knocked them together, mimicking Dawn-Waker's knock-pause-knock-knock acknowledgment. In minutes, Russ, Joseph, and Sarah were on the move.

CHAPTER TWENTY-EIGHT

Hunter Strand the Hot Dog Man carefully boarded his pontoon boat and set the newly filled propane tank amidships. Returning to the dock, he grabbed the extra bag of ice he'd picked up, tossed it aboard, then untied the lines and pushed away from the dock as he nimbly stepped across.

"Youse prob'ly lost out on fifty bucks already, Strand," he muttered at himself as he turned the ignition key and started the outboard. Pointing the bow of the pontoon boat toward the center of the lake, he began the slow trek to downtown McCall and the gathering boat parade. He would've been there already if he hadn't forgotten to check the propane tank; it had been running on fumes.

Once he was pointed in the right direction and ascertained there wasn't any boat traffic nearby, Hunter knelt and quickly installed the propane tank, then turned on the heating unit; water in the stainless-steel trays was currently room temp, and he'd need to get it up to 160 before he could drop the dogs in.

Hunter had grown up in New York City and "dirty water dogs" from corner hot dog stands had been a lunch staple when he'd worked in Midtown. After thirty years there, he'd had enough of city life and wanted to get as far away from the crowds as he could. Idaho fit the bill. Six months after moving to McCall, he'd bought a used center-console pontoon boat and rechristened it *Water Dog*. After painting each pontoon like a hot dog with mustard and relish, he'd installed the components of a hot dog stand amidships behind the captain's chair.

On the port side were the heated portions of his setup: the main hot water tray for the hot dogs, a smaller one for the unnaturally red spicy sausages, and a removable compartment and ladle for chili. Next to the heated section was a bun warmer, and then at the end, a "condiment zone" with all the fixings. On the starboard side were two ice chests, one to store the "on deck" dogs and sausages, the other loaded with soft drinks and water.

Motoring along the lake, Hunter Strand the Hot Dog Man delivered porky goodness to recreational boaters from first thaw to first freeze. Hungry customers always knew when he was coming: his floating food cart sported a large frankfurter-and-bun balloon tethered to a springy dowel. Vertically oriented, the hot dog sported a happy face with wide eyes and a smiling mouth. The kids loved him, and one tow-headed youngster had nicknamed the bulging cartoon balloon "Mr. Floppy"—on account of the balloon's tendency to partially deflate and sag as the day dragged on. Hunter's business was brisk, particularly when he came upon a cluster of boats at anchor. And now... a huge boat parade? He'd be surprised if he returned home with a single dog left.

Hunter stepped to the steering wheel and made an adjustment, then went back for the bag of ice. He'd discovered the lack of propane after he'd already iced up the coolers, so he surmised there would've been some melting during the time he'd been forced to drive to town and back for the propane. After topping off the coolers with ice, he scanned the lake again, made a quick course correction to avoid a one-man sailboat, then checked his hot water temp. *Close enough.* Hunter slid the stainless-steel chili compartment into its slot, then started loading up the hot dogs.

In his haste, he dropped one on the deck and it rolled under a bench. Hunter tracked down the errant tube steak and held it up to the sun for a spot check. *Salvageable? Nah. Give it up for luck.* He cocked his arm and called out, "Yo, Poseidon! I got ya sacrifice right 'ere!" then tossed the floppy wiener overboard, where it landed with a plop.

Hunter was turning around to grab the bag of red hots when a sudden movement flashed by in his peripheral vision. Behind his boat, something had snagged the floating frankfurter from the surface. Something *big*. Even with the pontoon boat's wake churning the water, Hunter could see the ripples expanding from the strike. *Dang... whatever that was, it was huge! Tiger muskie? Sturgeon?*

Still holding the bag of red hots, Hunter took two steps to the helm and throttled the engine down, bringing the *Water Dog* to a standstill. He stepped to the stern and fished a red sausage from the bag. *Let's see how you like a spicy one.* He tossed a red hot into the water at the stern and waited, eyes locked on the bobbing wiener.

Something was moving beneath the boat; he could make out shapes—roughly twenty feet down—as the unknown object came into view, swimming under the *Water Dog* from bow to stern. The first micro-thought Hunter had was that this was a school of large fish... but almost immediately, he realized the shapes he was seeing were a pair of large paddle-like legs extending to the side of a massive mud-brown body. And the shape at the front... he didn't have long to ponder what *that* was.

In the blink of an eye, a long head on an even longer neck shot up from the water, jaws pointed straight up and gaping open. The mouth engulfed the tiny sausage as the head continued rising, shooting into the afternoon sky. The pontoon boat lurched as the body of the creature surfaced underneath it, stranding the *Water Dog* on an island of glistening brown flesh. Suspended nearly fifteen feet in the air, the creature's head corkscrewed around on its serpentine neck. For a moment, it examined Mr. Floppy. Then it locked its eyes on Hunter.

Being somewhat new to the area, Hunter didn't immediately recall the name "Sharlie"—even though he'd seen it often enough around McCall—but he didn't need to know this thing's name to know its fangs meant business. The beast's jaws were closed at the moment, but he could see interlocking teeth along the sides of its mouth. Hunter started to turn and run for the front of the boat— maybe get the propellor spinning and chop up its back to scare it off. But then, the creature opened its mouth.

A strange hum radiated through the air. The sound seemed to resonate in a realm between the tone of a tuning fork and a single chord sung by an angelic choir. Hunter turned back around to face the beast, slack-jawed as he basked in the acoustic emanations. He shuffled to the edge of the stern and held up the bag of red dogs.

"Take them all... I...suh... sacrifice to you."

The creature's head lowered, and Hunter's rapidly dwindling thoughts defaulted to a routine question for a hungry customer.

"You... you want chili with that?"

Apparently, chili wasn't required. Sharlie extended her neck further until her head was right over the man in the boat, then her jaws plunged downward, engulfing him in a fleshy, fang-rimmed mouth. Withdrawing her neck into the sky, the Twilight Dragon of Payette Lake pointed her snout upward, unhinged her jaw, and swallowed her prey whole in three gulping pulses of her throat. Hunter Strand the Hot Dog Man went down easy, with a hint of cayenne heat.

As the creature sank into the depths once more, the *Water Dog* settled onto the surface of the lake. Grinning cheerfully, Mr. Floppy wobbled in the breeze as the boat floated south with the current.

"Anything?" Wolf asked, his impatience growing by the minute.

The team was currently finishing up a meal at the River Rock Café on the side of Route 95. After a fruitless search of French Creek with Ian's remaining drone, they had traveled west to Riggins. After stopping to gas up next door, they'd sat down to strategize while they ate a decent meal and made use of the café's facilities. The trip in the U-Haul had been cramped, with Wolf, Athena, and Merle stuffed into the cab and Ian and the intern riding in the back with the ATVs.

Athena had a laptop, a tablet, and a GPS tracker splayed out on the table in front of her. She clicked around, shaking her head. "The remaining tracking devices are still stationary at Sharkey's and Farley's houses."

Wolf waved that away. "Nae, I mean in McCall. Those reports of a monster on the police scanner... is it a Bigfoot?"

"Not a Bigfoot, no." Athena moved some windows around on her laptop. "It turns out there's a local legend about a lake monster called Sharlie who supposedly lives in Payette Lake. Kinda like a mini–Loch Ness Monster... who I'm sure you're familiar with."

"What do you mean by that?"

"Well... Loch Ness is in Scotland... and you're..."

"Oh! Yes! Aye! 'Tis true. Ach... good ol' Nessie. Seen 'er meself when I was a wee bairn."

"Mm-hmm. Anyway, it's probably just one of those sightings from some kook that ended up on the police scanner forum, and..." Athena trailed off and squinted at something on the screen. "Wait. Multiple fatalities... blood on a boat... roadblocks." She looked up. "Whatever is going on there, it's growing."

"That settles it! We go south to Payette Lake. Many of the waterways that lead to it connect to where Russ and his furry companions vanished. Perhaps we can head them off! And if we get some footage of a Nessie on top of that, so much the better."

'Man-machines!' Littlefoot signed excitedly from behind a copse of low trees. DawnWaker was crouched nearby.

'Danger?' she asked.

'I do not think danger,' Brighteyes signed back. 'I will ask...' Then he pant-grunted, 'Air-rah.'

Brighteyes had been referring to the blond female human as "Daughter of Beardface," but that had seemed lengthy and unnecessary. He had heard the other humans speak her name—Sarah—and was able to approximate it, although he was incapable of forming his lips and teeth into the shape needed to make the hissing sound that began the human name. He moved over to her in a low crouch and asked his question.

'Air-rah... man-machines. They friends?'

"Yes. One machine I know," she whispered and signed. "But I will make sure. Wait here."

Brighteyes passed the exchange along to Littlefoot and Dawn-Waker, and the trio watched as Sarah and the human known as "Russ" left their concealment and walked to the dirt road. Two human males—one quite tall—exited the vehicles and waited for Sarah and Russ to join them.

'You... hide well.'

Brighteyes was startled as the human with the long black braid of hair appeared at his side. He had not even heard him approach until the man was beside him, using some of Brighteyes and Sarah's simple sign language, not accompanying it with any human speech.

'You are quiet,' Brighteyes signed back. 'Like a puma.'

The man wrinkled his brow; Brighteyes had learned that human facial expressions did not necessarily indicate aggressive intent. The human signed back. 'I learn some sign language watching you and Daughter of Beardface... but I do not know that last word.'

Brighteyes panted understanding. He mimed a big cat stalking its prey, then pawed the air.

"Ah! Cougar!" the man said in human speech. "You honor me."

Brighteyes did not know what the man had said, but it seemed heartfelt. He offered his knuckles, and the braided-hair man bumped his own against them, then rose and went to join Russ and Sarah.

"You want to put three Bigfeet in our trucks?" Farley asked incredulously. "Are you nuts?"

"The plural of Bigfoot is Bigfoots," Russ said. "Sarah beat that into me pretty early on. Or you can just play it safe with Sasquatches."

"Oh, gee, I'm sorry... you wanna put three Bigfoots and/or Sasquatches in our trucks? Still just as nuts, no matter how you say it."

"That's what ya wanted the tarps for," Sharkey said.

Sarah nodded. "Correct. Look, Wolf Wallace knows they're with us, and we may have lost him back there... but maybe not."

"And knowing my competitor," Russ added, "if there's a chance for him to film a Bigfoot—or capture one—I doubt he'll give up. Our Bigfoot friends were traveling south anyway... so we can at least give them a big head start."

Joseph walked up at the tail end of the discussion. "We have reason to believe that the sphere we're searching for might have something to do with whatever is going on in Payette Lake. We'd like to get close to the lake and try our dreamcatcher again."

"That thing you got in Kamiah?" Sharkey asked. "You really believe that'll work?"

"It's worked already," Russ insisted, then went on to explain the fish and frogs the talisman had "pointed" at. "We'll travel down toward the lake, find a thickly forested area to drop off our friends, then continue on to McCall and see if we can get a hit on the sphere."

"The roadblock you mentioned," Joseph asked. "Where was that?"

"A quarter mile up Warren Wagon Road, just north of town, close to the south end of the lake," Sharkey said. "Might be cleared up by now, whatever it was."

"Our friend Liz said there were rumors of a lake monster attacking people," Sarah said. "If that's true, that might be what the roadblock was about."

"Wait... a lake monster?" Farley said with a snort. "You mean Sharlie? Oh please, that's just a silly story to get tourists to buy T-shirts."

"Maybe so," Joseph said. "But all legends come from somewhere... and if the Stone that Sings came into contact with a large predator, it could certainly explain this talk of 'monster attacks' on the lake. We need to hurry. Word of this incident is out, and if certain people make the same connection we did, it won't take long until others come looking."

Carson opened his eyes at the tapping on the executive cabin door. He had been trying to calm the urges inside, but his meditation didn't seem to be as effective this time around. On several occasions, as he pushed The Other into its mental cage, the bars didn't seem to hold. Fortunately, the voice was quiet now. At least the one inside his mind. The voice outside the door was quite insistent as it shouted his name.

"Cameron!" The tapping became pounding. "It's Bill!"

"Forgive me," Carson called out, "I was resting. Have we landed?"

"Five minutes, sir... but I need to speak with you rather urgently."

Carson took mental inventory, then spoke. "Come in, Bill... but stay by the door." He retreated to the rear of the stateroom and waited until Singleton opened the door and peered cautiously inside. Carson spotted one of the guards looking over Singleton's shoulder. "Both of you, come in."

The pair entered and Singleton shut the door. "Sir, we will land shortly, and the helicopter is ready and waiting."

"Are we on schedule, then? Any weather over Grangeville?"

"No, sir, but... you might want to consider an alternative location."

"Explain."

Singleton raised a tablet and read from it. "Our source in the quarantine facility says that something has the government DARPA types rushing to send a helicopter down to McCall, Idaho."

"Where's that?"

"It's a resort town on a lake, seventy miles south of Grangeville."

"And why are they going there? I thought they were searching the area where the... 'traditional' zombies came from."

"They still have a large presence there, but there are reports coming out of McCall of some sort of monster attacking people. Only rumors, mind you, but enough that the military is sending a small squad to investigate."

"They think the sphere—or something that came in contact with it—might have ended up down there," Carson surmised. "Or... if it *was* a meteorite... maybe there's more than one? The 'monster' you mentioned... is it another Bigfoot?"

"Unless it's a good swimmer, I don't think so, sir. The attacks all appear to have happened in or beside Payette Lake."

Carson thought for a moment. "My gut's telling me there's something to this, and I always listen to my gut." Carson's vision suddenly went a hazy red. *If that's true, then listen to your gut right now and feed it!* the inner voice shouted. *Your good buddy Bill is a little on the lean side compared to your babysitter, but I'll take either... or both!* Carson pinched his eyes shut, then spoke. "Tell the helicopter we're going to McCall," he managed.

The executive jet's cockpit announced their descent and asked that everyone buckle up. Carson gestured at the two men. "Go take your seats first. I'll be along shortly." At Singleton's hesitation, he added, "I'm fine, Bill."

"That's good to hear, sir, but..."

"Spit it out."

"It's Brick, sir. For the past half hour, he's been singing songs from *Cats*."

"I apologize... while I was meditating, I must have lost my concentration. I can control him, but it likely wears off after a time. See you up front shortly."

He ducked back in to the washroom for another steak, polished it off in seconds, then washed his face. Carson made his way forward and sat across from Brick. The mountain of a man had his head against the window as the plane descended into Missoula.

"O-O-O-Oklahoma," Brick rumbled, looking at the terrain as the plane touched down on the runway.

"Montana, actually," Carson corrected. "Listen, Brick... when we get on the ground, I want you to stick close to me. Do you understand?"

"If Ever I Would Leave You," Brick spoke-sang, nodding his crooked head.

"You won't leave me... nor I you."

The plane came to a stop and taxied toward the waiting Maiden helicopter. After equipment and personnel were transferred aboard, the Super Puma took off and angled to the southeast.

CHAPTER TWENTY-NINE

"Hunter Strand's hot dog boat is up ahead," Mark called out from the bow. "I can see Mr. Floppy."

"Probably on his way to the parade," Kevin remarked from the helm. "Let's pull up and get some grub."

Brady affected a gravelly, perverted voice: "I wouldn't mind a hot beef injection."

"Beat me to it," Stuart muttered.

Annabelle rolled her eyes. "Low-hanging fruit, fellas. Keep your eyes on the water to the sides. Kevin, your fish-finder working?"

"Yep... nothing to report."

When they had returned to the spot where they had retrieved the speedboat and its banana float, Dwight had taken the police boat to the north to search for survivors, while the Sharlie Hunters had gone south with the current. Five sets of eyes scanned the waters.

Annabelle focused on the pontoon boat to their south. Ever since it had started plying the waterways of Payette Lake, the *Water Dog* had become a familiar sight. "It's dead in the water," she observed. "And I don't see Hunter."

As they drew closer, the hairs on the back of her neck stood on end. Cilantro apparently agreed with her instinct, suddenly tensing up and growling. Annabelle lifted her rifle from the nearby bench seat and disengaged the safety. Mark readied his harpoon contraption and Brady hefted the Forest Service tranquilizer rifle. Stuart's weapon of choice was a camera with a telephoto lens.

When they came alongside the *Water Dog*, Cilantro once again whined and scooted away from the bow. The strange odor was again apparent, though not as strong as the last time.

Annabelle scanned the pontoon boat; while there wasn't the level of carnage as at the other three attacks, she quickly spotted several areas of spattered blood and a lonely shoe lying on the deck. She quickly called Dwight and relayed what they'd found.

"On my way!" Dwight reassured her.

"Good. Just look for the Mr. Floppy balloon and you'll find it."

"Where are you going?"

"To the waterfront. We've got to stop that boat parade."

Brighteyes was not enjoying his experience in the bed of the pickup. It was dark under the tarp, and the occasional bump in the road battered his tailbone. He hoped DawnWaker was okay. Even though the red-body had an adventurous spirit, she'd had no inter-action with humans before today. She had wanted to ride with him, but their combined size made that impractical. It had been decided that the diminutive Littlefoot would join her under the other tarp to provide reassurance. The tarps were secured at several points with strange elastic straps, but there were several points where the occupants could peek out.

They had been traveling for quite some time and Brighteyes had actually started to doze off when a sudden stench pushed past the musty odor of the tarp. Brighteyes jerked, now fully alert. He turned and lifted the side of the tarp closest to the front of the vehicle. Sarah had shown the three Bigfoots the windows on the back of the cabs, telling them that if they needed to speak with her or Joseph, they could rap on that window. Brighteyes did so now.

Joseph sat alongside Farley, eyes on the back of Sharkey's truck ahead of them. Russ was in the lead pickup with the dreamcatcher, ready to redirect their two-truck convoy if the talisman gave them a sign. Sarah occupied that truck as well; if the need arose, she would act as a translator for Littlefoot and DawnWaker. Joseph would provide the same service for Brighteyes, although his vocabulary was newly learned and quite limited.

There came a sudden tapping at the back of the cab, and Joseph turned to find a pair of brilliant blue eyes peering in the window. Brighteyes tapped the glass again with one hand while holding the tarp over his head with the other; they might soon encounter other vehicles, and Sarah had made it clear that they should remain under the tarps at all times.

Joseph slid the window open and signed and spoke. "You good?"

The Bigfoot pointed at himself, then tapped his nose. He gave two exaggerated sniffs of the air, then signed 'Bad.'

Joseph sniffed the air. Apart from the musky scent of a Sasquatch under an old tarp, he didn't detect anything.

Brighteyes watched him, then shook his head in a human gesture of negation. He tapped his nose again, then signed with a pair of gestures.

Joseph recognized the combination term from when Sarah had demonstrated it. "Alive-Dead," he whispered. He turned to Farley. "Roll up on Sharkey and toot your horn. We need to stop."

"I could just call him…"

"No, let's keep the phones off. Who knows who might be listening?"

The rumble of an approaching ATV came from the forested slope below the geologists' camp. Colonel Dosset turned aside from the growing excavation and peered through the trees. His men had been searching for additional meteorites, but so far, their efforts had been fruitless.

An ATV came into view and rolled to a stop at the edge of the perimeter. The lieutenant astride the vehicle snapped off a salute. "Sir! I've got flash intel for you. Eyes only."

In a digital world, a hand-delivered message was uncommon. Dosset took the proffered envelope from the lieutenant, tore open the side, then stepped away to scan the contents. He stiffened. "Who else has seen this?"

"Only the communications officer, sir. It was sealed when he handed it to me."

"Sergeant Jenkins!" Dosset called out to one of the men in the camp, who was currently speaking to someone on an encrypted radio set. When the man didn't reply, Dosset filled his lungs and bellowed, "Leroy!"

The man jerked and removed one of the headset muffs from an ear.

"Finish that call. Now. Then get me Grangeville."

Dosset examined the paper again.

A source at Maiden Labs has managed to contact us. Based on reports from several eyewitnesses inside the North Brother Island location, Cameron Carson is demonstrating unusual traits, including enhanced strength and accelerated healing. In addition, subject is prone to violent mood swings and erratic behavior.

Dosset thought back to several interviews with expedition

members, where they had described Carson "reviving" while in a body bag. He read on.

Carson's former bodyguard Brick Broadway was seen departing the labs with him; this same individual was declared deceased and was observed in the North Brother morgue for several days. Carson was last seen boarding a Maiden helicopter in Missoula, Montana. Radar indicates that McCall, Idaho, may be his destination.

Colonel Dosset had already ordered a small contingent to McCall to check on an odd report of a "monster attack" they'd received. *And now Cameron Carson is headed there?*

Sergeant Jenkins approached with the communications rig. "I have Grangeville, sir."

Dosset donned the headset. "This is Gandalf." He cringed as he said it. *Next time, we're using sports teams.* "Tell me quickly, what's the status on the airborne unit?"

"Departed a few minutes ago, sir."

Dammit. "Radio them with supplemental orders: in addition to determining the nature of these 'monster' sightings in McCall, they are to detain Cameron Carson if they see him, as well as his bodyguard, Brick Broadway. Warn them that the suspects may be extremely dangerous, but I want them alive."

"Yes, sir."

Dosset's lip curled in a wry smile as he ended the communication. *Technically, I'm not sure if you* can *take that man alive. I'm fairly sure he was* dead *after that Bigfoot bit him, just like the expedition medic reportedly said. If so... and he spontaneously resurrected... as well as his expedition bodyguard... then we may not even need that meteorite.*

He handed the headset back to Sergeant Jenkins. "Call base camp. Tell them to prepare a strike team and have one of the on-site helicopters on standby. I'll be there shortly." He turned away from Jenkins and strode up to the lieutenant on the ATV.

"Any orders, sir?"

"Yes. Get off."

Sitting between Sharkey and Russ, Sarah turned around in the cramped cab to check on Dawn Waker and Littlefoot. Currently, the youngster was amusing himself with an LED flashlight Sarah had given him. She had mainly offered it so that they could have some light under the tarp to aid them with their sign language, but the flashlight had proved more toy than tool.

"We're on the western side of the lake," Sharkey said. Farley's truck now led and Sharkey followed him south along Warren Wagon Road, a rustic route lined with spruce trees on either side. "Although, we're not actually at the lake yet," Sharkey added, then pointed out his window. "See that water through the trees? Locals call that The Meanders, on account of it meanders this way and that. That's the feeder for Payette Lake, so if your magic rock came down this way, it coulda gotten caught up in one of the twists and turns. Might wanna check your doodad."

"I don't think it's sensing anything yet." Russ was holding the dreamcatcher up, but its movements seemed more tied to the bumps in the road than to any external influence.

Farley's pickup slowed to a stop and Sharkey braked. Sarah watched the tarp in the truck bed ahead of them lift slightly. Brighteyes stuck his head out and sniffed the air, then lowered the tarp. In a moment, Farley was rolling again.

"Probably can't catch a proper scent under that tarp," Sarah surmised.

"Lucky there's no one else around up here," Russ commented. "Sticking his head out is risky."

Sharkey accelerated to catch up with Farley. "I think that festival down in McCall mighta drawn most of the people to the south side of the lake."

"What are they celebrating?"

"When Farley 'n' me drove through town to get around that roadblock, I saw a big banner for 'Vancefest'... whatever that is."

Mayor Vance surveyed his works and smiled. Atop the bandstand that had been erected south of the Mile High Marina, the mayor had a clear view across the McCall waterfront. The smell of funnel cake mingled with the sounds of a live band in Legacy Park and the beach area was packed. In the waters between the marina's docks and the docks alongside the mall, nearly a hundred boats were gathered, from humble bass boats to flashy pontoon boats decked out in decorations. Flags flew from many a mast and the mood was festive.

"Mr. Mayor, the fire chief needs to speak with you."

The mayor waved his assistant away. "Not now!"

"Yes, now," the fire chief insisted, pushing through the mayor's entourage. Though in his sixties, the man looked like he'd been chiseled from granite. "A little birdie just informed me you've got a fireworks barge out there. That right?"

"Yes. Well, not *here*. It's up north, between the narrows and Cougar Island. It's the climax of the boat parade. Everyone is going to gather in a great big circle around the barge and watch the display."

"You realize Idaho state law prohibits aerial fireworks without a display permit?"

"So?"

"You don't have a display permit."

The mayor smirked. "How do *you* know?"

"Because I'm the one who issues them. You never even filed an application."

"There was no time! Vancefest was an inspiration of the moment!"

"Inspiration is no substitute for preparation. No safety plan, no device list, no permit... no fireworks."

"Well, that rule doesn't count if it's in a lake," the mayor scoffed.

"This lake is lined with forests of highly combustible pine, fir, and spruce. One rocket goes astray, we could have a forest fire."

"But it rained quite a bit a few days ago," the mayor whined.

"The law doesn't 'switch off' after a rain. I don't know if it's the same where you come from, but things that get wet don't stay wet. No permit, no fireworks."

"I'm the mayor, and you work for me! I say the fireworks will go ahead."

The chief leaned forward, his deadpan manner giving way to a spark of rage. "I don't care who you are. I lost two good men fighting forest fires in the area and I'll be damned if I lose any more on account of your last-minute ego-fest."

"Okay! Fine. No fireworks," the mayor grumbled.

As the fire chief pushed back through the crowd, the mayor looked at his phone. That Graybill woman was calling again. He sent her to voicemail. Another call came in, this time from Officer Flynn. He sent that one to voicemail too. "Enough! I will not have my festival disrupted by a boating accident or two... or stories of an imaginary monster!"

"Mr. Mayor?" his assistant asked hesitantly. "You okay?"

Vance realized he had just shouted that last thought out loud. "Nothing, just... frustrated." He looked at his designer watch. "You know what? Let's get this show on the road! Give me the bullhorn."

"But the parade isn't supposed to start for another forty-five minutes."

"Close enough." He placed the bullhorn to his lips and triggered it. "Attention, boaters! We're going to get an early start! In a moment, I'll board my boat and lead off. Remember... no wakes! This isn't a race... it's a parade."

The mayor's request was ignored within seconds as the Osgood twins and their two buddies mounted their jet skis and roared away from shore, slaloming between boats as they raced for open water.

A quarter mile from the McCall waterfront, a local scuba diver had been trying out his new underwater metal detector. On the hunt for missing jewelry, he'd discovered far more than he'd bargained for.

Sharlie knew better than to try to eat the hard metal object on the back of the strange fish-human, and she had a devil of a time chewing the rubbery hide that encapsulated the tasty meat beneath. Working her jaws, she managed to separate flesh from neoprene, slurping down the insides and spitting out the wetsuit. That done, she resumed her southward trek. Ahead, a symphony of boat noise suddenly pulsed through the water. In the past, boats had meant danger. But now... they meant *food*.

"They're pulling over," Russ said.

Ahead, Farley's truck drove between a pair of evergreen trees and came to a stop near the winding river. Sharkey followed their lead and pulled up behind them.

"No boats in sight. And we may be concealed enough from the road," Sarah noted. "You think it's safe to let our friends stretch their legs?"

Russ exited the truck to let her past. "Can't see the road from here... but I'm only five eleven. Have them stay low."

In the other truck, Brighteyes raised the edge of his tarp and looked around. He lifted his head and sniffed the air, then pointed toward the shore.

"I think Brighteyes must have found something," Sarah said.

"He's not the only one," Russ replied. He raised his hand, palm down. Dangling from the loop on his middle finger, the dreamcatcher was floating almost level, pointing toward an area of reeds along the shore. He started to walk in that direction but came up short when Joseph interposed himself and held up a hand.

"Everyone...wait." The Shoshone closed his eyes and listened, then opened his eyes again and regarded the dreamcatcher. "This is the most that the stone has reacted during our journey. I do not hear any unusual tone in the air, but I suggest we have earplugs at the ready."

Sarah, who was letting DawnWaker and Littlefoot out from under the tarp, signaled for them to remain in the truck.

Emulating Brighteyes, Joseph took a slow breath in through his nose, then released it through an open mouth. "Russ... do you remember that smell when we first came upon the remains of those Spook Stalkers and the geologists?"

"Seems like ages ago, but... yeah."

"I smell it now. It's faint, but it is the same," Joseph said.

"Now that you mention it... yeah. I smell it, too."

Brighteyes had stepped down from the bed of Farley's truck. He pointed toward the reeds and signed.

Joseph nodded. "Yes. Alive-Dead." He went to the back of Sharkey's truck and retrieved the lead-lined sample box, sliding the broad strap over a shoulder. "Russ... put on those headphones of yours. Sarah, get some plugs. I'll follow with the box a few paces back and keep my ears open."

"Sharkey... Farley... you stay here with Brighteyes and friends," Russ said. "If the sphere is actually over there and it affects one of us, I think we can get that person under control. But I don't want to have to wrestle an enraged Sasquatch."

"You 'n' me both," Sharkey agreed.

Russ snugged the thick earmuffs onto his ears and followed the angle of the dreamcatcher's dangling feathers. Joseph and Sarah followed closely behind. In a few minutes, they found the source of the odor: an elk carcass. Or rather, a severed hoof, a massive rack of antlers, and bloody scraps of hide and fur.

"What on earth did this?" Russ asked aloud; his voice sounded muffled to him, thanks to the headphones.

The trio searched the area, but apparently this kill was what the dreamcatcher had been drawn to. No sphere.

Returning to the trucks, the group gathered near the shore. Sarah relayed what they had found to Brighteyes, then asked aloud, "So, now what?"

"The roadblocks you encountered," Joseph asked Sharkey. "They were on this road, yes?"

"Yeah. Much further south."

"If that was the site of a larger attack... then that's where we should go."

"We need to find a safe place to let Brighteyes off," Sarah said, examining her portable GPS. "There's a fair amount of forest to the west, about two miles south of here."

"Good," Joseph said. "Saddle up."

CHAPTER THIRTY

"Wait! Stop!" Annabelle waved her arms at the oncoming jet skis as the Sharlie Hunters' pontoon boat motored south toward McCall.

"It's the Osgood twins and their pals," Brady said. "Rich kid pricks."

"Doesn't matter... we need to turn them around!" She waved her arms again as they drew near. "Stop!"

Far from stopping, the jet skiers increased speed and split up, two going to starboard, two to port. Flashing by, all four of them raised their middle fingers in salute, then raced off to the north, laughing hysterically.

Annabelle watched them go. "Okay, maybe they do deserve to get eaten."

"I think I see the lead boats in the parade!" Mark shouted from the bow. His elbows were braced on the back of the forward bench as he tried to hold the binoculars level.

Sharlie was swimming at maximum speed when the sounds of approaching engines caused her to slow. From the sound of it, a great many human boats were on their way north, but these new noises were higher-pitched and closer.

She extended her head from the water for a quick peek. Four small, fast vehicles—each with a single human rider—were hurtling her way, hurling spray as they crisscrossed each other's paths. She recognized them from earlier in the day; they had been too fast to catch… but now… they were headed straight for her. She descended so that only the top of her head broke the surface. Eyes locked on the approaching humans, Sharlie lay in wait.

"Whoooooooo!" Henry Osgood screamed as he cut across his twin brother's bow, subjecting the trailing jet ski to his wake.

"Asshole!" Norm Osgood shouted as his jet ski became airborne before slamming back down and bashing his tailbone. Crushing the throttle lever under white knuckles, Norman tried to overtake his brother to administer some payback.

While the Osgood twins battled for aquatic supremacy, twenty yards to their left, their buddies, Randy and Kyle—aka Boof and The Gooch—played out a similar contest.

Norm managed to cut the corner and cross in front of Henry. Surprised, his brother overcorrected and fell into the water. With the removal of the ignition key on Henry's wrist lanyard, the jet ski's engine cut out; forward momentum carried it several yards away.

"Payback, beeatch!" Norm cried, but he didn't have long to revel in his victory. "Oh, shit!" A partially submerged log was right in his path. Norm steered hard and avoided the log… but then… it moved. As he passed the obstacle, it *turned* and he could distinctly see an eye. A semitransparent eyelid blinked.

Norm accelerated but the object lashed out with blinding speed, striking backward over its own body. Needle-sharp fangs clamped down on Norm from behind; upper teeth punched into his shoulder in countless places while the lower ones pierced his left side at his waist. Wrenching its victim off the jet ski, the creature whipped its head violently, ripping Norm in half. Buttocks and legs sailed through the air, landing beside Henry with a bloody splash.

Henry had seen the whole thing happen and was frozen with terror, but having a bisected twin smack into the water beside him broke the spell. Kicking furiously, he swam for his nearby jet ski. He didn't make it.

Boof and The Gooch watched in horror as the lake monster swam up on Henry Osgood, corralling him with a loop of its flexible neck and cutting the young man off from his jet ski. Its jaws shot forward with a rapid strike, engulfing Henry's head and upper body.

Screaming in terror, Boof and The Gooch roared away, fleeing to the north.

Sharlie turned to watch them go, half an Osgood in her mouth. Those tiny-boat humans were too fast... but there were so many more approaching. All she'd have to do was wait. She gulped down the rest of the Osgoods and descended once more.

"Old Man River," Brick rumbled, peering down at the winding river below.

"Yes, Brick... and the lake we're now flying over is...?" He turned to Singleton.

"Payette Lake, sir."

Carson triggered his seat's headset. "Pilot, let's make a low pass along the lake. See what we can see."

"Uh... Mr. Carson... we've got a problem."

Carson adjusted the headset to better hear the pilot over the roar of the helicopter. "Yes, what is it? Oh, wait... I believe I've spotted the issue." Outside the window, a Blackhawk helicopter was flanking them. The side was open and a door gunner had a wicked-looking machine gun pointed their way.

"They're ordering us to follow them to the McCall airport," the pilot announced.

Carson rose and removed his chair's headset, then rapped on the door to the cockpit. After the sound of a latch being thrown, the slender door opened. Carson stuck his head and shoulders inside. "Patch me in."

The copilot handed Carson a spare cockpit headset and triggered his mic. "Blackhawk, I have Mr. Carson on the line."

"*Maiden Super Puma, I say again... alter course or you will be fired on.*"

"This is Cameron Carson. What seems to be the problem, fellas?"

"*Mr. Carson, we have orders to take you into custody.*"

"Really? Whose orders?"

"*I am not at liberty to say. Is there an individual by the name of Brick Broadway with you, sir?*"

"Yes, he's here. He's a bit under the weather, but—"

"*We will need him as well. I repeat... alter course for McCall airport or we will shoot you down.*"

"I highly doubt that, if your orders are to take me in." He looked out the windscreen at the sparkling lake below. To the west, the sun was dipping toward the tops of the trees on the high ridge that rimmed that side of the lake. And just to the south, an outcrop gave a spectacular view of The Narrows below.

The Blackhawk called again. "*Maiden Super Puma—*"

Carson reached over and cut the mics. "That overlook on the

tip of that peninsula... not exactly a plateau, but there's a fairly flat parking area next to that access road. Can you set us down there?"

"Not a problem, sir."

"Good. Do it. And leave enough space for our friends."

"Yes, sir."

Carson flipped the mic back on. "Not sure what all the fuss is about, but we're going to set down right here and get it squared away. Carson out."

He killed the conversation before they could complain, then returned to the main cabin. Nearly all the seats were occupied—including the two that Brick took up. Seven sets of eyes looked up at him.

"Listen up!" he shouted over the engine noise. "I am about to meet with the military. Apparently, they'd like me to go with them."

"Sir, what—?"

Carson held up a hand and silenced Singleton with a meaningful glance. "I have no intention of becoming their prisoner. It is my belief this is a rogue element, operating outside the legitimate chain of command... no doubt they'd love to take me to one of their black site labs for a little Area 51 poke 'n' prod."

"What are we going to do?" Singleton asked.

"*You* will do nothing. Once we land, all of you will remain on the helicopter. Except you, Brick." When the man-mountain tilted his head to look at Carson, the billionaire crouched in the aisle beside him. "The two of us will approach them... unarmed. There is a chance this may get ugly. They may shoot at us."

"Chitty Chitty Bang Bang."

"Yes. That. If they shoot... you have free rein to defend me in any way you wish."

Brick managed a lopsided smile. "Anything Goes."

"Anything and everything," Carson replied. *Yes... yesss,* the inner voice concurred.

"Bill... fetch Brick's helmet and body armor," Carson

commanded as the helicopter came to a hover and descended. "Then close all of the window shades."

"What the hell are they doing?" the Blackhawk pilot asked as they circled the outcrop.

"No idea. Set down next to them. Cut the engines, but keep 'em warm." Lieutenant Stred left the cockpit. "Look alive, people! Once we're wheels down, Alpha Team, you'll fan out right, Bravo to the left. Higgins, you stay on the door gun. Portnoy, you're with me. Trigger discipline, everyone. Orders are to take them alive. If you have to, shoot to wound."

The red-and-gold Maiden chopper was sitting at the edge of a flattened area, its rotors completely still. As the Blackhawk settled to the ground twenty yards away, the squad's two fire teams disembarked and took up positions on either flank. Stred stepped away from the Blackhawk and crouched, his sidearm in hand. Portnoy joined him, assault rifle at the ready.

Lieutenant Stred waited until the Blackhawk's turboshaft engines had quieted before speaking. "What the hell are they playing at?"

"I don't see anyone in the cockpit," Corporal Portnoy observed. "And the shades are drawn in the cabin."

Stred was about to call for flashbangs when the door on the side of the Maiden helicopter opened and a set of stairs deployed. After a moment, Cameron Carson appeared, wearing a stylish suit coat and slacks. A silk shirt was partly unbuttoned, and his long hair appeared disheveled in a purposeful way. He flashed his trademark toothy smile.

"Gentlemen." He glanced around at the soldiers arrayed in a semicircle before him, then began to walk forward. "My goodness, this is quite the reception."

"Cameron Carson!" Stred shouted. "Get down on your knees and place your hands on your head!"

Carson continued his leisurely stroll. "I'm afraid it would be a crime against fashion to kneel in these Brioni pants. But there's no need for such abasement—I'm happy to go with you. And I believe you wanted my bodyguard as well, correct?"

A gigantic figure squeezed sideways through the Maiden helo's exit. Clad in body armor and a tactical helmet, the leviathan missed the top step, then tumbled to the ground, sending up a cloud of dust from the impact.

"My apologies. Brick is recovering from an injury he sustained while protecting me." The billionaire halted, then closed his eyes and continued to speak. "His sense of balance is a little bit off."

The enormous man rose from the ground, then dusted himself off in an oddly showy manner. He lurch-stepped forward to join Carson. In unison, the two of them raised their hands and walked forward again.

"No weapons, as you can see." Carson spun in a slow circle and Brick did the same, matching Carson's rotation almost exactly.

Stred holstered his sidearm, then reached over and took Portnoy's weapon. "Cuff 'em." He trained the rifle on Carson. "Either of you so much as moves a muscle, we'll drop you. I'll be more than happy to put some holes in the kneecaps of those fancy pants of yours."

"Such hostility," Carson admonished. He held out his wrists. Once again, Brick mirrored his movements.

Portnoy cautiously inched forward, cinched a pair of flex cuffs onto Carson's wrists, then did the same with Brick. The bodyguard stared straight ahead, not acknowledging him at all. "What the heck's wrong with this guy's neck?" the corporal asked.

"An overly aggressive Pilates session, as I understand it," Carson said, resuming his carefree walk toward the helicopter. Brick shambled along beside him. Once Carson reached the lip of the deck beside the door gunner, he paused. "Little help?"

By now, the eight men of Alpha and Bravo had moved in, with a pair from each team keeping a weapon trained on the Maiden helicopter. Two of the men from Bravo took hold of Carson and lifted him onto the bed of the chopper. Brick stood unmoving against the helicopter until two men from Alpha, along with Portnoy and the door gunner, combined their efforts to haul the huge bodyguard into the chopper. Their prisoners loaded, the rest of the team jumped aboard as the pilots spooled up the rotors.

"Why the hell didn't you just go to the airport like we asked?" Lieutenant Stred asked as he got aboard.

Carson smiled. "Because I had no idea what else might be waiting for me there. But here... in these cramped, close quarters... in this remote location... I count thirteen."

Stred felt a chill roll up his spine.

Carson held up his wrists. "Brick... 'Anything Goes.'"

Stred watched in disbelief as Carson and Brick both snapped their flex cuffs as if they were nothing, leaving bloody rings around their wrists. He tried to swing Portnoy's rifle up, but Carson struck him with a quick jab that shattered his jaw and plunged him into blackness.

"Everything's Coming Up Roses!" Brick howled as he tore Alpha Team limb from limb.

Carson, meanwhile, kicked the unconscious commander out of the helicopter, then plunged his fingers into the door gunner's throat on either side of the man's larynx. Ripping out his trachea and carotid artery in one swift movement, he turned his attention to Bravo Team.

A few squad members managed to open fire; bullets punched into Brick and Carson, with no noticeable effect. The same could not be said for the pilot and copilot, who took a fusillade of blue-on-blue rounds from one trigger-happy private.

Carson had just finished tearing a soldier's head completely free of his neck, when a sudden flash of light flooded his vision. Blood misted from his forehead, spattering the bulkhead in front of him. Reacting on instinct, he spun around and caught Portnoy by the arm, twisting and wrenching it out of the socket. The handgun the corporal had just used on him clattered away with the severed arm. Carson's arm shot out, clutching the man by the throat.

"You shot me. In the head. That was rude."

"That's... how you kill... zombies," the man managed to gasp.

"This isn't Hollywood," Carson growled. Although, admittedly, it was getting hard to think. Behind Portnoy, he could see Brick was finishing up, smashing the last of the soldiers to a pulp. With his free hand, Carson raised a finger to his forehead and found the exit wound, at least two inches across.

Need a little help? a familiar voice asked.

"If you can patch this mess up... I'll reward you," Carson said aloud.

"Wha...? I've... I've got a first aid kit," Portnoy managed.

"Oh, I'm not talking to you..." Carson murmured. *"He's talking to me,"* the billionaire finished in a completely different voice, brimming with madness.

Portnoy was rapidly bleeding out, but he stared in wonder at Carson's forehead as pseudopods of blood reached out from the edges of the exit wound... meeting... meshing... congealing. In his fading vision, he watched as the wound sealed itself in red, pulsing flesh. The thing before him looked down at him and grinned. "Tada!"

"Dear God, what are you?" Portnoy whispered.

"Something... *new.*"

Portnoy's eyes fluttered and Carson looked up at Brick, who stood over a pile of dead soldiers. "Nicely done, Brick. Impressive."

"I Could Have Danced All Night," Brick replied with a smile.

"There might be more opportunities to strut your stuff, but

for the moment... go keep an eye on the leader I tossed out of the chopper. *Don't* kill him. I need to ask him a few questions."

Brick grunted and went to the doorway.

"Wait!" Carson quickly stepped into the cockpit, killed the engines, and engaged the rotor break. "There. Wouldn't want you to lose any more of your skull. Okay, off you go. I'll be along shortly."

While Brick jumped down and trudged toward the unconscious lieutenant, Carson turned his attention to Portnoy. The man flailed his remaining arm, trying to reach another weapon. Carson kicked it away and leaned over him.

"Still got some fight in you? Good. The fresher, the better. If the heart's still pumping... the blood still flowing... it enhances the flavor."

Yes! Yes! Yes!

"No! Ple—"

Portnoy never finished his entreaty as Carson plunged his teeth into the corporal's neck. He gorged himself for several minutes, then forced himself to slow down before his control completely slipped. His inner friend wasn't pleased to be cut off from the feast, but Carson asserted his will and jumped down from the helicopter.

Brick looked up from where he was seated... on top of the lieutenant's chest.

"Well, that's one way of doing it." Carson approached the gasping man but paused when he spotted a window shade sliding up on the Maiden helicopter. Covered in blood, he strode up to the stairs and spoke to the cabin inside. "Close those shades. No peeking! Anybody looks, you'll answer to me. It's for your own good. Plausible deniability, etcetera etcetera. Now... retract the stairs and close the door. I'll be back in five."

He returned to the man on the ground. "Brick. Off." The prone man gasped, sucking in a lungful of air when four hundred pounds of ex-wrestler left his chest. Carson knelt beside him. "I'm feeling generous today, Lieutenant. You tell me everything I need to know... and I won't eat you."

Three minutes later, Carson thanked the man and snapped his neck with a casual twist. Lifting the limp body from the ground, he tossed it into the helicopter with ease, then looked around the outcrop. There was a bit of a slope there, a few yards from where the Blackhawk landed. "Brick... ready for a test of strength?"

"Anything You Can Do... I Can Do Better."

"I'm sure you can... but for this, I believe I'll take control." He focused, then willed Brick to go to the far side of the helicopter. Carson jumped aboard and went to the cockpit. One pilot was still alive, so he quickly remedied that situation, then released the rotor and wheel brakes.

Back outside, he crouched and placed his hands on the left landing gear strut, then controlled Brick to do the same on the right side of the aircraft. Straining, Carson pressed against the strut, then started to rock the chopper in short bursts of force. In moments, the wheels began to roll. With one final shove, Carson and Brick stepped back and watched the helicopter roll off the edge of the outcrop. Trees along the steep slopes bent and snapped as the Blackhawk plummeted down through the canopy. Carson and Brick walked to the precipice and looked down.

"Into the Woods," Brick observed.

Carson smiled. "Indeed. Well... that was an adventure." He looked down at himself, then took out his phone and called Single-ton. "Bill... bring me a wet towel and a change of clothes."

CHAPTER THIRTY-ONE

Sarah was scanning the wooded slopes to their right for a place to drop off Brighteyes when Russ suddenly yelped in surprise.

"Whoa! Check it out!"

The dreamcatcher was pointing horizontally toward Payette Lake on their left. The lake here was very close to the road; beds of dried pine needles formed a carpet on either side.

"I think it might even be glowing," Russ said, squinting at the stone embedded in the sinew webbing of the floating dreamcatcher.

"Sharkey, pull over!" Sarah said.

Their truck was in the lead, and Sharkey pulled over onto the needle-strewn shoulder beside the lake. Farley followed suit.

"The trees are quite thick on the opposite slope," Sarah said. "Let me check with Brighteyes... see if this works for him."

"We're pretty exposed here," Sharkey warned.

"I know. We'll need to be quick." She got out and went to the other truck.

"Good cover up there." Joseph nodded his head at the wooded slope as she approached.

"Exactly. But that's not why we stopped. Russ got a major hit off the dreamcatcher. Said the stone might have been glowing? You check in with him while I talk with Brighteyes." She went around to the right side of the truck bed and lifted one edge of the tarp. Bright blue eyes shone back at her.

'Air-rah!'

"Hello, Brighteyes."

'Why we stop?'

"Russ thinks there may be something by the lake."

Brighteyes appeared confused. He sniffed the air. 'But no Alive-Dead smell.'

That's odd. But there was no time to puzzle it out; although there had been very few cars on this road, it was only a matter of time before someone came along. "Brighteyes, the trees there..." She pointed at the slope on the west side of the road. "The forest is thick and extends for a great distance."

'You want I go?'

"No! I mean..." Sarah thought a moment, then attempted to articulate her quandary. "Yes... you should take Littlefoot and DawnWaker and find cover over there. But I want to spend more time with you, before we..." She wasn't sure what gesture to use, so she inverted the first two fingers on each hand to form legs and made them walk away from each other.

Brighteyes grunted and gave a nod, then imitated her improvised sign language. He pointed at himself and "walked" his fingers one way, then pointed at her and repeated the gesture in the other direction.

Sarah smiled wistfully. "Yes. But not yet. Go up there and hide. I will look for you at dark." She looked at the sky and noticed it was already approaching sundown. "I will look for you at *late* dark," she amended.

'Late dark. Yes. We hide. We wait.' He gave the tarp above his head a gentle push. 'Now? Safe now?'

Sarah looked both ways on the road and listened intently. Then she signed and said, "Yes. Go now!"

Brighteyes threw aside the tarp and vaulted over the edge of the truck bed, then ran to Farley's truck. He lifted the back to the tarp, grunted in a reassuring manner, then yanked that tarp aside, revealing DawnWaker and Littlefoot. The pair blinked in the fading sunlight. Brighteyes lifted Littlefoot onto his shoulders and held a hand out to DawnWaker. The copper-pelted Bigfoot took it and the trio dashed across the road and up the forested slope.

Sarah watched them go. When Brighteyes paused and looked back at her, she pressed a fist to her heart. The Bigfoot mirrored the gesture... then he was gone. She stared after them for a long while.

"You all right, Sarah?" Sharkey asked. He and Farley had gathered between the trucks.

"Yes. I will be." Then she remembered what Brighteyes had told her. She ran to the drop-off to the lake and called down to Joseph and Russ, "Brighteyes says he doesn't smell anything Alive-Dead!"

Russ looked up. "Whatever this thing is picking up, it's across the lake. Or in it."

Sarah went down to join them on the rocky shingle of beach that jutted out from the slope that fell away from the road. This stretch of the lake was undeveloped, though the remains of an old dock were present a short distance to their south.

"What's that?" Sarah asked, pointing straight out from the shore. A small island lay in that direction, but what had drawn her eye was a square boat about halfway to the island beyond.

"Don't know," Joseph said. "I noticed it, but the dreamcatcher isn't pointing at that... it's drawn to something in the south, in the main part of the lake."

"Hey, fellas," Sharkey called out. "It safe to come down?"

"Yeah, come join us," Russ said.

"Bring that hunting rifle you let me borrow," Joseph requested. "I left it in Farley's truck."

In moments, the two National Guardsmen joined them at the shore.

"Here ya go," Sharkey said, handing Joseph the rifle. "You plannin' on shootin' somethin'?"

"No... I want it for the scope." Joseph raised the rifle and pointed it at the vessel in the water to their east. "It's a barge... with a lot of cylinders on it. And an orange sign that says danger."

"Here, lemme see." Sharkey took the rifle and scanned the target. "Thought so. Yeah, that's a fireworks barge. Probably set up for the festival in McCall."

"What's it doing all the way up here?" Sarah asked.

"Well... I see someone you might be able to ask," Sharkey said. "There's a guy on a boat tied up on the opposite side, and it looks like he's about to cast off." He lowered the rifle. "Course, he could go in any direction..."

"One sec!" Farley ran back to his truck, returning quickly with a small air horn and some binoculars. "With bears and cougars around, I carry a bear horn around for hiking or camping. And... here." He handed the binoculars to Joseph. "Best not point a gun at a guy with a boat full of explosives." Farley stepped to the edge of the shore and triggered the horn, letting loose three short blasts.

Joseph glassed the barge. "He sees us. Wave him over."

The group waved and beckoned. In a moment, a small bass boat came out from behind the barge and motored their way. Wearing a red, white, and blue ball cap and a sleeveless T-shirt, the occupant appeared to be in his thirties, heavily suntanned. He slowed as he came into the shallows and nuzzled up against the ruined dock, tossing a loop of line over a wooden piling.

"Y'all with the mayor?" he called out.

"No," Sarah replied.

"Oh! Wasn't sure, with y'all calling me over. Well... what can I do for ya?"

"That your fireworks barge?" Sharkey asked.

"Yeah... well, it belongs to the company I work for. Wait... you're not with the fire department, are you?"

"Also no," Sarah reassured him. "But why do you ask?"

"Well... see... the new mayor hired us for the finale of his big boat parade, but then the fire chief called me, all pissed off, and said to shut it down. I started locking down the safeties, but then the mayor called about ten minutes ago and said it was back on."

Joseph stepped up alongside Sarah. "You said a boat parade?"

The man chuckled. "You must not be from around here. The mayor is throwing a big festival and it ends with a parade with all the locals' boats. The fireworks are for the finale. The boats are supposed to gather around the barge... at a safe distance, of course."

"And you run the show?" Sarah asked.

"Yup." He grabbed a metal case at his feet and popped the latches before raising the lid and showing off the interior. "I can run the sequence remotely with this control panel here." He indicated the yellow console inside, dotted with numerous red and green buttons and slots for batteries and fuses. "I was planning on running it from this old dock here. Y'all are welcome to watch."

Joseph looked out toward the lake. "This parade... what time are the boats supposed to get here?"

"Well, originally, the display was supposed to be at thirty minutes after sundown; the mix-up with the fire department permits might've thrown things off. But the mayor did say they've already left the McCall waterfront." The man turned in his seat and pointed down toward the main part of the lake. "They'll be coming up through there."

Sarah turned and confirmed what she already knew... the dreamcatcher was pointing in that very direction. And now, it was definitely doing more than pointing.

"Whoa!" Russ breathed. "That little rock in the web is definitely glowing now."

"Whatever it senses," Joseph said, "is getting closer."

Mayor Vance stood in the bow seating area of the gorgeous StanCraft Rivelle, looking up at the setting sun. He eagerly awaited darkness so he could trigger the LED lighting display that framed his boat. Well, it wasn't *his* boat, in truth. The beautiful wooden vessel, varnished and polished to a mirror sheen, was on loan from a wealthy friend who'd had it trailered up from Lake Cascade. As a recent California transplant, Vance hadn't yet gotten his own high-end boat, and he figured he ought to "dress to impress," boat-wise; this was, after all, *his* festival and *his* parade.

Looking around at the festive cavalcade that trailed in his wake, he could see all manner of merrymaking going on. Copious beers were in evidence, and a few people were grilling burgers and steaks on some of the larger boats. *I wonder where the hot dog boat is?* Vance had specifically invited Mr. Strand to take a position in the center of the parade.

The mayor's assistant was piloting the Rivelle. She had a worried look on her face, and he flashed her a thumbs-up to reassure her. *Probably concerned about my plans to have the fireworks after all*, he thought. But then, she pointed behind him, toward the north. Frowning, he looked over his shoulder across the bow.

In the distance, a boat was approaching at high speed. At least, as high a speed as a pontoon boat could manage. He recognized it immediately. It was that ridiculous Sharlie Hunters' boat he'd encountered earlier today. And sure enough, that park ranger was aboard, waving her arms.

"Those idiots are *not* going to ruin my festival," he muttered aloud. He went aft to join his assistant in the cockpit. "Ignore them!" he snapped.

"But they're coming right for us."

"Then go around, if you have to." He looked up at the sun as it finally dipped below the mountain range to their west. He grabbed his megaphone and the remote for the lighting display and moved to the stern. He triggered the bullhorn and swept it in an arc as he addressed the parade behind him. "All right, everyone! Light 'em if you got 'em!"

With that, he triggered the LEDs he had strung on the boat. Over a thousand red, white, and blue lights flashed to life. Behind him, other decorative illumination winked on, as other boaters turned on their own displays. He spotted an inflatable palm tree with Christmas lights on one boat and a neon flamingo on another. A trio of glowing drones—one red, one white, one blue— rose into the sky, controlled by a group of teenagers. Smaller kids on another boat lit up sparklers, and from one vessel near the back, a Roman candle coughed up glowing balls into the dimming sky, arcing the fiery orbs into the lake to extinguish with a hiss.

Bet the fire chief would love that, Vance thought. He was about to raise his megaphone again to praise some of the displays when the boat abruptly shuddered and lurched to starboard. He stumbled and was about to shout at his assistant when he spotted the reason for the sudden course correction: the Sharlie Hunters had arrived, their stupid sea monster flag fluttering as they cut across the Rivelle's bow.

Enraged, Vance raised his bullhorn and aimed it at the *Slimy Slim*, which had turned and was maneuvering to come alongside. "What the hell are you idiots doing?"

Annabelle winced at the amplified shout, but she yelled right back, "Mr. Mayor, you have to disperse the parade! Something is attacking people all along the lake!"

"Gee, let me guess... it's Sharlie. You've been hanging out with those losers for too long. It's just some boating accidents. Now quit trying to disrupt my parade! We are not turning back."

"You idiot!" Brady shouted across. "It's already too late to turn back! Every boat needs to make for one shore or the other, right now! Use any dock, just get off the lake!"

"You! You're the worst of them!" the mayor spat into the bullhorn. "I hereby ban you from all city council meetings!"

"Listen!" Annabelle pleaded. "Officer Dwight is up ahead with the Hot Dog Man's boat... Hunter is missing and there's blood on the boat."

"And I think we just passed a bloody wetsuit," Mark added.

Cilantro contributed her own thoughts with a barrage of barking... but it quickly became apparent that it wasn't the unpleasant man with the megaphone she was barking at.

"Oh my God..." Annabelle stared in disbelief.

"It's Sharlie!" Stuart yelled.

On the far side of the mayor's boat, a long-snouted head on an even longer neck rose into the air, lake water sloughing off its hide. The creature was pacing the boat, and the head swung around and looked down at the mayor.

Vance had his megaphone up and was about to yell something else at Annabelle and the Sharlie Hunters, but he must have seen the sudden change in their expressions. Bullhorn still pressed to his lips, he turned to look behind him. He found himself staring at something his mind couldn't quite comprehend: it looked like a slimy tree trunk, its wet surface sparkling in the blinking glow of the red, white, and blue LEDs on the boat. His gaze rose up the trunk and found a huge head with two eyes reflecting down at him. He screamed.

Mayor Gary Vance had cultivated a manly baritone while campaigning on the stump, but his terrified shriek was high and shrill... and amplified by the bullhorn. Overcome by fear and adrenaline, he impulsively crushed the trigger in a white-knuckled grip.

The blast of high-pitched sound seemed to startle the creature; it recoiled and shook its head violently. Recovering, it surged toward the mayor's boat. Vance's assistant had looked over her shoulder and reacted with the appropriate selection in the fight-or-flight response, wisely choosing flight and pushing the throttle to the stop. The mayor's boat lurched forward, the abrupt change in speed sending Vance toppling overboard.

The mayor's last thought was: *I should have worn a life jacket.* But it turned out that he didn't need one. Sharlie lashed out with such blinding speed that she arrested the mayor's fall mere inches above the water. Rows of razor-sharp teeth pierced his body in countless places. Megaphone still clutched in a death grip, the bullhorn amplified Vance's bloodcurdling screams and the squelching noises of Sharlie's fangs entering his flesh. Alternately releasing her toothy grip, then chomping back down, the beast turned the body in her jaws for an easier swallow and began gulping it down, her throat distending as the mouthful of mayor made its way into her gullet.

"Hang on, everybody!" Kevin yelled, squeezing a few more knots out of his outboard and steering to port to increase the distance from the aquatic horror.

"Arm yourselves!" Annabelle shouted.

"Stop!" Wolf Wallace shouted.

Merle slammed on the brakes; thuds and curses sounded from the back of the U-Haul as equipment and ATVs—along with Keith the Intern and Ian—slid forward from the abrupt deceleration.

"That looks like Sharkey's truck!" Wolf declared, indicating the two trucks they had just passed on the opposite side of the road. "Same make, same model... Athena?"

"Same license plate," she confirmed. "And the other truck belongs to Farley."

"Turn around. Pull over behind them."

Wolf's crew had been traveling northbound toward the area close to the termination of French Creek, intending to try and intercept Russ Cloud. Merle made a five-point turn to get the U-Haul back to their quarry, then brought it to a halt behind the two vehicles. "What're they doin' down here?" Merle wondered. "I thought they were still in Grangeville."

"No, just the swag with the tracking devices," Athena said. "Maybe they called on the National Guard to come to McCall to assist with whatever this monster attack was."

"Well, we'll just go and ask 'em," Wolf announced, opening the door and stepping down to the pine-needle-coated shoulder. He went around back and slid open the loading door. Ian and Keith were both lying on the bed of the U-Haul, Ian on his back with his legs thrown over an ATV.

"Next time... a little warning would be nice," Ian muttered.

"Stretch your legs, boyos. We're stoppin' for a wee moment." He stepped away from the U-Haul and looked around. Various forms of evergreen lined the road on either side. Next to the trucks, the lake was visible through the trees, while across the way, thickly forested slopes rose out of sight. He walked over to the first truck —Farley's—and noted a tarp in the back, attached in several places with bungee straps. He had a look inside the cab and spotted camping equipment almost immediately. He then lifted the edge of the tarp and immediately wrinkled his nose.

Merle walked up. "What is it?"

"Quite whiffy under that tarp. Unusual odor, it is."

Merle took a deep sniff. "Huh. Earthy. Maybe they were hauling mulch?"

Wolf looked down the road in both directions then removed the nearest bungee and lifted the tarp aside. "Ach, look ye here!" He reached in and came up with a clump of hair or fur. "What d'ye make of this?"

"Uh... maybe they have a dog?"

"I dinnae think so..." Wolf went to Sharkey's truck and looked under that tarp as well. "More hair! And the same musky smell. And..." He trailed off. On the ground, at the side of the truck, pressed into the bed of pine needles, was a pair of impressions. Rather *large* impressions, side by side, separated by about eighteen inches. This wasn't mud, so there wasn't a distinctive track, but to Wolf's semicompetent tracker's eye, these looked like indentations that could have been made by a Sasquatch. Perhaps one that had come from under a tarp and vaulted the side of the truck... leaving behind some of its hair.

Wolf was about to shout for everyone to kit up when Keith the Intern tentatively raised a hand.

"Um... hey. I think I hear voices down by the lake."

At the shore, Russ was squinting toward the narrows to the south. While it wasn't truly sunset yet, the sun had dropped behind the mountains, cloaking the lake in shadow.

"I see something coming this way," he said. "Two somethings."

Farley came over and raised his binoculars. "Jet skis."

"You think that's the lead element of the parade?" Sarah asked the fireworks operator.

The man shrugged. "Hell if I know."

Joseph suddenly appeared from where he'd been scouting further down the shore. "We've got company."

"They're still a ways out," Farley said.

"I'm not talking about the jet skis." He pointed up the slope toward the road. "Four men and a woman. Next to your trucks."

"Nobody better be messin' with my truck," Sharkey said, turning to run up the embankment. He only got a few steps when a voice called out in an atrocious Scottish brogue.

"Well, well, well... if it isn't Russ Cloud and his merry band."

Wolf Wallace descended from the road. Alongside him was a stocky-looking man in a camo ball cap carrying what appeared to be a cattle prod. He was followed by a smaller man with the look of a tech about him with a dart gun slung over his shoulder. He held a top-of-the-line video camera, its lens trained on Russ and company. Beside the cameraman, a woman with large glasses and shockingly purple hair carried an electronic tablet. Bringing up the rear was a nervous-looking young man who looked like he might've been plucked from the streets of a small Idaho town. Once Wolf reached Russ, the cameraman sidled to the side to get them in a two-shot.

Wolf struck a pose with hands on hips. "Ye've led us on a merry chase, Russ me lad."

"Hello, Willy," Russ said.

Wolf blinked. "It's *Wolf*."

Russ laughed as he slipped the dreamcatcher from his finger and handed it to Joseph. "Oh, please... your real name's William Peale, and you're no more Scottish than I am. Nice kilt, though."

"It's a top-of-the-line tactical kilt, I'll have you know! Besides, ye're one to talk, boyo, with that ratty do-rag of yours. The hairline must be in full retreat." He looked around at the others. "Sharkey and Farley I know." He nodded at Joseph. "And this must be some of that local flavor you like to include in your shows..." Wolf's eyes landed on Sarah. "But who is this bonny lass? A new cohost? Bringing a little sex appeal into the mix. Smart marketing move."

"*Doctor* Bishop has more brains in her pinky than your entire operation. Besides, she doesn't work for me... if anything, I work for *her*."

"Dr. Sarah Bishop is the primatologist Cameron Carson hired to lead the Bigfoot expedition," the goth-looking woman supplied.

"Ach, I recognize you now! But since we're on the subject of Bigfoot..." He held his arms out and looked around. "Where are they?"

CHAPTER THIRTY-TWO

"Where are who?" Russ asked.

"Don't play the fool with me! I saw your Bigfoot friends on our drone's camera! Oh! And you owe me a drone!"

"Why? Something happen to it?"

Wolf was about to lay into Russ when loud noises echoed across the lake, rising in intensity. Two engines... and what sounded like screaming.

"The jet skiers are getting close," Farley observed. He raised the binoculars and took a closer look. "Getting hard to see with the sun going down, but... it looks like two teenagers... scared outta their minds."

As the jet skis drew closer, the fireworks operator sat up straight. "That's Randy and Kyle. Their parents live off a cove about half a mile north." He took out a high-intensity flashlight and shone it toward them, then waved it around when it caught their attention. They abruptly changed direction and headed for the shore.

The two teens beached themselves and dismounted. One of them made an effort to calm himself and asked, "Are any of you cops?"

His friend lost all composure and shrieked, "It killed them! It killed them both!"

Joseph came over and put a steadying hand on the youth's shoulder. "Easy... you are safe, now. What happened?"

"Henry and Norm... it ripped them right off their jet skis!" He broke loose of Joseph's reassuring hand and ran for the road. "Screw this! I'm getting away from the lake!"

His friend followed, right on his heels.

"What attacked you?" Joseph called after them.

"Sh... Sharlie!"

Annabelle raised the hunting rifle again and took aim. Given the high velocity of the weapon's rounds, she'd had to time each shot for moments when no parade boat was in the line of fire. She leveled the barrel at the creature's broad back, then squeezed the trigger. Annabelle saw the bullet strike home, but it had no more discernible effect than the last two times she'd shot the beast.

After gulping down the mayor, Sharlie had charged the boat with the neon flamingo, her teeth scissoring through a hapless grill master and his amusing apron: "I Drink and I Grill Things." Boats that were close enough to witness the carnage began to scatter. Vessels further back in the parade had no idea what was happening and continued forward; numerous boats collided in a nautical traffic jam. But before Sharlie could strike another target, the teenagers with the drones sent the glowing quadcopters to dive-bomb the beast, distracting it. This gave the Sharlie Hunters a chance to close the distance and open fire. For all the good it did them.

"I've shot it three times!" Annabelle shouted, her voice competing with the engine and Cilantro's nonstop barks. "It didn't even react!"

"And I put two tranquilizer darts in it," Brady added. "But if they're meant for bears, I doubt they'll have any effect. Look at the size of that thing!"

"We've got to draw it away from the parade!" Annabelle nearly lost her balance as Kevin maneuvered sharply to avoid a strike from Sharlie's thrashing neck. She set down her rifle and crawled over to Mark, who was struggling with his unwieldy homemade harpoon gun. "Please tell me your gizmo is almost ready."

"It should be! The compressed air tank is good to go, but I had to attach a line to the shaft below the barbed head. Here... tie this to one of the aft cleats. Maybe we can drag that thing away from the other boats. And if it turns out that's a terrible, horrible, incredibly stupid idea... I've got a hawkbill knife that'll cut the line."

Annabelle took the line and tied it to the starboard stern cleat with a bowline knot. She glanced at the wickedly barbed spearhead. "Dare I ask... where does one even get a harpoon?"

"Antique auction. I took the head off the old wooden shaft and attached it to a short steel one." Mark blew out a nervous breath. "Okay... ready. Bad news is... we have to get pretty close. This'll shoot the harpoon harder than a person can throw, but it'll drop off fast."

"Kevin! Can you make a pass at it?"

"I can try, but I don't know if I'm her type," Kevin replied with a terrible Groucho Marx impression. "Sorry! Can't resist a good setup, even when terrified. Which side you want to shoot from?"

"Starboard," Mark grunted as he butt-scooted his way along the deck to the bench on the right side. He arranged the coil of the harpoon's nylon line on the seat beside him, then knelt on the bench and braced his contraption on the rail. "Stuart... make sure Cilantro's still clipped into her harness."

"She's secure!" Stuart shouted.

"Everyone... hang on!" Kevin turned the wheel hard to port

and lined up the bow with an area of open water between a random boat and the lake monster. Sharlie had just managed to catch one of the light-up drones in midair, crushing it in her jaws. Pushing the throttle to the max, Kevin sent the *Slimy Slim* shooting for the gap.

As the pontoon boat raced by the flank of the massive creature, Mark pulled the trigger. There was a short, violent hiss and the improvised pneumatic cannon hurled the harpoon through the air, the line unspooling behind it. The barbed shaft arced only slightly before it pierced Sharlie's flesh at the base of her long neck. As they raced by, the line continued to uncoil. Sharlie's head swung down, tracking the boat.

"Kev! Slow down!" Mark demanded.

"Are you nuts?"

"If we're going at full speed when the line goes taut, it might pull the barb loose or snap the line. Once I know it's set, you can floor it."

Kevin muttered something about "suicide" before pulling back on the throttle. After a moment, Mark shouted for him to increase speed. The line went taut and Sharlie reacted with surprise when she found herself being pulled.

"Oh, goodie... Mark caught the big one," Brady said. "Now what, Graybill?"

"Take us north! Away from the parade."

"Uh... what if she can swim faster than our boat?" Stuart asked.

As if to put this question to the test, Sharlie turned and pulsed her tail, following in the wake of the *Slimy Slim*. Her long neck extended as she tried to reach her tormentors.

"Probably shoulda used a longer line," Brady said as the jaws snapped in the air a few yards astern.

Annabelle placed a call. "Dwight! Are you still with the hot dog boat? We need you!"

"Hey! A helicopter!" Stuart shouted. He waved his arms above his head, trying to attract its attention.

"What the hell is that?"

Carson looked over at one of the Maiden technicians, who had his face pressed against a window of the helicopter. At Carson's instruction, the pilot had lifted off and taken them on a sweep across the smaller part of the lake to the east before crossing back over the peninsula to the larger part of the lake. They had discovered a parade of pleasure craft, many of them lit up like Christmas trees. But as they drew closer, it was apparent that something was not right. Boats were driving every which way, and there appeared to be some water rescues going on.

The technician at the window gasped. "It's huge!"

Carson crossed over to that side of the chopper and looked down at the darkening water. He could see a boat... and something chasing it. Something *enormous*. "Bill, tell the pilot to put a spotlight on that boat down there!"

The helicopter flew ahead of the boat, slowed to a hover, then rotated around and engaged a powerful spotlight. Carson thrust himself between the two pilots and stared down at the pool of light. The boat did not slow, nor did its pursuer.

"Jeez Louise, that looks like the Loch Ness Monster," the copilot declared.

Carson stared at the monstrosity bearing down on the pontoon boat. A few weeks ago, he hadn't even been sure Bigfoot was real... and now this? He spotted something: A line linked boat and beast as they passed below the helicopter. He had assumed that the creature was chasing the boat, but perhaps they were towing it.

That creature and the sphere are connected. They must be! "We need a boat," Carson declared. "Get ahead of them! Far ahead!"

The pilot did as instructed. To their north, a flashing blue light came into view. "Police boat inbound."

"It's going too fast. Find me another one."

And indeed, the patrol boat flashed by them, heading south. The pilot spotted another possibility. "How about that one? No one aboard."

"Looks like a floating hot dog stand," the copilot remarked.

One glance and Carson dismissed it. "Too slow. Take us closer to the houses to the west. There's bound to be something at one of the docks."

"Hey, I'm seeing some flashlights up ahead. The shoreline north of the houses." It was certainly getting dark, and the pilot flipped down his night vision goggles. "I see a bunch of people by the water... and a small boat and two jet skis!"

"Perfect," Carson said, grabbing a spare set of NVGs. "Let's get a closer look."

"Guys... there's a helicopter out there," Farley said. "Coming this way."

"They with you? Aerial photography unit?" Russ asked Wolf. He gestured at the faux-Scotsman and his four counterparts. "Never seen you shoot a show without an army of a production crew."

"Nae, it's not one of mine. Quit stallin'!" Wolf swept a flashlight across the surrounding trees. "Where ye hidin' your Bigfoot chums, eh?"

"I'm a bit more concerned about those two boys and their lake monster," Merle said.

"Those lads were probably high on skunk," Wolf scoffed.

"What about the reports Athena dug up, about attacks on boats," Merle urged.

Wolf hesitated. "True. Athena, lass... did those reports say where exactly those attacks occurred?"

But Athena wasn't listening. "That's the dreamcatcher you had in Kamiah!" she blurted. Everyone turned to watch her as she slowly walked toward Joseph, her eyes transfixed on the object dangling from the Shoshone's finger. "The one you picked up from that museum by the casino. How are you making it float horizontal like that?"

"I'm not making it do anything," Joseph replied.

Athena was now beside Joseph and she stared at the circle of sinew webbing. "That little stone... it's glowing!"

"Yes... and it has been increasing in brightness over the past few minutes." Joseph took his eyes off it and looked around at the others. "Whatever it is drawn to... it's coming this way."

"Faster!" Brady yelled. "It's gaining on us!"

"I'm going as fast as I can," Kevin shouted.

While Brady aimed a spotlight at the creature, Annabelle braced a foot near the stern and lifted the hunting rifle. She tried to draw a bead on the creature's head as it bobbed from side to side on its slithering neck. She only had two rounds left in the bolt-action weapon, and she missed with both shots.

"Well, fellas... we may be screwed."

"Hey! Here comes Dwight!" Stuart cried.

Racing in from the north, the police boat arrived on their port side. While his partner drove, Officer Dwight was in the bow with an AR-style rifle of some kind. He spun a hand in a circle while shouting back to the other policeman, then braced himself as the boat circled around and came up behind Sharlie, moving slightly to her right to keep the Sharlie Hunters out of the line of fire. When the police boat was mere yards away, Dwight leveled his weapon.

"You're too close!" Annabelle shrieked, her voice drowned out by the racing engines.

Dwight opened fire, looking to empty his magazine into the creature. He'd put about seven rounds into Sharlie's body when she suddenly coiled her neck and whipped her head around, lashing out at the police boat. In a fraction of a second, fifteen feet of neck went from one end of the creature to the other. At the last instant, the head turned on its side, jaws gaping, and clamped down on Dwight. Snatching him from the bow, the beast snapped its head back the other way, ripping the officer's torso in two, sending the halves sailing into the water in opposite directions.

"No!!" Annabelle shrieked.

The policeman at the wheel of Dwight's boat was crying out as well. The police boat dropped back, but then the shock on the man's face flipped to anger. He throttled up and the police boat leaped forward.

"He's gonna ram it!" Brady deduced.

"He'll end up crashing into us too!" Annabelle declared. "Mark, give me the knife!" She dropped her empty rifle and grabbed the knife from mark. "Kev! I'm cutting us loose! Make for the western shore when I do! Brady, grab my thighs! Any wise-cracks and I'll cut your head off!"

"You're no fun."

Annabelle leaned over the side of the boat while Brady held on tight. Opening the folding hawkbill knife, she quickly sawed through the line. It gave way with a snap. "Pull me up!"

"Kev! Go!" Mark shouted as Brady hauled Annabelle back aboard.

As Kevin steered to port, a loud, wet thud sounded from behind as the police boat slammed into Sharlie. The creature's slimy back acted like a ramp, and the patrol boat became airborne, thumping into the water on her opposite side. If the Sharlie Hunter's boat had remained where it had been, the police boat would have smashed into their stern. Before the officer at the wheel could recover, Sharlie struck, her jaws completely erasing the man's head.

As the Sharlie Hunters raced away, Sharlie lashed her powerful tail and took off after the fleeing boat, gulping down the severed head as she went.

"I count eleven," the helicopter pilot announced as they flew closer to the shore.

Through the night vision goggles, Carson peered at the group. There was one man in a small boat tied up at a dock. The rest were ashore, and if he was any judge of body language, they weren't all buddies. Two jet skis lay on the edge of the water.

"Find somewhere to set down," Carson demanded.

"Gonna be tricky, sir," the pilot said. "The road by the shore is too narrow. Trees too close to the shoulder. Maybe further north. Some houses up there. Might be some cleared areas."

"Wait..." Carson looked closely at some of the figures on the shore. Their features were hard to distinguish in the green haze of the NVGs, but at least one of them looked familiar. "Hover... hit them with the spotlight."

"Goggles off, unless you want to fry your retinas," the pilot warned, swinging his up above his forehead.

"I have the aircraft," the copilot announced, as he had been flying without the light-enhancing aids. "Spotlight on." He flicked a switch and aimed the light on the people below with a small joystick. The man nearest to them was distinctive, with a long black braid of hair hanging down his back.

"Joseph Washakie." Carson's face lit up in a smile and a pleased growl vibrated in his throat. "And there's Sarah Bishop... and Russ Cloud. All in one place." He gripped the pilot's shoulder and the man winced. "You have two minutes to find a suitable landing spot. If there is none, circle back and hover over the shallows."

"Uh... what...?"

The grip tightened and the pilot yelped in surprised pain. "Do it!" Carson withdrew from the cockpit to the cabin. "Well, Bill... I feel the object of our search is close at hand." After he explained what he'd seen, he turned to the four technicians. "Get your gear ready for a quick exit. Any unusual wavelengths or emanations in the area—radiation, acoustics, or what have you—I expect you all to locate the source. That's why I brought you. Whoever finds the source first, you'll be richly rewarded."

"We're in the Money," Brick intoned.

"And you, my muscle-bound friend... lose the body armor. I don't hold out much hope for your swimming abilities in your current state, and there's a chance we might have to get wet."

Brighteyes listened as the large whirly-winged man-machine— "maple seed machine," as Littlefoot liked to call it—moved away to the north. He was concerned for the safety of his human friends. They had not returned to their trucks. And then more humans had arrived in an even larger truck and had descended to the lakeshore where Sarah had gone. There had been raised voices. And now, this flying machine.

Brighteyes looked down the wooded slope to the road. The sun had set and it was dark; that made crossing a road quite easy, as an approaching vehicle's lights would give him plenty of warning. He turned to the others, his signing simplified in the gloom.

'I go. The new humans... they may not be friends to Air-rah. I go see.' He pointed to a thicker section of trees that lined the road on the lakeside. 'I hide there. They no see me.'

'I go too!' DawnWaker insisted. Littlefoot joined in with a basic grunt of affirmation.

'No. One hides better than three. Stay. I return soon.'

Brighteyes moved in a low crouch, quickly descending to the

road and looking in both directions. No lights were visible along it, but he could see lights below where Sarah had gone. Likely these were some of those small cylindrical lights that humans carried to see in the dark. He moved a safe distance away from the three trucks, then crouch-walked across the road and took up a position where he could just make out the shoreline. In the distance, he could still hear the helicopter... but there was another engine noise too... far out on the lake.

CHAPTER THIRTY-THREE

"Not good! Not good!" Kevin announced.

"What? What is it?" Mark asked, urgency in his voice.

"Our speed has dropped! Might have snagged something in the propeller. Fishing line or rope, maybe."

"Well, we can't just stop and untangle it!" Stuart shouted. "Sharlie's nearly caught up with us!"

Annabelle could actually feel the boat slowing; she looked astern and saw that Sharlie was indeed closing the distance.

"Come on, *Slimy Slim*..." Kevin coaxed. "I'm gonna slow down and pulse the engine in reverse... see if I can shake whatever it is loose."

"I don't know if we've got that much time, Kev," Brady warned.

Kevin rummaged around in the glove box next to the steering wheel. "Here! They're probably expired but should still work." He held out three handheld signal flares. "If Sharlie gets close, maybe you can drive her off. And if I don't clear the prop... she'll *definitely* get close."

Annabelle pocketed two of the flares and moved toward the stern with the third. Popping the red top, she swiped the striker against the tip and the flare ignited with a gout of red flame. "Okay, Kev... make it quick!"

Kevin slowed and tried his trick. The good news was, it worked. The bad news was, Sharlie caught up with them. She surged up to the stern, raised her head and neck in an arc above the boat, and opened her toothy jaws. An eerie harmonic tone emanated from the creature's throat, cutting through the engine noise.

Annabelle's initial surge of terror suddenly subsided into a strange sensation: a mix of contentment and puzzlement. She was semiaware of the others turning to face the creature as well. Even Cilantro ceased her barking. Kevin cut the engine. Annabelle forgot all about the flare and it dropped from her fingers, sizzling on the deck of the boat as it vaporized droplets of lake water. Sharlie bobbed her head from side to side, bathing them in the sound. But then... she abruptly clamped her mouth shut.

Annabelle blinked, her thoughts returning. *What just happened?*

High above the pontoon boat, Sharlie's neck was completely erect, her gaze no longer directed at them. She turned her head to one side and held it, then repeated the action on the other side. It appeared she was listening.

Annabelle snatched the burning flare from the deck before it ignited anything—or anyone—and whipped her head around. "Kev! Go!"

Kevin needed no urging. He started the boat back up and motored away. Behind them, Sharlie turned her head to face the northwest and began to swim.

"Something else has gotten its attention!" Annabelle shouted.

Sharlie didn't know what it was that drew her toward the distant shore. By all rights, she should have been feasting on the humans on the boat, but something else had taken her focus. At first, she had thought it was a sound, but she soon realized it was more than that. It was a compulsion. Some outside force was pulling at her. *No, that wasn't right...* It was pulling at the spherical object inside her, lodged deep in her stomach. And that sphere now urged her forward, directing her movements. Sharlie tore through the water, bearing down on the source of the sensations, unsated hunger building as she swam.

"That little stone... it's glowing even brighter!" Athena exclaimed. Her eyes were wide behind her glasses as she continued to stare at the dreamcatcher; the talisman now jutted straight out from the leather loop on the middle finger of Joseph's clenched fist, pointing to the southeast. "And it's... it's humming now!"

"It hasn't done that before," Russ said, coming over to Joseph.

"No... and it is no longer simply floating in that direction... it is *pulling*. If I hadn't made a fist, it would have yanked itself off my finger."

"Are you havin' a laugh with us?" Wolf asked.

Russ shook his head. "No joke, Wolf."

"Something is out there on the lake," Joseph said softly, "and it is coming this way."

"You mean... like a Nessie?" Wolf asked excitedly. "Then you believed those two lads?"

"I certainly did," Sarah said with conviction. "And earlier today, we received word about a monster attacking people on the lake."

"Aye... Athena heard about that, too," Wolf admitted. His shook his head, then kicked at the river rocks beneath his boots. "Right, then! Change of beasties, change of plans! Merle and... intern... let's go to the truck and grab any capture gear and weapons that might be useful. No idea how big this thing is. Ian, fetch your low-light and night vision cameras." He fanned his arms out. "Give me several angles toward the water. Athena... stay here and keep an eye on Russ and his pals." He turned to go but shouted back over his shoulder. "And, Russ, don't think I've forgotten about your Bigfoots! I know they're around here somewhere."

From his concealed position in the thicket many strides down the road, Brighteyes watched the other men return to the larger truck. They moved with speed and determination and spoke loudly as they gathered equipment from the back. The Bigfoot looked back at the shoreline, watching his friends. From their postures, they were tense and on edge. And they seemed to be focused on the dark lake beyond.

But then, their heads began to turn toward the sky. Brighteyes retreated further into the shadows as the roar of an engine and thump of whirling blades drew near. The helicopter had returned.

"Are you sure about this, sir?" Singleton asked. "The last time he saw you, Mr. Washakie seemed to wish you dead."

Carson thought back to that moment when he had been in the cage, and the expedition tracker had advised Singleton to kill the billionaire. Given what Carson now knew about his nature, he was amused by the irony of that suggestion. Although, to his credit, the Shoshone tracker had guessed at his condition before anyone else had. "Bill, I have little to fear from the man."

"But he's not alone."

"It won't matter," Carson said. *The more the merrier*, the inner voice concurred. "And with Brick at my side, nothing's going to hurt me."

"Not While I'm Around," Brick concurred.

"I am certain Joseph knows where the meteorite is... perhaps he even has it with him. And if that creature we saw on the lake is related, I can borrow a jet ski or that boat down there and go have a looksee."

"We'll be back on foot to reinforce you as soon as we can, sir," Singleton assured him.

Carson nodded. The flight crew had found a place to put down, but it was quite a hike from here, so he had ordered the chopper to return to the group of people on the beach and "drop him off" along with Brick.

"Coming to a hover. Get ready," the pilot announced over the intercom. "Overriding the door lock in ten seconds. Stand by."

"Everyone else, take your seats," Carson cautioned. "Brick... come here."

The big man rose. While he no longer wore his body armor, he retained the combat helmet atop his crooked head and a massive handgun holstered at his side.

"I will lead the way. You will follow after."

Brick grunted and wobbled his tilted head in agreement.

The helicopter dipped down and the side door began to open.

"Sharlie's really booking!" Brady cried from the bow of the *Slimy Slim*, his night vision scope held up to one eye.

"I see flashlights on the shore," Mark announced.

"Speed up, Kev!" Annabelle called out. "If Sharlie goes after those people, we may have to distract it again."

"Gre-e-a-at." Kevin drew the word out, sarcasm dripping from his pores. "Because that worked *so* well the last time." But he increased speed all the same. Whatever had been impeding the propeller was long gone, and the boat appeared to be behaving normally.

"There's the helicopter again," Stuart called out. "Looks like it's landing."

"I know that shoreline," Annabelle said. "It slopes and is right up against the road. No way can they land there."

And apparently, she was correct. The helicopter came to a low hover and trained its spotlight down at the edge of the water. Then... a man-sized object dropped to the shore.

Sarah looked up at the dark shape of the helicopter above them, then squinted as a powerful spotlight lit up the rocky shoreline, momentarily blinding her.

"Another helicopter? Who the bleddy hell is this now?" Wolf Wallace shouted as he and his crew returned from the truck, laden with equipment.

His question was soon answered. The spotlight pivoted below the helicopter, bathing the shallows and shoreline with light; a shadow dropped from above and landed in a half crouch at the edge of the water. The figure slowly straightened and stood before them, a toothy smile on its bearded face.

"Cameron Carson!" Sarah gasped.

Her surprise doubled as a second shape plummeted from the helicopter, but this one didn't land on its feet. The huge figure hit the shallow water behind Carson with an epic smacking belly flop. As the helicopter rose and accelerated away, Wolf's right-hand man —Merle, Sarah thought his name was—flipped on a wide-lensed flashlight to illuminate the two arrivals.

The enormous man rose from the water, apparently none the worse for wear, with the possible exception that his head was bent almost to his shoulder. A too-small combat helmet was snugged onto his head, but it was clear as day who this was.

Sarah couldn't believe her eyes. "Brick Broadway?!"

"But... he's dead!" Russ exclaimed, then pointed at the still-smiling Carson. "I mean, *you* were *probably* dead... but Brick was *definitely* dead."

"Ah, the miracles of modern medical science." Carson waded through the shin-deep water toward shore, nodding at the three ex-members of his expedition. "Russ... Sarah... Joseph. I suspect you know why I'm here. Joseph certainly does. Don't you, Joseph?"

No reply was forthcoming from the Shoshone, although his eyes were locked onto the billionaire. And while he continued to hold the levitating dreamcatcher's loop in his fist, Sarah saw his free hand drop to the hunting knife in its belt sheath.

Carson saw the motion too, but he didn't seem overly concerned as he reached the rock-strewn beach. Sloshing through the water behind Carson, Brick joined him and stood behind the billionaire's shoulder like a statue. Carson looked around at the assemblage.

"Gentlemen... ladies."

"Guys and Dolls," Brick added in a low rumble.

"I see some unfamiliar faces..." Carson continued.

"Wolf Wallace, Mr. Carson!" Wolf took several steps toward the billionaire, eager hand outstretched, but Russ intervened, intercepting him with a palm to the chest.

"Don't get too close."

"Now, now, Russ... no need to be hurtful." Carson mimed a sad pout before the unnerving grin returned. "As it happens, Mr. Wallace, I recognize you now. You were on a list of prospectives when we were assembling my Bigfoot expedition."

"Sorry I didn't make the cut," Wolf responded, a trace of bitterness in his voice.

"Yes, well... in the end, Mr. Cloud was clearly the better survivalist, and we decided on substance over flash."

"You son of a—" Wolf advanced on Carson but came up short when Brick shambled forward two steps.

"Shall We Dance?" the mammoth growled.

Wolf backed away.

Carson smiled. "Wise choice. As much as I'd love to make all of your acquaintance, I fear I'm pressed for time." He turned toward Joseph. "Where is it?" When Joseph didn't reply, Carson took a few casual steps toward him. "You either have it... or you know where it is."

"Are you talking about the Bigfoot?" Wolf asked. "Because they're nearby."

Sarah watched as Carson halted and lifted a hand to the side of his neck, rubbing the flesh beneath his fingertips. She remembered that was the spot where the teenage Sasquatch had bitten him... but there was no sign whatsoever of a wound.

Carson turned his attention to Wolf. "You said... *they* are nearby."

"Aye. At least two Bigfoots that I could see. I captured footage of them alongside Russ Cloud, but the bastard blasted my drone with a shotgun."

"Oops." Russ couldn't conceal his smile.

"I believe they transported them here in the backs of the two pickup trucks parked on the road up there, concealing them underneath tarps." Wolf puffed out his chest. "To try and escape from *me*, I suspect. But there's nary a man who can outfox—"

"Shut up." The billionaire's voice wasn't loud, but the menace it carried silenced Wolf instantly. Carson looked at Sarah. "*Two* Bigfoots. Well, well, well. And there *were* two of them that survived, correct?"

Sarah held Carson's gaze, although it wasn't easy. There was something disconcerting about his eyes... as if more than one person were looking back at her. She set her jaw and spoke with calm defiance. "There were. A young adult and a child. You met them before your... accident. After the last infected Bigfoot was destroyed, I helped them escape from the expedition perimeter. The last time I saw them, they were headed north; that was days ago and over fifty miles from here. I don't know what this skirt-wearing asshole is talking about."

Carson continued to stare at her, a grin beginning to grow. But then he shook his head violently, as if he were resetting his thoughts. "It's funny... last week, capturing a live Bigfoot was everything to me... but *this* week... I'm after something else. Something that I hope will shine a little light on what has happened to me." Once again, his focus returned to Joseph. "Where... is... the meteorite? Tell me now, or—" Carson halted. "What is that glowing thing you're holding? Is that it?"

When Joseph didn't reply, Carson advanced. Sharkey stepped in front of him with a hunting rifle held at his hip. Before he could bring it to bear, Carson lunged with unearthly speed and seized the weapon. Sharkey was far larger than the billionaire, yet Carson yanked the gun from his grip with ease and tossed it into the lake. Even though the sidearm throw appeared to be casual, the rifle sailed an astonishing distance, landing with a splash in the dark waters.

"Hey! That was my pap's!" Sharkey threw a brawler's punch, but Carson caught the Montanan's fist in midair with a meaty smack. The big man grimaced in pain as he was forced to the ground by Carson's white-knuckled grip.

Farley ran to help his friend, but Brick stepped forward and backhanded the guardsman, sending him sprawling. As the resurrected wrestler trudged toward his fallen prey, Sarah crouched beside Farley and dug the bear horn out of his jacket pocket. Pointing it toward the advancing man-mountain, she triggered an earsplitting blast. Brick staggered back and held his ears.

"Everyone, *stop*!" Sarah shouted. "Right now!"

Carson let go of Sharkey's hand, which the guardsman immediately cradled to his chest.

Sarah tossed the air horn on the ground. "You want to know what that thing Joseph has is? I'll tell you."

Brick dropped his hands from his ears and began to move toward her, but he abruptly stopped midstride, appearing frozen in place.

Sarah noticed that Carson was looking at his bodyguard when the big man went abruptly motionless. *Did Carson cause that?*

"You have the floor, Dr. Bishop," Carson said.

"Sarah... no." Joseph's voice was quiet but filled with conviction. "This thing will misuse any information you give it."

But he'll kill us all, if we don't give him something, Sarah thought. "There is a little stone in that dreamcatcher. It is *not* the one you're looking for, but they may be related."

Carson looked at the object floating in the air as if by magic. "Glowing... humming... defying gravity, from all appearances... and it seems to be pointing out toward the lake."

Athena suddenly spoke up. "Mr. Carson... I'm Wolf's technical advisor for *Man vs. Nature*. Give me a job in your tech division, and I'll tell you what I think is going on."

Carson's lip curled in amusement. "Done."

"I believe they've been using this dreamcatcher as a detector of sorts. The little rock appears to be attracted to something that is currently in the lake. In the time I've been here, I've witnessed the stone's illumination grow from less than ten lumens—a candle flame—to something approaching thirty lumens. And the low hum coming from it has been increasing by several decibels every minute."

Carson mulled this over, then began to chuckle. He shook his head as the chuckle grew to an eerie laugh.

Athena seemed thrown by this, so she plowed ahead with more conjecture. "We, uh... we met two teenagers who claimed a creature attacked them. These are their jet skis. Whatever is going on," she added, "maybe... maybe it's related to reports of a monster attacking things on the lake."

Carson's laugh ceased, but the smile remained. He pointed at Athena. "A gold star to my newest employee. What is your name, young lady?"

"Athena."

"Goddess of wisdom, how apropos." He looked out at the

lake. "As it happens, there is indeed a very large long-necked creature out there; we spotted it from the air about fifteen minutes ago. It was headed in this general direction if I'm not mistaken."

He looked again at the floating, humming, glowing dreamcatcher and the man who held it. "Mr. Washakie. Joseph. I know you are reluctant to engage with me in repartee, but allow me to provide you with a hypothesis. This beast may have interacted with the meteorite we both seek, and your toy is picking up on this creature. But here's what you might be overlooking—like magnets... opposites attract. If your little rock is drawn to whatever is out there... it may work the other way around."

As if to prove Carson's hypothesis correct, a deep, guttural bellow echoed across the lake.

"Blimey, that's close!" Wolf exclaimed, his Scottish accent slipping a bit. "Merle... fetch me claymore!"

"Wait, whoa!" Sharkey waved his hands. "You're not bringing a claymore mine down here!"

Merle snorted as he dug something out of the equipment. "Nah... he means his special machete. He saw that Liam Neeson *Rob Roy* movie and wanted his bushwhacking machete to look like a Scottish claymore, so I stuck a basket hilt on it for last season." He held out the sheathed weapon to his boss.

"Ach, good! Ian, get the lights and cameras set up. If something's out there, I want to see it!" Wolf strapped on the sheath of his "claymore" and struck a heroic pose... one that faltered slightly when the eerie bellow sounded again, much closer now.

Brick's mouth moved, even as he remained frozen in midstride. "Something's Coming," he rumbled.

"I've always wondered what a plesiosaur sounded like," Brady said after Sharlie trumpeted another loud call as she approached the shore.

"Not a plesiosaur," Stuart quickly retorted. "But whatever the hell it is, it's heading for that group of people on the shore."

Annabelle remembered the flares and dug one from her pocket. "Let's see if we can distract it... lure it back toward the water."

"And give it a second shot at eating us?" Kevin asked.

"No... we lure it away from those people... then make for the nearest shore before it catches up. Beach the boat and run for it. That thing doesn't look like it'd do well on land."

"We don't know that for sure, but... I'm game."

Annabelle extended the flare to Mark. "You do the honors. I've got another if that one burns out. I'll reload my rifle and shoot it a few more times, if the flare doesn't get its attention."

"Hang on!" Kevin announced, accelerating toward the creature as it neared the people on the shore.

Brighteyes gripped the tree trunk beside him, his powerful fingers digging into the bark. The newcomers that had dropped from the flying machine had attacked two of Sarah's friends—the men that had transported Littlefoot, DawnWaker, and him south. He had nearly burst from cover to come to their aid, but Sarah had made a loud noise with a device that hikers often carried; she'd then stopped the conflict with firm, confident speech. Brighteyes was pleased to witness this result.

In Bigfoot society, physical conflict was avoided whenever possible; a broken limb or deep wound could lead to severe hardship or even death, depending on the season of year and the purity of nearby water sources. If violence was imminent, another troop member would often play peacemaker.

Now, as one of the newcomers set up lights along the shore, Brighteyes could make out the man speaking with Russ, Joseph, and Sarah: it was the bearded man Sarah had introduced

Brighteyes to, many days ago at the human camp that Silverback had attacked. *But my brother Scratch killed that man. I am sure of it.* Brighteyes inhaled the night air and detected a familiar scent. It was faint and somewhat different from before, but it was there: *Alive-Dead.* The bearded man turned to speak to a woman with unusual hair the color of camas flowers.

Suddenly, a strange call echoed from the lake, sounding like no animal Brighteyes had ever heard. The humans on the shore, already agitated, displayed a mixture of excitement and fear. Brighteyes was about to cross back to the hilly side of the road to check on DawnWaker and Littlefoot when another sound reached his keen ears: the roaring of a man-machine out on the dark waters.

And then, as one of the humans turned on another bright light, something huge came into view in the shallows. The purple-haired female human screamed.

CHAPTER THIRTY-FOUR

When Ian triggered the bank of tripod lights, Athena shrieked and fled from the beach, sprinting toward the road.

"Holy shit... Sharlie's real!" the fireworks guy declared.

"Bleddy hell!" Wolf squawked.

"No fuckin' way," Russ stated flatly.

On the edge of the floodlights, a gigantic shape came into view, a massive neck weaving from side to side as it moved through the water, headed straight toward the gathering on the rocky beach.

"Magnificent," Carson purred.

"It's De-Lovely," Brick concurred.

"Are we rolling?" Wolf inquired at the top of his lungs.

"Rolling," Ian assured him in a nervous voice.

"It's comin' in hot!" Merle shouted, lifting the tranquilizer rifle they'd brought for any Sasquatch they came across.

Joseph moved his fist from side to side and the dreamcatcher pivoted on his finger, the webbed hoop and feathers pointing straight at the oncoming creature like a compass indicating north, the decorative feathers vibrating in the air. The creature reared its head back and trumpeted its guttural call again, but this time, Joseph detected a familiar hum underneath the bellow.

"Russ... did you hear that?" Joseph asked after the creature went silent again and resumed its advance. "Not the roar, but the after-echo."

"Yeah! It's like that chord I heard coming from the Stone that Sings. But it's weirdly muffled."

The Shoshone looked again at the dreamcatcher, jutting straight out at the oncoming creature; the tiny stone in the web was shining brightly. "I suspect the tone is muffled because the stone is *inside* the beast."

"That thing swallowed the meteorite?" Carson asked eagerly. When Joseph did not respond, the billionaire laughed. "It's *inside* it, isn't it?"

"Joseph! Get away from the shore!" Sarah cried out as the creature picked up speed.

"This is Wolf Wallace coming to you from Payette Lake in Idaho!" Wolf stood in front of one of Ian's cameras, pointing at the onrushing horror with one hand while brandishing his ridiculous machete in the other. "I came here looking for Bigfoot, but I found—nae, I *discovered*—something even better. Idaho's very own Loch Ness Monster... the creature from Payette Lake... Shirley!"

"Sharlie," Ian corrected.

"Shit... keep rolling, I'll dub it in post!"

"Nope nope nope nope nope." The fireworks guy shook his head repeatedly as he fired up the outboard to make a break for open water... only to realize he was still tied up to one of the pilings. He backpedaled the boat and rose to unloop the line.

Sharlie spotted the movement and her head snapped to the left as she reached the edge of the dock. Clamping her jaws onto the man from behind, she whipped her head to the right, tearing loose a sizable portion of the man's lower back.

"Jeezus!" Merle shouted. He raised the tranq gun and fired a dart at Sharlie's shiny body as the creature reached the shallows and began to rise from the water, hobbling onto the edge of the shore in a lurching, shambling gait, reminiscent of how a seal moves. Huge webbed, paddle-like claws scrabbled at the river rocks. An overwhelming stench of rot, pungent yet sickly sweet, permeated the air around it. While everyone scattered, two men stood their ground.

Carson pointed at the monster. "Brick... we'll need that hand cannon of yours."

"Annie Get Your Gun," Brick growled, extracting the enormous .50-cal Desert Eagle from its holster.

"That thing has something I want... would you be so kind as to kill it?"

As the shambling horror galumphed itself further onto the shoreline, the ex-ex-wrestler raised the handgun and emptied the seven-round magazine into its breast. The massive hollow-point bullets tore into the creature's flesh and the beast staggered back from the impacts. Its flanks shuddered like an elephant shaking off an attack of biting flies. Before the wrestler could reload, Sharlie's muscular neck swept down and across, whipping along the shore and slamming into Brick. The sledgehammer blow sent the huge man flying across the beach, where he smashed into a tripod camera and one of the floodlights, toppling them on their sides. The powerful spotlight lay upended in the rocks, throwing shafts of light and shadow across the shallows.

Sharlie's head swung back to center and froze, eyes locked on Joseph, who had retreated roughly ten yards from the water's edge. It raised its head and opened its mouth, and this time... the familiar tone wasn't so muffled. The bewitching emanations washed over Joseph and the humans around him, and the dreamcatcher's pull increased, lifting Joseph's arm toward the gaping maw. Rather than flee, the people in the cone in front of Sharlie's mouth stood in wonderment.

But one individual wasn't thus affected. Cameron Carson

dashed across the rocks and leaped high into the air, landing just behind the creature's head to straddle her neck. Reaching down to the beast's mouth, he grabbed one of the long, sharp teeth and yanked it out of its socket. This brutal act interrupted Sharlie's fascination with Joseph, and she turned her head, trying to reach her tormentor. Given Carson's position, she was unsuccessful.

Joseph shook himself as the effects of the Stone that Sings dissipated. He looked up at the beast, then down at the dreamcatcher... then over at the boat at the dock. And then a new distraction arrived: a pontoon boat with several people aboard, one of them waving a marine signal flare and shouting unintelligibly. Whether they were trying to warn the people on the beach or distract the monster, it wasn't clear.

"Joseph, you okay?" Russ asked.

"Yes. And I have an idea. Sarah, I'll need you too. If Carson keeps that thing distracted for a moment longer, this might work."

At that moment, Carson raised the pilfered tooth and rammed it into the creature's right eye, eliciting a shriek and a furious thrashing of the neck as the makeshift dagger robbed Sharlie of half of her eyesight.

"Go!" Joseph shouted. He dashed for the bass boat at the dock with Sarah hot on his heels.

Russ followed but called back over his shoulder. "Wolf! Make yourself useful and shoot that thing with anything you've got. Hell, throw rocks if you have to!" He ran to the shore, passing the jet skis to join Joseph and Sarah by the dock. "Is Fireworks Guy dead?"

"Extremely." Joseph reached into the blood-spattered boat and removed the metal case with the controls for the fireworks barge. He handed it to Sarah.

"I have no idea how to use this."

"You'll have a few minutes to figure it out." Joseph pointed at the pontoon boat with the waving flare. "And maybe someone on board that boat can help you. I'm going to drop you off there. Russ, you any good with jet skis?"

"Yeah... I used to ride one back in—"

"Good enough," Joseph interrupted. He slipped the dreamcatcher from his finger and gave it to Russ. "Your job is to play keep-away. No need to put it on your finger... just keep it handy. Put your headphones on and drive over near the fireworks barge... you can just see it there in the moonlight. When Sharlie comes after you—and I suspect she will—keep her occupied, but stay out of reach and don't stray too far from the barge."

"Where will you be?"

"On the barge. I figure the fireworks are full of safety features, so I'll be doing my best to make it all... *unsafe*."

"I see where you're going. When you're ready, you signal me... I lead Sharlie to the barge and throw the dreamcatcher aboard."

"And when Sharlie goes after it, I blow the barge!" Sarah finished.

At that moment, Cameron Carson came flying into the river rocks nearby; Sharlie had finally managed to shake him loose, and with such velocity that bones were surely broken. The billionaire tumbled to a jarring halt, several limbs bent at unnatural angles. Gunshots rang out and fleshy thuds sounded as some of Wolf's crew, along with Sharkey, pelted the monster with buckshot, tranq darts, and rocks. Wolf lifted his gussied-up machete and waved it in the air, yelling Gaelic obscenities. But Sharlie ignored all of it, focusing instead on Russ.

"That's my cue!" he shouted. Russ raised the headphones from around his neck and seated them over his ears in case the creature felt like singing a mind-warping encore, then he jumped aboard the jet ski and turned the key.

Sharlie swiveled her bulk around on the shore, trying to get within striking distance. By this time, Brick Broadway was back for more and grabbed hold of the creature's tail. Despite his vast strength, his feet didn't have enough purchase on the loose rocks and scree and Sharlie dragged him along as she lurched toward Russ.

"Catch me if you can, you Nessie wannabe!" he cried as he tore away from shore and veered to the left to draw her away from the remaining jet ski and the pontoon boat that was just offshore.

As Sharlie hit the shallows and dragged herself toward deeper water, Joseph mounted the remaining jet ski. Sarah squeezed on behind, gripping him around his middle with one hand while holding the control case's handle with the other. In moments, they were roaring toward the nearby pontoon boat.

"We've got incoming!" Brady called as he squinted past the blinding light of the marine flare toward the sound of an approaching motor. "It's two people on a jet ski!"

The flare in Mark's hand chose that moment to sputter and die out as it reached the end of its life. He tossed it overboard, where it hissed. Annabelle was about to hand him another when the jet ski arrived and pulled up alongside. A man with tan skin and a luxurious black braid was at the controls with a blonde sitting behind him.

"Permission to come aboard?" the woman asked as she held up a case she was carrying. "And can someone take this, please?"

Mark grabbed the case as Brady offered a hand to help pull the woman up from the jet ski. Annabelle leaned over the side to address the man but he abruptly rocketed away, riding off into the gloom. She turned to her new passenger and opened her mouth to introduce herself, but the blonde beat her to it.

"Hi, I'm Sarah... and that was Joseph. He's on a mission... and I've got one too." She took the case from Mark, set it on a bench, and flipped it open. "Any of you know how to work a fireworks display control box?"

As Brighteyes watched his friends race into the darkness on the fast water-machines, he thought about what he might do to help. He wasn't sure that he *could* help, having never seen such a large creature in all his time on this earth. What was more, the arrival of the beast had been preceded by the overpowering stench of the Alive-Dead smell. Brighteyes mulled over his options and realized he should first check in with Littlefoot and DawnWaker. They would certainly have heard the commotion, and the last thing he wanted was for them to come running to his aid with so many armed, fearful humans and a gigantic monster on the loose. Staying in the shadows, he crossed back across the road.

Sharlie tracked the single rider on the speedy little boat as she felt the strange compulsion continuing to tug at her, urging her to follow. Unfortunately, she felt something else pulling at her from the opposite direction, interfering with her ability to pick up speed. Arching her head up and back over her body, she spotted the unusually large human in waist-deep water, holding on to her tail. She swept her mouth downward, closing her jaws onto the man's head. As soon as her teeth clamped down, she felt two of them break; the human had some kind of hard head covering on— like a turtle's shell, but much tougher. Nevertheless, she found enough purchase to grip the head, which was oddly tilted on the man's shoulder. She twisted to the side to pull him loose from her tail; there was a loud crack as her tormentor was tossed aside into the shallows. Now unencumbered, Sharlie charged forward, reaching deeper water and picking up speed, following the siren song that was now coming from somewhere out on the lake, cloaked in darkness.

As the monster disappeared from the reach of the lights on shore, Wolf sheathed his machete and grabbed Ian's arm as the cameraman was lowering his rig from his shoulder. "Did you get any good shots?"

"Some, but only on this handheld. That thing trashed Camera One. And the light was all over the place."

"Ach, that won't do! We need more footage! If we can get some close-up action shots with that Idaho Nessie, they'll be shoving Emmys up our arses." Wolf abruptly snorted a laugh. "An Emmy enema! Good line. Write that down!" He found Merle and pointed at the bass boat. "Merle, help me get the corpse out of that boat! You and I will go out there and find the beastie. Ian, you too! Bring the night vision camera."

Merle shook his head, then threw down his tranquilizer rifle and let loose an Ozark-accented tirade. "Aw, *hell* no! You want me to go out there with a fifty-foot monster that just ripped that boat guy's spine out? That dog won't hunt. Go out there y'own damn self, ya fake-ass limey bastard. I quit." With that, he stormed off in the direction Athena had fled.

Ian watched them go, then looked at Wolf, his resolution fading.

"*Et tu*, Ian?" Wolf intoned.

"Sorry, boss... your health benefits won't cut it if I get my spine ripped out. We're taking the U-Haul. I'll leave you an ATV to get down to McCall." Ian set down the handheld, then retrieved another camera from a case. Walking up to Wolf, he handed it over. "Here's the night vision cam. That button starts her up. You can do the shoot yourself. You know. Like Russ Cloud does." He turned and trotted after Merle.

Wolf looked around for the remaining member of his crew. "You! Intern! Starts with a K... Keith! Come with me, and you'll be my new number two!"

Keith Henry Billings—a young electrician's apprentice with a bright future—replied, "If I go out there with that thing, chances are I *will* end up as a number two." He flipped Wolf the bird and went back to the road.

"That was a good line," Wolf admitted quietly as he watched the last of his employees abandon him.

Hefting the night vision camera, Wolf turned and trudged toward the bloody bass boat. He paused beside Sharkey and Farley, who were recovering from their encounter with Carson. "I'm shite with boats. Either of you blokes want to make a quick thousand bucks?"

"Fuck off," they snapped in unison.

"I would be more than happy to assist." Carson limped into the beam of the toppled spotlight; the ground-based illumination cast a long shadow out in front of him.

Wolf stared in amazement. "But I thought... I thought that monster broke every bleedin' bone in yer body."

"I'm a fast healer. And I'm also a fair hand with boats. Let's get you some good closeups of the beast. I *insist*."

Carson took Wolf by the shoulder and force-marched him to the dock; Wolf was surprised by the strength of the man's grip as he was propelled along the rocky beach and couldn't help but notice that Carson's limp was practically gone by the time they reached the boat.

Wolf looked down at the bloody remains of Fireworks Guy. "I don't know if I can do this..."

"Then allow me." Carson walked down the dock and jumped into the gruesome boat. Gripping the dead man by the back of his collar and bloody belt, Cameron unceremoniously tossed him over the side, where the corpse floated toward shore.

Wolf was about to step down into the boat but paused as he watched Carson look at his right hand—the one that had gripped the man's belt, right below the generous bite Sharlie had taken out of the poor soul. The hand was coated in blood.

Carson turned his hand over, looking at the red sheen on his palm. He blinked, then noticed Wolf staring at him. "Messy business. Why don't you untie the line to the dock while I wash this off?"

Wolf did as instructed, then settled himself in the bow with the night vision camera while Carson started the outboard and motored away from shore. Wolf shuddered, trying to make sense of what he'd seen as he'd unmoored from the dock: right before the billionaire had reached over the side to wash the blood from his hand... he had licked the palm. Several times.

Aboard the Sharlie Hunters' pontoon boat, Stuart pointed at the red buttons on the yellow surface of the fireworks control box. While the others had been trying to puzzle out the contraption, Stuart had simply brought up a YouTube how-to video for it.

"So... not that difficult. First, we turn this key to power it up."

Sarah did so and the display at the top lit up with two red zeros. "Looks like it's on."

"Good. Now, each of these twelve numbered buttons corresponds to a transmitter... and if you want them to all go boom, just start punching numbers, followed by that 'All Fire' button. One, all fire... two, all fire... three, all fire... and so forth."

"Okay... great!" Sarah looked out at the distant barge, where Joseph's jet ski had just arrived. Beyond the barge, she could make out Russ circling at high speed in the moonlight.

"Uh-oh. Problem," Stuart said.

Sarah looked back down at the control box. "What? Oh... shit." The red zeros had changed to "Low Battery."

"Too slow, ya rubber-necked bastard!"

Russ sent up a spray from his bow wave as he turned the jet ski hard to port, changing direction away from the fireworks barge. Sharlie followed, about ten yards behind... which was closer than Russ cared for. The creature's neck itself was about five yards long and could shoot forward in an instant if she reared back and struck... which she had done several times already. In the shadows atop the barge, Russ could just make out Joseph. He lifted one of his sound-baffling earmuffs from an ear as he made a close pass.

"Hurry it up, buddy!" he yelled as he roared past. "The low fuel light just came on!"

"Almost done!" came the reply.

Aboard the barge, Joseph stabbed his hunting knife into the cardboard casing of another mortar shell, slitting open the side to get at the gunpowder within. Many of the pyrotechnics for this display were in metal housings but, scouring the racks, he'd been able to find plenty that he could break open. Whenever possible, he left the ignition wires in place, then tipped the ruptured shells on their sides. When Sarah set them off, they should detonate across the multiple piles of gunpowder he'd assembled.

Joseph watched with concern as Russ made another pass; his friend had already experienced a few close calls from Sharlie's whipping strikes. Joseph figured he'd amassed enough explosives out in the open that an ignition would likely send the whole thing up, in either a fiery conflagration or—if they were lucky—a massive explosion. Either one should take care of this creature. If it had been altered in the same fashion as the infected Sasquatch had been, it would be resistant to many forms of physical injury. But fire... fire should take care of it. The bodies of the Bigfoots that had attacked the camp had burned just fine.

Hopping aboard his jet ski, Joseph roared away from the barge toward Russ, who was currently headed away from the barge, circling around for another pass. Barreling across the lake at full throttle, Joseph cut the corner and pointed the jet ski's headlamps at Russ, shouting as he neared, "Russ! Throw the dreamcatcher on the barge, now!"

With one earmuff still off his ear and on the side of his head, Russ heard the command. He banked sharply, nearly swamping the jet ski in the process. The nozzles lost some of their thrust and Sharlie rapidly gained. Russ managed to get up to speed just before she arrived, and he could smell the beast's fetid breath receding in his wake. Tearing across the lake, he reached the barge in seconds and brought the jet ski in close. Slowing only for a moment, he dug the dreamcatcher from inside his shirt and tossed it into the middle of the barge. He increased speed and turned the corner around the barge just as the sound of a tremendous impact reached him. Russ looked over his shoulder and spotted the waving neck of Sharlie silhouetted against the starry sky; the beast was halfway onto the barge, trying to pull herself onto it.

"Blow it! Blow it!" Russ shouted as he gunned the throttle to leave the likely blast radius... only to have the engine cough, sputter, and die... mere feet from the barge.

"We need four double-A batteries! Anyone?" Sarah shouted. "Brady, how about that camera?"

"It has a rechargeable pack. Kevin, don't you have a little flashlight in the glove box or something?"

"It uses triple-As!"

"Fuck me sideways," Sarah cursed under her breath.

The display with the "Low Battery" indicator had winked out

moments ago, and the group had been scrounging the equipment on the boat without success.

"Detonate the fireworks!" Joseph called out as he coasted up to the starboard side.

"The batteries in the control box are dead!" Sarah shouted. "The fireworks guy's boat must have some spares!"

"I'll go back there and... wait a moment..." Joseph revved his jet ski to steer it slightly to the side, redirecting its headlamps. In the beam, he spotted the bass boat that the fireworks display operator had been aboard. Wolf Wallace crouched in the bow with a camera held in one hand; another figure sat at the stern, operating the outboard motor.

"Carson!" Joseph accelerated toward the billionaire.

CHAPTER THIRTY-FIVE

Carson heard the shout coming from behind oncoming headlights. Wolf cursed and lowered his camera.

"Damned light blinded me camera! It's that Indian bloke coming on a jet ski."

"Native American," Carson corrected. "Shoshone, to be precise." He steered to port as the jet ski came alongside. "Joseph... just the man I was looking for. Where is the creature?"

Joseph ignored the question as he coasted to a stop and bumped against their hull. Grabbing hold of the side, he looked into the boat. "Is there a bag of tools in here? A backpack, perhaps?"

Carson glanced down at a black object under the bench in front of him. "Why? What do you need it for?"

Joseph did not respond, but Wolf let out a whoop. "I see the beastie yonder! On the fireworks barge!"

"Fireworks...?" Carson asked.

"Ach, ye didn't know... there was s'posed to be some big display tonight. The poor soul who was on this boat was in charge of running it."

Carson grinned at Joseph. "Ah... so that's your plan. Sorry...

but I have a plan of my own." With that, he accelerated away from the jet ski, heading toward the barge and shouted to Wolf, "When we get to the barge, you'll need to take over the outboard."

"I thought we were just getting some footage," Wolf said. "What are ye plannin' on doin'?"

"A little gastric surgery. That fancy machete of yours... give it to me."

Annabelle listened intently, trying to hear above the idling of the *Slimy Slim*'s engine. There it was again... a man's voice, carried across the water from the direction of the barge. She squinted, trying to make out the shape in the water near the barge. "Sarah, your other friend... I think he's in the water near the barge. I can see a jet ski with no rider."

"That must be Russ! Can you see him anywhere?"

Brady joined them and braced his night vision scope on the back of the port bench. "There's the jet ski... and I can see Sharlie on the barge... looks like she's hunting for something."

"Oh my God, Russ!"

"Hang on... there he is! He's swimming away from the barge." Brady pointed to a spot in the water where Russ was located. "Still too close, if the barge blows right now."

"Well, without batteries, we can't blow it anyway."

"Not with that control box," Annabelle said, digging in a pocket. "But you probably could set things off with this!" She held up the remaining marine flare.

Just then, Joseph raced up to them. "Carson's in control of the boat and he's headed for the barge. No joy on the batteries."

"We have another option," Annabelle said, removing the igniter top from the flare. "Will this work?"

Joseph's normally stoic expression lit up with a smile. "Provided I can land it next to one of the piles of gunpowder, yes! Ignite it for me?"

While Annabelle started the flare, Sarah leaned over the side, pointing toward the barge. "Russ fell off his jet ski. He's swimming away from the fireworks, but please make sure he's safe before you blow it?"

"I'll do my best." Joseph reached up and took the blazing flare, then accelerated away like an Olympic torchbearer, the bright flame lighting up his wake in an eerie red.

Where is it? Sharlie had managed to haul her bulk up onto the metal surface of the square boat and was raising and lowering her head like a crane, dipping her snout in between all of the objects that filled the vessel. The target of her search was here; she could *feel* it in her gut. She was dimly aware of other sensations: a sulfurous, metallic odor coming from powdery black dirt that lay in piles around her; a bright light approaching in the distance, flickering red; the sounds of a rumbling engine, approaching from a different direction. But all of these sensory stimuli faded into the background as a pulsing compulsion continued to drive her movements.

There! A yellow glow from beneath a metal drum drew her eye. She nosed the obstacle aside and looked down on a disc made of sinew, leather, and feathers. Freed from the drum, the object of her desire actually rose into the air, floating toward her. An approxima-tion of the thought that passed through Sharlie's mind was: *Well, that was easy.* She opened her mouth, and the object began its journey to join its counterpart, deep in her stomach.

Carson watched in eager anticipation as the barge grew closer.

"I'm having second thoughts about this, guv!" Wolf cried in his native Londoner accent, his put-on Scottish brogue jettisoned by fear as the massive creature filled the viewscreen of his night vision camera.

"What is it doing?" Carson pondered aloud as he brought the bass boat in close.

"Looks like it's... swallowing something. Blimey... you s'pose it's eating Russ Cloud?"

"Well, that would be a shame, wouldn't it?" Carson drew the basket-hilted machete from the sheath Wolf had given him. "This isn't a dull-as-a-butterknife prop, I hope?"

Wolf's alter ego managed to reengage and the brogue returned. "Nae... I keep her sharp for bushwhacking trails."

Not believing that for a second, Carson tested the edge on his skin, slicing it across his forearm. He was pleasantly surprised when blood beaded along the slice. "Yes... this'll do the trick." With only an instant of mental focus, the blood began to move across his skin and the edges of the cut knitted themselves together. "I'm going aboard. Take the boat a few yards away and wait for me. If you try to run, Brick will track you down and turn you inside out. Quite literally. He'll probably hum a Broadway tune as he pulls your liver and pancreas out through your nipples."

In truth, he wished he'd brought Brick along, but the wrestler had taken some damage during his scuffle with Sharlie, and Carson didn't believe the man healed at the same rate that he did. In addition, he doubted this small boat could have carried the body-guard's additional weight.

Reaching the barge, Carson stepped across. Keeping low and brandishing the blade, he moved through the drums, canisters, and barrels toward his prey. *I wonder where its stomach is?*

Russ paused his swim as a fiery red beacon left the distant pontoon boat and rapidly approached, a pair of small headlights visible beneath the flare. He treaded water and waved an arm over his head. In seconds, Joseph arrived, coasting to a stop.

"Climb aboard!"

With assistance from Joseph's free hand, Russ was able to mount the aft seat. "Thanks! Let's get the heck away before Sarah blows the barge."

"Change of plans. *You're* blowing the barge." Joseph twisted in his seat and offered up the flare. "With this."

'We must not run away,' Littlefoot signed. 'We must help our friends.'

Brighteyes gave a grunt-whine that indicated mixed apprehension. 'But... many humans. Some with boom-sticks. And a huge beast like I have never seen. I must keep you safe.' He looked to DawnWaker. 'Both of you.'

DawnWaker brushed her knuckles across his upper arm. 'I am not afraid. And Littlefoot is right. They helped us... we help them.'

Brighteyes sighed and nodded. 'Yes.' *But how would we fight such a creature?* He glanced around the copse of trees where they crouched. His eyes focused on a sturdy-looking branch that lay in the needles beneath a tree. He thought back to the final battle with Silverback... one of the humans had fashioned a weapon out of such a stick and used it to pierce the infected Bigfoot's leg. In the old lore of the forest folk, it was a common weapon among humans before the arrival of boom-sticks. He grabbed the branch, snapped off a few extraneous twigs from its length, then located a small rock. Placing the tip of the branch against a larger rock, he began to scrape the tip, sharpening it to a point.

Littlefoot watched, then panted in understanding. Locating another long branch, he offered it to DawnWaker. 'We make too!'

Carson pushed himself between a bank of metal drums and a toppled barrel of gunpowder to find himself beside Sharlie's midsection. Glancing up, he could see the monster's neck extended straight up into the air, its jaws open and gaping toward the starry sky. *I have no idea what it's doing and I don't care*, he thought as he raised the machete and dashed forward, eyes locked on a spot that he assumed would contain the creature's digestive system. The billionaire swung the weapon down and the blade slashed into its flank. A normal human would have likely failed to pierce the tough hide, but Carson's inhuman strength lent the swing a terrifying velocity; unfortunately, that worked against him as the edge struck a rib and the blade snapped off at the fancy bespoke basket hilt. Cursing, he tossed the remnant aside.

You don't need a weapon, Cameron... a voice insisted. *You* are *a weapon.*

Flashing a grin, Carson gave in to the savage urges and plunged his hands into the freshly made slit. He had just begun to tear it open when a bright light flashed in his peripheral vision. He whipped his head to the side and spotted a red shooting star arcing through the air toward the barge.

In an instant, the bloodlust abated just enough for Carson to realize he was standing on a fireworks barge full of gunpowder... and that "shooting star" was a flare.

"No!"

Unwilling to test the limits of his newfound durability, Carson vaulted the nearest bank of pyrotechnics and hurled himself toward the lake just as an acrid smell hit his nostrils. He was in midair when the sky erupted in white light.

Wolf Wallace had been busily filming what he suspected was about to be an Emmy-award-winning piece of footage: Carson had slashed Wolf's claymore against the lake monster and his precious weapon broke with the impact. Wolf didn't care, as he suspected the *next* thing he would capture in the night vision camera was Sharlie devouring one of the world's most famous celebrities.

Suddenly, his viewscreen was blotted out by an unexpected light source. As the software adjusted for the unexpected illumination, he could tell that it was a flare, arcing down into the middle of the barge. The *fireworks* barge. The fireworks barge that Wolf was far too close to.

"Oh... bugger me..."

A massive explosion lit the sky, gouts of flame reflecting off the surface of the lake. Sparks flew in all directions as the piles of gunpowder cooked off in a series of deafening booms. Some fireworks triggered properly and launched: errant rockets whizzed forth from the barge, and blazing stars detonated high in the moonlit sky. A tricolored smiley face glittered for a moment as a cascade of spinning sparklers floated downwind from an aerial burst.

Aboard the barge, Sharlie—the Twilight Dragon of Payette Lake—was blown into bloody, burning chunks. The latticework meteorite was blasted apart and propelled outward, fragmenting into numerous greenish shards. One of the larger fragments found a new home... punching into Wolf Wallace's chest cavity.

"Bullseye!" Russ crowed from behind Joseph as the pair roared away from the explosion. "You think we killed it? Whoa, watch out! Incoming! Veer left!"

Joseph skidded to the side just as Sharlie's head and three feet of lake monster neck splashed into the water beside them.

"Well, that answers that," Russ said as Joseph idled a hundred yards from the burning barge.

Joseph grunted. "And if we're lucky, Carson was still aboard during the explosion."

Ascending from the depths after his headlong plunge, Carson breached the surface. Instinctually, he opened his mouth to suck in a lungful of air before remembering that such was no longer required; that would explain how hard he'd had to kick, having little natural buoyancy left in his body. He smelled burnt hair and realized his precious beard and mane of luxurious locks had been partially flash-fried before he'd reached the water. Carson spotted the bass boat nearby; Wolf Wallace appeared to be standing in it, backlit by the blazing barge. Carson swam up to the boat and grabbed the side.

"I must confess, Wolf, I figured you for the type to hightail it out of here the moment you had the chance," he said as he pulled himself aboard. "Did you get some good footage at least?"

Wolf replied with an odd sound somewhere between a gurgle and a snarl. He reached toward Carson, then slumped to his knees, rocking the bass boat in the water.

Carson looked at the man. Wolf Wallace had clearly sustained a lethal wound, and yet... he was still upright and functioning. Carson spied a shard of something sharp and greenish embedded in the man's chest.

The faux Scotsman looked down at his own chest and gurgled, "I'm feelin' a wee bit peely-wally..."

"Well... here's your problem," Carson replied, pulling the greenish sliver out of the man's chest cavity.

The moment the object was removed, Wolf's body went boneless and clunked face-first onto the bottom of the bass boat. Carson held the object aloft, peering at its phosphorescent greenish hue... and instantly felt a kinship with it.

"I do believe that you are what I'm looking for."

Tucking the piece of meteorite into his pocket, he settled into place at the outboard and aimed the boat for shore. The shard in Carson's pocket exuded a pleasing warmth and seemed to whisper in his mind... and it appeared to be conversing silently with The Other. With a casual glance at the reality show host lying in the bilge of the bass boat, Carson reached down and tried to wrench one of the man's legs free of its pelvic socket. When the limb proved troublesome, the billionaire dropped to his hands and knees... and sank his teeth into the tender flesh of the thigh beneath the man's kilt, tearing loose a mouthful. The direction of the tiller on the outboard motor—and the overall physics of the boat's speed and trajectory—brought the gruesome tableau toward shore.

Annabelle had watched the tremendous explosion and subsequent display of errant fireworks, accompanied by chunks of lake monster sailing into the water. "Yes!" She pumped her fist, but the Sharlie Hunters were strangely silent.

"Such a waste," Stuart said.

"Well... there's probably enough of it left for a DNA analysis," Mark suggested.

"Good, we can finally settle the debate on what she is. Or... was." Brady scanned the waters near the burning barge. "The fire's playing hell with the night vision... but I can see... yeah, it's that bass boat again. It's heading to shore."

"Who's on it?" Annabelle asked.

"Hard to tell... looks like someone is crouched low in the bilge, but I can't make them out."

"Do you see Russ and Joseph?" Sarah asked nervously.

"Not with this thing." Brady waggled the night vision scope. "Too bright over there by that fire."

"I see them!" Kevin shouted, starting up the pontoon boat and motoring toward the onrushing jet ski.

In moments, Russ and Joseph arrived, their jet ski sputtering as it ran on fumes. "Well... that worked," Russ said with a breathless laugh.

"What about the Stone that Sings?" Sarah asked as she reached over to help Mark assist the two men aboard.

"What kind of stone?" Annabelle asked.

"Long story," Russ said. "I dunno, Sarah... that was quite a kablooey. Might have destroyed it."

"If it's a meteorite, then it survived the heat of reentry..." Sarah cautioned.

"Ah. True."

"But we no longer have the dreamcatcher to track it," Joseph lamented.

"Listen," Annabelle said, "now that Sharlie's been dealt with, I think me and the fellas need to go back to the boat parade and render aid."

"Totally understand," Sarah said. "Can you drop us ashore? We need to check on our... friends."

Annabelle watched an odd look pass between the trio, but she shrugged and swatted Kevin on the back. "Take us to that dock, Kev... then let's see what we can do back at the parade."

Brighteyes had watched as the woman with hair the color of camas flowers and three men unloaded a small four-wheeled vehicle from the large truck before driving away to the north. Satisfied that no one else was up by the road, he beckoned for DawnWaker and Littlefoot to follow him to the other side. Walking in a low crouch, they made their way into the copse of trees that Brighteyes had earlier used for cover. All three carried rudimentary spears they had carved from branches.

'I no see pretty lady or man with funny hat or man with long black hair,' Littlefoot signed.

Brighteyes grunted. On the shore, only two men currently remained upright—the ones who had driven them in the trucks with tarps. There was a third male figure—a very large one—but this one seemed crippled, lying on his back far down the rock-strewn beach and flailing his limbs like an upended turtle.

'I thought you said there were many humans,' DawnWaker said.

'There were.'

'And where is the big monster you saw?' Littlefoot asked.

'I do not know.'

Brighteyes sniffed the air. He could detect the remnants of the Alive-Dead smell on the breeze coming off the lake, but he detected something else on the wind. "Rain coming." Closing his eyes, he listened intently. 'Water-machine coming, too. No... *two* water-machines. Stay hidden.'

After a moment, a single small boat appeared, moving at a slow speed. It reached the rocky beach and grounded itself. From inside the boat, a bearded face rose into view: its facial hair was singed and patchy, its visage red with blood and gore. And it was chewing.

Moments later, a second boat came into view, and three figures stepped off it onto a man-made platform that jutted into the lake.

Littlefoot gave an excited squeak and signed, 'It is our friends!'

Brighteyes hushed his young half brother and gripped his homemade spear while watching the first boat, just as the occupant's head swiveled toward the sound of the new arrivals. Overhead, a light rain started to fall.

As the rain began, Russ helped Sarah step across to the rickety dock, lifting her from the pontoon boat and holding her to his chest as he pivoted and placed her on the boards, taking his sweet time releasing her. Joseph moved past them toward the shore as Annabelle and the Sharlie Hunters motored back into the lake. Sarah looked up at Russ.

"You know very well I could have stepped across on my own."

"I do. I do very well know that." Russ gave her a quick kiss. "But I saw my opportunity and took it."

Sarah gave him a smile, her teeth reflecting the moon's light. "Smooth. Listen, we need to get across the road and find Brighteyes..." she began.

"We may have a problem," Joseph said, his normally stoic delivery betraying an undercurrent of nervousness.

Russ followed Joseph's gaze and spotted Sharkey and Farley sitting in the middle of the shore... but that wasn't where the Shoshone was looking. The fallen lights from Wolf's crew were still casting sharp beams through the rocks, and Russ spotted the bass boat Carson and Wolf had been in earlier; it was beached on the rocks, and Carson was climbing out of it, his eyes locked on the two National Guardsmen.

Behind Carson, Russ could see Brick Broadway rising to his feet and moving toward his boss, but the gigantic bodyguard scarcely registered as a threat after Russ got a better look at the billionaire: Carson was soaked in blood, from nose to waist, and his long hair and beard appeared to have been partially burnt off. Most unnerving were his eyes; pupils dilated, they practically shone with madness. He had something in his hand that glistened with blood and a shiny white substance that Russ realized was bone. It was a femur. Carson tore a final morsel off the grisly trophy and tossed it aside as he began moving toward the guardsmen.

"Sharkey! Farley! RUN!"

MEAT...

The Other had a firm grip on the reins and steered its puppet toward the nearest source of warm blood, bone, muscle, and organs. Through the rain, Carson could see two men on the rock-strewn shingle, the two National Guardsmen that had been helping... who was it they had been helping? Carson couldn't quite remember but knew that these two could be—*should be*—consumed. He was vaguely aware of a large figure behind him, but he knew the meat on that one was a bit off. What was his name? *Brick*—yes, that was it. *Brick was useful.* He willed the man-mountain to follow.

Voices shouted from further down the rock-strewn beach and the two men nearest him suddenly looked up. Their eyes growing wide with surprise and fear, they scrambled backward down the beach as Carson broke into a run. One man—the shorter of the two—held up a hunting shotgun and racked the pump on it, raising the barrel.

Carson focused for an instant, and Brick suddenly charged forward, taking the first round of buckshot in the chest. Using him as a human shield, Carson darted around from behind the huge bodyguard at the last instant and grabbed the barrel of the shotgun, bending the metal before the weapon discharged a second time. With the follow-on shot, the barrel split with a bang and the man let go of the broken weapon and turned to run.

Acting in unison, Carson and Brick each took an arm and "made a wish," ripping Farley's arms off like a Thanksgiving wishbone. That left the big man, who screamed in horror at his friend's demise. Carson's eyes gleamed as he closed in on his next victim... but abruptly came up short.

A trio took up positions alongside the big man: a blond

woman, a man in a do-rag, and a very familiar Native American with a long black braid.

You...

CHAPTER THIRTY-SIX

Russ watched as Carson locked eyes with Joseph, who had drawn his long hunting knife and was weaving it in a figure-eight pattern in front of himself. Sharkey and Sarah both picked up rocks, and Russ spotted something that might prove useful. Stooping, he picked up the cattle prod that one of Wolf's flunkies had brought for a potential Bigfoot capture.

"You..." Carson repeated again, staring at Joseph, his face a mask of hatred and hunger.

"The meteorite has been blown to pieces!" Sarah declared—although Russ knew she was the one that suggested it might still be intact. "What you were looking for is gone."

Carson's gaze shifted to her and he grinned an impossibly wide grin, the corners of his mouth stretching far more than Russ had ever seen in any publicity photos. "Oh... is it?" the billionaire asked in a mocking tone before drawing a jagged greenish sliver out of his pocket.

As the only one of the group who had actually laid eyes on the Stone that Sings, Russ recognized the material immediately. He could hear a faint tone in the air, but the piece was small enough that it didn't seem to be having an effect, at least not at this distance. "Okay... so... you got what you came for," Russ said, holding the cattle prod at the ready. "There's no need for violence."

Now Carson's eyes found Russ. "Oh, but on that point... I must heartily disagree. I feel a great need for violence..." His southern patrician drawl was intact, but none of the charm remained, and the corners of his grin managed to stretch another half inch.

With the light rain continuing to fall, Carson started forward, but suddenly there came a tremendous roar—an unmistakable challenge. Everyone froze, man and monster alike, and looked toward the slope to the road.

Brighteyes stood in a wide stance, arms outstretched, with what looked to be a stout wooden spear in one hand. Beside him, the red-body female Bigfoot held a similar spear. Canines bared, Brighteyes roared again.

Brick Broadway looked at this shaggy newcomer, his head flopping on what might have been a recently rebroken neck, courtesy of Sharlie. He raised an arm and pointed at Brighteyes, his granite-jawed face twisting with rage. Song titles were gone as he spoke in halting speech. "You... killed... me..."

Carson chuckled. "Well... a relative did... but yes. This would be an excellent chance for a round two with a Sasquatch, don't you think, Brick?" He turned to the group. "As I recall, Brick's former death occurred from an impromptu piledriver, delivered by the father of *that* Bigfoot right there."

Brick appeared to be straining at an invisible leash, his fists clenching and unclenching. He looked at Carson imploringly.

"Oh, very well. Sic him, Brick."

Brick grinned. "Put On a Happy Face." He began trudging toward the Bigfoots.

"No!" Sarah threw a river rock, which collided with Brick's dented helmet, setting his rebroken neck to wobbling like a bobblehead, but he continued moving inexorably toward Brighteyes.

"Let him have his fun." Carson bared his teeth. "I certainly intend to have mine..." The Other took full control and Carson growled long and low in his throat before charging.

Carson reached out for Sarah, who was closest. She stumbled backward, but the billionaire moved inhumanly fast. Fortunately, as his fingers brushed her clothing, Russ rammed the tip of the cattle prod under the man's arm. Carson's muscles seemed to seize up, his teeth gritted together in a rictus grin.

Joseph did not hesitate, taking advantage of this momentary paralysis by stepping behind Carson and plunging his hunting knife into the side of his neck before ripping the blade sideways, opening up the billionaire's throat with a wide gash. Blood shot out of the wound... but then...

Sarah gasped as the fountain of blood seemed to coagulate in midair, then retreat into the wound.

Russ cursed as the cattle prod's metered shock concluded; before he could trigger it again, Carson swept his arm down and snapped the pole in half.

Sharkey, holding a large rock over his head in both hands, stepped forward with the intention of caving in Carson's skull, but the billionaire—muscles now free of the unexpected jolt—lashed out with a vicious shove, catching the guardsman square in the chest and sending him flying backward with a fractured sternum.

As Sarah watched, Carson turned to face Joseph, his grin widening as the blood around his neck appeared to retreat, flowing back into the wound on his neck. The Shoshone backpedaled, weaving his knife in the air. Sarah dashed around Carson, her eyes scanning for something—anything—to use as a weapon. As she did so, she spared a glance toward Brighteyes.

Brighteyes could smell the odor of Alive-Dead coming off the huge human moving his way, but the stench had a different quality than what he had experienced in the past. With one hand occupied holding his makeshift spear, his ability to sign was impaired, so he used basic vocalizations to impart a simple warning to DawnWaker —and to Littlefoot, whom Brighteyes had warned to stay in the shadows.

'Danger!' Brighteyes pointed the tip of his weapon at Brick. 'Death danger. No touch.'

DawnWaker acknowledged with a grunt and circled to Brick's left, gesturing that Brighteyes mirror her move to his right.

Brick ignored her, homing in on Brighteyes. The massive human tore off his shirt as he neared, revealing livid scars and an oozing wound where the 20-gauge shotgun had struck him minutes earlier. He tore off his helmet, which caused his strangely canted head to loll to the other shoulder. He dropped the dented head covering with a clatter as he closed the remainder of the distance.

Brighteyes held his spear up in both hands, waiting to make his move. Behind his opponent, he spotted DawnWaker flanking him.

Brick cracked his knuckles, the pops sounding like sticks breaking. "It's the Hard Knock Life," he growled. Then he charged, arms outstretched.

Brighteyes stabbed his spear at the man, who made no move to avoid the thrust. The spear punched into his stomach as he reached Brighteyes but appeared to have no effect.

Grasping the Bigfoot's wrists, Brick grappled with the much larger primate. His strength was inhuman, and Brighteyes could feel his arms being forced to the sides. He released the spear and tried to overpower the human with his own prodigious strength, but the man twisted his grip violently and Brighteyes felt something pop in his left wrist. He bellowed in pain.

Brick emitted a gravelly laugh and spoke-sung, "Poor Thing." He twisted harder, and Brighteyes tensed, waiting for his other wrist to give way. Brick threw back his head and prepared to sing the eleven o'clock number, when suddenly...

"Hurlk!" Brick gargled out a surprised sound as a wooden spear point burst through his open mouth. Caught unawares, the man released his grip on Brighteyes. The Bigfoot looked over Brick's shoulder and spotted DawnWaker, eyes flashing with fierce determination, both hands on the back end of her homemade spear.

Brighteyes looked her in the eyes as he grabbed the blood-soaked pointed end with his uninjured hand, then nodded his head to the right. DawnWaker grunted affirmation, then the two of them jerked the length of spear to the side.

The tremendous strength of the two Sasquatch was too much for Brick's already-damaged neck; the powerful movement tore his head completely free from his shoulders. It landed in the rocks, where it rolled to a stop, face up.

Blinking up at the night sky as the rain pelted down on his face, Brick managed to choke out a final song title from his tattered vocal cords. "A Little Fall of Rain..."

Brighteyes one-handed a large rock to make sure of the job when a shrill scream split the air. He whirled to look at the shoreline. 'Air-rah!' Dropping the rock, he started to go to his friend's assistance when suddenly he felt a grip on his ankle: Brick's body, deprived of its head, still had a little fight left in it.

Sarah had managed to find a tranquilizer dart gun that one of Wolf Wallace's crew had thrown down during their mass exit. It appeared to have a dart in the chamber, so she raised it to her shoulder and took aim. Carson had already tossed Russ aside like the minor annoyance he likely was and now focused on Joseph.

The Shoshone fought with great skill, managing to avoid Carson's attempts to grab him. The billionaire's movements had become more savage and feral, lacking some of the grace he'd shown earlier.

Joseph managed to slice across Carson's palm when the billionaire grabbed for him and danced out of reach again. Sarah wasn't sure her dart would do anything, and she had to wait until Joseph was out of the line of fire in case she missed. She moved a little closer, rifle at the ready. Finally, she saw her chance. When Joseph sidestepped a clumsy charge, Sarah fired. The dart took Carson in the neck. Joseph attempted to use the distraction to his advantage, but that was a mistake. Carson caught his knife hand and nearly ripped his arm from the socket; Joseph was able to break loose at the last second—even so, the move dislocated his shoulder.

The billionaire whirled around and was on Sarah in seconds, ripping the gun from her hands and grabbing her by the throat. She managed to scream once before she felt her oxygen being cut off. Carson tore the dart from his neck and tossed it aside. Mad eyes gleamed as he leaned in, perfect teeth yawning open.

A shrill call sounded from waist level. Carson turned to see what had generated the odd noise and Sarah saw his face register a flash of concern. Held in his vise grip, she could only drop her eyes to the side to look for the origin of the call, but she already knew who she would see.

Littlefoot stood mere feet away from Carson, aiming what Sarah recognized as Brick's high-caliber handgun. Sarah well remembered Littlefoot's unexpected demonstration of primate tool use, when the youngster had blasted Silverback's head apart with a mercenary's shotgun. But now, fear rose inside her. She had watched Brick empty that gun into Sharlie before being battered across the shingle. And that meant...

With determination in his eyes, Littlefoot squeezed the trigger. *Click.*

The juvenile Bigfoot looked confused and batted at the gun with his other hand before trying again.

Click click click.

Carson laughed. Maintaining his grip on Sarah, the billionaire reached out for the little Sasquatch.

"Cameron! Stop!"

A British-accented voice rang out from the slope to the road as a group of men descended to the rocky beach through the rain. Bill Singleton led what appeared to be a mix of mercenaries and technicians, armed with an assortment of weaponry and high-tech equipment.

As Littlefoot managed to scramble away, Sarah kicked and battered her fists at Carson's forearm; pinpoints of light began to sparkle in her vision as the choking grip threatened to rob her of consciousness.

Carson looked toward the new arrivals. "Buh... Bill..."

"Yes, Cameron... it's me. Let her go... you're killing her!"

"Oh, I intend to do far more than kill her," Carson growled, his eyes gleaming. "This here growing boy needs his lunch. And after her... all the rest of you!" He looked around at the others.

"No." Bill shook his head and raised a pistol. "I can't allow that."

"You can't allow? What are you going to do, you fussy little man?" Carson grinned, then opened his mouth wide, leaning in toward Sarah's face.

Pew-thwp! A small syringe with stabilizers zipped from the gun in Singleton's grip and buried itself in Carson's chest.

The billionaire laughed. "I told you; sedatives don't work on someone who no longer sleeps." He turned toward Sarah again, but a look of confusion appeared on his face as he tried to bite her. Suddenly, he dropped her to the rocky ground, his fingers twitching. "What's happening?"

"Dr. Schneider's paralytic," Singleton answered, a note of sadness in his voice. "You may remember, she provided us with several hypodermics as a safety precaution, but I thought it would be more prudent to have a projectile version on hand."

Carson growled low in his throat. "Sensible as always, Bill," he managed, then took two steps toward his assistant. Singleton darted him twice more and the billionaire's body seized up and collapsed onto the rocks.

"Get him to the helicopter," Singleton ordered. Two of the mercenaries started forward.

"No!" Joseph dashed toward Carson's prone form, hunting knife raised in his off hand, but came to a jarring halt as Singleton shot him as well. Wide-eyed and gasping, he collapsed to the ground beside the billionaire. His knife fell from his fingers and he clawed at the air. When the others moved to help, the mercenaries raised their weapons.

"Stay where you are, all of you!" Singleton commanded. "I'm afraid Mr. Washakie will need medical attention; the muscle paralytic was designed for Carson, and your friend may have difficulty breathing in moments. You'll want to remove that dart immediately."

Russ threw himself down beside Joseph and plucked the small cylinder from his friend's shoulder.

Singleton started backing away but raised the dart pistol again when Brighteyes charged toward the group. With DawnWaker's help, the Sasquatch had managed to pry his ankle loose from Brick's literal death grip.

"Brighteyes, no!" Sarah called out, then signed, "We are safe! Guns... dangerous!"

Brighteyes froze, then nodded acknowledgment. He gestured to Littlefoot to join him. DawnWaker hovered just behind the pair.

"Holy sh... Bigfoots!" one of the mercs gasped. His weapon's barrel drifted in their direction.

"Stop!" Singleton called out. "Leave them be. Our priority is Carson. Pick him up. Watch his teeth... I don't know how complete the paralytic's effects will be. Let's—"

"Sir!" One of the men to the rear was pressing his hand to his ear. "The pilot says there are multiple helicopters inbound. Military." As if to confirm the man's assertion, deep rumbles reached the ears of everyone on the beach.

"Brighteyes! Back to the forest!" Sarah shouted and signed.

As the shaggy trio retreated from the lake, Singleton and his men carried a stiff and unmoving Carson to the north.

Sarah dropped to her knees beside Joseph and Russ. "Is he...?"

"I'll be fine..." Joseph managed to whisper.

"The little vial on this thing still had half the liquid in it when I pulled it out," Russ said, tossing it aside. "Hey, go check on Sharkey."

Sarah rose and headed back to where the guardsman lay in the rocks, wincing as he held his chest. Gasping, he choked out, "Farley... is he...?"

"I'm sorry, Sharkey..."

The big Montanan swallowed and nodded, as if he'd known what the answer would be. "We gotta kill that freak," he hissed.

Overhead, the whumping of rotor blades signaled the arrival of yet another helicopter. In moments, ropes slapped into the river rocks and multiple soldiers fast-roped down, fanning out with weapons raised. After eight had landed, another slid down to join them. With a salt-and-pepper high-and-tight, this man had no weapon.

"Where is Carson?" he bellowed.

"You just missed him," Russ said. "He went thataway." He stabbed a finger to the north.

"Jenkins... take half the stick and sweep north. Find him and take him. Alive. Or... whatever he is." The man looked at Russ and Joseph. "I've been looking all over for you two. So...? Where is it?"

"Where is what, Mister, uh...?"

"Colonel. Colonel Dosset. Where is the meteorite from the geologists' campsite?"

"Gone," Joseph said from the ground. "Destroyed."

"Bullshit." Dosset turned to one of the soldiers with him who had a Geiger counter of some kind and was sweeping the beach. "Anything?"

"Traces... and it matches what was on-site in the camp."

"You guys aren't with the National Guard," Russ said. "Who are you?"

"That information is need-to-know, yada yada." Dosset pointed at the trio of adventurers. "You three have been a royal pain in my backside from day one." He looked around at the group. "Jiminy Crickets, you all look like you went ten rounds with a Mack truck. And you, soldier... where's your buddy? You two are thick as thieves."

Sharkey swallowed and choked back a sob, jerking a nod in the direction of Farley's body.

Dosset looked over his shoulder at it, then went over and crouched beside Farley's armless form and gave an appreciative whistle. "What did this?"

"Carson," Sharkey managed to choke out, "and that big bodyguard of his."

"Brick Broadway?" Dosset rose to his feet. "Did he leave with Carson?"

"No... he's dead. Lying over there. They tore his head off."

"They? Who they?"

"Carson did it," Sarah said quickly, silencing Sharkey with a glance. "He went all feral or something and attacked everyone on the shore."

"Shedd! Bag and tag him. The head too. What's the ETA on the Humvees?"

"Twenty minutes, sir."

"What's that fire out there?" Dosset asked, looking out toward the lake.

"Fireworks barge," Russ said. "Went boom."

Dosset looked at him, eyes narrowing. "There have been reports of a lake monster of some sort... know anything about that?"

Sarah didn't see any point in dissembling on this point; they'd find the remains soon enough. "Dead. On the barge."

"Jeezus Huckleberry Christmas, did you bastards burn up *another* cryptid? You better hope there's still some viable tissue samples, or I'll have your asses for treason! Regardless, you'll all be enjoying my hospitality for a lengthy debriefing. Shedd... you have flex cuffs?"

"Yes sir, I—"

Shedd was cut off by a cacophonous sound to the north. A hail of automatic weapons fire from multiple weapons split the air. Dosset drew a handgun and Shedd immediately held a hand up to an earpiece and listened.

"Sir... Jenkins found the Maiden helicopter... they've been fired upon. At least two heavily armed hostiles." He listened. "The helicopter is taking off!"

"Dammit! Shedd, watch these four! The rest of you, on me!"

With that, Dosset and three of the remaining soldiers dashed through the rain and sprinted up the slope to the road, angling north. That left Shedd, who held his submachine gun on the quartet on the beach.

"Guys... any of you want to spend the next few years in Guantanamo Bay?" Russ whispered. "Or Area 51?"

"We'll have to rush him," Joseph said quietly. "But none of us are in the best of shape, and I imagine he knows how to use that thing."

Suddenly, there was a sharp pair of knocks echoing from a nearby tree on the slope... and then a large pine cone bounced into the rocks at Shedd's feet.

"Grenade!" he shouted, instinct getting the better of common sense.

That was all the time Joseph needed. Before Shedd could bring his weapon up, the Shoshone dropped him with an expertly aimed rabbit punch to the back of the man's ear.

Sarah grunted a quick thank-you toward the trees and spotted Brighteyes beckoning toward them. "Guys, come on!"

Russ quickly followed her. Joseph grabbed the soldier's carbine and threw it into the lake, then offered his hand to Sharkey.

"No, man... I gotta... I gotta stay here and see to Farley. Don't worry, I never saw your furry friends. Y'all get on out of here. Take my truck, if you need to. Or I could get Farley's keys..." He swallowed as he looked in that direction.

"No... we'll do better on foot," Joseph said. "But thank you." He placed a hand on the big guardsman's shoulder. "I am sorry for your loss."

Sharkey nodded. "You better go. They said something about Humvees being twenty minutes out a few minutes ago."

Joseph nodded and took off after his friends. In moments, humans and Bigfoots climbed the steep wooded slopes above the road, heading west.

CHAPTER THIRTY-SEVEN

Singleton gripped the bulkhead behind the cockpit as the Maiden helicopter roared across the lake, rose above a hill, then dipped down to follow a creek valley. The pilot had his NVGs on and was flying nap-of-the-earth to avoid radar detection. After a brief firefight, they had only just managed to escape.

"I'm not comfortable with this," the pilot said. "Those guys were military, and—"

"We've already had a run-in with the military," Singleton snapped. "And as you recall, it didn't end well for them. We are all accomplices. Now turn off the transponder."

"I could lose my license..."

"You'll lose far more than that if they catch us! Need I remind you, you are working for one of the most powerful people in the world? And Mr. Carson takes care of his own. I'll extend a quarter-million bonus for each of you if you get us safely out of here."

"Well, would you look at that; the transponder's on the fritz," the copilot said as he reached forward and flipped it off. "I'm with you, Mr. Singleton, sir."

The pilot sighed. "Well, fuck. Okay, then... where are we going?"

"How's your fuel? Can you make the Canadian border?"

The copilot made a quick calculation. "It'll leave us on the edge of bingo fuel, but yeah, we can make it."

"Good. I'll give you a precise location once I make some calls on the sat phone. Maintain radio silence and continue flying north." Singleton retreated to the cabin to check on Carson and found his employer staring at him, duct-taped securely to a seat and still pumped full of paralytics. Carson's face was caked with blood and his beard was patchy and singed. Carson's eyes followed him as he approached, and Singleton thought much of the madness had left them.

"Sir, I am taking us across the Canadian border. We have a team in Vancouver that can likely reach us before the authorities do."

"Bill... I'm... sorry," Carson managed to rasp, his speech slurring somewhat. "Lost... control... still... hard to... focus."

"I hope you don't mind, but... I believe I should inject you again, sir."

Carson managed a grin. "Prudent... as always... but one thing first. Do you have... one of those... shielded sample boxes handy?"

Singleton retrieved one from a member of the technical team and brought it over to Carson, who remained rigid in his chair.

"Right... pocket." His eyes flicked down at his side. "Piece of... sphere. Put it in box... quickly."

Singleton swallowed, then nodded to one of the surviving mercenaries who had on a pair of shooter's gloves and instructed the man to retrieve the object while he stood by with another dose of paralytic.

The man found the small sharp-edged shard of meteorite and was about to drop it in the box when his eyes went unfocused. Singleton thought he heard a very faint tone in the air, but with the cabin noise in the helicopter, it was barely perceptible. Quickly, he snatched the object from the merc's hand and dropped it into the box before sealing the lid.

"As I thought..." Carson said. "It was... affecting me. My mind is already clearer. I suppose I'm fortunate that I did not come across the entire sphere. It must have been blown apart by the explosion on the barge. But hopefully that piece is enough for Maiden's scientists to research what exactly happened to me." Carson chuckled. "Although... I imagine that research will need to occur at one of my overseas facilities."

"Yes, sir." Singleton frowned. "If that was just *one* piece of the meteorite... what happened to all the rest?"

"Over here, sir! Another one!"

Colonel Dosset brushed off the annoying medic who was still trying to clean up a graze wound on his cheek from the earlier firefight with the Maiden mercenaries. He went over to where one of his technicians was using an extendable pole grabber to retrieve a second piece of the meteorite from the water. "I suppose we can thank our lucky stars that the stuff floats," Dosset said as he watched the man drop it into a sample case.

"We'll have boats here within the hour, sir," one of his soldiers announced.

"Good. But go ahead and take those two samples back to Grangeville. I want analysis to start immediately!" He turned to Shedd. "Any word on the prisoners you were supposed to be watching?"

"No, sir... sorry again, sir. We can send out another search party if you want, but I assumed you wanted to prioritize personnel toward finding more pieces of that meteorite, sir."

"You assumed correctly." Dosset sighed. "We'll find them soon enough... they can't have gone far."

"How much farther?" Russ panted.

"Another two miles and we should reach Highway 55," Sarah said. "But right here... this is some of the thickest forestation on the southern slope of Brundage Mountain." She turned to Brighteyes and spoke-signed, "This is where we must part." She pointed to the north. "You will be safe there for now. When it is safe for me and my friends to return, we will try and find you again."

Brighteyes's eyes shone with moisture. 'Air-rah. I will miss Air-rah.'

"I will miss you too, Brighteyes. But you have Littlefoot to keep you company. And your new friend." She gestured to DawnWaker.

"He may have more friends than that," Joseph said. He stepped off the trail and crouched. "Here." He gestured to the ground. "And another over there."

"Bigfoot tracks!" Russ declared, leaving the trail to lend his eyes to the search for additional prints.

Suddenly, DawnWaker stiffened and scented the air. She signed excitedly. 'I smell our kind!'

Sarah examined the tracks Joseph had spotted. "Looks like we weren't the only ones to consider this patch of forest to be a good home." Together, the three humans and three Bigfoots located additional sign and quickly determined the direction this mystery Sasquatch had taken. After final goodbyes, the two groups parted, Bigfoots heading north and humans heading west.

"So, what's the plan once we reach the highway?" Russ asked. "Hitchhike?"

Joseph shrugged. "As good a plan as any."

"Where to?" Sarah asked. "We can't go back to Grangeville. Honestly, I'm not sure *where* we can go, if those black-ops guys are after us."

"I may have an option." Joseph smiled. "I have family in Canada."

Brighteyes looked over at DawnWaker as the red-body crouched behind a pine tree overlooking a tiny alpine lake, likely a pool of runoff from the nearby mountain. On the grassy shore below were a pair of young Sasquatch, probably teenagers judging from their size and playful demeanor.

'Do we greet them?' DawnWaker signed.

'I want to!' Littlefoot declared.

Brighteyes flexed his injured wrist, working the fingers; he thought it was only a sprain, but he would need to favor it for a time. He scented the air, searching for the muskier scents of any alpha in the area. At the moment, he detected nothing apart from the two below. 'I do not smell another troop.'

The two teenage primates appeared to be trying to fish, but an isolated body of crystal-clear water like this would have no fish, unless humans put them there.

DawnWaker said as much. She signed, 'They search for fish where there are none.'

Brighteyes chuffed playfully. 'As you often tell me... *you* are the best at fishing. Perhaps you can teach them where better to look. Let us go and say hello.'

With that, the trio cautiously rose from cover. Retrieving a fallen branch, Brighteyes rapped it twice against a tree trunk, signaling his presence to the newfound tribe.

AFTERWORD

Well, it only took me eight years. And on that note, I'd like to start off this afterword with the answer to "what took you so long, Sully?" Back in 2017, I was a third of the way into the writing of *Zombie Billionaire* when inspiration struck for a thriller involving a narco submarine being built for a cartel... only to be hijacked by terrorists, who swap out the coke for explosives. With my longtime love of scuba diving, I knew I wanted a divemaster as the central character, and The Deep Series was born with *Deep Shadow*. And when that took off, I just kept writing more and more of that series.

But meanwhile, on the wall of my writing room—looming over my shoulder for the past eight years—was a corkboard of color-coded Post-its with the storyboard of *Zombie Billionaire*. Every time I looked at it, I had the urge to jump back in and finish. And after eight years, I had an enormous pile of ideas that had accumulated—which is probably why this book is so *long*! Finally, after one of my Deep books was put on hiatus due to Hurricane Beryl flattening the island I was writing about, I decided it was time to return to Brighteyes and Russ/Sarah/Joseph and Carson.

Weaving together five storylines was a challenge; it took me far longer than I expected and the word count grew and grew. I debated splitting it into two books, but the "act structure" didn't really allow for that. If I'd bisected it to make a trio with *Zombie Bigfoot*, I think the middle book would have suffered. Incidentally, I *had* originally planned for a third book: *Zombiesaurus*. But I felt Carson's story and Sharlie's were intertwined, so I opted to keep it all in one. More value for your buck, right?

One of the things I've enjoyed doing with my Deep Series afterwords is to let the reader in on some of the sausage-making behind the scenes. What's real, what isn't, and where it all came from.

First off, even though the Creature Quest books are full of cryptids and zombies and future tech, I try to keep one foot on the ground of reality—or a single toe, at least. The major locations are all real, with the exception of Maiden Industries' underground lab on North Brother... although the island itself is real, as is all of its history. The headquarters of Maiden Industries is in an actual building in downtown Manhattan on, of all places, Maiden Lane. I swear to you, that was a complete coincidence. I wanted a location near the helicopter pads with a view of the bridges on the East River, so I looked at Google Earth and picked a tall one with shiny windows. It was only later, when I was searching for nearby bagel places Carson might visit for his meeting with the board, that I discovered I had placed Maiden Industries on Maiden Lane.

Speaking of food businesses and coincidences... when I started novelizing my screenplay of *Zombie Bigfoot* back in 2016, "Sassy-Squatch Ice Cream" in Kamiah, Idaho, and "Squatch Sweets" in McCall were not there! But when I sat down to finish *Zombie Billionaire* last year and pulled up locations where my characters were, both of those perfectly named locations were on the map, right next to where I had set some of the action. And, yes, Kevin's ice cream cone—the Notorious B.I.G.foot—is a specialty cone they serve at Squatch Sweets. And the breweries in McCall and

Grangeville are real places; I like craft beer, you may correctly surmise.

Sharlie is an actual legend in McCall and I had a lot of fun delving through various accounts of sightings over the years. And, yes, the Loch Ness Monster's exact nature is an area of controversy, so I had fun giving each of the Sharlie Hunters a different opinion as to Sharlie's nature. One fun tidbit: when I wrote the epi-epilogue in *Zombie Bigfoot*, I gave Sharlie scales. When I wrote this book, I realized she couldn't turn out to be a pure plesiosaur because they don't have scales... or so I thought. Two days ago, I spotted an article about a remarkably well-preserved plesiosaur fossil discovered in Germany. You guessed it: It had scales! The skin seemed to have rougher scales along the flippers (like a green sea turtle) and smoother skin (like a leatherback sea turtle) on its back. Rigidity on the flippers gave power for swimming, and smoother scales on the back gave a more hydrodynamic form. Attached to this article, I found a link to another article from 2022 about the discovery of plesiosaur fossils in Morocco that indicated that some plesiosaurs lived in fresh water.

As for the Sharlie Hunters, they are all based on a group of actors I worked with when I was performing on Broadway in *Newsies*. While the bulk of the cast of *Newsies* was quite young, there were a number of roles that required actors of a certain vintage. Thus... "The Oldsies." Heck, we even had our own T-shirts made. The Oldsies were all crammed into a dressing room on the fifth floor and spent much of our spare time laughing our asses off and playing practical jokes on each other. Many of us would leave the Sunday matinee to go yuk it up at a craft beer pub, so that gave me my inspiration for where the Sharlie Hunters would likely gather for their meetings. And, hey, if this series gets picked up for television or film, there's a ready-made group of actors available to fill those roles.

Back to Sharlie... you may remember that the epi-epilogue from *Zombie Bigfoot* followed the progress of the Stone that Sings as it made its way from the Nez Perce-Clearwater National Forest to Lake Payette. In this book I interjected a little more of that journey. The inspiration for that came from an old children's film they would show us in elementary school, when the teachers needed a break. *Paddle to the Sea* was a short film about a boy who carves a canoe with a Native American occupant, and it follows this wooden toy as it goes from snowy mountain to creek to stream to river... and onward to the ocean. Even the frogs that appear in this book are inspired by that old movie. Go look it up on YouTube! You may realize that you watched it too.

On the subject of Mayor Gary Vance: no, the name Vance has nothing to do with the current vice president. I just wanted a name that was similar to another fictional mayor who ignored warnings of an aquatic killing machine, Mayor Larry Vaughn. If only he'd listened to Roy Scheider...

I've also had folks ask me who Cameron Carson is based on. The answer is: He's an amalgam of a number of billionaire adventure-seekers I've watched over the years. Another fictional character with real life inspiration: Alan Dusk. You can probably guess where his inspiration comes from. But I'll say this... I just read an article where a certain billionaire was offering to rescue some NASA astronauts stranded on the International Space Station. My section where Dusk one-ups Carson by offering to recover the bodies from his failed moonshot... my fictional scene's creation predates reality by roughly six months. Life imitates fiction!

I modeled the behavior of my Bigfoot tribes on some of Jane Goodall's studies of chimpanzees and researched various accounts of encounters with Sasquatch for aspects of behavior such as signaling and vocalizations. And BearFriend's full-body alopecia and his coat of roadkill was a bit I had intended to put into the first book, but I ultimately decided I needed Silverback's troop to be fairly small to make the book work.

Cameron Carson's specific "zombification" was a lot of fun. I wanted to do something different, and the idea for his blood taking on a life of its own came from reading an article on nanobots. I needed a way for him to sustain tremendous damage and keep functioning, and that seemed like a unique way to do it. I researched a number of longevity treatments as well, and there is indeed a "Wolverine" peptide out there, although you certainly can't walk into a CVS and get it.

Brick Broadway simply *had* to come back from the dead, and the idea that his damaged brain would fall back on his career in the ring and spout Broadway songs seemed like a no-brainer (pun intended). And, yes, the copyright laws don't allow song lyrics to be used in a book without permission... but song *titles* are not copyrightable. I had tremendous fun searching for Broadway song titles that could convey contextual meaning, allowing the big lummox to communicate with Carson.

Some quick thank-yous are in order. To my beta reading team, Chris Sorensen, Kevin Carolan, Tom Alan Robbins, Mark Aldrich, John Brady, Dan Sharkey, and Kristie Dale Sanders, thank you so much for your notes and encouragement! All of you made it into this book in one form or another.

My editor, Eliza Dee, did a bang-up job keeping my multiple plotlines from tripping over each other, and I should give credit where credit is due: Did you notice how the Bigfoot dialogue was done with single apostrophes? That was her idea, back when she edited "ZBF"; I thought it was brilliant, helping to set their method of communication apart from human speech. And thank you to Gretchen Tannert Douglas for your eagle-eyed proofreading; I swear, typos just spontaneously generate themselves each time I shut my laptop.

And finally, kudos to Claudio Bergamin, who created the artwork for *Zombie Bigfoot* and *Zombie Billionaire* from scratch. Claudio is an accomplished artist of rock albums and I was fortunate enough to discover that he was a big fan of Bigfoot. Sorry we didn't get to do the lake monster... maybe next time!

ABOUT THE AUTHOR

Born in East Tennessee, Nick Sullivan has spent most of his adult life as an actor in New York City, working in theater, television, film, and audiobooks. After recording hundreds of books over the last twenty-five years, he decided to write some of his own.

For something completely different, check out Nick Sullivan's action-adventure novels:

THE DEEP SERIES

Visit Nick at
NICKSULLIVAN.NET